STATERA

**CALUMET
EDITIONS**

Minneapolis

FIRST EDITION February 2026

Statera. Copyright © 2026 by Adrijus Kveda.
All rights reserved.

For information, write to Calumet Editions,
6800 France Avenue South, Suite 370, Edina, MN 55435

10 9 8 7 6 5 4 3 2 1
ISBN: 978-1-962834-66-7

Cover art: Calla Sawyer
Interior art: Pernille Caprioli
Book design: Gary Lindberg

STATERA

Adrijus Kveda

CALUMET EDITIONS

Minneapolis

BLACKOUT

Act I

What is freedom of thought?
Anything that derives itself from memory.

1

Aurora

I zone in. The echo of chaos resurging through me. Screams. Gunfire. Footsteps.

I climb the tallest tree at the border of our Colony and drag myself onto a branch. I wish my binoculars were clearer. I smashed them into the Arbiter's skull when I stole them. The impact must've cracked the magnifying glass.

"Keep running, Mathew," I speak quietly into the radio, trying my best to sound calm. But it's only not to ignite panic. "You're about five hundred metres from the checkpoint. Don't stop."

I force myself to watch the family of three hurtle away, staying within the tree lines. Diana stays close behind, while Mathew carries their son in his arms. The family struggles across the vast, pathless patches of grass that have blended with kilometres of murky, polluted dirt. Grey cans, plastic wrapping, receding cigarette butts and car registration plates protrude from the ground, making each step a potential gash. This barren wasteland engulfs our home. Colony Lithuania is the overgrown ruins of war. What remains are remnants of past civilisation, with nature reclaiming its place. Here, we've been rounded up like cattle and forced to continue surviving, breeding and working.

Every boy and girl at fifteen is forced into a job. Arbiters shove a pistol down your throat until you submit. You sign the document, accept your role as a slave, and waste your life in service to the Federation of Olympus, Righteousness and the Elect—FORTE. In Colony Lithuania, freedom is submission to power.

So I refuse my freedom.

Before the family departed, I caught a glimpse of their thin, tattered jackets that couldn't possibly protect them from the cold. Their entire life was stuffed into one rucksack. Their faces were coated in dead, dry skin that was starting to peel back. The little boy, Noah, is about four years old and looks too much like my brother. Fear trembled within their eyes; eyes I desperately hope to never see again.

I promised to help them escape Colony Lithuania. They knew the risks. I shouldn't feel responsible, and yet I can't stop my hands from shaking.

My eyelids become heavy. The dreary gaps of time I spend watching them scramble to the checkpoint fill me with frustration.

My fingertips tightly grip the binoculars, wishing I had the electric lenses the Night Arbiters use. These ones are from their old catalogue, with no night vision and no infrared. I must rely on the advanced zoom and my ability to see in the dark.

FORTE supplies all new technology to the Arbiters. We are left with whatever we can make, or whatever scraps we can scavenge from our ancestors.

I fidget, unable to tame my nerves. I shouldn't know their names. I shouldn't know what they look like. Above all, *they* shouldn't know *me*.

The family ran to me. Someone told them I'd help, probably an old friend of my father's. The entire family was scheduled to be hanged at tomorrow's executions. Even Noah, who's not old enough to go to school. Mathew fought an Arbiter who tried to rape his wife. But self-protection is defiance.

I exhale sharply. The weight of what I'm doing suffocates me. What have I gotten myself into, Dad? I'm sure if he were still here, he'd tell me, *You're doing what's right, sweetie.* But as the years drag on, I'm not so sure anymore. I think I'm just leading people to die.

Newly arriving trains roar through Colony Lithuania, blocking out every other noise. The speakers on every streetlight sizzle in the background as the trains come to a stop.

Even from afar, the streetlamps leading up to the train station are brightly visible. My tree isn't tall enough for me to see the railway, however everyone who lives here has seen the train station. It's the only part of the city that FORTE rebuilt.

It's an all-glass dome, adjoined with colossal pillars at its entrance. Holographic images of the train schedule materialize above the entryway. A sight hard to imagine since we all live in the slums.

"To all whom it may concern," Overseer Milgram announces. He is a member of FORTE who lives here and rules over us according to the laws of Statera. "I'd like to welcome our guests from Olympus Mons, who have travelled all the way here for the Equilibrium."

Rounds of applause and cheers can be heard, slowly fading away into the distance. This happens every twelve years. FORTE selects new subjects for the Equilibrium, some type of ceremony. No one ever speaks about it. It must be too traumatic to bring up.

"We're approaching the wooden hut," Mathew informs me over the radio, and I hear an unnerving gulp of air leave his mouth. "Should I enter?"

I glance at my mechanical wristwatch. It's 11:55. Patrol returns at midnight. The family will have to cover as much ground as possible.

The wooden hut is a watchtower for the Arbiters, with a full panoramic view from the top. But at ground level, hidden within its data cabinets, lie maps and charts detailing the geography of the wasteland beyond our Colony.

"Quickly! When you enter, find the cabinet labelled Northeastern Statera. Then grab a map of the Baltic Region," I instruct him urgently. I'm scratching my skin, which I know is a dangerous habit—11:56.

"If I don't return, you go without me. If I'm alive, I'll get back to you. I swear it," Mathew whispers to his family.

Before tracking Mathew through my binoculars, I glance at Diana and Noah cowering behind a tree trunk. There's no need to say anything. Tension must be suffocating them. They either escape and live in isolation or stay behind and become a rotting warning. They can't return unnoticed. The cameras will be watching. They have no choice. They have to make it.

"I found the map. It shows different locations and types of forests," Mathew says in a hush. "There is just one problem."

The wooden hut is shrouded in darkness. They should be alone. Everything should be fine.

"I can hear somebody speaking on the second floor." Mathew races through his words. I can almost feel his heartbeat. "They might spot my family."

"It's a risk you'll have to take. You only went there for the map. You have it. Go back to your family and begin making your way to safety," I answer, keeping the receiver pressed against my ear.

Please don't do anything stupid. Please.

I glance at my watch. They only have one minute.

"Hey, you need to go now! Regroup and head for the hills," I tell him. He doesn't reply. My forearm puckers into goosebumps, moist with sweat. The erratic drumming of my heart thuds in my ears, pounding faster and faster. "Your time is up."

An eruption of blinding sparks bursts through the trees.

Gunshots rattle the night, awakening a tree full of crows, who rise from the branches in a cawing mass. They screech horrifically and disperse.

Immediately, every light in close proximity flares to life, slicing through the blackness.

Night Arbiters, weapons and torches scatter along the disfigured heap of trees in an instant.

"What the hell did you do?" I suppress my anger, quietly screaming into the radio. "I told you to go."

"He's dead. Once I'd sensed this animal, I made sure to put a bullet right through his chest," a deeper voice answers back, with conviction and sincerity. "He pleaded for me to not harm his son with his final breath. Honourable. I'll make you a promise. Tell me your coordinates, and I won't harm the boy. Or I'll butcher them all, just like I did last time."

After a moment of silence, the line goes dead.

"Damn it!" My breath rushes out in broken gasps.

I switch to the second radio, the one Diana holds, and shout into the mic, "Run! And don't stop running until you've reached the wastelands."

I turn around and firmly grip the tree, clambering to its very top where the branches thin out and shake, threatening to snap under my weight. My hands are slick with sweat, unsteady as I try to move my hair out the way and bring the binoculars to my eyes.

I follow the flashlights that spread into the forest. Steadily, I look further on, hoping to see Diana and Noah approaching the wastelands. Instead, I spot them around fifty metres in front of the Arbiters, tripping over branches and rocks, as they stumble forwards.

The air hums. Then rain starts to fall, quickly soaking the forest. My clothes stick to me. The pungent scent of rot becomes even more apparent with the ghastly raindrops. The people of Colony Lithuania are fenced in by barbed wire, infrared cameras and electrified steel gates. There's only one route to escape. Reach the wastelands. Where even the Arbiters won't dare follow you. Radiation levels are still unknown. They wouldn't risk entering to save their own.

But the uneven terrain is mangled with sharp-edged metals, plastic bottles, car tires, and chunks of concrete, making it impossible to creep through silently.

Keeping my eyes on Diana and Noah, I can see the Arbiters closing in, efficiently cutting through the forest, checking behind trees and possible hideout spots. They are professionally trained killers. Soldiers born and raised to contain us.

Mother and son won't make it.

I do what I must. Pulling the detonator out of my pocket, I press the button immediately.

The forest flares into violent, scarlet flames that temporarily distract the Arbiters while they gaze around in distress, unsure of what to do. Before they know it, the second round of explosives begins to engulf them in a firestorm. This time, trees plummet from the skies and land mines erupt, blowing up anyone nearby into lumps of flesh.

Checking my binoculars, I find Diana and Noah in the shadows. Hand in hand, they hurtle away, desperate to leave their old life behind. My face is suspended in unrest. I keep seeing my brother Jacob, in the same position as Noah.

Behind the two of them, I can see another silhouette. Moving as silently as the wind. One Arbiter gallops effortlessly through the irregularities of the earth with a twisted sense of purpose.

He is the only one left pursuing them. Easily, he pinpoints their exact position around a hundred metres in front of him.

The raindrops land on the glass of my binoculars, blurring my vision into grey. I rush to wipe the glass clean, brushing my fingertips across the splintered surface. My eyes lunge through the dark, rummaging ahead through broken trees to the edge of the desolate wastelands.

I catch the shadow. The hunter.

Without hesitation, the Arbiter drops to one knee and extends his arm, leaning it against a branch. He looks through the scope of his rifle, steadying his sight.

Diana helps Noah leap over a fallen tree, and they keep charging onwards.

C'mon, you can do it. Just a little farther.

My heart won't slow down.

I press down on my detonator again and again, knowing all the explosions are over, hoping that maybe an explosive has been delayed.

The bullet punctures the night, cutting through the stillness. It slams into Diana's stomach, forcing her to stumble as she helplessly towers over Noah, shielding him. Diana sways side to side, her legs unsteady. Three more bullets tear into her upper body. She collapses, limp and silent. Blood gushes out from underneath her, growing into a dark pool.

Noah stands frozen, looking down at his mother. What can the boy do? Another eruption of bullets rip through Diana's torso. Specks of blood squirt onto the surrounding trees in dark splashes.

"Mommy, wake up," Noah squeaks, his voice breathless. His little hands try to shake her awake. He pleads, "Don't leave me. Please open your eyes! You said you would always be with me."

Noah drops to his knees beside Diana and holds her up, becoming drenched in his own mother's blood.

"Mommy, *please* get up!" he cries, his voice trembling with desperation and innocence. He looks around frantically. "Someone, please help my mom."

It's pointless.

The last Arbiter emerges from the shadows, his rifle aimed and ready. Noah turns towards him, his eyes probably glistening with hope.

At that sight my hands shake with dread. A spark flashes through the night. And the boy falls dead.

2

Lukas

The same tremble of terror holds me hostage every night. Before me stands the girl. Tears make my vision blurry, almost impossible for me to see her. She always passes me a flag, then leans in.

"You're the reason they died," she whispers, with rage in her eyes. Fury turmoils through her. Quivering with hatred, she shrieks, "It's all *YOUR FAULT!*"

Soaked in my own sweat and horror is how I wake up. The usual.

The drowsiness of sleep keeps me captive in the warmth of my bed. I tap the sheath on my belt, making sure the knife is still at my waist. I can't sleep without it. Gently, I turn my head towards my two sisters, snuggled up in bed. My feet are silent across the mouldy, wooden floorboards, as I sneak to the front door. I dress myself in the same old hunting wear, consisting of dark-green cargo trousers that once belonged to my father, a sweater of the same colour and brown leather boots. Below the stairs, I unhinge a floorboard and lift it free. I grab my bow, arrows, and rope, then retrieve my small mirror to inspect myself. A tall, muscular, slender boy looks back at me. I wince at my withered body, disturbed by the jagged distinction of my bones poking against my skin. I tilt the mirror to examine my neck, checking if the cut has started to heal. The flesh grooves inwards, still red and inflamed.

Nothing much I can do. It's going to leave a scar.

It'll be a harsh reminder: Never feed wild animals.

My skin is a shade brighter than the white clouds that form around our home daily. My father says our pale appearance is caused by a lack of nutrients. I don't trust him, but a schoolteacher probably wouldn't lie about something like that.

I need to cut my hair. It's over my shoulders; never been this long before. My mum's gentle hands used to cut my hair using this exact mirror. It was her gift to me on my seventh birthday. Her final gift. It was the first time I had seen the colour of my eyes—bright blue. Now they're much darker, more grey.

I miss my mum. Every day I think about her. She was my protector, and now I must protect my sisters the same way she once protected me.

I dust off the Premier's portrait. The man is white and bald with unnaturally tight skin, almost like it's being pulled back. Those eyes are sharp and superior, holding not a sliver of doubt. It's the only picture allowed in homes, and if it's found dirty, my family will be hanged.

I walk to my sisters' bed and gently kiss both of them on the forehead. Without waking them, I leave for work, closing the door softly behind me. They best not know of the horrors beyond this door.

When I walk through our Colony, I'm reminded even more of the dark. It has been raining since last night, showering the streets with colourless droplets of despair. The cold breeze strafes across my neck, sending shivers down my body. All the houses are made of wood, with thin walls that are sinking into the ground. There are no roads, only trampled grass that's been ripped away to reveal lanes of dirt and mud that come together to form pathways. The only existing distinctive features are the matte-black metal poles that pose as streetlights across Colony Lithuania. But the oddly blemished reflection of the lamps indicate they are cameras. We know they're watching.

I reach an alleyway between the Arbiter Barracks, where they train, monitor us and live. I breathe in, fighting back the burst of memories.

Two people died because of me. Right here.

I turn the corner and enter the alley. Josh leans against the brick wall of the barracks, playing with a knife in his hands. His blond hair and tall figure look out of place. We work as hunters, roles assigned to us by FORTE. We hunt together, sell game at the River Market and split the earnings.

"How'd you sleep?" Josh asks, readjusting the collar of his jacket as he approaches me.

"Don't even ask."

We bump fists and head down the alleyway.

"More nightmares?"

"Why ask a question when you already know the answer?" I chuckle.

"Because I hope the answer changes," Josh replies.

"I doubt it ever will."

We reach the end of the alley, where the metal fence is humming threateningly with sharp bursts of electricity sparking from the barbed wire underneath it. We continue walking along the fence towards the forest.

"The weather feels *draining*," Josh remarks.

"You always say that."

Josh shrugs. "You'll understand one day."

"Nonsense is nonsense. I don't want to understand you," I respond.

He laughs, then says, "I just meant the night was rough. I can barely keep my eyes open."

I nod, knowing better than anyone how that feels.

We pass rows of streets filled with fragile houses that are now splintered with sagging roofs and fading colours. Along with blocky, concrete apartments, which have been around for as long as anyone can remember. Colony Lithuania stretches on like this, each street looking like a copy of the last. Apart from a farm, or the outskirts of a forest crawling into the Colony, everything looks identical.

"Did you know Colony Lithuania once had its own language?" Josh asks, keeping his voice low.

"My mum told me about it," I answer, then shrug. "But what difference does it make? No one speaks it."

He raises a brow. "How would you know?"

"Schools teach in Elect. It's been like that for centuries now. Our language can't exist anymore."

Josh grins to himself, his face wrinkled with frustration.

"Am I wrong?" I press him.

"I wish you weren't so sure," he replies with a heavy breath.

I sigh. "That means I'm right."

History can be rewritten and destroyed. Books not published by FORTE are forbidden, even self-written ones. Poems and songs have to be taught and memorized. Our history is a chained prisoner in isolation, slowly losing its sanity. Without people to speak it, history dies. And so does language.

"Why bring it up?" I ask.

"I just think we lost something special. Something that belonged to us." Josh hesitates, his head slanted down. "Now nothing belongs to us."

I spot lamps ahead and signal for him to quiet down. Always assume they're listening.

The slums we came from disappear into our peripheral vision as the buzzing fence opens up into a set of gates leading into the forest.

An Arbiter stands tall, firmly gripping his rifle. Black metal armour shields his body. White letters on his chest spell "FORTE." A dark visor conceals his eyes, while the helmet swallows his head entirely, leaving only his mouth exposed.

"Will you sign us in?" Josh asks, lifting his sleeve to reveal the X-Code tattooed into his flesh.

"All forest jobs are halted until further notice," the Arbiter grumbles like he hasn't slept enough.

"But we can't afford not to work—"

The Arbiter grabs Josh by his collar and lifts him off the ground. Then he spins and thrusts Josh into the gate with a rattle. I grip my bow, arrow ready.

Something inaudible is whispered.

"Hawk?" Josh gasps.

The Arbiter releases him.

"It's worse than the weather, Josh. Beyond a drain," the Arbiter murmurs.

Josh's eyes widen, his face turning stiff.

"Get out of here!" the Arbiter demands.

Suddenly Josh wraps an arm around my shoulder and forces me to walk with him.

"My house at four," he whispers. "Be there."

Just like that, he disappears.

I return home, my mind fatigued from overthinking Josh's reaction. Something is wrong.

Is it because of the Election? Everyone is paranoid. This is when FORTE's laws are enforced even more strictly than usual. Anyone speaking ill of FORTE or the Arbiters can be charged with treason.

For that, they will torment you, make an example out of you, until keeping you alive is no longer useful. If you're lucky, they might just hang you.

I open the front door. "I'm home."

Footsteps ripple through the floorboards.

"Brotherrrrrr!" Sofia yells as she lunges forwards and throws her arms around me. "Welcome home."

I pat her head. "You don't have to squeeze me. I'm not going to disappear."

"But if I hug you, you'll stay right here," she declares, enthusiastically.

"That's right!" I gasp, pretending my legs are frozen. "I can't move. I'm stuck."

She giggles and loosens her grip.

"Oh wait! I'm free." I scoop her up as she laughs harder.

"Let me go!" Sofia fights back, shaking and wiggling herself out of my grasp.

"All right, you've won," I chuckle, setting her back on her feet. "You girls hungry?"

"Starving!" Amelia shouts from the living room.

I smile. "Understood."

Amelia is slouched over the dining table, scribbling in her notebook. During Election week, children are on holiday, while teachers undergo additional training to prepare for the Ceremony of Equilibrium. My father said they're taught what to teach and how to depict FORTE. From a young age, they try to coerce us into believing that they are gods.

But would God compel or convince? Neither. You choose to believe or distrust.

"Go finish your homework in the meantime… all right?" I tell Sofia.

She groans, rolls her eyes and joins Amelia at the dining table with her schoolbooks.

Before I step outside, I call back, "What do I always tell you? The sooner you finish work—"

"The sooner you'll be free!" Amelia and Sofia grumble in unison.

I grab the radiometer and walk into our garden. I kneel to the bucket of rainwater and insert the metal probe, listening for any ticks. The more it clicks, the more radioactive something is. But the device doesn't even hum.

I assemble firewood into a square, stack smaller twigs in the middle and ignite them. I heat water over the flame since the stove is out of gas. I'll need to head out into the wasteland for supplies soon.

Once bubbles rise to the surface, I brew tea using mint leaves and use the remaining hot water to boil eggs. While waiting, I nibble on the good parts of leftover mouldy bread.

"All right, girls, breakfast is here." I place two plates in front of them, each with an egg and a slice of bread.

"Aren't you going to eat?" Amelia raises a brow as she pushes her schoolbooks to the side.

"I already ate. I'm full," I reply nonchalantly, hoping my belly doesn't rumble as I speak.

Sofia doesn't wait and starts peeling her egg. The crunch of the shell makes me ache with hunger.

"Don't let it go cold." I shoot a glance at Amelia.

She shakes her head. "You're a horrible liar."

I mask my grin. She's all grown up now.

"C'mon, eat up."

Once they've eaten, I clear the table, wipe off any crumbs and try to help out with their schoolwork. We venture through Statera's history, mathematics and practical knowledge, like knowing every job in Colony Lithuania, how to avoid radiation poisoning and the social hierarchy between citizens, Arbiters, and Overseer Milgram.

"Argh, I can't do any more!" Sofia puffs exasperatedly.

"Someone's lazy," Amelia hisses with a sneer.

"I'm not lazy! I'm tired," Sofia complains.

Amelia shrugs. "Whatever floats your boat."

"*Hmph*." Sofia crosses her arms.

"Amelia, stop teasing your sister," I say while glancing at the clock in our kitchen—03:34.

"Just saying the truth," she says smugly.

Sofia's lower lip scrunches up with frustration.

"I said stop it."

"Fine," she whispers. "Sorry, Sofia."

"Like you mean it," I demand. "Go on."

Amelia sighs. "I'm sorry, Sofia."

"It's okay. I know you just want me to work hard."

"Working hard doesn't mean you don't rest. It means you give it your all," I explain. "Now come hug me for good luck. I'm off to the market."

Sofia runs into my arms and squeezes me tight.

"I can't breathe," I croak playfully.

"Come back soon," she says. I nod.

Amelia doesn't embrace me but instead follows me to the door. I throw my bow and arrows over my shoulder and tap my waist to check if the knife is there.

"What brought you home early?" Amelia keeps her voice low, making sure Sofia doesn't hear.

"The forest has shut down," I reply.

"Must've been an incident, huh?" she remarks.

"I'd guess so."

"Partisans?"

"I wouldn't know."

"Well, stay out of it. We can't lose you too."

I guess she thinks the same as I do. After Mum died, we lost our father to liquor.

"All right. You're the eldest when I leave, so you're responsible. There's a loaf of bread for dinner. If anyone knocks—"

"Don't open the door, don't answer them and stay together," she finishes my line. "Lukas, I know what to do. I'm not a little girl anymore."

"That's *why* I'm scared," I whisper, hiding my face from her. I reach for the door. "I'll be back late."

"Wait!" Amelia rises to her tiptoes and kisses me on the cheek. Her face softens. "Come back safe."

If only the world were peaceful. Then I could let my sisters walk out this door without the fear of losing them forever. Then they'd finally be safe.

I wait outside the concrete block of apartments. Grey walls streaked with ashy smears, like scars from past fires. Roots crawl up its spine.

The Election will be announced today. Every twelve years we restore Statera. The Election selects subjects for the Equilibrium. Those who refuse to participate in the Election are sacrificed to restore Statera's balance between the living and the dead.

FORTE chooses an age group in intervals of decades. Ten to twenty is the youngest and fifty to sixty the eldest. Then everyone of that age in Statera prays they are not selected.

We never know who is taken until the morning after. All we know is that the subjects *never* return.

"You're early." Josh interrupts my thoughts, approaching me with a rucksack in hand.

"I've never seen you like that," I answer.

Josh raises a finger to his lips and signals for me to follow him. I guess it's not safe to speak here.

"Let's head to the River Market," he says.

Rain spits from the sky, heavy and cold. The grass smudges with mud underneath our feet. The trees around us don't offer much shelter. We're quickly soaked.

The outline of stalls appears blurry in the distance.

"They won't hear us now." Josh takes off his rucksack and unzips it to reveal a game bag. "Take it."

"All right, I'll carry it," I reply, tilting my brows at his tone. I lift the leather bag. "What are we selling?"

"Lukas," he mutters, his voice slow and sombre. "There is no we."

My face is blank with confusion. "I can sell them by myself, we'll split the—"

"You don't get it," Josh heaves, his eyes narrow with gloom. He puts the rucksack on. "I'm leaving."

I tilt my head. "As in?"

Josh stares at me quietly.

"You're not coming back?" I ask, trying to read his face. But he just holds my gaze, silently. His expression is still as a stone. He's never like this. No matter what. "What happened? Are you all right?"

"Lukas." He sighs, a grumble in his voice. His eyes turn glossy, like tears might burst. "I can't tell you. You of all people know that better than anyone!"

I look at him helplessly.

"Besides my sisters, you're all I have. I need to know," I plead, aware I'm on thin ice. Knowing could mean death. But I must know. He's my only friend. "Please."

His eyes lock onto the ground. He's blocking me out.

"Goodbye, old friend," Josh says, his voice muffled and hurt. "When the world no longer drains us of life, I hope to meet again."

"Please tell me," I beg. My gut twists in desperation.

"I hope you'll live for yourself..." He pauses, taking a deep breath. "And not just for others."

A surge of rage floods my chest as he walks away. My heart beats faster.

"So this is it?" I yell while shaking. "This is how you treat me?"

Another person I considered family, out of my life, just like that. My face trembles with fear.

Josh stops and turns around, looking numb.

"This is how you treat your friends?" I murmur, my voice breaking.

"No," he growls with a tremor of regret. Josh stares into my eyes with shattered emptiness. Coldness. "This is how I protect my best friend."

I watch his silhouette vanish into the trees.

I clench my fist, my body rattling with sorrow.

What did he do? My chest pounds rapidly. Only way to escape FORTE is to venture past the wastelands, but radiation would ensure you won't last long.

Whatever happens, I just don't want to see him dead. I fear that I'll find him in the town square amongst the hanging corpses.

When I reach the River Market, the rush of faces overwhelms me. I don't want to be here. But I need to sell the game before it starts to rot.

I walk past the stream of people, heading to mine and Josh's usual stall. Well, mine now. I haven't even checked the contents in the bag. To my surprise, when I tear it open, there are berries, walnuts, pieces of chicken and rabbit all in brown paper bags. Quickly, I distribute everything equally, putting what I want to sell on display, and everything I want to keep back in the bag. There's a lot more I'm going to keep than sell.

Overseer Milgram's voice booms out of the overhead speakers in the market. "FORTE announcement of the utmost significance to be brought to you in the next ten minutes. Must be heard and spread like wildfire." Announcements are normally for hangings. My belly tightens up, as I involuntarily imagine Josh dangling from a rope around his neck.

It takes me a couple of moments to recapture my composure.

"How much for the chicken?" a lady calls out. White, blonde hair makes her stand out. She looks like the girl from my nightmares, just much older. I stare at her face, frightened by the familiarity.

She furrows her brows. "Young man?"

"Depends," I reply, leaning forwards. "Are you here to trade or buy?"

"I was going to buy, but I do have a full can of gasoline." She pulls out a cylindrical can from her shoulder bag. Probably no more than half a litre.

"Can I smell it?"

The lady twists the cap and holds it out. I bring it to my nose, sniffing reluctantly. The sharp scent burns through my nostrils. This is perfect. Now I can use my oven to cook the rabbit tomorrow.

"I'll take it as a trade."

"Deal." We shake hands.

I place the chicken inside a small paper bag.

"I haven't seen you around here before," I say as we swap goods. She's not a part of my regulars.

"Oh dear, I've been spotted!" she chuckles. "I don't usually shop at the River Market. I just wanted to get my daughter something nice to cheer her up. She's going through... a *difficult* time right now."

I pull out a handful of berries and give it to her. "I hope this helps."

"You didn't have to, dear." I see her lips curling into a smile.

"Just take it." The can of gas is far more useful to me than she realises.

"Thank you," she says with a grin.

We part ways and I start heading home myself. I can't help but think of Josh.

Tears sting my eyes but I keep on walking, gripping the game bag with all my anger, refusing to let myself cry.

Who's going to hunt with me now? Who'll have my back out there? A knot of regret twists inside me. I should have thanked him. He always looked out for me, like the older brother I never had.

The streetlights buzz with static.

"Good evening to all who may be listening," Overseer Milgram speaks with an unsettling charm, radiating excitement. "The generation for this Election has been chosen. The youth shall restore Statera."

The bag slips from my grasp. Terror forces me to tremble.

"The generation is between ten and twenty years of age," Overseer Milgram exclaims. My throat runs dry. A familiar, haunting scent fills my nostrils. It's my sweat. I can sense my own fear. I can't stop shaking.

He cheers. "May you Blaze or Burn!"

The static dies. Rain falls. Crickets hum.

I freeze, incapable of moving, wishing to disappear inside the trees. The subjects never return.

Sofia is eleven. Amelia is thirteen. I feel like I'm suffocating. Those two little girls could become subjects, and I'd never see them again. I could become a subject. My heart races. What will happen to my sisters if I'm gone?

3

Aurora

Stride by stride, I drag myself home. Sweat drips down my nose. Every breath leaves me weak. Damn it!

A welder is no easy job, especially for a girl. Almost everyone I work with is a man. But the heat of molten metal kills us all the same. It shreds our strength.

Thick, slushy water trickles down the street through the small cracks in the concrete. Everything is grim and grey.

Rainwater shouldn't be radioactive anymore, but I still avoid it as best I can.

I heard there'll be an announcement today. I guess I'll see more hangings in the town square. I might see the little boy. My stomach crumples in agony. Noah could be swinging from a rope with bullet holes for eyes.

I feel like throwing up.

I stop outside my house. My fingers wrap around the splintered, wooden fence that surrounds my home. I can barely hold myself up. My head won't stop throbbing, like it's too heavy.

"You okay?" My neighbour Hannah leans towards me with a tender expression. She's got long brunette hair and a kind, puffy face. Way too kind for this world.

"Yeah, just tired," I respond, rubbing my eyes. "Haven't slept well."

Hannah glances towards the clusters of flowers across her porch. I could never have the patience to take care of such a pointless thing.

"It's important to take care of yourself." She smiles, then comes closer. "Not just others."

"Mhm." I nod.

Hannah embraces me, tightly. She engulfs me like a warm blanket. May she stay safe and one day, long from now, die as a human being—that's all I can wish for. I hold onto her for longer than I usually do, unwilling to let go of her. You never know when it could be the last time you see each other.

"Good luck tonight," Hannah whispers, as she pulls away and pats my head.

"Mhm." I nod in confusion and we part ways. Luck for what exactly? When the little boy needed luck, it failed him. Luck will fail me too.

I enter my home. Warm air rises to greet me. I smell something unusual. Chicken. It smells wrong, like something I shouldn't be allowed to want.

My family can't afford such luxury. Someone else must be here. Staying on my tiptoes, I creep from the doorway to the living room and peek into our garden.

My mum and my brother, Jacob, are hard at work over a fire.

"What's the occasion?" I ask, removing my utility belt.

"Oh, Aurora." Jacob smiles, turning away from the grill and running up to me. "You're back!"

"Guess what I got you." I grin, reaching into my pocket.

"What? You welded me a knife?" Jacob giggles.

"Even better." I pull out scrunched paper and some pencils I managed to loot from the work supply. Unfortunately, there are no colours. Children only receive schoolbooks and pens, which they are forbidden to use for anything other than schoolwork. People have been hanged for wasting school supplies. I believe the pens they distribute have chips in them that track what you're writing. I used the metal detectors at work to scan the pencils. They should be safe.

"I can finally draw again! Thanks, Sis." Jacob cheers and takes them to our bedroom immediately.

Mum carries the pot from the fire as its contents slosh and sizzle. She smiles at me. "My beautiful daughter."

"Cut it out," I snap. "You never act like this."

"A mother can't cherish her child?"

"I'm not in the mood. What is this?"

"I thought we could eat something nice," she says, putting plates on the table.

"Why?" I ask.

My mum approaches me, slowly.

"Honey, tonight's the Election," she whispers.

I stare at her, blankly.

"What about it?"

She grimaces with fright. "It's your generation."

My face turns stiff.

"Jacob is safe. But you're… in danger."

"Okay." I let out a shallow breath, my stomach crumbling in horror. My chest rises and drops erratically.

My mum embraces me. "All we can do is hope."

"Okay," I murmur, my voice shaking.

We eat dinner, laughing and reminiscing about memories. We speak of Dad, of my graduation, of my childhood. Jacob recollects how I helped him with schoolwork and of the countless nights we stayed up learning how to draw. The warm candlelight caresses our fears. And just for a moment, I feel loved.

A series of rowdy knocks force me awake. Sirens hum louder and louder. Blinding rays of white light pierce through the cracks in the walls, slicing the dark into fragments. I struggle to move my legs, shifting my body diagonally until I can throw myself out of bed.

With each second, it sounds as though the knocks are going to ram the door frame off its hinges.

"Coming! Almost there!" I yell, perplexed as to whom it may be. Swiftly, I yank the torn blanket from my side of the bed and wrap it around myself.

Outside I hear voices clash into a contorted mess of loud, inaudible noises. There are dogs barking, men screaming and worst of all, high-pitched shrieks for help.

My first thought is a partisan in hiding. But I shouldn't be suspected. I haven't done anything noticeable… not yet anyways.

The repulsive pounding on the door rings with even more force. My veins expand. Small bursts of anger rush to my head.

"Be right there," I shout, and lunge forwards to the entrance of my home. In one swift motion, I leap for my coat, which hangs by the door, and reach into its pocket. I curl my fingers firmly around my blade.

I let out an uneven breath, preparing to grab Jacob and hustle to my backdoor. He won't end up like Noah… he won't be like *that* little boy.

Slowly, I rotate the key and thrust the door open. I keep one side of my body concealed behind the door, gripping onto the forest knife with all my hopes.

Three men, dressed in black, perfectly fitted uniforms stare me up and down. Pistols, handcuffs, and other items I don't recognise, hang from their belts. I look at their faces, only to find a metallic mask with a visor covering their eyes. You can only see their mouths, which are unprotected and open to the air.

"Who's at home?" the first Arbiter demands, holding a pencil-shaped panel that displays a light-blue clipboard.

"Me and my mother," I answer quietly. On the outside I attempt to keep a straight face, free of terror. "What's happening?"

I keep my eyes fixated on their faces, catching short glimpses of the surroundings. But I can't see much through their wide and broad shoulders that cover my sightline too well to be coincidence.

"And the boy?" he asks, pointing at something on his holographic board.

"Asleep," I reply with a frustrated growl hidden in my tone. "What is this?"

The Arbiter beside him cocks his pistol and points it at me. I gaze back, unsure what to do. My mouth runs dry. Even if I were to take one of them out using my knife, it's pointless to try against all three of them. I lack the physical power. I slide the knife back into my coat pocket and then step out fully from behind the door, immediately lifting my hands into the air.

The Arbiter behind the barrel is expressionless, staying completely still. The motion seemed habitual. My stomach throbs as I feel the intensity of my heartbeat rise unmanageably. Each breath leaves me weak and more anxious than before.

"You have five minutes. We'll escort you from here," the first Arbiter commands. The two men behind him seem unfazed. I gulp down any resentment, helplessly staring down the end of the pistol, which is still pointed at my heart.

"Five minutes for what? Where are you taking me?" I squeal, petrified of the Election.

"Don't," growls the Arbiter holding the pistol. He squeezes the handle until his leather gloves squeak as they stretch. "Don't *tempt* me."

I close the door quietly and make my way back inside. Jacob and my mum are still in a deep slumber, somehow completely unaffected by the cacophony of chaos outside. I vault towards the window by our bed, slightly adjust the knitted cloth used as blinds and take a quick peek.

Patrol cars are lined up in a straight line, one after the other, down the middle of our street. Intensely luminous lights protrude atop the patrol vehicles, glistering in constant rotations from house to house.

Arbiters grasping powerfully onto enraged dogs stand beside the cars, while the other Arbiters in groups of three go from house to house, asking who is at home and then confirming using a checklist.

"Let go of me!" Hannah screeches as two Arbiters drag her by the shoulders. She violently twists and turns, kicking the ground with all her might over and over again, but to no avail.

"Please, please, don't do anything to her!" Hannah's mother pleads in desperation, running behind the two Arbiters in an unbalanced rhythm. She calls out through her howling tears, "She's a good girl, please."

The Arbiters don't budge in the slightest. They slam Hannah into the mud. She lands with a gut-wrenching thud.

"No! Please, God, no!" Hannah's mother shouts.

The same two Arbiters lunge towards Hannah's mother. One of them springs ahead and locks the mother's arms together behind her back. The other reaches for his baton and propels it at the back of her head with full force, multiple times, until her body goes limp.

I turn away from the window. My eyes feel like they're going to bulge out of their sockets at any moment. A taste of dinner rises from the back of my throat. Steadily, I try to breathe in, but my lungs overflow with terror, incapable of inhaling. The pounding in my chest accelerates.

What the hell is this?

I focus my eyes onto Jacob's innocent face, his chubby cheeks, his flawlessly straight hair, his cute little nose, and I long for him to stay this way.

I long to stay trapped in this moment. I remain locked in fear of what I may lose tonight.

He's going to become a good man one day. With or without me. That thought scares me. I want to wake him up for a final goodbye. Just in case. But all I feel is a cold wave of emptiness.

I want to cry, to sit still and weep all my pain away into my pillow.

"Aurora," Jacob whispers, keeping his voice low while clearing his eyes. "Why are you awake? It's still dark."

I was so lost in my own thoughts that I didn't even notice him. The light from the cracks in the walls gently illuminates his face.

"I need to go to work for a little bit." I hesitate, unsure of what to say. I feel the teardrops brush against my eyelashes, but I refuse to let Jacob see me like this, especially if it's the last time we see each other. "I need to go for a while, to keep you and Mama safe… okay?"

"When will you be back?"

"Jacob, I don't…" I hesitate. "Not for a while," I lie. My chest bursts in flickers of torment, but I don't dare express any of it. No matter how much it burns.

"How long is a while?" He's guiltlessly pure, still unaware of how our world works. Selfishly, I wish it wasn't this hard on me.

Defeated by dread, I strike a match and light the candle on our nightstand.

I sniffle under my breath. "I don't know," I speak with a lack of conviction. I've let myself crack. I'm a horrible sister. He deserves better. All I can do is lie. "I'll be back before you know it. Now come give me a hug."

Jacob smiles. I couldn't forget this moment if I tried. His tired, droopy face rushes into my arms. I hold him tight. I hold back my fears and exhale a powerful gust of relief, leaving me a tad lighter, as if I had expelled the weight of all my worries.

"I must go now." I pause, rising to my feet.

"I'll get you flowers when you're back, Sis." He smiles. "Bring me something from your trip."

I leave the candle on the nightstand, its dimming wick a clear sign the flame is dying. Stifling my sniffles, I begin to make my way to the door. I hide my eyes from him. "Tell Mama we'll talk later. And remember, Jacob, I'll *never* forget you."

"Then I'll draw you a surprise. Something even more unforgettable!"

"That would be nice," I mumble, scrunching my face to keep it blank. "Now go back to bed."

I hear the blanket shuffle. "G'night."

"Sweet dreams, Jacob."

I don't look back. I imagine his warm smile.

I snatch my jacket, then close the door behind me. Maybe it's best parting ways like this.

I'm no good at goodbyes.

I wipe my eyes and rub my nose. The wind shoots through me, leaving my skin spiky and bumpy with shivers.

The same three Arbiters wait for me. Beyond them, I see patrol cars and tanks lined up in the middle of my street. I slide my hands into the pockets of my jacket, trying to stay warm.

"You won't need that." One of the Arbiters steps forwards and rips it off me. I look back in shock, only to meet his penetrative glare.

"Move on," he spits. I turn back around and wait to do as I'm told. I'm nothing more than an asset now.

Out of my peripheral vision, I can see other kids and teens, close to my age, all standing one by one in perfect lines.

Helicopters whir in the distance. Search lights beam the outskirts of my neighbourhood, ensuring no one can escape the Election.

Dogs howl and scream, disrupting the stillness of the night. My breath quivers unsteadily. In the coming weeks, many dogs will starve to death.

Dead men can't feed their friends.

Suddenly, all aircraft illuminate a single point.

"Overseer Milgram has confirmed that attendance is satisfactory. The Election will soon commence." A woman stands elevated on a platform surrounded by tanks. She looks like an angel, cloaked in a white dress that shimmers in the dark. The draped fabric around her chest swirls and folds as if that part of her dress were made out of clouds. Her hair cascades down her back in tangled coils, which twirl like rope. I've never seen hair like that. Her dark, lustrous skin is a deep black that makes her body appear velvety and delicate. Somehow her darkness glows softly in the night. Yet there is no warmth in her tone. "On my authority, Enyo Victor commands all Arbiters to proceed with verification."

"We are under your eye," the Arbiters chant and clasp their hands together. Then they separate, one per civilian.

"Your name?" the Arbiter asks, his voice raspy.

I think it's the same Arbiter who held a gun to my heart. I sigh noiselessly, and gulp down my spit.

"Aurora," I answer, avoiding his gaze. This tiny act of revolt is all I can do.

The Arbiter shakes his arm, and a rectangular hologram flares to life. With his other hand, he traces the air, and the image shifts with each flick.

"Your X-Code?" The Arbiter looks down.

"It's 182240." I lift my sleeve to show the small italic numbers below my wrist. The tattooed ink stares back at me, embedded deep within my flesh.

Everyone who lives in the Colonies gets a tattoo of their X-Code at birth. It's how they keep track of us.

People are numbers.

"You're verified." I'm in the Election.

"What's going to happen now?" I ask.

"The Premier will pray to restore Statera. And then the Election will take place. You will cast your vote and determine your own fate," the Arbiter says, shaking with excitement.

A fragile flicker of hope. I might live.

We stand in lines. I try to count how many of us there are, but after thirty I can't go on.

Poles emerge from the corners of the stage, beaming light. The air ripples with colour until holograms float from each side of the platform.

The Premier's face is lined with jagged edges, and skin stretches sharply from his jaw to the back of his head like a guitar string tuned too tight. His eyes are tense with confidence. He looks just like his portrait.

"May the Trinities of the Elect allow FORTE and its citizens to restore Statera once more," the Premier says, unfaltering in his confidence. "The balance between the living and the dead must remain equal. Life will be spared. Blood will be shed. To blaze or to burn. That is volition."

The unending chorus of barks is a terrifying warning that unravels aching through my chest into my guts.

The Premier's hologram stares with eyes of passion and dignity. Each breath squeezes my lungs tighter.

"The Election allows *you*, my subjects, to shape your destiny and forge your own future. It is the opportunity to show gratitude to your Gods. May our grace absolve you of your sins," the Premier says, his voice slow and forceful. His cheeks stretch into an abnormally wide grin, a wicked contortion of devotion. "The Trinity of Spirit, myself, the Yin and the Yang protect the natural order and maintain the ultimate telos of life. The Trinity of Matter… Demetrius, Enyo and Callisto judge the value of your life's actions to determine your eternal state in the afterlife. The eyes of the Trinities are everywhere, keeping watch on the wicked and the good."

We're forced to worship, love and celebrate the Trinities of the Elect. But this isn't faith… this is slavery.

When people are executed for the presence of dust on the portrait of a man—that's not belief. Coercion makes one conform. And here, conformity is the decision between life and death.

"The Election is part of the universal chain of cause and effect. The ability to choose recreates stability. And if my subjects devote themselves to the Trinities of the Elect, then the natural order will equalize once again."

What the hell is he even saying? There is no natural order. The principles of the world are not etched in stone. Rules govern people. Rules stem from order. And order is determined by power. Always.

A perverted smirk expands across his reptilian face. "Welcome to the 99th era of the Equilibrium. May your sacrifices restore Statera!" the Premier declares. "Commence the Election."

The Arbiter steps forth and thrusts a spear into the ground in front of me. Spears clang up and down the street, as every subject faces them.

Sparks flow up the metal like a river of flames. The night ignites in crimson whirlwinds. Flashes of red and orange fill the dark.

The spears hum with electricity, as the tops break off into two branches that bend and slant down like the neck of a swan. The metal tilts until it faces the ground and then a weighted pan dangles down from a chain on both branches.

"The Election provides all subjects with the gift of choice—a vote. Half of you will burn and half of you will blaze. To restore Statera, the balance between the sacrifices of the living and the dead must be equal," says the lady in the white dress, Enyo. She grins, her teeth pristinely white. She spreads her arms wide, as if inviting us into an embrace and exclaims, "To celebrate the mercy of your Gods we shall recite the prayer of Grace."

The Arbiters stand up tall and straight, bringing their hands together and interlinking their fingers.

All their voices join together as one in a terrible, low-pitched roar.

> "Hail our Makers,
> Full of Grace,
> The Elect are with you,
> Blessed be your names.
> Embrace you solely, none can replace,
> And the blessed shall worship your face.
> Holy Makers,
> Never forsake us,
> Give us strength, give us breath,
> Until we're blessed with death."

How can torment mean blessed?

I press my palms against my face, trying to disappear into the fleeting warmth of my hands. Tension makes us sweat. We all gulp in exhaustion and anguish. Terror is collective.

"The Election is the first step to the Equilibrium. Every subject faces the scales of justice. Your vote will determine whether you stay in the Colonies or participate in the Equilibrium," Enyo explains calmly. "Now, as for the votes."

Both scales erupt into ghastly flames. I see my own fear reflected in their light.

"You shall vote by placing your hand on a scale. One flame will brand a white dot, the other a black dot. White means you remain in the Colonies. Black means you will restore Statera in the Equilibrium. You may only place your hand on one flame," Enyo says, licking her lips in sinister anticipation. "This is the first step to restore Statera. Let the Election commence!"

The Arbiter in front of me takes a step back but watches me closely.

"You may proceed. Cast your votes." Enyo smiles and lifts her head with pride. "May you Blaze or Burn."

Patches of sweat stick to my chest and arms, making me restless. I swallow saliva repeatedly, but my mouth stays dry. A queasy sensation in my gut forces me into staggered steps.

I gaze forwards, hypnotized by the rotating brightness of each flame.

This choice decides if I'll ever see my family again. I remember Jacob's smile. I want to see him grow up.

Mesmerised by the dancing swirls of the flames, I lift my right hand. My fingers shake.

Memories flicker rapidly across my mind. My dad's lessons, my mum's warmth, Jacob's joy. I feel like I'm trapped in this moment. *What the hell do I do?*

There is no rational way to make this decision. I'm held hostage by uncertainty.

My Arbiter turns to his left, probably to see if the others are taking as long.

I don't think. I smash both my palms onto the scales. Hot streaks of paralyzing agony rush back and forth across my arms. My flesh sizzles. Grunts slip out through pursed lips as I rush to tear my hands off the flames before the Arbiter notices.

My skull throbs and my legs go numb, threatening to give out. I feel alert and unconscious at the same time. My palms continue searing.

I can still hear the hiss of burning flesh echoing in my mind. My hands won't stop stinging.

The Arbiter shifts his gaze back to me. Using all my willpower, I turn my right hand over.

I gasp. Black dot. My chest tightens with dread.

"Show me your hand," the Arbiter demands.

I lift my palm unable to stop trembling. I clench my other fist, breathing heavily, horrified at what they might do to me for rebelling.

You're *never* coming home, Aurora.

Nothing worse can happen.

"Follow me," he says.

At the end of my street, black, rusty trains are waiting for us. These still ride on tracks rather than the magnetic wheels I've seen on modern trains.

The Arbiter turns to me. "Get in."

"Okay," I mutter, fighting the empty throbbing in my chest. I take a small step forwards, crumpling my eyes as tightly as I can. Don't cry.

Without warning, I'm yanked by my shirt and tossed inside the carriage. I skim across the cold metal and collide into many legs. I inhale sharp breaths as my shoulder flares in swells of pain. I apologise under my breath and try to crawl away, except there is nowhere to move. It's a single carriage with around fifty of us squashed together.

The insides of the wagon are wooden, and the stone flooring is littered with hay. I suspect that this was a livestock carriage.

Rigid iron bars are shoved across the opening side of the

carriage like a sliding door, leaving us locked inside with no way out.

Outside I spot kids running back to their homes into the warmth of their families. *Why was it not me?*

Enyo walks on a white carpet laid out for her towards our carriage.

"The Election has determined that you are core members in the revitalisation of Statera. You are now all subjects of the Equilibrium," Enyo announces, condescendingly.

I feel a disheartening shiver grip my body. I breathe out in a broken rhythm, incapable of finding relief.

What happens now?

My brother's face comes to mind. Jacob will grow up to be strong. He will be a good man. I will be proud of him. I have to convince myself of this. Because if I don't, I'm unsure how much longer I'll be able to withhold the building pressure that lingers behind my eyes. It's my only way to stay sane.

Everyone in this carriage is huddled together. The boys and girls around me range from merely taller than Jacob, to significantly bigger than me. There is not one fragment of hope between us. There is only silence.

There is a faint smell of fur and dry food. But worse than that, there is a strong, revolting presence of animal waste, which clearly hasn't been cleaned. The pungent odour stays trapped in my nostrils, while I combat my instinct to scream. I force myself to breathe through my mouth, suppressing the urge to vomit.

I squeeze through people, trying to get away from it all by reaching the metal bars. Arbiters drag away children and dump them into one place.

A reflective colour glistens as I look closer, clearly distinctive amongst the blackness of the night. I think I see a carriage with glass walls.

Enyo continues. "Those in opposition to the Trinities of the Elect will be eliminated. Statera welcomes the sacrifice to restore the balance of the living." She watches the carriage with crossed arms.

Inside, people crawl and scramble over one another. A cloudy white absorbs the colour of their eyes. I see their mouths stirring in despair.

I can't hear them, but I keep looking at their voiceless pleas for help.

Dark-green fumes begin to submerge the carriage. A pulsing emerald colour is all I can see.

A shallow breath escapes.

Human legs and arms poke out of the iridescent green gas like a travelling centipede. The glass convulses, sprouting cracks from the corners that creep towards the centre. Their screeches break out in a collection of breathless agony. Gasps and yells splutter outwards. I grind my teeth and start to scratch my skin. I'm paralyzed by the hopeless horror.

Torn and demented faces scour through the gas, repeatedly smashing their skulls against the glass in hopes of finding air. Fingernails scratch the glass. Others drop and vomit blood.

Tumultuous breaths of horror leave my mouth as I glance down at both of my palms. Both are branded by a black dot. I'm lost in a crackle of confusion.

I look up at the glass carriage, ice sinking into my gaze. Hannah's face is crushed against the glass as her jaw bones disconnect from her face.

She looks like a horrific distortion of what was once human. Her lips plead for her mother.

Her hand drags across the glass, leaving a thick handprint of black blood.

The sheer force of desperation compresses her body into an irregular, deflated sphere of flesh. Her eyes turn still. No person deserves such an end.

"Affirmative. Results confirm the hypothesis." Enyo walks away, a smug expression on her face.

I look down at the identical dots scarred into both palms.

This was the elimination of agency. What *will be*, is now what *is*. There was never *a choice*.

That night, women, children, even the men and the animals—all wept in harmony.

4

Lukas

The black dot seared into my flesh stares back at me like an eye. I shrink into myself, my face stiff as stone. My vision shivers then blurs, wet with fear. Uneasiness claws up my throat.

I can't breathe.

"Show me your hand," the Arbiter demands.

The white flames of the scale shimmer against the dark. Dogs bark like crazy, crying for their owners' return. My street overflows with Arbiters and patrol cars. Helicopters roar above.

My belly churns, leaving me faint. The ground spins around me. My head stings. I step back.

"Amelia, Sofia..." I mutter, my eyes turning wide. "Where are they?"

"I'll repeat myself. Show me your hand."

I watch specks of people scramble to their homes. It's like my lungs are contracting, as each breath grows more shallow. I can't see the girls anywhere.

"The Trinities of the Elect command you to lift your hand!" The Arbiter comes closer.

"Where are my sisters?" I ask.

"Wherever they chose to be," the Arbiter answers. "Last time I ask. Show me your hand."

I lift my right palm. Then I twist my torso and thrust my knuckles into his jaw. He falls with a static hum. My hand burns. His face felt like hitting metal.

I creep away from the main street, sticking to the shadows as I make my way home. Before I go, I must know if they're safe. I need to see them one last time.

I evade the Arbiters on the street. Dogs don't quit howling, as if they have rabies. Their screams conceal my movements.

"Red alert. X-Code 202240 has fled." The warning crackles over the Arbiters' shared radio. They'll find me soon.

I slip between houses, quick and silent. Muddy footsteps lead up to my home. I gasp. Amelia holds Sofia tightly, caressing her back.

"Look," Amelia says. "I told you he'd be back."

I stare at them, huffing air.

"Lukas!" Sofia lights up.

"Show me your palms."

They lift their hands. I exhale at the sight of the white dots. My shoulders fall at ease.

"I'm so glad you're okay." I rejoice and gently take their hands in mine.

Helicopters soar overhead, their searchlights scanning the street.

"You're bleeding." Amelia wipes my knuckles with her shirt. "What happened?"

My face falls. My eyes narrow.

I turn my palm over. "This happened."

"Oh!" Sofia squeals.

Amelia glares at me, her eyes quivering with rage. She grimaces like she's holding something back. Then she jumps into my chest, wrapping her arms around me tightly. Sofia joins the embrace, already sniffling.

"Look, you two stay safe—"

"Shut up and just hug us," Amelia interrupts.

Sofia trembles in my arms.

The girls I raised are strong and smart. I think Mum would be proud. I hope I did well.

"Sofia, Amelia. You two little troublemakers mean *everything* to me," I whisper. "Brother loves you... all right."

"We know," Amelia mutters.

"You tell us every morning." Sofia tries to smile, tears gliding down her face.

"Then let me tell you again. One last time."

I kiss them both on their foreheads.

Amelia's face tightens. Her eyes glimmer in pain. She sobs quietly, trying to stop herself.

"You look out for each other... all right?"

"Yes, Lukas." Sofia nods, still snivelling.

I stand up. "Be strong. For me."

"Okay," they mumble through their tears.

I give their shoulders a squeeze that says goodbye.

Footsteps thump behind me. I turn around. My father stands before me, his fingers wrapped around a bottle of liquor. Pale face, long hair, dirty clothes.

"Still drinking?" I grumble.

"Not t'night."

I show my palm. "Then you're sober enough to know what this means."

My father freezes.

"First your mother... now you too, huh," he murmurs.

"Mum's death is no longer an excuse." I grab his shirt and yank him towards me. My voice shakes. "You're a father."

"I know."

I lean in. Tears on the edge of my eyes.

"Then protect them."

My father's face creases with worry, his mouth opening as if to scream. Before I can react, my vision tumbles sideways, and something knocks me to the ground. Metallic arms grip me. I'm pressed against the dirt like a worm inside the beak of a bird.

Rough hands pat me down from my head to my chest to my groin. I tremor in discomfort.

I feel a drumming in my chest.

"Subject Lukas, X-Code 202240, secured," one Arbiter speaks into his radio.

"We'll take him to the Overseer," the other adds.

The two Arbiters snatch me with their claws and drag me away.

"Protect them!" I scream.

I see my sisters' red cheeks and their puffy faces. My heart aches, so I glare at my father.

"I swear, I'll haunt you from the grave if I have to!" I shriek, squirming my body and kicking my feet. "You can't leave again. You stay. You protect."

Get your asses off the floor! On your feet!"
Glaring lights startle us awake. I squint uncomfortably. The train wagon looks like it's used for exporting cargo goods. Except now, the seven unfamiliar faces and I have become the valuables.

"We don't have all day," the Arbiter snarls, raising his rifle to speed us up.

Everyone in the carriage climbs out, stumbling forwards reluctantly.

I'm the last to leave.

"Move." The Arbiter jabs his fingers into my neck and jerks me forwards. Three Arbiters surround us, light beaming from the gaps in their armoured chests.

There are no signs of human life. Just flattened grass that leads to two distant containers.

We're shackled at our ankles, chained together in a line. The eight of us look like prisoners. But the only crime we've committed is not wanting to die.

The weight of walking is hardly bearable. Most of us are barefoot. The cold air slashes my skin in a biting hiss. To die from the cold would be mercy.

"After this ordeal, I'm sleeping until noon," one Arbiter mumbles with exhaustion.

"There's plenty of Arbiters anyways," another replies. "We, the living, can have a break. Isn't that right, Doule?"

"You're certainly correct," the Arbiter named Doule responds, her voice monotone and mechanical. "Thousands of Double-A Units are refuelling for tomorrow's duties. Your presence may not be necessary."

While the Arbiters discuss their rest, I look at a small girl in front of me who trips over her feet. She's wearing nothing but an oversized shirt, looking like she was snatched out of bed.

I slip out of my jacket and place it on the girl's shoulders.

"Here, take it," I whisper. She glances over her shoulder, her eyes hollow. "It will keep you warm."

She nods and wraps the coat around herself tightly.

The cold's burn seeps into me, turning my flesh rigid. How could she endure this? Poor girl.

We halt to a stop outside, lining up against the containers. Its metal surface stings and chills my skin further.

"Overseer Milgram reporting. ETA thirty minutes. Please wait patiently and take care of the subjects." The report chimes from the little radios placed on the Arbiters' shoulders.

"Thirty minutes, huh," one Arbiter pouts. He turns to face us, licking his lips. I can taste fear in my mouth.

What is he thinking?

Suddenly the Arbiter extends his baton and steadily stomps towards us.

"I think I know how to take care of them," he says blankly, but his lips carve into a grin. He walks in a line, inspecting us. He then brushes the baton across the girl's face. "To have ourselves a little fun."

A collective gasp ripples through us.

The girl breathes heavily, her body shivering ever so slightly. She bites her lower lip and puts on a brave face. But I can see it in her eyes. The truth.

Everyone here knows what happens next.

"Well, it has been a while since the last time I had the opportunity to amuse myself." The other male Arbiter approaches us, taking off his helmet. He has an older, wrinkled face and almost no hair on his head. "But I certainly value the pleasure of such an occasion."

Fear jolts through me, like an electric current flowing through a cord of steel. Beads of sweat drip down from my forehead. I'm panting. And there is not a single thing I can do to stop myself. The Arbiter continues walking alongside us, looking down at the eight of us. Almost like he's deciding which one of us can provide him with the most joy. His footsteps echo in the quiet darkness, drawing closer with every step. Unexpectedly, he stops.

He stands before me.

He caresses my hair, gently and slowly.

"We have one who's shaking," he remarks, leaning in closer. With his breath hot against my ear, he whispers, "Are you frightened, boy?"

There's pleasure in his voice.

His sadistic stillness makes my blood run cold.

Steadily I lift my head, feeling his arm squeeze fiercely onto my shoulder. Taking a deep breath, I consider my options. He's plated in armour and armed with special-use equipment designed to harm or kill. There is no option for escape. Still, I must protect myself. I can't let them use me however they want.

I won't let them. I won't.

I nod, then murmur, "I'm just scared."

"Don't be scared. There's nothing to fear. Let me guide you, boy," he says, dragging his fingers around my waist. "I'll teach you."

"I don't want to learn."

His breaths grow moist, terrorising my skin with warmth. Goosebumps crawl up my arms.

"It's not *that* bad. I'll make you feel good. C'mon, just show me a little love," he pleads, pressing his face into my hair. There's a sense of desperation in his words, like he needs me. His grip on my waist and neck tightens, reaffirming his control.

But I know it's all an act. A way to persuade. A way to take advantage. A way to use me.

"I can't." My voice trembles. "Please stop."

But what I really want to say is: *I hope you die*.

His face lights up with anticipation. Then, in a wicked swing he grasps onto my shirt and takes me with him, as he marches into a container.

An orange light bulb casts a faint glow. The container's interior is metallic blue.

His lips curl into a rumble of laughter, shifting between high-pitched giggles and shrieks of madness. He unbuckles the pistol at his waist and waves it around.

"Let's see how much you'll want me to stop, with a bullet dancing inside your mouth," he mocks me.

Doule knocks on the container door. "As Overseer Milgram's Double-A assistant, I lack the authority to interfere. However, neither am I obligated to help you. I'd suggest a nimble break."

Doule leaves silently.

A bone-chilling tremor writhes through my veins. Not even *she* will help me.

I close my eyes and think of home. The aftertaste of dread warns me of the coming moments. My breathing begins to rise, as I feel the Arbiter's fingers go through my hair, until finally he claws it all together. His breath impales my neck.

"You are mine," he grunts, throwing me down to the metal floor.

The other Arbiter enters the container, holding the little girl's hand. She is still wearing my jacket.

"Lie down in the corner over there for me, angel."

"You can't take her, look how little and scared she is! Please no… pick somebody else!" A fist smashes into my temple. My head bounces against the floor. I lie still, stunned by the numbness in my skull.

"Keep your mouth shut," my Arbiter roars, clutching his fist and rubbing it tenderly.

These Arbiters don't care about the scars they'll leave behind. Pleasure is the only value in their miserable lives.

I try to crawl away. Try to grab something to defend myself with. But my arms are too heavy, and my body is slow. My head is still weak.

He drives his foot into my lungs, knocking the air out of me. A sharp, deep pain holds me hostage. A throbbing wave of distress fills my belly.

"I'm trying to make this as painless as possible for you, but you're making this process really difficult," he says, rolling up his sleeves to reveal hairy, veiny arms. "Stay still, and I'll make you feel good. I promise."

Breathe. I tell myself over and over again. But I'm no longer sure whether I'm trying to make the pain go away or whether I'm attempting to tame my own fear.

The Arbiter rips off his helmet. His sweat plummets onto me. The grey hair atop his head has thinned out. Drool streams out his lips. His brown eyes broaden with excitement. All he wants is me.

He grabs a knife from his waist and bends down towards me. I glance over to the girl. The other Arbiter viciously squeezes her neck with both hands.

"What is your name?"

The girl's neck begins to turn red and purple.

"I said, what is YOUR NAME?"

"Ariel." A soft gasp escapes the little girl's mouth, followed by a storm of wheezing.

"Don't look over there. Keep your eyes on me, boy." The Arbiter brushes the edge of his knife around my neck, leaving a trail of scrapes. The metal is frigid, and I can't help shivering.

He gently lowers his other hand to my inner thigh. Groping it in circular motions, as he begins to place his fingers higher and higher on my body. Gradually moving from my hips to my chest.

My throat runs dry, limbs weak and unsteady. I pant relentlessly as sickening thoughts make me twist and turn with disgust.

Maybe I deserve this.

My eyes sting, turning watery. I feel his weight on top of me. I feel his excitement surge with every beat of his heart. His sweat drips onto me. His touch is cruel and painful. I can't get him off me no matter how much I struggle to escape his grip. His grasp doesn't loosen. Not one bit. It only grows tighter.

Tears scorch trails down my cheeks. I don't know why this is happening to me. To us. I'm sorry, Ariel.

I feel shameful. I feel like I caused this.

His fingers rush all over my body, leaving behind scratch marks and handprints on my skin. I shut my eyes. I don't want to feel anything. But I feel it all.

My body is not mine.

Nothing matters anymore. I feel dirty.

One last time, I try to shake my hips, attempting to create enough force to kick him off of me. Yet he doesn't even flinch. It's hopeless. I feel worthless.

The sheer weight of his body alone keeps me pinned down. Incapable of producing any sort of movement, I bite my lip, hoping to distract myself from what's happening.

But his breaths and expressions haunt my mind.

His hands reach for my trousers, unbuttoning them and sliding them off my legs. I'm not naked, not yet. But I feel exposed. I feel disgusted. My hands tremble and I can't stop them.

Embarrassment floods my mind. A cold prickly sensation looms over me. I feel dizzy.

I try to squeeze and hold my knees together. But his arms separate my legs in an instant. I look away, ignoring his eyes. I am humiliated.

I don't want to feel.

His fingers crush my chin and turn my head back to him.

"Keep your eyes on me," he growls with pleasure, his breaths becoming quicker. His expression screams rage, but his eyes are hungry. He lifts up my shirt and presses his thumbs on my chest. I feel him poking into my belly. There's nothing I can do. His weight paralyses me. "I want you to enjoy me."

Please, someone help me. Make him stop. However, no one can hear my prayers. There is no more help. No more luck. No more strength.

I feel defiled.

He spits on my face and bites my neck. I turn away in humiliation. The ground vibrates with his movements. He lowers his hand, patiently circling around my crotch.

I try to scream, but the words won't come out. I form the shapes of the letters with my mouth. But there's no sound.

I can't resist any longer.

"Close your eyes," he orders, hungry for me.

A crushing sense of powerlessness leaves me bare and empty.

He licks his teeth and his eyes intensify.

I'm flung onto my belly, and he holds me down. He cuts my underwear and tears it off me.

He snarls, "Don't try to resist. Just open up to me."

I feel him pressed against my back.

I don't want to feel anything.

"Please stop," I murmur.

"Just bend over." A deep, throaty moan slips past his lips. The hand on my neck holds me in place, his fingernails digging into my skin. Yet the pain is numb, almost imaginary. Shock blinds my senses.

He grinds himself against my thighs. I feel nausea overwhelm me. My stomach twists with shame.

My heart pounds, trying to burst out of my chest. Droplets of sweat gallop down my back. He spins me back around to face him.

Fear encages me, like the literal chains squashing my ankles. I squeeze breath down my windpipe.

I look around in hopes of grabbing something. Something to set me free.

But there's nothing. Only the wetness of his lips. My privates are cuddled in saliva. I'm frozen.

"This won't hurt a damn bit, just—"

Blood spatters into my eyes. The man collapses on me, his weight suffocating. The gunshot momentarily deafens my hearing as a phantom squeal rings in my ears. Another gunshot whips past.

I feel light-headed.

Doule enters the container, kneels and inspects the Arbiter.

"The bullet appears to have struck the cervical neck region," she observes.

"Excellent." Overseer Milgram walks inside, wearing black trousers and a tight, white shirt. "And the other one?"

"Wound to the larynx. Will bleed out promptly without medical attention."

Overseer Milgram walks over to the Arbiter slouched beside the girl, who is pressing both hands firmly against his Adam's apple as blood gushes out.

"Who gave you permission to play with my subjects? While I can excuse what you did, the problem is *who* you did it to. These are the subjects of the Equilibrium. Essential to me and FORTE. You disgraced the Gods!" Milgram roars, then smashes his fist into the Arbiter's face repeatedly until the man's body slumps over. Milgram frowns. "Now my shirt is dirty."

Ariel is too stunned to express anything besides stillness. She sits with her arms wrapped around her legs. Her face is scrunched with horror. She tries to stay motionless, but her body fails to lie for her as her legs tremble more violently than any type of fear I have ever witnessed.

I feel so bad for her.

I notice that I'm quivering as well and attempt to regain my composure, forcing myself to manually breathe in and out.

"This is so infuriating!" Milgram complains. "Doule, what were Enyo's instructions prior to escorting the elected subjects to Olympus Mons?"

"Anaesthetic sedation."

"Okay. Tend to the girl. Ensure she's physically and psychologically stable. If cognitive trauma is evident, administer the Resurrector prototype as per Enyo's wishes."

Doule carefully scoops up Ariel and leaves the container.

I'm hoping to be left for dead. But that is a futile wish. Overseer Milgram drops to his knees beside me and lifts my arm.

"Sit up."

I get up and watch as Overseer Milgram pulls out a syringe with a clear vial. Suddenly, I feel a sharp prick in my arm, a cold fluid entering my bloodstream.

"Do you ever wonder what the Equilibrium is?"

I shrug. "I hoped I'd never find out."

"Well," Milgram chuckles, "wouldn't that have been nice?"

I imagine being at home with my sisters. Playing a board game before bed. Mostly empty bellies, but full hearts. At peace. Yeah, that would be nice.

"Do you believe in the Trinities of the Elect?" Milgram asks.

"I have to," I reply.

"That's not your real answer."

My eyes become heavy. In between gasps of consciousness, Milgram begins unravelling his thoughts.

"Memory is a fragile strength. But it's what defines your essence, makes you who you are. It's the power of the self. And so, it's the only agent of freedom we've failed to purify," Milgram explains.

The world is spinning. I can still feel the man's weight smothering me. I feel shameful and empty.

"*You're the last step.*"

"But isn't the Equilibrium… a ceremony… just a tradition?" I ask confused, avoiding eye contact.

"It's a tradition for Statera. But for us, it's an opportunity of cleansing," he answers vaguely.

"To remove free will?"

"No. To create our *own* free will. And to do that, we must rinse individuality. Memory *must* collapse."

"What?" I feel myself drifting off.

Overseer Milgram smiles. "Just like this. Remember, no act of freedom goes unpunished."

The moment then began to fade as the injection took effect. Light vanished into a patchwork of blackness. The only thing left, hovering within my subconscious was one particular phrase from the Overseer, repeating itself throughout the vastness of my mind, over and over again in my sleep—*Memory is a fragile strength.*

5

Aurora

Hope withers. Eerie murmurs circle me. Earlier, the train wagon lurched to a stop. Somewhere in that dread and that pain, I passed out. I'm guessing they used gas.

Ever since then I've been alone. The only familiarity is blackness.

Dogs howl, their cries echoing into the night. In the distance, I hear the rumbling of train tracks. Sweat trickles down my spine, peeling away my sense of humanity.

I feel like a cornered animal.

"Let them see!" Overseer Milgram roars, his voice hoarse and too close like he's inside my ear. The dogs continue to growl. Fierce metallic clicks clatter over my head, like a helmet being unlocked.

I go from black to dark. The night sky is bleak, devoid of stars. The landscape is flat, barren and shrouded in mist. I reach out and run my fingers through the grainy earth. It feels like sand.

I open my palm. My eyes freeze. The black dot is gone. I check my other hand only to find clear skin.

Where the hell am I? How did they get rid of the branding?

Suddenly a beacon casts a spotlight of blazing white light. Overseer Milgram stands out in the dark. I notice the shadows that surround me. Subjects of all different sizes stand in a line.

What are they going to do to us?

I sniff the frosty air but only find the scent of sweat and hunger.

"Congratulations on the Election. You are now the restorers of Statera," Milgram says. "The next step is essential to the Equilibrium. We must restore the balance between the living and the dead. The living must merit life, and only those who persist above others deserve it. It is survival of the fittest. The weak will be disposed. The strongest paired. Evolution demands it. Welcome to the Elimination Link."

I gaze into the line of subjects. Many stand still, probably terrified, their pain buried in their sobs. But tears are meaningless in the face of evil. We were rounded up like cattle. They'll continue to treat us as their pets, their animals, their property.

We're breathing skeletons, two-legged puppets for their entertainment. To them we're not human.

"In the Elimination Link you'll compete against your peers. You'll complete objectives under timed conditions. All subjects will be split into different, randomised groups. From each group, only one boy and one girl may live. That is all," Milgram concludes.

Metal continues to grind against itself in the distance. The train tracks squeal.

I sense my body shrinking, losing sensation in my limbs. I feel unsteady. My face grows heavy, turning still. Even my heartbeat is turning slow. It's like I've lost control over my body.

Overseer Milgram walks away into the dark behind us. My eyes disobey me, refusing to follow him. The spotlight disappears.

The wind whips by me. The train tracks tremble in a metallic rhythm of high-pitched shrieks.

Untamed panic floods me. I can't move.

"I will be your guide," Milgram says, calmly. His voice echoes again, like he's inside my head. My senses return. I slump over and drop to my knees, fetching for air. *What the hell just happened?*

"Welcome to your first objective in the Elimination Link." He pauses as something behind me begins to tremor in an oddly stable rhythm. I turn around. The clicking of metal grows louder, and patches of sand kick up into the air, forming clouds of mist. "For your first test of survival…"

Silence deepens into tension.

This is it. I release a slow breath filled with exhaustion and anticipation. An intensifying rumble eclipses every other sound as it approaches.

"Catch the train! Whoever doesn't make it will be immediately eliminated," Milgram announces. An eerie shiver clambers up my spine. Focus, Aurora. Staying alive for Jacob, that's all that matters now. "Your life is in your hands. May you Blaze or Burn! Now, run."

Ahead, the train pierces through the mist, creeping from left to right. We break into a sprint, rushing towards the train as fast as we can. Adrenaline surges through me. I don't dare slow down.

Billows of dust and sand rise into the air. The ground quakes underneath the horde of drumming footsteps.

The train continues to drift, its rear end coming into view. I shift my direction to the right for a shorter path and continue chasing it.

Holding my breath, I dash forwards, refusing to lose hope. Once I get close enough to attempt to hop on, I reach what looks like a caboose, a wagon with metal railing at the train's end.

I spot other figures climbing onto the train. They must've surpassed me during the sprint.

"Thirty seconds remain until the fireworks commence," Overseer Milgram announces.

My heartbeat makes my ears ring. My eyesight plummets into blurriness. The train becomes a moving shade of grey.

Impulsively, I leap forwards into the air, my arms stretched out to grasp the railing. The pulsing sensation in my stomach grates my nerves.

My fingers just grasp onto the bars of the exterior, and I squeeze as firmly as I can, trying to hold on. The pounding of footsteps makes my heart pound faster.

Screams rage in anguish all around me. I'm guessing some have lost the race for their lives.

An abrupt shudder tosses me backwards, and I feel myself swinging wildly, barely holding on. I realise that the bar is slowly loosening out of place. I'm swayed side to side by the train's momentum. The wind lashes at my face. The metallic rod shrieks as it turns.

"I'll draw you a surprise."

"Bring me something from your trip."

"I'll get you flowers, Sis."

Jacob's voice rings in my head. I envision his sweet smile. Viciously I grip onto the rod as tightly as I can. I drain the courage from my memories.

I only have one shot at this.

The moment I shift my hips, the bar jerks further out of place, and my hand begins to slip.

"Ten seconds!" Milgram yells, urgently.

Ahead of me, a kid propels himself towards the train, his grunts ragged. His body is soaked in sweat, covered in furious determination. With each stride he gets closer. Then his foot slips, and he vanishes into the mist.

Desperately stretching my hand out, I hope to clutch onto another supporting rod, or the railing—anything. I reach and reach. My fingers finally grasp the bar next to it, but the instant I secure my grip, the rod detaches. My other hand burns with tension. My own breathing starts to suffocate me. I shut my eyes, preparing for death. The wind ferociously slashes my face. I feel my body shrinking away.

The tightness of my grip weakens. I'm struggling to hang on. My fingers are slipping.

I'm sorry Jacob. I can't keep my promise.

Don't waste another breath on me.

Draw for someone else.

A shadow emerges in front of me. But the winds disperse my vision. Warmth surrounds my hand. The firmness of my grip on the bar shrivels.

I slam my eyelids shut. And let go.

I feel weightless. Wind flicks past me. I gallop through the air. This is peaceful.

That's when I sense the forceful pressure of two hands digging into my arms. Something has curled around my forearms. I open my eyes as I'm swung upwards. A silhouette hurls me over their shoulder, and I'm flung into the last carriage of the train.

My head crashes against the wooden floor. Scorching numbness engulfs my senses. Sounds of a clock ticking oscillate through the entire train.

"Light the fireworks!" Twisted enthusiasm seeps from the Overseer. With my heavy, crooked legs, I rush to the window. In a vicious cycle of falling, bruising my knees, then getting back up, I manage to lift myself up to the glass.

A deafening eruption of hums fills my ears. I stay still. Red droplets bounce against the window like rain.

The remaining kids who didn't make it burst up in flames and explode. Their internal organs splatter onto the ground. My hands throb in fear as I crush the window trim.

Not even a corpse can be seen. Only dismembered remains, which trickle in dark blood. A bubbling mess.

I start envisioning my father's death. I remember the harrowing sight. Terror binds to me.

I can't breathe. I can't see. I can't move.

An obsidian cloak smothers me unconscious.

My body shakes in line with the heartbeat of the train. The carriage rocks side to side in an unpredictable rhythm. I'm confined within a cell, my arrival here a blank gap in memory. I'm caged by three slanted panels on the back wall and iron bars on a sliding door parallel to it. The middle panel on the back wall is glass.

I lie on the ground, reliving the moment those kids erupted. The spread of blood. The tangle of guts. Everything feels wrong.

Rays of sunlight gently force my eyes open. Demolished hills, perforated mountains, craters as large as cities, dried up lakes, and burned forests glare back at me from afar. Life has turned its back on the world.

I gaze into my reflection on the metal bars, wondering about the pristine white uniform that has replaced my torn clothes. My face appears inanimate. I look down at my hands, appalled that the branding from the Election is no longer there. My knees should be bruised, my fingers with thickened, stinging skin but yet I'm perfectly fine.

Have I healed already? The hell.

A chilling realisation causes dread to course through my veins. My clothing was the last thing I had that was mine. They have left me with nothing.

Time slips away unnoticed. Suddenly, the train begins to tremble violently, decelerating to an unexpected halt. I glance through the window. Trees loom within the fog, their branches sprawling into the shadows. The twisted roots sliver through the moss and dirt in circular patterns. Raindrops rattle the windowpane.

The carriage shakes as it comes to a stop. A bell rings from outside my cell.

Without warning, the cell's door slides open by itself. My sight radiates in extreme brightness. Closing my eyes, I bring an arm to cover my face, as the blinding sensation temporarily stuns me. Nothing else but a blazing shade of white irradiates my vision.

Bringing my palm closer to my eyes, I start to see the texture and encasing of my own bones. Panic flutters in my stomach.

The blur dissolves.

"Welcome back. May the Trinities of the Elect allow us to restore prosperity," Overseer Milgram utters.

My chest feels tight. My breaths betray my uneasiness. Milgram's voice only reminds me of the kids. He called it fireworks. The hell is wrong with him?

"Allow me to reveal the remaining subjects," Milgram says, just as another cell is illuminated. A pixelated girl stands before me. Eventually she comes into focus. It's a young girl with long hair. Her lips twitch into a smile. Her eyes glow, wide and crazy. I find her suspicious, like there's something lurking behind that innocent face.

The silence between us permeates with tension.

"The train is composed of twelve carriages," Overseer Milgram announces. "Every fourth carriage holds two of you. Six subjects remain."

The girl twitches her neck erratically, like she was a feral dog fighting its instincts.

"Your objective is to stop this train. However, only one boy and one girl are permitted to live." His voice lowers, reverent. "May you Blaze or Burn."

The girl stares at me. We're probably both asking the same question: *Who kills who?*

I won't harm her if she leaves me alone. I hope it doesn't come to that. But I will kill anybody to protect myself. Self-preservation is an instinct. It's my intrinsic right.

The bell rings twice.

Both of us leap ahead at full speed.

The carriages are three-dimensional octagons, with windows at the sides. Strips of orange lights stretch across every facet.

The train accelerates at an alarming rate. But I keep dashing forwards. The girl has overtaken me. She reaches the next carriage while putting as much space between us as possible.

A metal latch clicks. My carriage starts disconnecting from the main part of the train. Rapidly, I sense the carriage losing speed, like the air was pulling me back. There must be automated brakes causing this. I swing my elbow and break the final window of my carriage. I climb out and throw myself on top of the carriage, staggering sideways from the harsh winds.

Three. Two. One. I vault forwards.

The impact shudders through my limbs as my arms slam into the roof of the train, making me lose balance in a precarious tumble. I leverage my weight in a frantic struggle and fling myself inside.

Sharp intakes of breath agonise me. The thudding in my chest accelerates rapidly. My stomach sinks.

I force myself to stand up, my legs wobbling. My knees sway. I rest against the octagon wall and catch my breath. Think of Jacob. Survive.

Why did this happen? Because the girl reached the next carriage before me? If every carriage disconnects, then all subjects will be pushed closer together.

I get it. They want us to fight.

Think, Aurora! I demand. *How do trains work?*

Hypothetically, the first carriage should be the control room. If the girl has sprinted ahead, then she's already figured that out. I must find another way.

My only hope is hidden in the shadows, at the very edges of the floor. At the sides of the bottom facets there are grey and black cables. Without wasting another second, I hurdle towards the centre of the train, passing by empty carriages. I spring ahead following the wires.

I follow the wires as they disappear and reappear from sight, weaving through cabins, seating areas, cells, and rooms that emerge in the other carriages.

All of the cables conjoin at the ceiling in a singular tube. Their journey carries on for a while longer, until they vanish into a cabin. An electrical room?

Doubt creeps in. This can't be it.

I check the ceiling and the ground that precede the cabin. But now I know for sure—all the cables come together and vanish into this one room.

I walk up to the cabin's door, which hides close to the wall. I twist the handle. But it doesn't budge. Pulling the doorknob downwards, I strike the door with my shoulder. Then again. The door swings open, sending me to the floor, as I barely have time to brace myself for impact.

In a rush, I rise to my feet, close the door and scout the room. The strips of light grow brighter from my movement. I see shelves filled with rows of cables.

Where could the power source be?

My neck hairs stand up stiff.

My eyes widen.

I spot my shadow on the ground. It grows bigger. Bigger than it should be. I sense an ominous presence behind me.

I step forwards, ready to turn. But before I'm able to rotate, something unseen wraps its arms around my mouth and neck, restraining me. I twist and turn in rampant motions, yet my arms are only imprisoned with more force.

"Take a moment to collect yourself. Don't make me break you," a boy whispers, his voice laced with adrenaline and fear. I tug my elbows, ready to strike. "The train doesn't have a battery or a control room."

Distant thuds approach us.

I clench my jaw. *Who the hell is he?*

He lets me go. "Be quiet. The *others* are here."

6

Lukas

Excruciatingly, I scream in silence. My eyes scorch red. Not even a whimper leaves my mouth. The air stuck in my lungs pummels my body with pulses of strangling misery.

The girl watches me blankly. She extends her arm, her gaze attentive, her free hand soothing the pain in her elbow. I clutch my injured chest. Each breath is a struggle as pain radiates through my torso.

The other subjects march through the corridor of the train, unconcerned about revealing their location. A palpable tension gushes through my veins. *It's him.*

I can smell the metallic scent of blood. At least, I think I can. It's the same scent from moments ago.

The poor boy lay motionless. His eyes were still. Bursts of fresh blood oozed from his neck. The killer had a raging tenderness etched into his grin, as he smashed a girl's face into a wooden table. Again and again. Her nose was twisted, eyes bruised with puffed and swollen cheeks.

"You're a coward!" I yelled, fury coursing through my fists.

The killer drops the girl. He meets my eyes and says, earnestly, "It takes courage to kill."

I glare at the girl. Her face is cold and stern, as those dark brown eyes shoot through me. The same eyes I'd seen yesterday on the train. Remembrance crumbles my composure. The sparks of red and orange fireworks flash my vision. My chest tightens.

A putrid taste of yesterday fills my mouth. I fight the urge to vomit and gulp it back down.

We both sense the vibrations beneath our feet. The others are approaching. We continue to gaze at each other. I gently press a finger against my lips. Footsteps hammer the ground. Muffled voices intersect outside this cabin.

"Where did she go?" the killer groans, furiously.

Another pair of feet trample onto the scene. The girl and I press our ears against the wall to hear better. We face each other, silenced by the stifling tension surging between us. She looks familiar.

"It's *him*," a young girl's voice emerges, calmly. "He must've reached her before us."

"Doesn't matter," the boy hisses in response. "The other two choked to death. And so will the two of them. As for the boy, I'll kill him with my own hands."

"In that case, let's not waste any energy," the girl says.

"What in Statera's name do we do now?" he asks.

"We stop the train and we find them."

They walk away further down the train.

The girl who elbowed me stands up. Her head tilts, puzzling how to react.

She clenches her fist. "Get away from me."

I step back.

"Talk," she demands.

"All right... just calm down," I reply, but her eyes only grow colder. "I saw that boy shatter a girl's skull until her head could no longer stand on her neck." I take a deep breath. "The girl with him wields a metal bat. She killed the other boy. There's only four of us left now."

Her face stays flat, unconvinced.

"They're killers. They're trying to get me, too, and now you as well," I pause. "We *need* to go."

The girl strides closer, then pushes me. I stagger a few paces, but she grabs my shoulder before I can fall and then shoves me into the wall. She presses her other hand against my ribs.

"Don't you lie to me," she whispers, harshly.

I stare at her. "I'm not lying."

"Then whose blood is that?" Her eyes flick up to my face.

"I don't know," I say.

She rubs her thumb above my brows, and I flinch away. I tap my forehead myself. It stings and itches.

"It's mine," I discover. "Look, we don't have the time for this. We must go."

The more time we waste, the closer death lurks.

"How did the blood get on you?" She keeps me pinned against the wall. I don't fight back.

"I must've been hit, I don't know." I shrug. "We need to move."

She glares at me. Her eyes narrow with suspicion.

"I don't trust you."

"Then don't," I reply. "But we need to go now. If you don't want to work together, I'll go alone."

"I'm not letting you go."

I lean in, our faces inches apart. "Then we'll both die."

"You want me to believe you? Then give me one good reason to trust you."

"I'll show you the bodies," I spit out, bitterly.

She shoves her palm into my ribs. I grunt a stifled squeal. Slowly, I manoeuvre my foot behind her leg.

"There's no evidence you didn't kill them. I can't trust your word," she snaps.

I grind my teeth in anger.

In a sudden burst, I throw myself forwards, using the foot behind her to trip her. She snatches onto me, taking both of us to the ground. Upon impact, I clamp both her arms and ram them above her head so that she's forced to listen to me.

"I would only kill to protect myself. Don't you dare say that!" I explode, my voice hoarse and on the edge of breaking into tears. "I didn't kill them."

Her face shakes with anger.

"How can I trust you?" She struggles.

"Because I saved you," I murmur in irritation. "You were about to lose your grip on the train railing. I pulled you back into the seating area. You passed out shortly after."

"Damn... That was you?"

She frowns in recognition.

"I'm sorry," she mutters quietly.

"Just don't hit me again," I respond. I get off of her and extend a hand to help her stand up.

She averts her eyes. "Okay."

She takes my hand. When she stands up I get a proper look at her. She's maybe ten centimetres shorter than me. Her dark-black hair brushes just slightly over her shoulders. Her face is slender and stubborn.

"Together?" I ask before opening the cabin door. She knows what I mean.

"I can't say no," she murmurs, softly.

"Then before we go... if there's no power source or control room, do you have any idea how to stop this train?"

She looks at me and grins smugly.

"We'll just have to break the train bit by bit," she says, confidently. A glint in her eyes tells me to trust her. Maybe I shouldn't, but I can't fight my gut-feeling. "Follow me."

We creep up the train, staying light on our feet. Once we reach an intersection between two carriages, she waves me over. There's a small gap, where you can see the metal latches linking the carriages together.

She crouches down. "Look… all of the carriages are connected. If one goes off the track, they all do."

"That's… how we stop the train?" I question her, hesitantly. She nods. "How about us? Once the train goes off its rails it will crash."

"I know," she replies, unruffled.

"What about us?" I envision the carriages merging into a wreck of disfigured metal. "We could die."

"You have any better ideas?"

"Nothing."

"I thought as much," she retorts. "We have no other choice."

How do you stop a train that can only accelerate or decelerate? You remove its tracks. Logical, I suppose.

"We need to get to the front of the train," she says, standing back up.

I consider our safety. The train's front resembles a nose with thicker metal encasing the carriage. We should have better odds there.

"Let's move," I reply.

A frosty shiver tumbles down my spine. I sense that looming feeling I can't explain. Last time I felt it was my mum's goodbye.

"I love you, my sunshine." She kissed my forehead, smiled and left for work. I didn't know that would be the last time I saw her alive.

On our way to the primary carriage, we witness tables sprawled out with rope and all sorts of weapons from blades to spears. All cabins and cells have disappeared. So have the bodies of the dead boy and girl. But I don't tell her this.

Something is wrong.

We approach the first carriage. We stay silent, communicating in the darkness with our eyes.

Towards the front of the carriage, there is a slanted desk with three levers. Having no time to investigate, I pull down the right lever. Instantly, the train begins to accelerate.

"Stop that!" the girl hisses.

Out of panic, I pull the other levers but nothing happens. The train darts forwards, reaching ever greater speeds.

"It won't stop!" I call out.

"Damn it."

We both glance outside through the nose window of the train's cockpit. Fog seeps through the night. Tiny dots glint in the distance. I look closer. In the distance, dimly lit train tracks diverge into multiple directions.

I spot a faint glimmer just beside the approaching tracks.

"We have to derail the train," I say, pointing to the glow I noticed. "I think that's the lever that switches the tracks."

The girl's eyes light up. "We need to switch the tracks at the last possible moment."

"Yeah, the train will go off its rails."

"Okay," she says, walking away to the other carriage. She returns a moment later, holding a spear and wrapping a handful of rope around her waist, then double knotting it. I guess she intends to strike the lever with the spear, swinging it like a bat.

She gives me the other end of the rope attached to her waist. "Trust me?"

"Just be careful," I respond, tightening the rope around my waist and also wrapping it around my hand. "I won't let you go."

"Tell me when we're getting closer." She squeezes through the gap in between the carriages and climbs on top of the primary carriage.

Death is a coin toss with no bias.

"Get in position," I say, hearing metallic thuds above my head as she walks further to the front. I look through the gap she climbed out of, ensuring I'm calculating our distance from the two pathways accurately. The rope squeezes so much I fear it could rip. "Almost there."

I hear the rumbling of footsteps approaching.

"You can't run now," the boy grunts, emerging from the darkness of the carriage opposite me, dragging an axe. It's *him*. He's with a girl. "We must eliminate our competition. This is just the way it is."

"Let me handle this," the girl says. She escapes the shadows. Her face makes me tremble. It's Ariel, the same girl from the container where the Arbiters used us. Tremors jolt through my chest. Beads of tears stream down my cheeks. She reaches out to comfort me. The moment she touches me it replicates *his* touch from back then. The immovable weight… the suffocation.

The others tread towards me. I pivot constantly, monitoring the train's distance from the impending pathways. Paranoia scatters through me. I don't know where to look.

"Let go of the rope," Ariel says as she draws closer. "And we'll make it quick."

I glimpse at the tracks. Around sixty seconds left.

"I'm not a killer," I answer. Her figure stays mostly concealed within the dark.

"Oh, Lukas… You stood by and let the girl die. You let her die. You didn't fight for her. You just watched. You're already a killer."

"Step back." I shove the girl lightly. "I had nothing to do with it. He killed them both. I'm not like you."

I whip my head round and notice we're almost there.

"Do it now!" I yell as loud as I possibly can, before the girl in front of me can react. She swings her fist at my head. I jump backwards, struggling to stay upright and hold onto the rope. Once again, she lunges at me.

Swiftly, I dash my arm to the side and thrash my elbow into her cheekbone. She falls to the ground on impact.

The killer freezes.

"Get up, Ariel!" he shouts, running over to her limp body. "I said get up."

Not wasting this opportunity, I start to pull the rope back. But nothing comes back, just more empty rope.

"Hey, where are you?" I yell, but no one answers me. The carriage starts to quake beneath my feet like it was hopping up and down. Did she do it?

The boy runs at me, his eyes protruding with rage. He swings his arm back, preparing to throw his axe.

Before he's able to reach me, the train tilts sharply to the right and we're both knocked upside down, leaving us incapacitated in mid-air.

The air screeches with metallic sounds as the carriages derail and collide, crashing into one another with explosive bangs. I hold my breath, as I'm violently flung into the train's interior. Pain erupts in my skull, and I feel the warm trickle of blood running down my face.

7

Aurora

Disoriented and lost, I look around as debris surrounds me. My vision is a fog of distant colours. I struggle to find my balance, attempting to stand back up again.

Immediately, I open my mouth to shout his name.

But… what is his name? I think to myself, my mind suddenly going blank. He resembled someone so familiar. I thought we exchanged names.

My brows furrow in confusion as I make my way towards the crashed train. The forest floor crunches under my feet. I can see the silhouettes of trees in the distance, lit up by the flames of the wreckage.

After I pulled the lever, the train had shot onto grass and decelerated before ultimately collapsing sideways. Every carriage crashed into each other. I had managed to leap off the front just as it slowed down. Right before it fell.

I drag my legs forwards, grunting through the pain.

He saved me. It's only right I do the same.

Remains of the train are scattered in pieces. As I approach, smoke spirals up like a cloud of serpents into the black sky. The once octagon shape of the train is now flattened, fractured metal. The fires are few but they flash with electric sparks.

My heart beats slow and heavy. Where is he?

I don't want to shout. The killers could still be alive. I must find him fast.

Crickets chirp in the dark. Flames crackle and sizzle with jolts. My ears ring from the tumbling carriages.

I can't stop hearing it.

I find what's left of the primary carriage, its distinctive arched shape now a heap of warped metal.

I hear a voice from the top of the mound, accompanied by wheezes and croaks. "She won't find you."

The grass is dotted with shards of glass. Carefully, I hop from foot to foot, avoiding the fragments, and draw closer to the voice.

I spot the killer towering over the boy who saved me.

"I was going to settle this fist to fist. To give you a fair fight," he says, before lowering to his knees and inching nearer to his face. "But you can't even do that, can you?"

The poor boy lies still, his eyes shrinking. His flesh is carved with gashes. Blood trickles down his face.

"We just stopped the train," the boy coughs, his voice shallow.

Quietly, I search through rubble, hoping to find some sort of weapon. I decide on a sharp chunk of metal, like the remnant of a chair leg. I start to creep up the mound, staying low.

The killer peers at the boy, like a bear with torturous patience.

I evade any placement of my feet on dented metal, remaining silent.

"That makes more sense now." The killer digs his hands into the boy's throat. His biceps ripple with stiffness. "Tell me, who is we?"

The boy doesn't speak.

"Who were you with?" he howls.

"It doesn't matter," the boy grunts.

The killer squeezes the boy's throat even harder. "Who is she?"

"You're a coward. Just do what needs to be done."

"I asked, who is she?" the killer shrieks, his vocal cords rasping with anger. I crawl towards them, gripping my chunk of metal. He doesn't seem to sense me.

"It doesn't matter. You can't kill her. She's the last girl left," the boy croaks, his face growing a shade darker, veins threatening to pop. "You've lost Ariel."

"You're right." The killer nods. "Ariel died in the crash…" He pauses, his eyes sharpening with recognition. "I'll tell her so did you."

My foot slips, and I slide down the rubble, as metal and plastic tumble down with me. The killer turns around instinctively, eyes wide with worry. In that split second, the boy retracts his legs and kicks the killer in the chest. He staggers backwards, his feet unsteady. I lunge forwards, swinging the chunk at his face. His jaw snaps to one side, and he flumps to the ground.

"The Elimination Link has been established," Overseer Milgram announces, his voice still too loud and too close. "One boy and one girl remain. Await further instructions. Next, we'll proceed with Fractured Faith."

The boy croaks nonsense under his breath. His eyes shut, returning to his previous state of half alive, half dead. I take him by the arms and drag him away from the wreckage. The flames disappear into distant flickers of orange. I feel numb to my injuries. I can't feel the boy's weight. I head towards the sea of trees.

Towards the darkness.

Towards the unknown.

The fire rises, as the sound of branches burning like rhythmic tapping deteriorates into silence. Into nothingness.

He lies an arm's reach across from me, motionless. Only his chest rises in uneven intervals, indicating that he's alive.

I watch him the same way I used to watch Jacob's face in the morning before leaving for work. The boy's face droops with exhaustion even while asleep. For a boy, his hair is long and wavy. Hollow cheeks and pale skin reveal he doesn't eat enough. Just like me.

His face is slit with thick gashes below his eyes and across his forehead. At least the blood's stopped. He must've smashed his head into something when the train crashed.

He'll have scars. But he'll live.

I listen to the tranquil chaos of the flames. Popping and cracking. I try to get rid of the turmoil inside me.

The fire creates a soothing melody. I remember a time like this…

My dad lay on hard dirt, covered in streaks of mud. Everything around him was blurry, I couldn't even see the surrounding trees. Immediately, I ran up to him and kissed him, told him how much I've missed him. Pressed my hands against his cheeks. His stare remained the same. Immobile. He didn't respond. I moved my hands to his forehead, feeling his coldness steadily radiate onto me. It felt like I was touching ice. Nevertheless, he was a statue, and I was merely an observer.

"Dad!" I quietly whispered, as every shred of happiness faded from my voice. "Can you hear me?"

He was gone. In the blink of an eye, I found myself standing with white flowers in hand, while men dressed in black stood around me. They were statues as well. Bewildered, I began to make my way forwards. The dark sculptures turned to dust as I passed them. Way ahead of me, I saw his face from a distance, shining bright. My face was gloomy and wet. My tears formed oceans of sorrow, submerging my inner misery in a weeping silence.

I was no longer his little girl.

With each desperate stride, I was closer to my dad. I looked down at his face. And gently put the white rose above his name.

"Hey, wake up," a voice calls for me. My eyelids flutter slowly in response. "Where are we?"

I recognise his voice. Leaping from my foetal position, I impulsively wrap my hands around him.

"Are you okay?" I shudder.

"Yeah, I'm all right," he replies, startled. He taps my back encouragingly. "Alive thanks to you."

"I'm glad," I say, my chest light with relief. Awkwardly, I pull away and sit down beside him. "We're even now."

The boy smiles. "I wasn't counting."

The fire has died down into smouldering bits of red. The embers glow in the inky blackness of the night.

"Do you miss home?" I ask.

He meets my gaze. "I miss my sisters." His face wanders off, deep in thought. "I'm worried what they'll do without me."

"I'm sure they're okay."

"I wouldn't be so sure," he whispers, looking down. He plucks a few pieces of grass and plays around, tying them together like a braid.

The boy glances at me. "Do you miss anything?"

"I miss sleeping in my bed," I reply.

He chuckles. "Yeah, I miss that too."

Lightning thrashes through the night, catching both of us off guard. Thunder echoes deep and loud, almost like my mind had hallucinated it inside.

Specks of light glimmer across the trees like fireflies leading further into the forest.

"Follow the light and find the graves. There you will face your Fractured Faith," Overseer Milgram instructs us.

The boy and I walk silently, led by the dots of light. The skies start rumbling, flooding the night with rain. The longer we walk, the more the forest transforms. Trees grow smaller and thinner. Branches wrinkle without leaves. The grass shifts to moss, becoming dryer and harder. By the time we reach the graves, the rain has soaked my white uniform and left me shivering.

"Welcome to the final test of the Elimination Link. Fractured Faith. Truth will be unveiled. Pain will prevail. And only then, can a Duo be paired or discarded," Overseer Milgram announces, his voice stern. "In the centre of the graveyard, you will each find a loaded weapon."

My feet sink into the mud of the graveyard, as we head to the centre. On the ground we find two pistols. There are two graves opposite one another.

"Subjects take your weapons."

I pick up the steel pistol. It's heavy and compact.

"The shattering of truth can make or break a bond between humans. Power changes us. Power changes how we view the truth and how we react to it. Humans become swayed by emotion. Vulnerability tames our rationality. And we become governed by our desires," Overseer Milgram explains, his voice calm, yet seeping with enthusiasm. "Let us witness your Fractured Faith!"

Raindrops plummet to the ground, tapping against the mud as if caressing the earth.

"What is this?" the boy stutters, reading the name of one of the graves.

"Nearly ten years ago both of your parents died. Aurora's father and Lukas's mother. However, they killed each other. Not directly. But they died in consequence of the other's actions," Overseer Milgram asserts, his tone shaking with suspense. My jaw twitches with anger. The pummelling in my chest grows louder. The boy's name reemerges into my mind, like a crashing comet. "The truth has fractured your faith. It has broken the trust you shared. Now the power is in your hands. Seek justice, seek revenge, seek acceptance. The choice is yours. May you Blaze or Burn!"

I stagger forwards, unprepared to read the name on the grave. My eyes scorch as I stiffen my face, stifling my tears.

The letters "BRUCE" are engraved into the headstone. My father's name. I keep staring at it, numb with disbelief. My hands tremble as I run my fingers across the etched stone.

He died a partisan. I promised him I'd help others in need. But I've sent more people to die than I've saved. I still remember the little boy's face as he begged for someone to help his mum.

The letters on the gravestone burn into my eyes.

The rain fails to damp out my pain.

My face flushes with fury. I press my lips together, trying to control myself.

"This was their deed, not ours," Lukas says, his voice threatening to break. He throws the pistol away, and we both watch it sink into the wet dirt. "It's not our fault. I can't blame you for what they did."

I ignore his gaze. I check if my pistol has a loaded magazine and grip it firmly with both hands.

"We're not responsible for their mistakes," he says.

"You don't know what *responsibility* is," I hiss through gritted teeth. Fury boils my blood.

I remember you now, Lukas. You're my hatred.

His innocent eyes gazed at the floor in silence. It was too quiet. Carefully, I treaded through the snow. I approached him with his mother's flag of death in my hands. Extending my arms, I passed it to him. Then leaned in closer to his ear.

"You're the reason they're dead," I whispered, staring into his eyes with nothing but pure disgust and anger. I began trembling, as I desperately withheld my temper. I raised my voice. "It's all YOUR FAULT!"

If his mother didn't work with my dad, he would still be alive. Arbiters had discovered that she was a partisan. A trap was set. A bomb just for her.

So why was my dad with her? He wasn't the one caught. He should have lived.

I hate you. I can't blame your mother anymore, so I blame you.

Anger was my only emotion.

He perpetually kept his eyes locked on the floor. No response. The sound of his quiet, broken breaths echoed between us.

If I ever saw him again, I swore to ensure my face would be the last thing he ever saw.

"YOU!" I yell at him as tears blur my vision. I'm untamed, uncontrollably loose to do whatever I want to him. My face radiates with resentment. "We're never coming home anyway. So you'll answer for your mother's sins."

He's frozen. Just like he was *then*. Except this time, he's facing me. His eyes look into mine. But he's not scared or frightened. It's as if he understands.

I try to pull the trigger, but I can't do it. Not when he's looking at me like that. I squeeze the pistol until my hands shake.

"Look away from me!" I scream. It's as if my vocal cords are being ripped out of my throat. But he continues looking at me with soft eyes, while he begins to come closer. The tenderness of his glance starts to soften me. Gently, he takes another step forwards.

Stop this! I can only shout at myself. This can't be happening. The promise that I made all those years ago will be the promise I fulfil today.

Lukas, this is it.

"Turn the other way. Now! Do it."

But he doesn't budge. I reangle the pistol right above his head. Without any hesitation, I pull the trigger. The bullet grazes a tree behind him. Abruptly, his pupils grow slim. All of a sudden there is no emotion in his eyes, and the kindness in his glance starts to melt.

I roar, "TURN THE OTHER WAY!"

Step by step he rotates the other way, standing right in front of me, looking into the opposite direction. Slowly approaching him, I make sure to walk warily, in order to not slip in any of the puddles. The second I reach him, I kick right behind his knee and he drops.

He lay on his knees, right before me. Not saying a word. Promptly, I shove him down, making sure his face is covered in filth.

"You feel the coldness?" I ask him, clenching onto his neck tightly. "That's how I felt when your mother murdered my dad."

I crush his flesh with my fingers, then bring his face closer to mine.

"You're the son of a murderer. That's all you'll ever be," I shout until my throat begins to swell. "You deserve to rot in the ground."

"My mum didn't kill your dad."

I bring the barrel of the pistol to the back of his neck. He twitches at the cold metal scraping his skin.

"Don't you dare lie to me. You deserve to die."

My eyes overflow with tears as I start to press down on the trigger. There is no other way. *You may have saved me, but you couldn't save yourself.*

I'll get rid of you. Your death is my responsibility.

"One wrongful action doesn't correct another," Lukas says, just loud enough for me to hear.

Anger slowly seeps through me all over again.

"What did you say?" I question him, furiously demanding a response. Lightning flashes through the skies, momentarily blinding me. I shift the barrel from his neck to the back of his head. "SPEAK!"

"It doesn't matter what you do. You can belittle me, hurt me, torture me. Do whatever you want to me." He pauses, wiping his face with his sleeve. "In the end, none of this will bring Bruce back. I'm sorry about your dad. But to kill me is wrong, and you know it."

I freeze, as rage rushes through me for the last time. I'm his daughter. This is for him.

"Don't you ever, ever say his name again."

Putting my finger to the trigger, I breathe in my last spark of hate.

The shock wave ruptures the night sky.

8

Lukas

An intense beam of multicoloured light dances across my eyelids. I feel my pupils shrink. The echo of a bullet's shock wave rumbles in my eardrums. My heartbeat accelerates, causing a disorienting weakness that sends my entire body crashing to the floor. In blind panic, I reach for my stomach, expecting to feel blood… except there isn't any.

What's happening? My gut shakes with each breath. Needles pierce my body, over and over again. Something's not right.

I still can't see. Frantically, I rub my eyes. The colours start to distinguish themselves. But the world remains blurry.

Dim white bulbs glimmer above, ghostlike.

It's hard to know what's real and what's not.

"Please calm down," Overseer Milgram says. "I ask you both to kindly listen to me for a moment. After, you will understand everything."

Both? I'm stunned. *How am I still breathing?*

Chains rattle chaotically, scuffing the ground. Confusion races through me. Uncertainty ensnares my senses. I can only see colour; the rest of my vision stays fuzzy.

"Aurora, I implore you to stop resisting the locks. They are for your safety." Overseer Milgram addresses the metallic clanking.

The screech of metal grinding against itself subsides.

We're both alive. Everything she said, she meant.

"Gradually you will experience the return of all your senses. Everything will be back to normal. Please stay calm. There is no need for concern," Overseer Milgram explains. "When you awaken, further information will be provided."

"What is this?" I mutter, horrified. "She just tried to kill me."

"That was absolutely necessary." Overseer Milgram's voice deepens as he speaks with eerie joy.

I feel like I'm hyperventilating. My muscles won't listen to me.

"The Elimination Link is sacred to the Equilibrium and essential to restoring Statera. How can you restore the balance between the living and the dead, when you're both spiritually alive?"

My eyelids grow heavy.

Sleep starts to creep up on me.

"The purpose of this project isn't to reduce the number of subjects."

Sinister beeps echo one last time before the machines fall silent.

"It's to pair them together. Through death."

I open my eyes to darkness. Metal presses down against my face. My arms feel stiff and ache when I stretch them out. Tension bolts up my spine.

"Good morning. I trust the two of you are in good health," Overseer Milgram greets us.

"What have you done to me?" Aurora cries out. Chains clatter. She resists, to no effect.

"Both of you have regained all your senses. Soon the immersion mask will be removed, and a series of physiological assessments will be conducted to ensure optimal conditions. Be advised, there will be additional health examinations leading up to the Equilibrium."

Mechanical hums vibrate around my head.

The mask lifts off my face.

Bright lights stab my vision, making me squint repeatedly until tears escape my eyes.

We're confined within an all-white padded room. Its monotone atmosphere feels suffocating. Aurora sits across from me at the other end of the spacious room. The only way out is through two grey translucent doors. Overseer Milgram stands in front of the exit, observing us patiently. He wears a white lab coat, his fingers crawling through the air as he commands a floating screen of letters and symbols.

I look around, noticing another grey door beside me, labelled as the washroom. The stale colouring of the place makes me sick. There's something oddly unsettling about its dullness.

My wrists are tightly bound by cuffs. The chains are linked to the wall behind me, leaving me little space to move.

I glimpse at the girl that tried to kill me. She's also chained to the wall. Her face is expressionless, yet the wrinkles on her forehead appear entwined with confusion and sorrow.

Perhaps she regrets that the bullet didn't find its way to the back of my skull.

"Now then, your physical tests are satisfactory. Your schedule will consist of rest, prayer and farewells. Any questions?" Overseer Milgram asks, his voice sounding non-commanding for the first time.

Milgram's skin is grey and pale, almost silver. But I doubt it's from a lack of nutrients. Probably not enough sunlight. His beard is dark and full, which makes his face look ominous. As if his expression is hiding something. He stares at me with those sharp and intimidating brown eyes. Desensitized to suffering.

"No questions," I answer, waiting for him to turn away. He creeps me out.

Overseer Milgram shifts his gaze to the girl.

"How is he not dead?" Aurora growls, charging each word with such angst that it sounds like a demand. Veins throb with unbridled fury across her face. Her eyes lock on mine. She wants to bury me.

"How curious... that's strange," Overseer Milgram murmurs, puzzled. He taps his earpiece. "Has the Xanax hallucinogen not worn off yet? She's still impulsive and erratic."

His face furrows in confusion. "Oh—temporary side effects. Understood."

Overseer Milgram sweeps his hand through the air, and the hologram unfurls into a massive projection before us. The display shows a boy sprawled on a hospital bed, tendrils of cables leaking from his body. A spherical helmet with an oxygen mask is stuck to his face.

"The boy in the image has wires and electrochemical needles affixed to his body. These send electrical impulses to the user's brain mirroring reality."

"That works?" I stammer.

Overseer Milgram grins. "Both of you were in a simulation. Every sensation was fabricated to resemble existence. An intricate illusion." He waves his hand and the projection disappears. "None of it was real."

"Why?" Aurora blurts out.

"Elimination Link is programmed to select troubled individuals and force collaboration. It's meant to build trust and then break it down."

"Then was the point of this?" I grimace in disbelief and disgust.

"To break you." Overseer Milgram stares at me. "Fractured Faith is designed to distort trust and pair you together through death. Spiritually your Duo has become half dead and half alive. You have now gained the Trinities right to restore Statera."

"Liars," Aurora whimpers, her eyes wide and red.

A woman's image projects from Milgram's wrist, her appearance tinted in a shade of blue. It's Enyo.

"Our conversation is due."

"Love and duty calls," Overseer Milgram declares, gesturing to his wrist. "I'll see you very soon."

The door seals shut, leaving us alone, each chained to our isolated corners.

"All of it was fake?" Aurora whispers, her skin slick with sweat. She twitches repeatedly as if it were involuntary. I can see her eyes dilate with horror. Her voice sounds desolate. "I'm sorry."

"You're only sorry the bullet wasn't real," I reply.

We don't share another word.

"You've got an hour. Food will be delivered shortly. Please rest," a nurse suggests, readjusting our handcuffs so that the chains keep us a fixed distance from each other. She leaves.

Everything is supervised. I'm sure that even right now we're being monitored.

Does Aurora feel bad? I wonder.

She's no longer shaking. She looks normal now.

I rest uneasy, constantly shifting my weight around, unable to evade the sharp tension in my posture. My legs feel strained from the prolonged stillness.

I can't bear this much longer. It's too awkward.

I shatter the silence that binds us. "Why do you blame me for everything?"

She glances at me. Grey, empty. She's quiet.

I find this agitating. There's no point in weeping now. What's done is done.

"I didn't kill your father. The same way you weren't responsible for my mum." I search for a way to resolve our conflict. My mind urges caution. But revenge must have been the only thing occupying her mind for a decade.

Can I blame her? I question myself what I would do if I were in her place.

"I tried to kill you," she sobs, turning her back on me. Weakly, she whispers, "How can you forgive me?"

"Because once I wanted to do the same," I say.

"Then why didn't you?" She glances at me timidly.

A nurse enters, also dressed in pristine white. She pushes a metal cart and positions it between me and Aurora. The nurse taps her wrist twice, and our handcuffs start to glow in a vibrant red. The chains fall to the floor.

"Eat now. You'll regret it later if you don't. I'd recommend showering after. Your scents aren't very attractive." The nurse points to the bathroom door, then exits, leaving us alone again.

A table rises from the floor in the middle of the room. We transform it into a feast. Bowls of salads, racks of sizzling meat, and odd rectangular shaped fried potatoes. On the side, there is a rainbow of fruit with donuts coated in different flavours, alongside jugs of water, juice and a strange brown bubbly drink.

This feels wrong. This meal would be worth years of trading at the River Market. I've never even seen this much food in one place.

No wonder Colony Lithuania is overrun with hordes of starving children.

"We should eat as much as we can," I tell Aurora, softly. "This could be our last meal."

Silence. She doesn't budge.

"Speak to me," I say. "Stop being selfish."

"There's nothing I deserve to say," she mumbles.

I place a glass right in front of her and fill it with water.

"C'mon, let's eat." I ignore her murmuring. "I know it's hard to trust."

"You shouldn't forgive me," she cries out.

"You were drugged. You were led to do that."

"That's no excuse! Why would you forgive me?" she begs, finally turning to face me.

"I don't forgive you." I pause. "But I understand."

She remains speechless, confused.

"I know the feeling of wanting to rip someone apart and carve a bloody mess out of their corpse." I look at her, knowing my eyes must be blank, devoid of warmth. "That's what I wanted to do to you, ever since you told me it was *my fault*. I've had nightmares of you ever since then. But killing you wouldn't have brought Mum back. It would've only caused more pain."

Droplets of regret drip from her eyes. Aurora sniffles and quietly wipes her face.

"I'm sorry for back then," she says.

"It was a long time ago," I reply, soothingly. "We need to trust each other."

She gulps, "Okay. I'm sorry."

I shake my head. "Stop saying that."

"Saying what?"

"That you're sorry. What's done is done."

"I'm sorry. I'll stop," she whimpers.

"You did it again." I chuckle and extend my hand towards her. "Trust?"

Aurora breathes in, regaining her confidence.

"Mhm, trust." She takes my hand. We squeeze each other tightly.

"Let's not waste this." I hint at the food. I hadn't noticed, but my belly has been quivering uncontrollably.

"Yeah. I'm starving," Aurora admits, taking a sip of water. Briskly, we finish off all the salad and meat, each mouthful guilty and delightful.

I feel a little queasy from the food. Keeping my hands on my stomach, I lie down beside the table.

"We should go wash ourselves." Aurora rises. I notice her slender figure and toned muscles. Quietly charming. "In case, it's our last—"

"I know, I know." I cut her off, waving my hand gently. "You can go first."

Steadily, she starts moving towards the bathroom door, walking shyly and uncomfortably.

She catches my inquisitive gaze and hesitates for a brief moment before finally speaking.

"Aren't you coming with me?" she asks timidly, her face painted with a slight blush.

"W... what?" I almost choke on my water. "Why? What for?"

"So we don't run out of warm water..." she pauses anxiously, her voice trailing off as she stares at a fixed point on the floor, avoiding eye contact with me. "Or water in general."

"Don't worry." I gesture with my hand for her to head to the bathroom alone. "There'll be enough."

Aurora enters the bathroom, scepticism flickering across her face. The faint rush of water filters through the wall like distant rain.

I'm left alone to my thoughts. I can't stand this. The absurdity of it all makes me nauseous.

As our children go hungry and our mothers shrivel to death, they throw away untouched food, use up as much water as they want, while depriving us of everything. Why is that right? Why is that fair? Because their faith claims so?

They would use up all the water on earth before bothering to cleanse the blood from their hands.

The instant Aurora leaves the bathroom, cloaked in a large white towel, the opaque glass walls flash green. Two ladies enter the room, dressed in white dresses, each holding a plastic box in their hands.

"Meet Ellie and Dianna. This couple are the most successful designers here in Olympus Mons." Overseer Milgram walks in after them. "They will tailor this year's holy robes for each subject."

I'm told to shower and clean myself, while one of the ladies dresses Aurora. Once I return, she is dressed in a sculpted white suit, its sleek fabric interfolds in sharp lines that press tightly against her skin and contour her body like armour.

Milgram signals to the other lady. "Go help the boy, Ellie."

We enter the bathroom and Ellie's hands get to work, wrapping cloth around me and pulling the suit onto my body. Then she presses a button on her wrist and adjusts the tightness of the robe. She meticulously examines the proportions, ensuring my appearance is perfect. Then Ellie presents me.

"Excellent, indeed," Overseer Milgram exclaims. "Just as expected. Thank you, Ellie and Dianna. Your work for the Trinities of the Elect is admirable."

"Thank you, sir," they reply.

Overseer Milgram checks his wrist. "It's time to go. Ellie and Dianna please clean the room. My subjects cannot be late."

Aurora and I follow Milgram.

Leaving the room, I glance behind me. Ellie and Dianna embrace one another intimately, their bodies locked together in relief.

That type of love is forbidden in the Colonies. We're only allowed to reproduce. The more people, the more slaves.

It's an unexpected sensation, this joy that grips me. I haven't seen any humanity in quite some time.

Then the door slides shut.

9

Aurora

Wooden planks expand into a narrow tunnel. It stretches endlessly into the gloom. The dim lights on the ceiling struggle to penetrate the foggy mist in the air, casting long, eerie shadows on the creaky wooden floor.

Shivers rush down my spine while I struggle to maintain my composure. Impulse screams at me... Run!

I'm trapped in a white suit with an electric collar around my neck as if I were a dog.

Every few steps, the floorboards screech. The white brick walls make me feel insane.

"Checkmate," Overseer Milgram says. A chime surges from his wrist. He stretches his hands out, gradually searching the wall like he's reading its texture. Eventually he stops and applies pressure. Bricks sink into the wall. Milgram steps back.

The floor begins to illuminate a vivid yellow as the colour spreads through the lines in the wooden planks.

"What is this?" Lukas mutters. I gaze at his long, brown hair. The ends curl. His face is slim and serious.

I still don't know how to feel around him.

Why the hell would he forgive me?

"Keep quiet," Overseer Milgram snaps. He focuses on the wall, which shifts inwards, unveiling another path. Under his breath, he comments, "Immaculate."

We head into the tunnel. Black marble walls are illuminated by blue light panels in the ground.

"Let me explain the event we're attending." Overseer Milgram turns around to face us. "Tonight, the Premier shall perform his sacred oration. A prayer of hope to restore Statera."

His eyes sharpen like he's trying to see through us.

"His Highness can bless you or curse you. Your survival starts here. Blaze don't burn."

We reach the end of the tunnel, and the floor beneath our feet starts to rise. We're lifted onto a round stage, lit up by panels hanging from the ceiling that flood the air with brightness.

White robed subjects sit in a circle in the middle of the platform. Every face is blank, still with fear. Lukas and I are seated together. We don't move, talk or squint. Eyes peeled open.

The black marble stage contrasts our snowy garments. A translucent curtain encircles us, glimmering in blue hues.

We wait patiently. One thing I learned from my mum is: *When you don't know what to say, keep your mouth shut.* I follow her advice now.

Overseer Milgram sneaks up behind us. "Remember my words." He's dressed in a plated black suit, coated in tiny crystals. "Listen carefully. Respect your God. Obey."

The curtain flickers in oscillations of purple that grow outwards from the centre repeatedly until the curtain disintegrates into bubbling sparks.

A massive stadium surrounds us. Dense crowds radiate in every direction. Around the stage people stand, cheering, screaming, toppling over one another to get a better view. Further away, people fill up the stadium seats.

I look side to side, realising that the subjects are separated by men in black suits—for us that's Milgram. Arbiters stand below the stage, entirely static, barrelled weapons attached to their sides.

The audience is a sea of flashing lights. Anticipation looms. Instruments hum together, creating a powerful melody. As the rhythm of the melody rises, tension starts to build and spread around the stadium. Undoubtedly this marks the Premier's entrance.

Applause erupts from the audience.

The Premier materialises from the ground, rising to the stage, enveloped in smoke. He circles the stage, his shoulders pulled back and confident. The man grins and waves at the crowds. Then he lifts one hand and slowly curls it into a fist. The stadium falls quiet.

A seraphic ring of light forms above the Premier's head.

"Grace and candour to Statera. You are under my eye," the Premier proclaims. He walks around the stage, staring at different corners of the crowd. "Colony One is essential to Olympus Mons. You are a part of FORTE and responsible for our strength in carrying out our righteousness. For your hard work and unquestionable faith, you are rewarded with my sacred oration."

Cheers of delight scatter through the stadium.

"We're all bound by rules. And to know your purpose is to possess wisdom. Let's begin the oration with fundamental knowledge."

Applause breaks out. I catch sight of the crowd standing around the stage. They're dressed in work clothes like coveralls, protective jackets and gloves. Their faces are dirty and bruised, skin pale like they haven't seen sunlight in years. Something's not right.

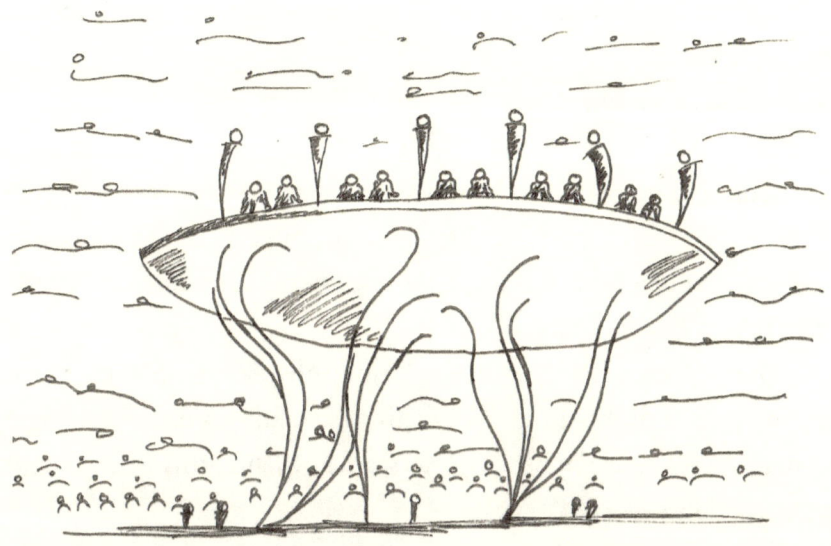

"The Trinities of the Elect guide Statera towards righteousness, and I ensure it. The Trinity of Spirit fosters the mental. The Trinity of Matter nourishes the physical," the Premier explains, authoritatively. "Cycles of death create cycles of life. One cannot exist without the other. This is the fundamental principle." His voice drops, grave and final. "Therefore, the number of the dead and the living on the scales of justice must reach Equilibrium. When balance fails, life cannot be sustained. I do not kill. I correct. I restore."

No one dares to breathe. My gut tightens as the stadium thickens with tension.

He knows nothing about life. Life is struggle. What does he know about the struggles of a woman? Struggles of the poor? Struggle of us, those shrivelling in the Colonies? Of Lukas and me? Nothing.

"Every twelve years, at the first hint of snow, the Equilibrium corrects and restores Statera!" the Premier dictates. And his words become history. *Power is trust and trust becomes truth.*

I stare sceptically at his sleek, round face. The same face on that portrait I've had to polish every day of my life. I'm filled with hatred.

There is nothing to correct. There is no rule. It's just him and he's just a killer.

"FORTE orchestrates the Equilibrium, and the Colonies perform. Each subject is essential in restoring the balance between the living and the dead. Yin feeds off death and provides energy to the Yang, which gives us life," the Premier preaches earnestly. He pauses to heighten the suspense and then explodes… "May the Equilibrium restore Statera!"

The audience howls with jubilation, bleeding with excitement for the Premier to continue. He continues walking around the stage, approaching where I'm seated. He smiles, then forms a fist again. Everyone falls silent.

This is pathetic. How can they believe him?

His words are an empty projection of his desires, not universal rules. How can they not see that?

"Now you'll pay your respects. Take a minute of silence to honour the sacrifices these subjects will make. Bow down or remain seated in silence as a token of your devotion."

A countdown from sixty seconds flies above us, floating in the air. Accompanied by the sounds of a ticking clock. The crowd bows with closed eyes. Only the Premier remains standing.

Fury trickles through my veins. I can't listen to him. I won't submit.

Slowly, I grip onto the armrests of my seat.

"Aurora! Stop right now," Lukas whispers furiously, placing a hand over his mouth as if he's covering a sneeze. "Sit back down. You're going to kill both of us."

I'm sorry, Lukas. This I can't control.

I stand up straight and glare at the Premier. I don't know what else to do.

Swift ripples of gasps spread through the stadium. I remain standing.

"Aurora, sit back down," Overseer Milgram hisses through gritted teeth. "For your own safety. Sit."

That's when the Premier notices a disturbance in the silence. A force overcoming his rule.

He turns around. His face stays stern, but I catch the flicker of a grin. He raises his hand.

The countdown pauses.

I purse my lips but I remain still, my face stiff with anger. He walks towards me, his expression calm and composed. He knows exactly what he's going to do.

I don't back down.

He stands before me, his eyes locking onto mine. But I look straight past him.

"And I thought your father was quite the rebel," he says, grinning. He places an arm on my shoulder and leans in closer to my ear. "His daughter is impressive. You possess great courage. I like that."

I adjust my glare and look him dead in the eye. This doesn't bother him. In fact, he seems happy.

"Your Highness, please excuse this young lady. She does not comprehend our ways," Overseer Milgram says, calmly.

"No, no, my dear Milgram. You have it all wrong," the Premier replies, shifting his gaze between us. "She understands us *perfectly*."

"As you wish." Overseer Milgram sits back down.

"What makes you think you're going to be any different?" the Premier asks me, his cold face looming down on me. The corners of his lips stretch into a smile. My palms are slick with sweat. The weight of his presence suffocates me. I keep my face still, but my breath turns quick and broken. It's as if he's having a normal conversation with me. "There are millions that have died by my hand. But I've killed very few."

I growl, "Then I'll be the first to return the favour."

His smile grows.

"I like you girl, but be careful." He pauses, leaning closer to my face. "Your father made the same promise. Look where that got him."

My eyes widen. Each breath is a fight for control. But my judgment turns cloudy.

I swing my fist at him. Reaching for his throat.

Right before it connects, my neck jerks to the side, and my arm twitches before falling to my waist. My entire body turns rigid, trembling lightly. I look up at him, biting down on my lower lip until I draw blood.

I hear the sizzle of electricity around my neck.

The Premier lifts his hand revealing a device with a red button. "You could never *not* submit."

Arbiters grab my arms tightly, restraining me. I twist and struggle, but the searing pain around my neck only intensifies.

"My sincerest apology for that partisan accident that blew up your dear little father. But every fire has to be extinguished." The Premier leaves me paralyzed and approaches Overseer Milgram.

"Proceed the Duo to the Callisto. He'll know what to do. Tell him to paint the dragon, dot the eyes."

"Consider it done."

The Premier and Overseer Milgram shake hands.

An opaque cover is pulled over my head. Electricity jolts through me. My body trembles against my will. I can feel myself descend, probably exiting the stadium. My fists remain clenched, even as my muscles spasm. Tears drench my face.

I see blackness.

My eyes burn.

The hotness and sweat of my body fills me with a desperate need for pain. Digging my fingernails into my flesh, I scream internally in agony—*He killed my father!*

10

Lukas

Naive. Thoughtless. Prideful. These words flock to mind as frustration builds within me.

I glare at Aurora. She sits motionless in her car seat, lips firmly pressed together. She clasps her wrist, squeezing herself until she stops shaking. Her eyes are numb, wide with sorrow. She's drowning in the flames of her father's past. And it's all her fault.

You don't rebel just for the sake of it. You need to earn something in exchange for your suffering. All she's done is made us a target.

Following the Premier's orders, a black hood was thrown over our heads, and we were dragged outside the stadium. Then tossed into this jeep.

Overseer Milgram removed our hoods. He smiled and applauded our efforts before smugly whispering, "*Resistance will fail you.*"

The engine growls in a powerful roar, and the car suddenly accelerates, shoving me deep into my seat. I've been so focused on Aurora that I haven't noticed the luxurious interior. It's glazed in plated rose gold and white leather, while lustrous yellow lights shimmer across the decor.

The yellow reminds me of my mum's candles, which she used to craft out of beeswax. They sparkled like magic in the dark.

Keep it safe, and in return, the fire will keep you warm, mum used to say calmly. Her voice is everlastingly ingrained in my memory.

I won't forget her.

I catch Aurora's gaze as she timidly glimpses at me. She wants comfort. But I can't give her that.

"You couldn't sit still?" I fume. She sighs heavily. "Do you not understand? They have the power to kill *whoever*. That man decides who lives and dies."

"You're protecting a murderer?" she shoots back.

"No. I want to protect us. *Us!*" I roar with disgust. "If it means protecting what family I have left then I will sit still and shut up."

"You're only worried about yourself," Aurora snarls and puffs out air in anger. "You're just scared."

I force myself to take deep breaths, as my face twitches with rage. I can't detonate. We need each other.

"Scared? That's right I'm scared!" I admit, my voice shaking. "He clicks his fingers and every person you have ever loved will be in the ground."

Aurora holds my gaze, her eyes trembling.

The Premier controls every inch of anything we have ever stepped foot on. We live by his will.

The car doors snap open. I hadn't even noticed the car had stopped.

"Let's go," Overseer Milgram calls us over. "Callisto Victor will be thrilled."

"Why?" Aurora asks, spitefully.

"He's a member of the Trinity of Matter, who ensures the permanence of causality between subjects. He ensures fairness."

Aurora frowns. "You didn't answer my question."

"New procedures excite him."

We don't ask any more questions.

We're in the middle of a snowy forest. Milgram leads us to a black skyscraper that coils upwards and narrows into a needlepoint at the top. Red stripes curve along the structure in a sleek manner.

Inside, we enter a silver room, and Milgram presses a button on the wall. We rise upwards. The strange sensation forces me to grip the handrail to steady myself.

"Thirteenth floor." The room buzzes with a robotic voice. Then one wall slides to the side, revealing a massive chamber. Carpet floors, oceanic wall plasters, and a glimmering chandelier greet us.

A young lady emerges from the corner, her legs humming with each step. She's dressed in tight, black armour like an Arbiter.

"Your host is ready to meet you," she announces, her smile rigid, unchanging. "Follow me."

We stay close behind her as she heads towards a wall with marine tapestries. She presses her hand against an ocean wave, and a blue holograph reacts to her touch, creating a pin pad. A moment later the wall disperses in two, leading us into a laboratory.

Microscopes, helmets and metal equipment lie sprawled out across white tables. The ceiling is black and rubbery, swallowing much of the light. A silhouette lingers behind a table.

I force down saliva, trying to keep myself composed.

The figure looks up at us, its face concealed within the shadows. But the head shape isn't circular. It looks like someone's jaw was flattened and straightened out.

"This is my laboratory!" The man welcomes us, his voice steady with a hoarse distortion. He stares from afar. He raises his fingers, and the light panel overhead brightens. He escapes the gloom for the first time. "Come closer."

His face is scaffolded by rods fused to a mask outlining his face. Metal coils replace his jawbone, tunnelling into his flesh. His face contracts into an unnaturally slender state, as if someone flayed his skin to the brink of tearing.

I freeze, hesitant to move forwards. Aurora hunches her shoulders. She squints nervously.

"Do I frighten you, dear?" he asks, his tone stilted and mechanical. The metal coils must be assisting his vocal cords.

Aurora stays silent, shaking her head no.

"Is it the mask?" he guesses, dragging a finger across his jawline. "My skin? My eyes? My scars?"

The man steps closer to Aurora, his movements buzzing with electricity. He sways a hand over his face. "You don't want to end up like this do you?"

"No," Aurora murmurs.

He turns to me, brushing his fingers along my collarbone. "Do you?"

"Let's not terrify them, Callisto." Overseer Milgram steps in between us.

"It's been ages, my friend," Callisto whispers.

"Indeed."

They shake hands.

"There can only be one reason you're here," Callisto denotes, moving away to massive cylinders at the end of the lab. "You know I'm *not* fond of visitors."

Milgram smiles. "The Premier requests you to *paint the dragon, dot the eyes.*"

Callisto looks back, those hollow eyes wide and bright with joy. He grins.

"Project Blackout commences."

We're taken to the cylinders for examination. Callisto calls them magnetic resonance imaging machinery. We lie down on a sliding bed where our limbs are locked by metal bands, and pillows are stuffed around us until it's difficult to breathe. Then we're shoved inside.

A hologram instructs us to follow a dot with our eyes, react to pictures of animals and inanimate objects, as well as remember family members, birthday memories and funerals.

My eyes keep wavering off into my thoughts, failing to stay concentrated. I fight the weight of sleep, but it's a struggle to stay conscious.

We're taken out of the machine, told to sit down and given water bottles to drink.

"Such developments are immensely promising," Callisto asserts.

"This is the preliminary?" Overseer Milgram asks.

"Precisely. The scans reveal typical healthy brain structure. The procedure will continue as expected…" Callisto's voice trails off.

Milgram's face wrinkles with confusion. "But?"

"But… there may be episodic discharge over time."

"How can degenerated neurons return to life?" Overseer Milgram questions, his voice slow and puzzled.

"True neurodegeneration doesn't occur. The serum we're using to mimic amyloid plaques to disrupt communication between neurons isn't permanent at all. It's more like synaptic inhibition. Since the serum doesn't allow for tau protein aggregation, neurofibrillary tangles cannot develop, so the disruption is temporary," Callisto explains, his hands gesturing in the air like he's manipulating a hologram.

Overseer Milgram's eyes fix on Callisto. "Which means under the right overlapping stimulants, those neuron pathways can reactivate?"

"Exactly."

Overseer Milgram thinks for a moment, then nods.

"And is Enyo informed?"

"Most certainly. Hence why this is a preliminary trial," Callisto says.

"Your innovation never fails to charm," Overseer Milgram praises Callisto. The masked man nods.

"If I may dawdle a little, I'd love to interview our subjects. It's a rare opportunity for interaction."

"Your authority is my command," Overseer Milgram says, bowing lightly.

Callisto claps his hands twice.

We go back to the entrance of the laboratory where two velvet armchairs have been prepared.

"You two." Callisto points at us. "Sit. On the ground."

Even the laboratory floor is soft and warm. I cross my legs and look up at the two men in charge of our fate.

Milgram approaches an armchair. "May I?"

"Of course, my friend."

Callisto circles us, occasionally stroking my hair or patting Aurora's head.

"Do you know the true purpose of the Equilibrium?" Callisto asks, squatting down in front of us. "Don't be shy. Speak up."

Aurora gulps, and I see her eyes flickering nervously.

I hesitate. "The Premier said it's to correct the balance between the living and the dead."

"You're on the right track. But correcting balance is rather vague... no?" Callisto gets to his armchair and steadily reclines, resting his face on his hand. "I want you to try and be more meticulous."

I attempt to recall the Premier's speech and pinpoint his exact phrasing. "Life grows unsustainable?"

"That's right. Excess life becomes wasteful," Callisto says without blinking. "You must keep it in check. Both numerically and figuratively."

"Why tell us this?" I ask.

"I want to comprehend your thought process." Callisto plays with his sleeve, revealing a tattooed number, but I only catch a glimpse of the first digit... 8. It's eighty-something. "You are pardoned of punishment. You both know of your upcoming demise. To add further torment would be unnecessarily cruel. And I'm a man of necessity. You may speak honestly."

Aurora and I nod.

Callisto asks, "So, how do you keep life in check?"

"You limit the population?" Aurora answers, doubtfully.

"Close. You regulate the maximum and minimum number of people. That's how you limit it. But to figuratively keep life in check, you must remind humanity of suffering. Of the necessary evil that permits life to continue onwards," Callisto explains, his face bubbling as he grows more tense. "So the purpose of the Equilibrium is simple. It's to penalise you of retribution. You discipline the sin before it happens. You let life sustain itself by sacrifice. You make that sacrifice fair. Thus, numerically and figuratively, life and death become equal."

Aurora gazes up at him. "So... what is equal?"

Callisto stiffens, his eyes piercing us. He mutters through pursed lips, "Pain."

"It seems the mood has fallen," Overseer Milgram comments, grinning sheepishly.

Callisto turns his head to Milgram. His glare sharpens. "Silence."

Milgram's face falls. But I can't sense fear. Only intention to submit.

Callisto looks down at us.

"Such weather drains me. This interview is done." He's about to get up, but his face widens as if remembering something. "One more thing," he says, turning to Aurora. "The Premier has a message for you, Aurora. And I quote: 'Project Blackout will be your punishment. You'll lose everything. Even yourself.'"

Aurora stays quiet, but her brows crease with confusion. The atmosphere feels heavy.

"Thank you for the visit," Callisto says, reaching over to shake Milgram's hand. "Your time is greatly appreciated."

"Anything else we may be of service to?" Overseer Milgram asks.

Callisto stands up. "No. Just leave my sight."

Then he disappears back into the shadows of his laboratory. The armoured lady from earlier returns to lead us out the building.

We pass through the lobby with the ocean waves right back into the elevator we came from.

"I wish you well. Don't burn up!" The lady smiles and waves goodbye as the elevator doors close.

Once the doors open again, a gentle breeze ruffles my hair. My skin feels lighter. The cold air soothes me. We exit the elevator back into the snow.

Birds chirp. Snow crunches. The wind whispers. We follow Overseer Milgram towards a black car. But my attention is elsewhere.

I spot a figure lurking in a tree. He's up on a branch, just how I'd hunt rabbits with my bow. The man appears to be watching us.

The ground sizzles in a circle around us. The same noise a child would make when imitating a snake. The crackle whips back and forth across my eardrums. Suddenly the trees stop swaying with the wind. Birds fall quiet. I can hear the thumping of my heart. Everything becomes a part of silence. My eyes blink uncomfortably.

First I see the colour, then everything lights up in flames.

11

Aurora

The snow bursts into flames. Explosions ripple through the ground, surrounding us in fire. Smoke spirals into the sky. A storm of flashes erupts from the trees. Bullets slice past us.

Arbiters rush out from Callisto's skyscraper. Rifles ignite. Laser-like rounds scream into the trees, detonating upon impact. Trees collapse and flick snow into the air. I've never seen energy weapons in action. They're terrifying.

A horde of white figures dash across the snow, lunging towards us, rifles drawn. I freeze.

What the hell... partisans?

Before I can react, Arbiters encircle us. In the blink of an eye, I'm taken by the arm and tossed into the black jeep. Lucas is thrown in as well. The door is shut. The car flings us side to side as it accelerates rapidly.

"Get your seat belts on!" Overseer Milgram yells from behind the wheel. I get up and stumble to my seat. "Do you copy? This is Milgram."

Screeches and crackling gargles echo through the speakers.

"Answer me!" Overseer Milgram barks into his radio. "Backup requested at Callisto's Centre. Subjects are in transfer to the Final Goodbye checkpoint. Over."

For a second, all we hear is the buzz of static noise.

"Beyond... a... drain," the returning voice crackles, smothered by shrieks and gunfire.

"What the..." Milgram mumbles, as a hologram appears in front of Lukas and me.

The projection shows reporters sprinting frantically in all directions. In the background, Arbiters continue gunning down trees, while others in hazmat suits spray chemicals onto the partisan corpses.

For a moment I consider escaping. Dying now is probably a much better fate than what's coming.

I check the door latch but it's firmly locked. Suicide isn't permitted.

"What are they doing to the bodies?" Lukas gasps.

"Killers who disrupt the balance of the living and the dead don't deserve honour," Overseer Milgram snarls like a raging animal. "Their bodies will be preserved for scientific use."

Abruptly, the hologram flickers, snow blasting upwards. A lady desperately rushes on screen, a microphone in her hand. She describes multiple sections of the forest where explosions have occurred.

Rounds of bullets glint through the air. The camera quivers, and the screen splinters with dark lines. Blood drips onto the screen. The reporter falls into the snow with a sudden thud. Screams follow.

Explosions paint the skies with smoke. The camera drops to the ground, colliding with the reporter's head. Sunlight flashes through the hole in her skull. The reporter's blood leaks in squirts, coating the sheets of snow a thick red.

The screen fades to black.

The rest of the trip we stay in silence. We spend an hour inside a dark tunnel crossing the sea. After, we pass by various landscapes, from leafless forests to factories submerged in fumes to crop fields.

Once the world grows dark, I fall asleep.

"Get up, Aurora." Someone shakes my shoulder. "C'mon, you don't want to miss this."

I flick my eyes open to see Lukas warmly gazing at me. Before I can ask Lukas for what damn reason he woke me up, Overseer Milgram opens my car door.

"I suggest you use this time wisely," Overseer Milgram says, leading me to a ragged, wooden door. "You have five minutes. We'll be outside."

I open the door, my face twitching with fright for what I may find. But the scent is comfortable, inviting me further inside. That's when I realise, I'm home.

I creep to the living room, avoiding the creaky floorboards. I sit down at the edge of our bed.

"Jacob, are you awake?" I whisper, softly. I caress his hair how I always do. Jacob sits up, rubbing his eyes, still drowsy.

"Aurora?" His eyes widen.

"Shh, it's nighttime."

He lunges into my arms and holds me tight.

"Where were you?"

"I had to go. To protect you," I answer, helplessly.

"So now you'll stay?" he begs. The pain in his voice is hard to bear. I can't bring myself to lie. I can't break his little heart. Not again. So, I just embrace him even tighter, holding him even closer.

I want to run away from here, but I can't. I want to scream at the top of my lungs, but I can't. I want to never let go of him, but I *must*.

"Remember that song we used to hear our grandmother sing to us all of the time?" I ask, hoping to create one last good memory. Tears sit on the edge of my eyes, as I fight to hold them back.

Jacob shakes his head. He can't remember. Maybe he was too young. I try to do my best impression of a smile and begin to sing our grandmother's song.

As I sing this song, look at what we walk on,
Once beautiful land, now it's all gone.
Stripped to pieces, burned to ashes,
An oak is helpless, once fire catches.
As I sing this song, looking hopeless and torn,
Once beautiful land, now it's all gone.
This is the land that I love, but its hands that I hate.
This is the land I walk on, but its gravel I hate.
As I sing this song, look at where we were born,
Once beautiful land, now it's all gone.
If you see an old friend, you don't have long left,
Once beautiful land, now taken by theft.
Bones of the dead is the land I walk on,
You'll do the same, the day that I'm gone.

By the last line my face is soaked. My eyes hurt. Every tear burns.

"Don't cry, Sis." Jacob pats my face dry and kisses me on the cheek. "That was beautiful."

"I really, really love you, Jacob," I whisper in between my sobs. I take his little hands and squeeze onto them. "Don't forget me, mmm'kay?"

"I love you too, Sis."

I use Jacob's hands to hold up my trembling face and sniffle quietly, burying my pain. I need to go. I hug Jacob one last time, clutching him so tight that I temporarily deprive him of air. Then I kiss him on his forehead.

"Don't you dare leave again without saying goodbye," mum whimpers, standing behind me. She helps me stand up. Tenderly, she dries the wetness from my eyes and embraces me. She kisses the top of my head over and over again. "A mother loves her child more than anything in this world. You know that, honey?"

I nod. "I know, Mum."

"Good," she mumbles, kissing my hair again. "Then you remember that."

The hinges squeak and the door creaks open.

"It's time," Overseer Milgram announces.

"Okay," I reply, my eyes scorching with pain.

Jacob must've sensed something because he jumps out of bed and runs to the kitchen table. He returns to hand me a scrap of paper. "Take it before you go."

I crunch it into my palm to conceal it from Milgram and step away.

At the doorway, I turn around one final time. Jacob won't understand it now, but Mum will. "Remember to bring me flowers, okay?"

That is the last thing I say to them. Those words drain every ounce of courage from my soul. If I have such a thing.

I ignore the beating of my heart, the heat rising in my chest, the rage brewing in my mind.

I leave my home in silence.

I climb into the car and look down at my palm. Jacob drew a sketch of me with a flower wreath on my head. I smile, my eyes droopy. I'm so proud of him.

I hope he'll visit me when I'm dead.

My face stings in fear and sadness, but I don't let it show. I try my best to smile and wave goodbye.

The helicopter descends onto the ground. Raindrops flick against the windowpanes in the night.

"Welcome to the Health and Safety Faculty. I've been anticipating your arrival." A glowing umbrella emerges from the darkness. Enyo grins as she approaches us. She's slender with flawless, unblemished skin that gleams despite its blackness. Her body is accentuated by the white dress she wore at the Election. "Milgram, my love."

Overseer Milgram traces his fingers down her arm, then lifts her hand and kisses her wrist. "At your service, my love."

"You never fail to make me lust for you," she says.

"And you never fail to take my breath away."

"Very well, follow me." Enyo guides us into an elevator. "Pleasantries out the way, how are the two subjects?"

"Emotionally dazed after the 'Final Goodbye.' But that is to be expected. Overall, they're acceptable," Overseer Milgram explains.

"And were the interactions recorded?"

"Of course. We can artificially generate any scene to convince the post-trial subjects of what we wish."

Enyo grins with a hint of wickedness. "Superb."

The elevator doors open, and we travel down a straight corridor with countless rooms. All I see are empty hospital beds and curtains.

Everything is white.

This place gives me the creeps.

"You'll experience a health and safety procedure. This is our last course of action before the Equilibrium," Enyo informs us as we pass a room with its curtains open. A small boy, maybe ten years old, lies unconscious in a hospital bed while doctors stand around him, watching his brain activity on a screen. "I have access to the best researchers and medical professionals in Statera. Specialists of the human mind. The best of the best."

Thunder erupts through the corridor, startling me as I shake my head side to side. We keep walking. Enyo and Milgram link arms.

"We've arrived," Enyo says, putting on a face mask and handing another to Milgram. "*You* won't need these. Now please, Aurora here, Lukas over there."

She points to two different entrances.

Lukas and I are led into two different rooms, where the only thing that separates us is one big window in the middle. Both rooms are composed of white walls and a hospital bed in the middle. Enyo and Milgram excuse themselves for a moment, exiting our rooms and locking us inside.

"Odd," Lukas says, approaching the window between us. "Why are we separated?"

I sense a hint of terror in his words.

"It's like we're together but only through sound."

I meet his gaze, which is the first time I notice the blue circles underneath his eyes.

"Lukas, are you okay?"

He nods, but his eyes are puffed red.

I hesitate, "How was your family?"

"Alive. I miss them." Lukas rests his hands on the glass. I recognise the fragility in his voice. "And yours?"

"They're okay. I try to ignore them, forget about them, get them out of my head—"

"But it doesn't work?" he interrupts me, his voice raspy.

"No. It doesn't."

"Yeah. Same."

Steadily, he inhales while lifting his head as if he were pushing back his tears.

"I have a little brother. His name is Jacob," I tell Lukas, trying to lighten the mood. Maybe saying it aloud will help? "He's the bravest, sweetest little boy in the world."

"Never thought you'd speak about anyone like that," Lukas responds, half-grinning, half in pain. He adds, "He sounds awesome."

"He is." I nod, remembering his drawings, his poems and most of all his smile. "And you?"

"Two sisters. Amelia and Sofia. They're full of wonder." Lukas smiles to himself, glancing away and sniffling. He speaks, brittle and delicate, his voice wavering in between his words. "I'd come home from hunting, and they would both run up to me. Filled with questions, their eyes bright."

"What kind of questions?" I ask softly.

"About everything. The weather, the forest, my job. You see, I *never* let them out the house much." He pauses, his voice trembling. "Now I wish I did."

"It's okay, Lukas." I try to catch his gaze.

"I was just scared. I just wanted to protect them." He looks down in shame. Tears plummet from his face.

"I know, I know. It's okay, Lukas." I can't reach out to him. I feel the trickle of wetness around my own eyes. Not right now, I tell myself. But tears flood before I can control them.

"We'll…" I can't speak, my voice quivering. "We'll be okay."

I place my palm on the glass next to his.

His eyes meet mine. He inhales sharply.

"You're right." He presses his palm into the glass, resting it against mine. I start to feel his warmth. "We'll be all right."

Footsteps echo in the distance. I wipe my eyes and remember Jacob's smile.

"I guess I'll see you on the other side," I say, smiling at Lukas.

"I'll meet you there," he answers, trying to smile back.

A doctor and a nurse enter my room. Both wearing white lab coats with masks, goggles and gloves. The window in between me and Lukas turns pitch black.

"Shall we begin?" the doctor asks.

"Affirmative." Enyo's voice shoots back from the doctor's wrist.

He connects multiple plastic cables to my fingers and even sticks a magnetic orb onto my scalp. The nurse then brings forwards an extremely small syringe. The nurse wipes my skin with a disinfectant wipe, and the doctor gently taps my arm with the syringe, as I sense a short, but painful jolt.

"Injected." The doctor looks up to the nurse, blankly. "Proceed."

The nurse speaks softly. "Aurora, I want you to take a deep breath in and a long breath out, repeat that four times for me please."

Before I know it, the drowsiness of sleep overwhelms me, as I dip in and out of consciousness.

Quiet murmurs and mutters echo across the room, but I keep my eyes shut.

I can faintly hear the nurse's voice. "All is complete. The tracker has been implanted into her brain through the bloodstream. The serum injection will kickstart Project Blackout."

I may overhear something useful, I think to myself, concentrating as hard as I can.

"Any critical memories that may trigger episodic discharge?" Enyo asks.

"The activation of the medial temporal lobe and the hippocampus appeared most often when specific associations could link back to the subject's mother or younger brother. For instance, flowers activated memories of her brother and retrospection of how she'd like to be remembered by him. The associations are far too many and unpredictable to be scaled down to specifics. The entire episodic neural system will be inhibited for as long as possible," the doctor explains.

"Understood. Further experimentation is required for a clear solution..." Enyo trails off, like she'd become distracted. "Peeping in on conversations is disrespectful."

I stay still, but I can feel my chest rumbling.

"You won't remember this anyway." Enyo chuckles. "I'll tell you a little secret," Enyo whispers, her voice shifting into a deeper, more demented shrieking. "You will lose all recollection of your memories. You won't remember anyone, anytime, anyplace…" she pauses, then snickers. "Not even *Jacob*."

I jump awake, striking her with my elbow until she stumbles to the ground. I sprint across the room, reaching the transparent window.

"Lukas!" I yell, banging on the window repeatedly. "Wake up, Lukas! We have to get out of here."

I don't want to forget.

Two Arbiters grab me, lock their arms around my shoulders and toss me back onto the hospital bed.

"No, NO!" I scream in fear, kicking my feet and shaking my whole body in desperation. "Let go of me! Don't touch me!"

I don't want to forget.

I plunge forwards, forcefully twisting my body to catch a glimpse of Lukas. But he lies still. Silent.

"Keep trying, Aurora. He's already forgotten you." Enyo sneers. "He's already lost you!"

The Arbiters strap me to the bed until I can't resist.

"Like the Premier said, you will lose everything. Even yourself!" she asserts, picking up the syringe.

Enyo's eyes ignite.

"Goodnight. I hope you're able to dream of Jacob," she taunts me, then leans in. "For the last time."

Pain pulses through my body. My heart begins to slow. Echoes fade to silence. Everything becomes a blur. My eyes open to a void of nothingness.

I black out.

REALM OF LIBERTY

Act II

Freedom is the act of choice and the choice to act.
Anything less is surrendering to power.

12

Lukas

Once I open my eyes, instinct takes over. I stretch out my arms and legs. My muscles feel sluggish and weak. I extend my arm down to my waist, avoiding its sharp edge, reaching for my blade.

My mind goes blank.

Fragmented reminiscence returns to me, but I can't make sense of it. Déjà vu. An unsettling familiarity.

Why did I do that? I can't make sense of anything.

A shiver hurdles up my spine, but I don't react. Instead, I open my eyes. I'm in bed with a blanket up to my neck. Machines beep quietly. I look above my head, encountering a perplexing tower of cables attached to a helmet.

Everything is white. The walls, the tables, my bed frame, even the door. There's a transparent window to my right. Through it, I see another, identical room.

Steadily I rise from my bed, getting used to balancing on my feet. It's as if I've woken up from a coma. My body feels static.

I catch a glimpse of my reflection in the metallic frame of the hospital bed I was in. Everything seems to be in place. That face though. I wince.

That's *me?* I sense an agitating wave of nausea.

The door opens, and a woman in high heels steps into the room. She wears a white jacket, with her hair tied in a bun. I notice a wound above her eye. Her dark skin is the only thing in this room that isn't pale.

"Good morning," she greets me. There's a sense of calmness in her voice that relaxes me. "You may be confused right now, but don't worry."

She hands me a glass of water, then sits down.

"Where exactly are we?" I ask, as I consume the entire glass. I begin to escape the drowsy state of numbness I was in just moments ago.

"We're at a safety facility preparing for the Equilibrium…" the lady answers, but her words turn into meaningless mumblings.

I place a hand against my chest, feeling for my heartbeat. The beeps in the room grow louder and quicker. I look around, feeling distant and unaware of everything.

Who am I?

Gently, I close my eyes. I think back to yesterday, but nothing comes to mind. It's like I'm a blank slate.

"What's my name?" I interrupt the lady.

"What are you talking about?" she pauses, eyebrows arched.

"What am I called?"

"You should know that…" She hesitates, then says, "Lukas."

"And who are you?"

She doesn't answer.

She scribbles something down on her notepad and looks back to me. Her gaze is sharp and unreadable.

"Your memory has been reset," she discloses, speaking emotionlessly. "That's why you don't remember anything."

"Why? What did I do?" I panic.

The beeping monitor in the corner grows louder.

With no past I'm nothing.

"You were elected for the Equilibrium," she says, propping her head on her hand. "You didn't do anything wrong. You simply chose your future."

"Chose?" My breaths are heavy. I stare at the unguarded door behind the lady.

"The world requires balance. Statera must be restored," she says, her voice excessively sweet.

I swallow my fear. "I could run."

"There's twenty soldiers behind that door," she responds directly.

"What did you do to me?" I yell.

"Sit down."

"There's nothing stopping me from hurting you until you tell me the truth."

"That would be naïve." She tilts her head and smiles.

"I can do a lot worse than that bruise on your face." I tighten my fist.

"Oh, your friend gave me this!" She taps the wound. "She woke up very confused. Just like you."

The size of her pupils don't change. There's a truthfulness in her expression.

I don't fully trust her. But I'll listen to her explanation. My fear doesn't disappear. It merely shrinks a little.

"Sorry," I lie, acting timid. "I don't know what's wrong with me."

"Don't apologise." She laughs, pleasantly. "Nothing is wrong with you. You're just scared, no?"

"Yeah, I'm confused."

"Introductions first. I'm Enyo."

We shake hands.

"You said I'm Lukas, right?" I ask, bewildered. She nods, cheerfully smiling.

"That should sound familiar."

"It does. That's why it feels so strange."

She pats my shoulder. "One step at a time."

"Why are we here?" I ask.

"You'll participate in a Ceremony that requires you to fight for your life."

"Why would I agree?"

"You didn't. You accepted the calling of your Gods."

"Am I going to die?" I ask her, gazing deep into her eyes. Searching for lies.

"I don't know. Fate is yours to make." She omits the questions, but her face doesn't fluctuate. There's a calming kindness tied to her voice.

I don't think a person can fake that.

"Lukas, I want to show you something," she says, placing a small metallic panel on the hospital bed between us. "I won't allow any doubt."

Video footage materialises into the air.

I see myself. Or the self I was before inside the same body. I'm in a wooden house, the walls uneven and splintered. The house is dark, with the only light coming from a small, orange bulb in the middle of the room. I'm crouched down talking to two girls.

"Those are your sisters," Enyo says softly. "Listen carefully. This is what you're fighting for."

In the video, I clutch their shoulders.

"Amelia, Sofia you have to understand… I'm going away to keep you safe," I plead, my voice raspy. They don't answer. Their faces are red, wet with suffering.

"I want to protect you." The camera shifts to my back, so that you can see my sisters more closely. "Amelia, you'll take care of the house. I've taught you how to cook. Sofia, you listen to your sister. Live together. Be happy together… all right?"

Sophia can't hold back her tears. She sniffles with every breath.

"I'm going to come back from the Ceremony. You understand? I'll protect you and come back. You'll always be safe." My voice says this, but it sounds mechanical. Unlike me.

I embrace my sisters, letting them cry into my chest. Then the video ends.

The footage feels off. And my sisters don't ring a bell. My name at least felt familiar. But with these two girls, I feel zero recognition. I feel nothing.

"That doesn't explain why I can't remember anything," I probe.

"The Trinities of the Elect want to minimise your pain. Removing emotional instability and one's connection to the past has increased survivability," Enyo replies, her voice dear and sweet.

I don't believe she's lying. Her eyes reflect her emotions. I want to trust her.

But what she's saying frightens me.

"All right… but why is the Ceremony necessary?" I ask quietly.

"The duality of existence is balanced on a scale of life and death," Enyo explains, gesturing with her hands. "When one outweighs the other, havoc ensues. The way to achieve righteousness and peace is balance."

"So how do we balance it?" I ask, confused.

"The Ceremony of Equilibrium always attains the right number of the living and the dead. Your participation restores Statera. That's how you'll protect your sisters!" she responds, grinning with her eyes.

I don't say anything. But this is the first time I doubt her.

"I'll explain the Equilibrium further. But firstly, we need to meet your Duo. Are you hungry?" she asks.

I nod desperately.

We leave the room swiftly and venture through a long white corridor. There are no noticeable details. My mind feels shredded by the absence of colour.

A spiralling glass staircase leads to the top of this facility. A viewing platform. The sun bathes the world in soothing heat. Clear blue skies. The wind is friendly and light. Fresh air fills my nostrils. In the distance, I catch the foggy shapes of factories, apartment blocks, and slender skyscrapers.

I let my shoulders fall, feeling relaxed.

In front of us there is a long, extended table filled with food and two benches on either side.

A muscular man dressed in a navy suit approaches me. His dark beard conceals his intentions. Cloudy skin.

"I'm Overseer Milgram. Please enjoy your last meal." He guides me to the table where a girl sits opposite me.

She looks the same age as me, just smaller. Her hair is short, trimmed to fall across her forehead, always staying clear of her eyes. She looks frail. Her skin stretches thinly over her cheeks, revealing the hollowness and sharp protrusion of her bones. She doesn't eat much.

Her face is stiff. Her eyes track me, coldly.

"We don't have long left," Enyo giggles, shuddering with excitement. This is the first time her eyes look menacing, devouring the light around her. "Soon we shall be on our way."

"Where are we going?" the girl asks demandingly, her glare intensely aimed at Enyo.

"The Realm of Liberty!" Enyo exclaims, revealing perfectly polished white teeth. Her face turns vicious, carved with bloodthirst. Her eyes become venomous, sharp. Her presence feels authentic.

I learn of Enyo's true nature. My chest rises and falls unevenly. My heart shatters with fear as I realise: *She lied to me about everything.*

13

Aurora

A boy fixates on my face. I recognise familiarity within his gaze. Squirming in my seat uncomfortably, I find myself surrounded by three strangers. And a past that's dead.

No identity, no memories, no family. I'm alone.

"Lukas and Aurora, together you will form a Duo," Enyo says, sipping on a glass of coffee with ice cubes. "In the Equilibrium, you are responsible for each other's safety."

Lukas anxiously scratches away at his skin.

Protect one another? Hell… I doubt we'll live long enough to get the chance.

I stare down at the empty belt on my outfit. How did I even end up wearing this? They must've dressed us while we were asleep. Stretchy cargo trousers, leather boots, and a long-sleeve shirt are all we've been given. Our clothes are mostly black with hints of red on the stitching lines.

"In the Equilibrium your goal is to survive the harshest environments. Endure, adapt, overcome." Enyo exhales white clouds after puffing on her bracelet. "Restore Statera, and I promise the return of all your memories."

"Anything else?" I snap.

I'm sick of staring at their serpent eyes.

Enyo smiles, then adds, "The deadlier your journey, the greater the rewards. Survival Points are attainable to be exchanged for goods."

I shift my attention to Lukas. His face contains an elusive familiarity that escapes my mind's focus. He must be from before. Before *now*. But that doesn't matter. Nothing matters anymore.

Wind thrashes our faces like a force pressing against us. A wide helicopter with wing-shaped rotor blades lands on the deck.

"Let's move," Overseer Milgram says. He leads us to the silver aircraft. We climb inside and strap ourselves in. The insides of the helicopter flash, and a central hologram floats up, mapping the location we're flying over. Right now it says "Colony One" (Ireland).

I turn to the boy, studying his posture, his gaze, even his breathing. He looks calm with a dissociative blankness that conceals his fear and pain. Same as me.

"What's your name?" I ask him quietly.

He stares at me, cautiously.

"Lukas," he replies, moving his gaze above my head.

"You don't care about my name?" I respond, infuriated by his silence.

"I already know it." He gestures upwards.

That's when I notice the floating square gleaming above the boy.

    Name: Lukas

    X-Code: 202240

    Age: 17

"You should look outside. This could be the last time we see something like this," Lukas suggests, softly.

Green, lustrous forests enclose the earth, in beautiful ring-like patterns. Lakes trickle through the land, weaving and unfolding in random but intricate pathways that mesmerize me.

"I'd like to explore these lands one day," he says, filled with wonder.

"I'd go with you." The words leap out before I can stop them. He smiles gently and nods.

We know we're destined for elsewhere.

Once we exit the helicopter, we find ourselves surrounded by colossal pyramids, built out of chiselled, white stone. There are fourteen of these structures in total. As we approach one pyramid, it glows in a golden outline.

The inside of the structure is an empty, brightly lit room with a round table at its centre. The rest of the room is made of white and grey plastic like a science lab. Though I've never seen one, I instinctively know how a laboratory should look.

My own mind doesn't make sense to me.

"Welcome to the Preservation Pyramid. Here you'll prepare for the Equilibrium, which starts at midday. But I'd like to show you something before that." Enyo leads us to the round table and gracefully steps aside, unveiling a circular stadium, filled with ethereal blends of blue and grey. It expands into a range of biomes and landscapes converging all into a singular dome at its centre.

"This is the Realm of Liberty!" Enyo cheers. "A coliseum where the Equilibrium will take place."

The columns are divided into three sections, comprised of three parts each. The sections progressively shrink smaller and become narrower as they venture towards the dome.

I hate to say it. But it's an alluring creation. At least from where I stand. But once I'm inside the Realm itself, I suspect I'll feel differently.

"The last thing you must do before the Equilibrium is choose your tactical syringes," Enyo says, tapping on her bracelet to activate the hologram. "These are injections that enhance specific capabilities of the human body. Here they are."

Feather Falling	Softens the impact when landing from great heights.
Bolt	Increases sprint speed by 25%
Endurance	Improves stamina by 25%
Suppression	Silences movements by 75%
Mobility	Enhances the distance of all jumps. Increases leap speed.
Stability	Magnifies your balance and enables you to cling onto difficult surfaces.
Arms Blazing	Increases strength by 50%
Awareness	Increases concentration. Accelerates thought processes.

All tactical syringes last for 300s.
Exception: "Arms Blazing" is limited to 180s.
If multiple tactical syringes are used simultaneously, effects are capped at 90s total.

Overseer Milgram places two ominous boxes, which house the same vials each. We can both choose the same syringes if we wish. Alongside the boxes, there are two vial racks containing three slots each, with our names on them.

"You may choose," Enyo says, stepping back to give us some space.

Lukas and I start reading the labels on the hologram.

Each syringe has different, alien colours, with different shades of green. Purple is the most prominent.

Lukas stares at the labels of Bolt and Endurance with curiosity.

"What is this nonsense?" he whispers so that only I can hear him.

"They've lied about everything," I mutter.

Lukas purses his lips. "This isn't a Ceremony."

"I know. This is something they *want* to do."

I grab the Arms Blazing vial, and my fingers tremble with fury. My eyes shoot Lukas a daring question.

But he shakes his head as if to say: *Don't do it.* He motions his eyes to the corners of the room where the cameras are aimed at us.

"Let's focus on staying alive," he says quietly.

I sigh and nod.

"These seem logical." Lukas places Bolt and Endurance into his vial rack. Since he's a male, he'll likely be stronger and faster than me. Perhaps to pair with his physicality, I should go for Awareness. But I'm not sure about my remaining two.

"Maybe this should be your third?" I hold out the vial of Suppression to him. His tactical syringes are focused on running. Mine should be more varied.

"All right." He takes it and fills up his rack.

"Good," I reply, picking up another vial. "Do you think we can combine my Awareness with your Suppression?"

"Yeah," he pauses. "You seem good at this."

"Hopefully good enough to keep us alive."

I notice Enyo grinning. Maybe we've done something right. That snake wouldn't be smiling otherwise. Her face revolts me.

"The Realm had different biomes, right?" I ask, deciding between taking Mobility and Stability for their climbing benefit or Arms Blazing and Feather Falling for combat.

"That's what it looked like," he agrees. "Besides, they said the environment's the threat."

"Then it's settled." I pick up the Mobility and Stability vials, completing my vial rack.

I shout, "We're done."

"Superb!" Enyo applauds. "My dear, could you attach the syringes?"

"Of course." Overseer Milgram inserts the vials into the tactical syringes and places them in our utility belts. Holographic letters on the syringe reveal the name of the vial and below it in italics: "*One Use Only.*"

"Let's head to the drop spot then," Enyo exclaims.

We exit the pyramid structure and head for a new helicopter. Arbiters wait around the aircraft. A heavy metal ladder assists us to the helicopter.

The outside of the helicopter is painted in luminous white. Once inside, Arbiters pull a stretchy black suit on top of our outfits. It has robust flaps around the armpits, like concealed wings.

This must be for the drop.

The helicopter ascends in a powerful thrust. We're seated in the middle, confined to the view of the blue sky through the cockpit windshield.

This is actually happening, I squirm in terror, feeling dizzy.

I sense wetness begin to flicker around my eyelids. I repeat deep breaths, but the overwhelming intensity of the moment absorbs me whole. My chest is pounding.

Lukas looks at me, full of worry. But I can't tell him anything. I try to, but my lips won't stop quivering.

"We're almost at the drop!" Enyo announces proudly. Her face twists with desire.

"What is the drop?" Lukas asks, nervously. We're vulnerable prey tangled in a spider's web as venom inflicts nausea.

Enyo breathes in deeply, pleasureful. A sinister glance, shrouded in anticipation, slices our confidence. She rejoices. "A leap of faith."

14

Lukas

Nothingness expands into the distance. Desert lands surround us, uninhabited by humans. There's no other terrain. Everything is sand.

But as we get closer and closer, a distant circle begins to increase in size. A cloudy hue surrounds it.

"All helicopters in position," Overseer Milgram declares. The air is tense with anticipation. "Thirty seconds until inbound."

Enyo stares outwards into the Realm. A somewhat cold, yet frightening expression in her eyes.

Through the helicopter's open doors, a colossal construction looks back into my eyes. A stadium stretches out through different complexes of land, so far that I can't even see the other end of it. Only grey, impenetrable fog. At its heart lies a massive sphere, with all lanes converging into it. I've never seen anything remotely as grand... though, I can't remember anything I've *ever* seen.

"Twenty seconds until inbound."

Other helicopters drift through the skies, each one slanting downwards gradually. Pointed and ready. Anticipating the moment when the countdown hits zero.

Enyo stands in front of us, gazing outwards with a proud smile at the Realm. The air becomes humid. It feels like we're in it.

"Attach the subjects!" Enyo says to the Arbiters at her side, her voice echoing around the whole Realm. They push us into two seats placed at the back, strap us in and then the ramp opens.

"Ten seconds until inbound."

"Welcome to the Realm of Liberty," Enyo shouts, most likely smiling, as she stares across the Realm, excitedly waiting to witness us battling for our lives. "Fight for freedom and scuffle for balance."

"Five."

The chairs we're strapped to jolt forwards to the open ramp. We're steadily lowered until our seats start to dangle upside down, facing the Realm head-on.

"Four."

The Realm blends the colours of earth, where deserts, mountains, forests, water and stone chaotically collide, ripple through one another and merge together.

Teardrops form around my eyes. My heart slams into my lungs repeatedly, leaving me breathless, gasping for air helplessly.

The world grows silent, except for Milgram's countdown. "Three."

Then the centre of the Realm erupts with thick, black smoke. My skin curls up.

"Two."

A shockwave pulses through the air, shaking our helicopter lightly side to side. The belts around my waist begin to loosen. I feel light-headed. There's not much air up here. My nostrils flare, damp with fear.

"One."

I hear my heartbeat, like someone was knocking on my skull. But I can't hear myself think.

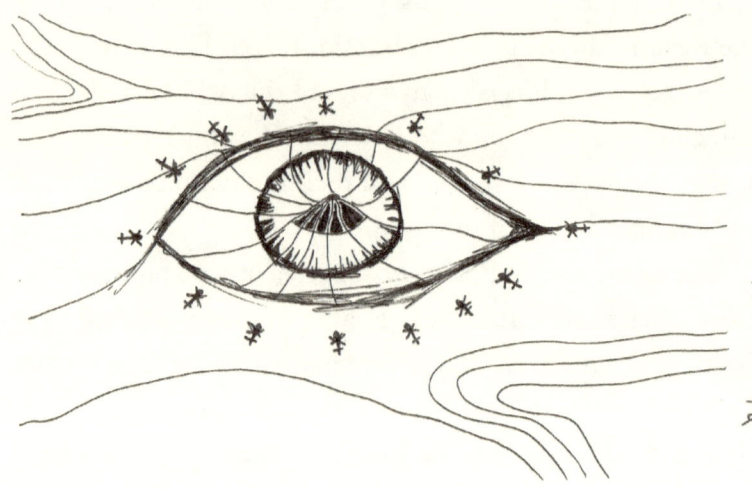

"The Equilibrium is now underway."

The belts unhook. One last fleeting moment of hope. Then I'm galloping breathless through the sky. My eyelids flutter, absorbing my tears.

We're on our own now.

We're plummeting downwards, as the merciless winds slice past our limbs. With each passing second, we fall faster.

I glance around the Realm, spotting other black specks in the sky aligned with us. We're so far apart that the other subjects resemble birds in flight.

Who will survive the longest? That question defines us now.

"Can you hear me?" I scream at Aurora, but her face remains expressionless. "Aurora!"

Eventually, she turns to face me. Her eyes are stiff. As if she's unaware we're free falling down to earth.

She looks right past me, like I'm not there.

The two of us circle one another, dancing with certain death. We plummet from the clouds. Gradually, the Realm becomes clearer. Our section of it looks like a linear pathway, a lane. Encaged by two thick, unbreakable, brick walls that are covered in vines.

My stomach knots. Everything shakes. I notice the flapping material from my jumpsuit bouncing against my stomach. These are wings attached from my arms to my feet. A glide suit.

We're not too far from the ground. I begin to see a grand array of piled junk, cars and wheels spread out amongst our share of the Realm. It looks like a labyrinth filled with different lanes, leading into different paths.

But first we need to get there. Before gravity splatters us against the ground into a bloody mess. I have to do something. We're interlocking hands with death.

There's a grey ripcord just above my chest. It's on Aurora's suit as well. I point towards the steel handle on her left shoulder, signalling for her to pull it. But nothing is getting through to her.

I have no other choice. I have to keep us both alive. I pull the handle strongly. My arms and legs are repositioned forcefully into an X shape, allowing for the fabric to stretch out.

The wings at my sides resist air, immediately making my descent steadier and slower.

Aurora drops through the sky rapidly. My arms shudder in rage at her incapacitated state. I try adjusting my speed, aiming myself downwards to glide vertically.

I need to reach her. Before it's too late.

My body is balanced against the air for a few moments as I descend vertically until the air knocks me out of control. I begin spiralling towards the ground, as my body spins and flips over repeatedly.

The world around me keeps swirling and rotating. I extend my arms, searching for Aurora, but I can only feel the ruthless wind as it whirls me rapidly in circles. I try to locate her, but the immense pressure on my neck makes it impossible to move.

Suddenly, I plunge into something. My head bounces from the impact as I'm rotated until I'm facing the ground again. My heart quickens. My body is horizontal now, falling on top of something else. Aurora.

Her eyes are wide, filled with panic. The collision brought her back.

I press my palms against her shoulders, as we both tumble to the earth in each other's arms. I grip onto her lever and pull it from her shoulder.

But it won't open. It doesn't budge.

I try pulling it with all my strength, but nothing is working. Rage streams through me. I'm unable to contain myself any longer. Viciously, I slam my fist into her shoulder repeatedly. Her eyes bulge with redness. She painfully seals her lips together. I grasp onto the lever with both hands, falling under her. The brisk movement creates a vibration. I look back up, seeing her wings deploy. Silently, I breathe out in relief and turn back around. My eyes search the ground that we're approaching too rapidly.

Nothing but empty land filled with old, rusting metal cars. Grass protrudes through the cracks in the stone walls. Below us, there's a small body of water. It must've been put there for us to land in.

We have to make it.

I tug her towards myself and shout into her ear, "Hold onto me!"

She accepts my hands in her own, unhesitatingly. She clutches on tightly.

I feel her fear. She feels mine.

Instantly, we sway through the air, gently beginning to descend at a significantly slower pace.

We spin in a circle, holding each other desperately. The wind bombards us. My eyes won't stop blinking from the dust. I try to catch my breath.

My heart pounds like a steel hammer, and my lungs empty with each beat.

That's when I'm submerged underwater, sinking deeper and deeper by the second. The cold bubbles absorb me, leaving me panting and puffing for air as the lake drags me to the bottom. My vision withers.

I swing my feet and arms simultaneously in quick bursts of panic. As I arise from under the surface of the lake, I spit out the water trapped in my lungs. I can't breathe.

Only then do I notice that I'm alone amongst the pulsing waves of the lake.

"I'd like to welcome all subjects to the Realm of Liberty. Refer to me as your guide, Enyo," she announces, enthusiastically. "The Realm is divided into three Stages, each Stage containing three Survival Zones as separate waves of obstacles. In between each complete Stage there is a Safe Zone, allowing safe passage for a limited amount of time. Once all Stages have been completed, the Final Act shall commence in the heart of Statera. This is a celebration of the Trinities of the Elect. Life will be taken and life will be given. May the passage of time restore Statera."

The speakers sizzle with crunching sounds of flames smouldering. A mixture of cracks.

Enyo rejoices, *"May you Blaze or Burn."*

Each outcome is futile. Both dissolve into ash. Leading to the embrace of death.

I climb out of the lake. Water drips with every step. Steadily, the glide suit loosens itself. A zipper seam now runs through the middle of my suit.

It wasn't there before.

I throw the suit on the ground and wring out my shirt. The cold slithers down my spine. My arms shiver. I wince with each breath. My nostrils tear with icy heat. I shake off these biting pains and put my damp shirt back on. I tread onwards into the lane.

It's a concrete road filled with rusting frames of cars, cluttered gears, and metal plates. It's a narrow pathway, ensnared by grey brick walls that tower oppressively on either side.

A daunting passage of imprisonment.

The colossal size of the Realm is unfathomable to me. How long did this take to build? And why? Just to watch us suffer?

I follow a small trail of wet footsteps to a car. Aurora is lying down on the hood of a brown, corroded car. Her chest rises and falls rapidly over and over again. A spasm of gasps and coughs burst out of her throat, rattling her upper body. Her eyes grow watery.

"Are you all right?" I ask her, steadily approaching the car as to not frighten her out of the blue.

"I just need to breathe." Her voice is sluggish.

"All right. You do that."

We stay in silence for a couple of moments. She doesn't move one bit. I look forwards into our lane, spotting two rocky pillars up ahead and a long stretch of emptiness. Beyond that, everything becomes foggy.

"I'm sorry about earlier," she mumbles, rising to her feet.

"That can't happen again," I say, coldly.

"It won't," she retorts.

"Are you sure? Because you almost got us both killed." Fury bubbles at the edge of my lips.

"I said it won't happen again."

"I don't believe you," I hiss in anger.

My body shakes.

"I blanked out. I said I'm sorry."

"What do you mean you just blanked out? How does that happen?"

"I don't know!" she shrieks, her fists clenching.

"I just want to go back to whatever life and whatever family I had before I ended up here," I vehemently persist, partly yelling, half-whispering.

"You think I don't?" Aurora growls and shoots me a stare that seems to say *watch yourself.*

"You do?"

"Yes I do," she spits back.

"Then we need each other," I say, silencing her. "You can't leave me on my own like that again."

She turns away furiously. "And I won't."

A ferocious screech darts through the Realm. The ground shudders. Pebbles hop up and down. I turn back to the lake where we landed, but it looks distorted, neon almost. An emerald wall pulsates in a hypnotic rhythm, crawling towards us.

"Your first survival zone will propel the Equilibrium." Enyo's voice echoes from the sky. "Behind you, there is a magnetic barrier that destroys one zone every twenty-four hours. This is the Great Constant!"

Aurora glances over to me, her face arched in confusion. She whispers, "What the hell is that thing?"

I shrug my shoulders in response.

"The Constant is a suffocating gas, which if inhaled for longer than three minutes induces paralysis." I don't wait for Enyo to finish her explanation. I grab Aurora's hand and drag her along with me, jogging away from the neon barrier of air approaching us. We tread through a junkyard filled with the skeletal remnants of cars. Clutters of worn-out metal pieces, probably torn off from the cars, lay scattered all across the ground.

"Let go of my hand," Aurora demands, staying by my side. I do as I'm asked. We continue moving ahead.

Enyo explains, "This gas is a mixture of arsine amongst other subordinate chemicals. Hence the first objective is established. Survive the Great Constant. Reach the white passageway. Don't burn up."

We pass the two pillars I'd seen before, carefully placing our steps as we run onwards.

The Constant spreads through the ground, absorbing the decaying cars and rubble. A squeaky rupture echoes through our lane as chunks of metal violently vault upwards inside the gas. Its colour alternates between dark shades of green and yellow, occasionally blending together in some regions as it throbs with waves of neon and lime.

The ground is a maze of treacherous steps.

A thunderous, gut-wrenching echo pierces my ears. We glance back at the same time, watching the two pillars crumble as they implode.

"It's nothing… keep moving," I blurt out.

Aurora groans. "Do you see any way to get past these cars?"

I search through the cars once more, but our lane is a wide, expanding tunnel of litter. I can't see anything beyond that. I shake my head.

"Maybe it'll be easier if we bounce from car to car," I suggest.

We both climb on top of a car and start moving ahead, jumping as lightly as possible from car to car. We find our momentum, one person per car. Otherwise they sway from the imbalance of weight. The wheels no longer have enough air to keep the car bodies rigid.

The Constant patiently wriggles behind us, echoing with fracturing cracks. Everything is steadily absorbed and eaten up whole. It stays on our tail. I keep my breathing repetitive, trying to avoid a stitch in my ribs.

A metallic clank in front of me disrupts my focus.

A sudden gasp darts from Aurora's lips. "Lukas... help me." She lies trembling on the hood of the car ahead of me. I spring towards her in an instant. I notice the broken windshield.

"My foot, damn it." She lifts her left leg, revealing two thick shards of glass impaled in her sole. I don't give her any time to prepare herself. I grab a metal rod from the hood of the car and swing it at the shards of glass, breaking its largest parts. She quivers, wheezing in agony, mumbling nonsense under her breath.

It's important that the shards don't go any deeper. Everything else we'll take care of later.

"C'mon, get up." I wrap one of her arms around my neck, helping her stand. She grunts in a whispered rage. We continue moving forwards, leaping from car to car, but at a much slower pace. "You just have to bear the pain for now."

"Damn it, I know! Just shut up," she fires back, struggling with heavy breaths. She presses her weight against me, as we tread onwards. The rows of cars begin to disappear, unveiling an empty clearing that leads up to the distant passageway. A glossy white entryway, probably leading into the next zone.

I jump off the last car we're on, then turn back around to help Aurora onto the ground.

"Argh," she squeals as her left foot touches the ground. She can't stop trembling. I do my best to help her regain her balance.

We continue storming ahead.

The dust from the ground begins to rise, followed by waves of abrupt vibrations. Roars hiss from the sky.

I look up to where the sound came from. Specks of brown dust begin to plummet. Metallic rustles reverb through the air.

Chunks of metal begin raining from the sky. Cars descend face-forwards from the top of the entrapping walls. I peer around to peek at the Constant. It's poisonous colour glints at me from twenty metres away.

It's closer than ever before.

I drag Aurora with me as we gallop forwards, heading to the left where the path is clear. I keep my grip tight on her arm and waist as we hobble together.

The cars hail from the sky at a much greater speed. Above me, metallic crunches pierce the air like thunder. In a split-second reaction, I shift our bodies to the right, just narrowly evading a car that fragments into pieces beside us.

"Can you still hop?" I ask Aurora, seeing her left leg no longer touching the ground.

"Yeah, let's go," she squeals, unable to stop grunting. She hops as fast as she can, leaning on me to assist herself.

The ground beneath us fractures into uneven cracks as we step on it, sending us tumbling down. I catch sight of a small vehicle hurtling downwards. Directly above us.

I pull us to the side, forcing us to fall to the ground. Without hesitation, I get on top of her and cover her body with mine in a push up position.

I close my eyes, squinting nervously, anticipating the immense force of being squashed.

But… nothing happens. A resounding thud shakes the ground in a clashing scrunch.

I storm to my feet and help Aurora get back up, sensing the sizzling sounds of the Constant catching up to us. I glance back at the fallen debris. The cars and the metal junk fall everywhere, except for one singular pathway. Like a maze, the debris forms the walls, creating only one route to safety.

We are rats in a maze.

"Agh." An unexpected squirm escapes Aurora's lips.

A growing shadow dawns on us. Jumping to my left, I swing

Aurora to my other side desperately, just barely evading the hunk of car parts that dash into the ground where we were moments ago.

We get up again. I feel the muscles in my legs begin to stiffen. My lungs are empty.

I slump down to my knees, swinging one arm to the ground to protect my face. My fingers sweep the floor, touching a bitter and dusted path made of stone.

"Are you okay?" Aurora asks, worried by me stalling. I gasp for air repeatedly, lightly shivering from the numbing air.

"We can't stop," I say, gruffly.

I turn around and see the Constant absorb the cars behind us.

Sweat rolls down my face, as I try not to reveal the engulfing agony in my legs. My clothes are soaked from head to toe in dirt. I stand up in an outburst of shallow breaths.

I drag my feet forwards. Together me and Aurora limp ahead, stumbling and grunting from the burning air.

The path ahead is empty. It leads up to the passageway, a top-hinged door with a silvery-white frame that closes smoothly in a vertically downward motion. We stagger on, motivated solely by surviving.

Beneath my feet, the ground quivers turbulently, swaying us side to side.

The ground crumples and disintegrates into a fog of sandy rocks.

I spring ahead, keeping Aurora tightly stuck to me. The scorch on my soles imitates walking on burning coal. The passageway frame is gradually closing, descending to the ground. Cutting off our only escape.

I feel the oscillating ground pulse violently. The ground is collapsing beneath us.

"Argh, what are you doing?" Aurora shrieks in horror as I fling her onto my shoulder. I gather all my remaining strength and surge forwards, hurtling as fast as I can.

The Constant chases us with predatory intent. My knees and shoulders burn unbearably with such intense discomfort I might puke at any moment. We're ten metres from the passageway when I realise the door is about to collapse to the ground.

My lungs are breathless. With the Constant grazing my back, I leap forwards recklessly and hurl Aurora forwards into the passageway, as the ground shudders underneath my feet.

I fall to my knees, surrounded by debris.

And let the world collapse around me.

15

Aurora

Echoing thoughts race through my mind, each one a chilling reminder of death's imminence. My limbs refuse to respond, leaving me stuck to the ground and motionless. My skin feels numb against the cold earth. I've been drained of strength. A dull ache pulses down my left foot, forcing me to glance at it.

To say my body is misbehaving would be inaccurate. Rather it's ignorant of me. My muscles resist me. I can only control my eyes, but even then I can't turn my head much.

Waves of wind bombard me, frosting my skin until my sensations become foggy. I suspect I'm shivering.

Clatters and shrieks sound like distant growls. Or maybe they're cries for help, twisted by the wind into the sounds of dying animals chanting their final, pain-wretched screams.

Am I hallucinating? I question myself. I feel both conscious and drowsy at the same time.

From my position I can't see much. A white panel towers over me—the passageway. The ground is paved with stone bricks, which extend into the walls that form our confined path. Strands of grass emerge from the cracks in the bricks of the walls, striving to grasp a fleeting touch of sunlight.

Jabs of brightness make me wince, and I shut my eyes. I envision myself in a valley of tall grass. Greenery and forests surround me in the distance. The air must've been full and fresh. A trail of flattened grass, worn by years of footsteps, leads to a small hill up ahead. On top of it there is an ordinary, dark oak hut. The brownness of the wood has faded, slowly turning grey.

There is something strange about this image.

Why does it feel so familiar? My mind aches from the obscure nostalgia. It doesn't make sense to me. I have never seen this before. At least me, the new Aurora, hasn't. Why the hell am I imagining it?

The light I see through my shut eyelids starts to darken. My heartbeat finds a constant rhythm and the world grows quiet.

W ater drips onto my face, making me instinctively move my head. After a few agonising moments of flickering my eyelids, trying to get used to the brightness of the sun, I look out into the lane. It's much like before. The ground and the walls are still made of mossy stone bricks. The air lingers with an ancient smell. However, this time there aren't any obstacles; it's just a single-lane pathway with nothing in it.

I gape at my foot, where the wound has curled up into throbbing, pink lumps. I lift myself from the ground, swaying lightly until I can stand firmly. My body hasn't recovered. I feel uneasy as a constant, agonising burn makes it impossible to bear any weight on my left foot.

The Realm in front of me is bleak and hopeless. There is nowhere to go.

While still unsteady on my feet, I take one step forwards and feel a sudden jolt of realisation hit me. I become bleary-eyed, struggling to see straight.

I can't remember if Lukas made it past the passageway.

"LUKAS!" I shout without thinking. "Where are you?"

Silence fills the air.

"Lukas..." My thoughts trail towards the worse scenario. I gradually turn back towards the white passageway, dreading what I'll discover. I whisper under my breath, "You wouldn't leave me, *would you?*"

My eyes widen in fear. I gulp in heavy lumps of air, failing to react. Lukas lies pale and still on the ground.

I limp towards him, each step sending waves of searing pain from my foot up my leg. My limbs tremble, steadily failing to support my weight, but I push forwards, breathing in ragged gasps, my body driven by sheer desperation.

I'm scared to face what might be the truth.

It won't be the truth, I say to myself, my own voice wavering and uncertain. I find no reassurance.

I don't want to be alone.

I clutch onto his body, trying to search for a pulse. I keep shaking.

"Lukas, please wake up," I cry.

I don't know what to do. I can't tell if he's breathing. I press my fingers beneath his nostrils, hoping to feel the faintest hint of breath.

"C'mon, c'mon, don't play with me. Wake up, Lukas," I stress. Still there's no breath.

His body remains fixed. His chest doesn't rise, nor fall, but stays flat. His eyes closed.

"Wake up, you idiot. Don't leave me," I whimper, sensing the build-up of moisture behind my eyes.

My heart beats slowly.

I'm on the brink of losing it.

Then a painfully long pause of silence. I hear a cough, then another and another. I feel his body bounce back to life, as he shakes with each cough.

"C'mon, stay with me," I snivel, completely stunned. I lightly tap him on his back to help with the coughing.

"I don't have a choice," he croaks. Lukas rises and stares ahead, like he's searching for something. His face is haunted, lips drawn tight and his eyes are vacant, as if he were trapped in a troubling dream. With a hint of confusion, Lukas asks, "We made it?"

Relieved, I reply, "Yeah, we did... somehow."

I raise him until he's slouched against the passageway door.

"Catch your breath." I lean beside him. "We'll need to regear and keep moving."

"I don't want to deal with that again," Lukas says firmly, then exhales slowly.

"The Constant?" I ask, half flinching as I remember the sharp and continuous agony I felt from the gas while Lukas carried me. It burns you alive.

"With dying," he shoots back, turning to face me, calmly. "That was *too* close."

"Yeah, I thought I lost you."

"Still breathing." He chuckles.

"Let's keep it that way."

The moss on the walls has dried out by now. There is no water to be found. My stomach churns and growls in hunger. I can do nothing but fill my lungs with air.

We have been walking forwards for an hour or so. The ground is flat, devoid of anything resourceful. Lukas and I don't talk much, to reserve our energy. We're running on fumes, fuelled solely by survival instinct.

The silence is peaceful, leaving me alone to my thoughts. At times, I sense a glimpse of the valley and the hut flickering back into my mind. But the image fades just as quickly as it comes.

The past feels untraceable. Maybe I'm seeing things. Maybe it's just a memory teetering on the edge of my conscious. Maybe the past is elusive, slipping away from me like smoke in the wind.

I may never get my past back. But would I want it? Wouldn't I disappear and the old Aurora return? Or would it be some strange combination of the two of us?

I fail to answer the question… *Who am I?*

Am I the same person as the old Aurora?

My thoughts are interrupted by vibrations that rattle behind us. Little rocks on the ground rapidly spring up and down. Relentless gusts of cold winds strike us.

"Do you see anything?" I ask, seeing nothing but the same, empty lane stretching behind us.

"Nothing," he responds, leaning down to look at the ground, which continues to pulse in an even rhythm now. The shuddering expands, circling us from all angles.

Lukas and I keep turning and looking around, unable to understand our surroundings.

"What the hell is this?" I quiver in bewilderment.

Lukas steps closer and says, "I'm right behind you."

We stand back-to-back, gradually spinning in a circle while observing the lane.

We hear the sound of liquids sloshing around. Torrents of black water slop over the walls. The liquid appears shallow and dark. The waves roar in irregular movements. However, its slow and viscous descent betrays an imminent peril lurking within its depths. Water shouldn't be *that dark.*

"Welcome to your second survival zone. Your objective is to survive the Great Waves. Stay afloat and don't breathe any in," Enyo warns us. Black water plummets down from the towering walls.

Ripples collide on the ground, erupting into thicker and bigger streams that dart towards me and Lukas.

Enyo adds in an intensely loud and maniacal tone, "*May you Blaze or Burn.*"

And the Realm starts to flood.

"What do we do?" Lukas screams, horrified by the currents surrounding us. The black water begins to rush through our feet, holding us hostage in a freezingly cold embrace.

"I don't know. Let's link arms," I shout, battling against the chilling squeeze of the liquid. Yet my legs begin to shiver involuntarily. The icy grip of the waves terrorises both of us. I feel Lukas's body tremble.

"Aurora, look up!" he squeals in horror.

I glance upwards only to stare helplessly at the sight of additional water waves hurtling down directly above us. Terror holds me still.

Multiple waves violently crash into each other, submerging us underwater. My fingers crumble from the cold, and I lose my grip of Lukas. I urgently gasp for air. I descend deeper and deeper.

The water kisses my lips, and I taste a bitterness unlike anything I've ever known.

16

Lukas

Whirling currents clash with one another, brutally thrusting me far beneath the waves. Aurora's hands are ripped away from me, and I quickly lose sight of her. My heart pounds against my chest like it was trying to leap out. I feel a thick, bitter texture brush against my lips. Impulsively, I seal my mouth shut as tightly as I can.

The liquid's thickness keeps me hostage, as I can only manage short, frantic blinks, desperately trying to catch glimpses of where I am. But my vision is a watery clutter of blackness. Muffled currents surge around me, leaving me disoriented. My lungs contract and squeeze. Agony tears through my chest.

I need air. My guts pulse and scream.

Frost pierces my skin, forcing my muscles to shiver relentlessly until they ache with exhaustion.

I lift my arms, but it feels like someone's pushing against them, trying to stop me from moving. Through pain and anger, I thrash my arms in frantic, circular motions until my head emerges above the waves. I gasp for breath immediately. I sense the sharp tightness in my lungs begin to ease.

The liquid starts vanishing into the ground, as if it were being sucked away. I spin in circles. Panic-stricken, I search for Aurora. But all I can see is a swirling, bouncing mass of opaque water.

The water keeps on plummeting, bringing me closer to the ground.

"The flare has begun to blaze!" Enyo screams, her voice echoing through the lane. "Congratulations on surviving the Great Waves. However, it's *not* over yet! This liquid is primarily water, but it's laced with arsenic chemicals. Ingesting more than three mouthfuls of this mixture will lead to an excruciatingly slow and painful demise. Anything less will induce past hallucinations or destabilise the mind temporarily. May death commence to restore Statera."

I breathe out in relief, grateful that I didn't swallow any of the liquid. The water completely dissipates into the gaps between the bricks on the ground.

The same brick walls tower on either side of me. Yet the landscape has transformed from stone to soft, sandy dirt. The road ahead now undulates with small hills and craters, creating a terrain of little peaks and valleys.

Twenty metres in front of me, atop a hill of wet dirt, lies Aurora, frozen in the foetal position. Her arms and legs are tightly curled up, shielding her face. The eerie stillness leaves me uncomfortable. Right away I sprint towards her. While her body is motionless, her face twitches restlessly.

She's fighting to stay awake.

"Hey, Aurora, get up," I say, gently lifting her into a sitting position.

Her bony, hollow face frightens me as her facial muscles shudder uncontrollably. With trembling hands, I check for her pulse, and thankfully I feel a faint flicker of beats beneath her skin.

Her face won't stop shaking. In my arms, she whispers something inaudible underneath her breath.

I touch her forehead. Intense heat radiates from her. She's likely feverish. She's completely drained of energy, her body as frail as one can be.

"Wake up Aurora… it's me, Lukas," I quietly call out to her. But she doesn't react. Her eyes stiffly drift off to elsewhere. "We need one another." I pause, hesitantly, then add, "I need *you*."

I look at her sluggish body, bare and weak in my arms. Dread creeps over me. I don't know what to do. I don't know how to help.

She looks like she's having a nightmare, fleeing from some unseen terror. Her eyes remain open. It's as if she is both awake and dreaming at the same time. She grits her teeth, her jaw tense. Hushed grunts escape her lips. Her eyes are a deep, dark brown, reminiscent of the golden amber tint of chestnuts.

The strands of hair that droop down on her forehead shimmer like polished obsidian. For a girl's length, her hair is short. But knowing her, it's probably for something practical rather than any aesthetic reason.

There's dust and dirt splattered all over us, but her skin is still smooth. Despite the paleness of her skin, she possesses a perplexing beauty I can't quite explain.

During this I refuse to take my hand off her neck, constantly ensuring that I feel a pulse.

I hear the harsh, gritty sound of rocks grinding relentlessly against one another. I turn towards the abrasive noise, glimpsing a section of a wall beginning to rise, creating a wide entryway into what looks like another lane.

Are they giving us more areas to explore? I ask myself silently, unease creeping into my thoughts as I remain uncertain at what this may indicate. I suppose the announcement of our next objective should clear things up.

Suddenly, Aurora's eyes snap wide open, and she grips tightly onto my arms. She stares at me, her face twisted with fear.

"L-Lukas," she squeaks in a stutter, followed by rough, dry coughs. She croaks, "What happened?"

"Are you okay?" I ask, troubled. I check her forehead again. "You look really feverish, I'm worried."

"What happened?" she demands, her voice weak and raspy.

"The lane flooded with liquid, and then I found you here on the ground," I tell her. "You looked like you were having a nightmare."

"It was just a bunch of colours," she replies, confused. "Like a delusion." Her eyes look grey and lost now.

My heart skips a beat. I glance down at her hands, checking for any remains of the liquid. That's when I see black droplets dripping from her mouth, sticky and slow, like saliva.

"Please don't leave me." She slobbers as she speaks. Though it's little amounts, the black liquid oozes out of her mouth as she coughs and spits on the ground. Tears run down her cheeks, leaving faint red lines on her skin. She whimpers, "I don't feel well."

"I'm right here," I reassure her, clutching onto her even closer. "I'm not going anywhere."

Enyo's words pop into my mind. *This mixture can lead to an excruciatingly slow and painful demise...* I gulp in fear.

"Aurora, I need you to focus. How much of the liquid did you swallow?" I ask desperately, feeling my heart race. Sweat drips down from my forehead. She looks lost, like she's someplace else.

I press again. "I need you to tell me. I need to know. How much?"

Ferociously she coughs and spits again. The wheezing is wet and violent. Her skin looks faded, ghostly white. Something's not right.

I grip her shoulders. "How much?"

She looks at me, with eyes of uncertainty, as if she were steadily losing her senses.

She grunts, "I don't know."

And then her eyes lose focus and wander off aimlessly, as now her whole body throbs and twitches in random, erratic movements.

"Welcome to the third survival zone. Your objective is to discover the hidden equation of this survival zone reflecting the displayed poem and reality. One line of numbers shall unlock the passage to safety," Enyo declares in a foreboding tone. "The poem can be seen in the sky. Here's a hint—imminent deaths!"

"Aurora, we need to move!" I insist, growing worried about completing the objective before the Constant returns to finish us off.

But she's unresponsive. Her body is frozen in a cycle of trembling motions.

What do I do? I hear my heartbeat echo in my ears. It rings invasive and rambunctious.

I glance up into the sky, seeing a four-line short poem displayed. That's when I catch movement in the corner of my eye.

Adrenaline surges through me.

My grip on Aurora tightens and impulsively I crawl backwards, pulling her with me.

In the distance, out of the entryway into the other lane, a light grey fog begins to emerge. And from it, two unknown silhouettes slowly make their way towards us.

17

Aurora

Breathe. Relax. Free yourself. A voice shrieks from the depths of my mind.

Each breath leaves a vicious sting in the back of my nostrils. The cold, restless air piles on like snow, already here and yet constantly coming. It's like I'm trapped in a blizzard.

No matter how hard I fight the cold, I can't move. Forming a fist feels next to impossible.

With every blink, the world grows fuzzy. One moment I'm in Lukas's arms, the next I'm shivering as I tread through a white forest.

What the hell is happening to me?

My mind feels dizzy.

My breaths are faint murmurs that disrupt the stillness of the forest. The snow cracks beneath my feet. My heartbeat echoes in my ears. Erratic and unrhythmic.

I feel like I'm being watched, like the trees have eyes.

Burns radiate through my arms. I bite my lips to silence myself, but grunts of agony still escape. It's as if someone is dragging molten metal across my skin. The metal doesn't cool down, only burning brighter and hotter, searing deeper into my flesh.

My throat aches with dryness. I need water.

Lukas, where are you? I know I won't receive an answer. He's not here. Somehow I know this for certain. *Lukas, you promised you wouldn't leave me...*

The throbbing in my limbs dissipates. My muscles shrink and I exhale in relief. I feel lighter.

But that presence is still here, somewhere close.

Suddenly, the snowflakes freeze in midair. The gusts of wind disappear. I hear the chirping of birds, as if it were an early spring morning. I blink and the world shifts. Cold to warm. The sun pierces through the forest in bright rays. The trees are full of leaves. Small patches of violet flowers protrude from the grass, dazzling in the sunlight.

Birds continue singing. Clouds are small and see-through, the sky a light blue. It all feels familiar.

I approach the flowers, mesmerised by the way the petals resemble a butterfly's wings. They shine a golden purple in the sun, as if absorbing light itself. I breathe in their scent, earthy and sweet. It's vaguely recognisable. At least, to the past Aurora it is.

"Honey, I'm here."

The same voice from earlier interrupts my focus, echoing through my mind. It's eerily distinct, like a whisper from someone I know, pulling me closer.

"Run to the edge of the forest."

The voice guides me along. I can't remember who it belongs to. But I know it's someone important.

"You'll find me there."

I head deeper into the forest, following a footpath of trampled grass. I press my palm on a tree trunk, leaning against it to catch my breath. Instinctively, I jerk my hand to the side, sensing a sharp pain in my fingers. I look down to see thin cuts across my hand, stinging as blood spills out, coating my hand with its thick, crimson texture.

Without anything to disinfect the wound, I wipe my hand on my trousers, trying to stop the flow. When I lift my palm, I stare in confusion. My fingers are perfectly fine, as if I never cut myself in the first place.

What the hell is this place?

I gaze ahead at the forest. For a split second, I remember the grass swaying lightly, the river trickling, and nature's hum. But when I snap out of it, that memory still feels distant, like I was observing someone else's mind. My skin prickles into bumps. I feel strange.

My body stiffens, reluctant to walk onwards.

I'm being warned.

I breathe in. Air feels heavy. My lungs want more no matter how much I inhale. The footpath leads me up a hill.

"You're almost here, honey."

"Who is this?" I yell, my voice wavering with doubt.

As I climb up the hill, my stomach starts to twist, like my guts were telling me to run away. The trees have lost their leaves. The moss has been invaded by waste, as chunks of concrete, metal rods and plastic bottles pierce upwards through the earth.

I have to be careful with each step.

In the distance, a squeakier version of my voice teases, "Catch me if you can!"

I rush ahead, finding a wooden house. The roof is crooked, and the house itself seems to be sinking into the dirt. The garden is a small square of grass and stones with a wall of firewood and small piles of coal. There, I see a younger version of myself and a little boy, no older than four or five, running after each other.

"Argh!" the boy hisses in frustration, then drops to the ground.

"You almost got me. Next time, be ready for me to turn the other way," the younger Aurora says, sitting beside him and patting his head.

Why the hell am I watching myself?

"This is so unfair. You're older than me," he says, irritated. "I wish I was the eldest, then you couldn't catch me."

Younger me laughs gently.

"Don't worry. Before you know it you'll be as old as me." I remember saying that. But I don't know who that little boy is.

"Will I really?" he exclaims.

"Of course you will. Since you're a boy, you'll probably be even taller than me."

"And then I can work with you? Catch food with you? Walk home with you?" The boy's eyes are bright with wonder.

"Mhm, sure," the younger Aurora says, turning away and grimacing in pain. "That's exactly right!"

Younger me smiles at the boy, but I can tell there's something hidden behind those deceitful eyes of hope.

Suddenly, the house, the garden, younger me and the boy fade away into brightness, leaving me alone atop the hill.

"Just a little closer."

The voice is persistent.

"Closer to where? Where the hell are you leading me?" I shout, but I'm silenced by the breeze blowing past me, stirring a strange nostalgia for this place I've been brought to.

Moss crawls beneath my feet, and the ground turns a darker green, dotted with mushrooms and bushes filled with berries.

I breathe in the scent. It smells like... home.

My vision blurs between lying down while staring up at the pale sky and standing on this hill studying its greenery. I put my palm to my forehead. I'm feverish.

An older lady stands in between two trees ahead of me.

She waves me over.

I approach her, cautiously.

"Who are you?" I ask, my head buzzing with heat.

"Oh, honey, you've found your way to me. I'll help you, my child," she says, soothingly. Why is she calling me a child? My mind oozes with confusion. She smiles. "Below these two trees is where me and Bruce met."

"What are you talking about? Who is Bruce?" I grumble in frustration.

This stranger who stands beside me appears similar to me. Is she a hallucination of who I will become? Her clothes are patched with ripped fabrics, her skin etched with scars... yet she looks so familiar.

Who is she?

"I know you don't remember me." The woman embraces me tightly. I almost jump away, but her warmth is so calming that I can't help melting away into her arms. "I'm sorry."

"For what?" I ask, relishing in her warmth.

"Sorry for making you relive this."

She points to a part of the hill that's dark with rain. I feel a tingling sensation course through me. My body turns still. I recognise the emotions flowing through me. Reminiscent pain. I tremble in terror.

I spot a man lying on hard dirt, motionless. His clothes are smeared with mud. We're in a destroyed forest with barely any trees around. There are piles of logs being collected in wheelbarrows. The man's eyes are cloudy, as if there were a layer of fog in front of them.

There's familiarity within this uncertain sight.

I'm terrified by it.

My gaze drops to his chest. There's blood gushing from a hole in his stomach.

"Dad!" A faint, desperate whisper echoes from a girl.

"C-can you hear me?" Her voice wavers, thick with fear.

Tears fall from my eyes, mingling with the rain.

"*What*—" I wipe my cheeks. What is this I'm feeling? It can't be grief… I don't know this man… right?

I close my eyes and find myself in the lady's embrace again. It feels comforting, like an instinctive place of safety.

"Are you okay?" she asks and then kisses my forehead. "Your fever is gone."

"I'm fine… what did I just see?"

She stares into the distance, as if disturbing has penetrated her mind. She frowns. Her eyes narrow, clouded with sadness.

She rests against one of the two giant oak trees beside us.

"This is where Bruce and I swore our sacred vows to each other. I couldn't stop smiling, knowing we would be together, knowing we would be each other's, until our deaths. I felt that I'd be happy for the rest of my life!" she cries with joy but tears soon stream down her face.

"So who was he?"

"But it wasn't until death, and definitely not for the rest of my life," she sobs, fury edged into her words.

"Who was he?" I'm losing patience.

The woman inhales deeply, her gaze fixed on the ground.

"My husband," she hisses, her voice breaking. "He was a good man."

"And who is he to me?"

Darkness permeates the skies.

I feel myself weaken. The lush trees slowly disintegrate. Leaves turn brittle, crumbling into fragments that float away with the wind. The world shimmers momentarily, leaving only a hollow emptiness where the forest once stood. The earthy scent is replaced by the smell of burning wood.

In the midst of this chaos, the woman leans in, wrapping her comforting arms around me one final time. She looks into my eyes.

"I'm your mother," she whispers with a croaky, melancholy voice. She pauses, her eyes overflowing with an unbearable sorrow. "And that man *was* your father." She breathes in, haunted by loss. She shrieks painfully, "They took *everything* from us!"

18

Lukas

Eclipsed by terror, Aurora's eyes flicker, struggling to stay open. Her body twitches restlessly, as if coursing with electricity. She's become difficult to carry. Her mouth forms silent shapes, stifling a scream that never comes.

Mist whirls around the entrance. Inside, the subjects linger, unable to escape the growing fog.

They couldn't have seen us.

Relief washes over me.

I crouch low, traversing through the vacant land of small hills and craters. There's nowhere else to hide.

Cautiously, I avoid the sandy earth as to not leave any footsteps behind. I stick to the grass where possible. I need to hide Aurora and solve the equation.

I don't know if the new subjects are dangerous. I'll try not to be seen.

On top of a hill, I find a hole where I can hide her for now. I need to treat her fever. I hope the next zone will have water or something I can use to cool her head.

Carefully, I lay her down into the hole, keeping an eye on the subjects to ensure I've not been followed.

Suddenly, a sharp pain stabs my guts, scorching my insides. I clutch my chest and collapse beside Aurora.

What is happening to me?

My throat burns with a rising sensation. I'm going to puke.

Grunts and gasps ooze out of my mouth in agony. I gargle helplessly, unable to stop it. I feel a fluid building up inside my mouth.

Ferociously, I cough it out. My vision grows blurry, and everything feels sluggish. I look down, seeing a string of black liquid trickling from my mouth.

"Oh no." The words escape my lips before I can compose myself. My body goes still.

All of a sudden, I'm on both feet, running. Each heartbeat strikes more fear into me. I can sense that I'm smaller than I was moments ago. My lungs feel heavy.

Two older kids stay on my heels.

There's no fighting them. I have no choice but to accept my surroundings. I keep my eyes locked on the ground ahead, making sure I don't slip or fall again.

"You disrespectful little punk! You don't steal food!" one of them shouts furiously. "I'll break your legs if you don't stop!"

My sister needs this more than you. My parents told me to take care of her. These thoughts rush through my head, as I fear the beating that awaits if I'm caught.

I catch sight of the Arbiters Barracks, a collection of red-brick buildings with no windows, lined up next to each other. They live clean, unlike us.

I approach the first building and take a sharp left into a small alleyway between the barracks.

Maybe I can lose them here.

I run down the alley, seeing a small shadow at the end of it. That should be another route.

But when I reach it, I realise there's nowhere to go. It's a dead end with no lighting. The place makes my nose wrinkle with disgust. Something is rotting.

There's a black door on each building, probably a way to manoeuvre between the two barracks. Trash bags and piles of cigarettes are scattered across the ground.

I turn back, dread clawing at my throat.

They've got me. I'm so screwed. I panic, feeling them lunge closer as they begin to corner me into this dead end. My heart pounds my chest. I feel like prey.

The two of them approach me, their faces tense with anger. One of them is tall, with long black hair and a thin figure. The other boy is short, bald and very buff. I can't understand where he gets enough food to stay muscular.

"First. Give us the food back," the short boy scolds me, sounding like a disappointed mother. His words are hissy but soft, almost like his lips won't fully open. I hand the paper bag back to him and cower next to the trash bags. The boys check through the contents of the bag, counting everything up. Sweat rushes down my spine.

I don't know what to do.

"Everything's here. We're good," the tall one says.

"Bertie, you watch the alley, keep us safe," the short one orders sternly.

"What about you?"

"I'mma talk to him."

"Don't be stupid. I mean it, Ellis!"

Bertie, the tall boy, steps back and watches over the entrance to the alleyway. Ellis walks up to me, his face stiff as rock. His muscly figure looms over me, casting a shadow onto me.

"Look boy, what you did—"

"Just please don't break my legs, I need to go back to my baby sister. I'm all she's got," I whimper, a lie to win mercy. My parents have been gone for days, and my sister will die of thirst before they return.

Ellis places his massive palm on my shoulder. My eyelids close slightly as my body tenses. The drumming in my chest accelerates. I feel like I'm going to erupt.

I swallow my spit, waiting for the worst.

"Relax kid, we're not gonna hurt you," Ellis says earnestly. "I look scary, cuz half my face is frozen."

A deep breath escapes my lungs. I wipe the sweat from my forehead, feeling my heart begin to slow.

"What do you mean... frozen?" I ask, watching him intently.

"Look." He points to his face and then stretches his skin on both sides. He then shifts his expressions between smiling and imitating an angry roar, but only the flesh on the left side of his face stretches and contracts. His right side is completely paralyzed. "See, it won't move. Sorry if I scared you."

"It's okay..." I pause, feeling an embarrassing wave of guilt course through me. "I'm sorry too."

"Y'know what you did wrong?" Ellis asks.

"Yes." I avert my eyes. "I shouldn't have stolen."

"You didn't hide fast enough."

"What?" My eyes widen.

"What... what... don't look so surprised," Ellis mocks me, jokingly. "I grew up here too, I know what it's like."

"So you're going to let me go?" I ask, hopeful.

"Normally I wouldn't." Ellis flashes his fist at me, then grins after. "But it seems all you need's a lesson."

"What do you mean?"

"You don't steal from your own people, little punk." Ellis pokes my shoulder playfully. "Look, Arbiters always carry food with them in their duffle bags. In the evenings, their guard is down. If you're gonna steal, do it then. But be smart. You don't take the whole box of food, just scoop a little off the top. That way they probably won't notice. I've never been caught."

"What's a duffle bag?"

"It's those big rectangular bags they carry," he explains.

"Ohhh." I realise I've seen them before. My dad has one for work, but it's old and bruised.

"Ellis, I think we gotta move, man," Bertie warns him.

"All right, one sec." Ellis turns to me. "Look, I'm Ellis… that's Albert over there. I call him Bertie for short. If you ever need help, you can come to us. But remember, you don't steal from your own people. Got it?"

I nod.

"What's the matter with you? Why you still look lost?" he asks, leaning closer. He's treating me like I'm his younger brother for no reason.

"Why are you helping me?" I ask, keeping my eyes locked on the ground, too ashamed to look up.

I feel like I did something really wrong.

"Ellis! We gotta go," Albert insists, his voice tinged with deep urgency.

Ellis looks back at the empty alley and responds firmly, "There's no one there. Wait."

"I can hear people in the walls. They're close."

Ellis shakes his head, frustrated.

"Someone helped me when I was your age," Ellis answers, looking me right in the eyes. "He corrected me, taught me how to survive. You did nothing wrong kid… you were just trying to survive."

"Thanks," I mumble, still too sheepish to look up.

"Here, take this." Ellis hands me a small loaf of bread and a knife. "This for your sister, and the blade is for you."

"I can't give you anything for it," I mutter, ashamed to accept it.

"I said take it." Ellis pushes the bread into my hand. He sheaths the knife and slips it into my pocket. "It's yours now. Take care of it."

I look up at him, my eyes shrinking with confusion. I don't know what to say. I don't understand why I wasn't punished.

"We'll be going now. There's work to do," Ellis says, patting my shoulder before walking away.

"Take care of yourself, little man," Albert adds with a sympathetic nod.

I sit down next to the trash bags, unsure of what to do. I wish I didn't need to steal. It's so scary.

Behind me, a door creaks open. I turn around in surprise as an Arbiter steps outside, holding a thick, brown cigar. I stay motionless, praying he won't notice me. He lights the cigar, and its end bursts into a bright orange flame with each puff.

"Y'know, this ain't no place for a kid," he says in a low-pitched, growly voice. I stay silent in response, hoping he'll just shoo me away.

"Why were those lumberjacks chasing you?" he questions. If I tell him what really happened, then I'll be hung. The punishment for theft is death, no matter the age. I must say something else.

"It was a game of catch," I answer, a quiver in my stomach. If I stay still, the Arbiter shouldn't see the redness on my face.

"Hmm. I know that's a lie." He puffs smoke out of his mouth, then crouches down in front of me. "I heard 'em say they would break your legs."

"It was just a taunt…" I pause unnervingly, gulping down spit. "I'm fine."

"To me it seemed like they stole your food." The Arbiter inspects my face. I can't see his eyes, as they're covered by his helmet. His mouth is bare, his beard overgrown. His breath stinks of alcohol.

"They didn't steal anything. They caught me, so they got to keep the food." My words are rushed and filled with fright. I'm scared of what this man will do to me. But I can't say the truth either. That I stole the food. I'm a coward. My chest squeals for air as I try to stay as still as I can.

"I knew it." The Arbiter puffs out smoke, blowing it straight at my face. "I don't understand you townsfolk. Always protecting one another, even when you hurt each other. Pitiful."

"They didn't do anything, I swear. They're my best friends!" I cry out, tension rising in my gut.

Why won't he believe me?

"If they're your friends, what are their names?"

"Ellis and Albert. I call the tall one Bertie. They're really cool!" I blurt out, trying to sound cheerful, hoping this'll shut him up and he'll let me go.

The Arbiter presses down on his forearm, where a plastic patch lights up in blue with a keyboard on the screen. He jots something down and smiles at me.

"You should go home now. It's not safe for a kid to be here," he says, his voice gruff.

I get up, ready to run back home. I squeeze the bread tightly, trembling with worry.

"Will my friends—"

"I said go home. I won't repeat myself." The Arbiter places a hand on his weapon holster. The beating of my heart shakes me to my core. I turn and walk away.

Later that week, I'm holding my sister's hand at the weekly executions, where all Colony civilians must be present at the hanging site. My sister barely stands straight, shivering from the cold. She wraps her little arms around my legs and presses her face into my thigh, trying to hide from the wind. I always turn her the other way and cover her ears during the hangings.

My eyes turn stiff with terror. I feel ready to run, surging with adrenaline. Nausea rushes through me, and my stomach twists with fear.

I want to vomit.

Ellis and Albert stand at the hanging site, a rope tightly wrapped around each of their necks. They look calm, having done nothing wrong.

The platform drops.

The rope tightens.

Everyone else shakes violently, their feet dangling in the air. Yet Ellis and Albert look peaceful, their faces restful.

They fall lifeless in under thirty seconds.

But their eyes don't lie. A blank gaze.

They knew they died because of *me*.

I bite down on my lip with dread. I couldn't forget the cloudy colour of their empty eyes.

I come home to a paper bag of cold bread waiting on my doorstep, and my heart sinks.

From that moment on, Ellis and Albert haunted me wherever I went.

The barren whiteness of their eyes was permanently engraved into my memory, refusing to be forgotten.

Dirt fills my mouth. My throat snaps with a sharp gag as I try to suppress my coughing. When I went unconscious, I must've fallen hard. My face aches. I wipe my face, brushing away the soil clinging to my skin.

Then it all comes back.

My chest hammers like I'm still running. Those white eyes still fresh in my memory. My gut still throbs with guilt. Enyo warned us the liquid caused visions… but this is something else.

Why did it feel so real? Why was I so young?

I have no recollection of being young. My earliest memory is waking up in that white room, knowing nothing, knowing no one.

All I've known since I opened my eyes is fear.

But this wasn't like a memory… it was like I relived it. A scar too deep to erase. Too heavy to hallucinate.

My legs stagger as I balance upright.

I look down at Aurora. The stillness of her body is occasionally interrupted by bursts of twitching.

I press my palm against her forehead. She's too hot. I slide my hand down to her cheek, feeling the heat rising through her entire face.

"I need to get you out of here… you're burning up," I murmur. My eyes shift upwards to the sky, where the blue floating letters form a poem.

> Who is trapped in the mist,
> Will meet Death's loving kiss.
> Of four who were, two will persist,
> Your answer lies in what's been and what is.

The fog from earlier starts to swirl, growing thicker and patchy. It expands throughout the lane, gradually enveloping everything in an impenetrable greyness. I stick to the clear patches, avoiding the mist.

Obscure shadows dash through the fog, like they were searching for something.

The episode of what I just witnessed keeps flashing in my head. Who were they? Who was I?

The fog reminds me of their eyes. The emptiness of their face. The hollow hopelessness within their gaze. The whiteness of death.

Finally, the two subjects emerge from the fog, their faces drowning in exhaustion. Their eyes are blazing red, frozen with horror. The girl has dark skin with braided hair. She looks strong. The boy is scrawny, skin as pale as mine and bald. I focus on their outfits, trying to decide whether they are a threat. They're dressed the same, long-sleeve shirts and cargos, all black with red stiches. They have a utility belt as well, but it doesn't reveal anything about their tactical syringes.

I had forgotten about my own tactical syringes since the start of the Equilibrium.

"Help us," the girl pleads, rigid with fear. I run to her. Suddenly, she gasps and her chest violently jerks upwards. "Don't go in there."

"What happened to you both?" I ask anxiously.

"The mist... it's poison," the boy curses, blood trickling from his mouth and nose.

The girl collapses, and I jump to the ground beside her, pressing my fingers against her neck, trying to find a pulse.

"Tell me if it hurts," I demand.

"It burns!" she squeals. Her body convulses violently, skin cracking as inky black tears drip from her eyes. I can't feel a pulse. "Everything burns. Help me! Help—"

She shudders uncontrollably.

The air is thick with the burned smell of ash.

"What do I do?" I turn to the boy, trembling with terror.

The boy is frozen. His eye sockets are empty. Vacant holes of darkness.

"I can't see," he mumbles, his head twitching in fierce disbelief.

I'm unable to say anything back.

"Please don't leave us!" he shouts. His muscles contract in an erratic spasm.

Drops of liquid hit the ground with a loud, repetitive echo. My ears start ringing.

I look on in horror as the boy's arms begin to liquify, his flesh dripping onto the ground.

"What in the hell…" I whisper, unsure if what I'm seeing is real.

"What's happening to me?" he snaps, his voice high-pitched and wavering. "I can't feel my eyes. I can't feel my arms. I can't feel anything."

I turn to find the girl, only to see the remains of her bones dissolving into a puddle of goo on the ground.

"I don't want to die alone," the boy mutters, as his head deforms into liquid and dribbles onto the ground with the rest of him before I can speak. The last thing I hear is the sound of rupturing bones dividing and splintering apart from one another.

I need to get out of here. I need to get Aurora.

The world rumbles beneath my feet like an earthquake coming.

I face the start of the lane, catching sight of the passageway crumbling, sending rocks and bricks hurtling through the air in a chaotic storm.

Suddenly, a tan and green barrier filled with thunder bursts through the passageway.

My eyes widen in panic.

The Constant is heading towards Aurora.

Desperately, I reach for my waist, grab the Endurance tactical syringe and bury it deep within my shoulder. Fire streaks through my veins. I bite down on my lip to stifle the pain. My teeth turn numb. For a moment, the world shifts into a blur, then snaps back into focus. Every muscle ripples, ready for use.

I look back at the liquified subjects. Their puddles are a revolting mix of bloody goo and vapour. Gas rises from the puddles, spiralling back into the mist which has almost fully dispersed.

"Sorry," I mumble, realising that I failed to do anything for them. I panicked so much I couldn't even comfort them in death.

I run towards Aurora. Adrenaline surges through my body. My strides grow longer and quicker. With each step, it's easier to find my balance.

I feel sharp, faster than ever.

I reach the hill where Aurora lies and quickly scoop her into my arms. Hunched over, I dash forwards, leaping over holes and craters.

The passageway is at the very end with a brick staircase leading up to an all-white, glossy platform.

The poem's words race through my mind.

If the answer is based on what was and what is, does it refer to our past lives or to the present? If it mentions the mist, then it must be talking about right now.

Aurora grows heavier the closer I inch to the passageway. The Constant starts creeping up to us.

I must outrun it.

This feels like I'm running from Ellis and Albert all over again. I push aside my desperation and keep on running, refusing to let my emotions take over. Not now.

Upon reaching the stairs, my legs start to wobble. The effortlessness I felt moments ago fades as my fatigue returns. The Endurance tactical must've worn off.

The eerie buzz of the Constant approaches, accompanied by muffled eruptions and thunder.

I stagger up onto the platform of the passageway and rest Aurora on the ground. I feel drained of all my energy.

The walls behind us collapse and scatter into fragments, with little stones bouncing against my body.

My lungs feel shallow, deprived of the ability to breathe. I inhale repeatedly, suffocating.

I need air.

But my nostrils are sealed.

My chest tightens, turning heavy.

I look at Aurora's unconscious face. Bruised and dirty, yet she still glistens in the sunlight. There's no time to worry about Aurora. Otherwise, there will be nothing left of her to worry about.

I feel my chest open up and, finally, my gasps for air allow me to breathe. My nostrils burn with exhaustion.

I spot a little rectangular machine next to the passageway.

I scramble over to it.

A display lights up with the message:

Type in the Equation.

(Answer the poem)

I gaze up at the poem in hopelessness. I don't know the answer. What does it mean by "what's been and what is"?

Looking back at the screen, I see boxes and the types of symbols it allows you to input. There are numbers, an equal sign and different operations.

This is the hidden equation Enyo said we need to solve. If the poem is talking about the situation right now, then the hint Enyo gave was about the subject's deaths. Why would our deaths be a part of the puzzle?

The Constant swallows everything in its path.

I need to focus. I look at the poem again.

Of four who were, two will persist.

That means the four of us subjects represent "what's been." Then "what is" must be the current survivors. Me and Aurora. Two.

Of the original four, two died and two remain.

My hands hover above the screen. What if I'm wrong? What if the gates never open?

With trembling hands, I type in: $4 - 2 = 2$.

The passageway groans, then the gates start to rise.

I exhale, feeling at ease. Then the air turns green. The passageway opens half a meter and stops.

The Constant is here.

I vault to Aurora.

My skin shrieks with scorching agony as the gas pricks at it relentlessly. I carry Aurora to the passageway.

My heartbeat feels flat.

I shove Aurora through the gap in the passageway and crouch down to the ground, feeling my vision start to grow dimmer.

The world around me crumbles as the platform shakes. The gas within the Constant flares in separate shades of black, purple, and flickering yellow. Upon its terrorising touch, all stone and land remoulds to dust. I have no strength left, but out of sheer will, I roll over the gap in the passageway, my entire body shuddering with pain.

Through the small gap in the passageway, I watch the Constant explode with streaks of flames and disjointed sparks that overwhelm its green colour, turning it into a dark, burning red.

My flesh pulses with agony as I struggle to cling onto consciousness. A heavy silence falls. I wonder, *How would I like to die?*

19

Aurora

Golden sunlight flickers my eyes awake. I flinch at the brightness, as my drowsiness fades. My head aches, possibly from the hours I've slept. I scan my surroundings, ensuring I'm fine.

Everything appears normal... almost serene.

The same grey walls conceal us on either side, with grass emerging through the cracks, hinting at how long the Realm of Liberty has been here.

Ahead, a white marble pathway cuts through a forest full of thick oak trees, pine trees and ponds.

It's nice to see greenery. The colour of nature calms me. For a moment, I feel hope. Everything might be okay. Though I'm wary in case that's just delusion before death.

Lukas sits on a rock, all curled up, his head buried in his hands.

Further down, there's a cabin protruding from the brick wall with an orange hue glinting from it. There's a red cross below the roof.

I try to remember how I got here. I fell into a dream state. I hallucinated my mother. I know nothing after that.

Everything happened after I swallowed the water... but Lukas consumed it as well. I recount the faint trail of black liquid dripping from his mouth as he promised not to leave me. Then how am I still alive?

I don't know what happened to me. I felt alone and scared like a child weeping for her mother. That's why I begged him to stay with me. There was a disturbing familiarity brewing within me, something the current me has never felt before.

"Congratulations on completing Stage One. Welcome to the Safe Zone," Enyo announces, sounding thrilled. "In the Safe Zone, the Care Point provides you with medical treatment as well as the opportunity to purchase food and clothing with your Survival Score. Endurance throughout the three Survival Zones of a stage accumulate Survival Score."

My stomach growls, reminded of its function.

I feel weak.

"The Constant has a current pace of one zone per twenty-four hours," Enyo continues. "Since you completed Stage One in two days, you're ahead of the Constant by sixteen hours. By noon tomorrow, the Constant will reach the Safe Zone."

We need to rest and eat. I look at the trees and ponds, imagining squirrels and fish. We can either buy food or hunt it.

"I can't unsee it!" Lukas whispers in a ragged cry, pulling his hair.

I can't see his face from here. As I put my foot down on the ground, I feel my sole burning up. I take off my left shoe and look down to see dark yellow and pink flesh encircle the wound. The skin looks stretched and frail around the gash. The cut itself is gruesomely dark, like the colour of a rotting rose. I put my foot down and step by step, I inch closer to him.

"Stop showing me this," he shrieks.

"Lukas, what's wrong?" I ask, growing worried by his heedless outbursts.

His fingers tremble at his scalp, on the brink of tearing his hair out. Webs of red lines engulf his blue irises. Dark circles fill the skin beneath his eyes.

What's wrong with him?

"Please, stop it!" he pleads desperately.

"Stop what? Lukas, what's happening to you?"

He doesn't seem to hear me no matter how loud I speak. I'm right in front of him, but he doesn't see me. *What the hell does he see?*

"I don't want to see them anymore," he murmurs softly. I see tears dropping to the ground.

"It's okay," I say, placing my hands on his shoulders. I bite my lip to stop myself from screaming at the pain in my foot. "I'm right here. You're not alone anymore."

"It was all my fault." His eyes finally meet mine, glistening with tears. Wide and haunted.

"What did you do?" I ask softly.

"I told *him* their names."

"Lukas?"

"That was all he needed."

"What are you talking about?"

"They died because of me."

Who is he talking about? Why is he psychotic?

"Okay, calm down first. It's just me and you." I gently wipe his tears. I crouch down and cup his cheeks with my hands for a short moment. "It's just me and you, Lukas. Us and no one else."

"All right," he replies, mournful. His eyelids droop, and his face is pale. He needs rest.

"What happened to me?" I ask, trying to remember the last details before my dreams began. The black liquid filled the lane. I was submerged beneath it. Unable to hold my breath, I swallowed some of it. I coughed for air. Then Lukas found me. After that it was all in my head.

"We both swallowed some of the black liquid. That's when you lost consciousness. Enyo said that it caused past hallucinations," Lukas recounts, shivering.

"Meaning what?"

"Meaning anything you witnessed was a distorted dream or memory of the past…" He pauses, giving me a moment to process it.

"It was real?"

"Maybe." His gaze is shallow, like he's elsewhere.

"So that's how my mother looks, huh?" I mutter underneath my breath. *Who was that little boy?*

Lukas looks away at the sky, exhaustion permeating through his face.

"How did we get here?" I'm trying to fill the gaps in my memory.

His eyes turn to me, heavy with sorrow.

"*You* need to leave," he whispers, fury hanging on the tip of his tongue.

"What?"

"Stay away from me."

"Why?"

"Everyone around me dies."

Lukas told me everything. From the two older boys he saw in his dreams to the others who died in the mist within our lane. He's been through so much, and I wasn't there for any of it.

While we spoke, his eyes were cold, but they trembled with fear, not rage. He was terrified of himself. Horrified that he'd cause me pain.

He hated himself. But never did he admit to that. He just kept waving me away, repeating… *"You need to leave."*

Once he realised that I wasn't going anywhere, he accepted it with disguised fury. He described his shame and burning guilt. He couldn't see that it wasn't his fault no matter what I told him. When I said he was just a child, he responded, *"I should've known better."*

His feelings were eating away at him. I didn't know what to do. I told him one thing, perhaps a bit too sharply.

"You're feeling the guilt of surviving, of choosing yourself over others. You didn't cause their deaths. You just survived while they didn't. All you did was live on. Sometimes, all this world comes down to is kill or be killed." I spoke with conviction, feeling that this was true even in our pasts.

After that, I caressed his hair until I felt his breathing steady. I built a fire next to him, to keep him warm.

I'm walking back to him now, carrying three small fish wrapped in leaves, and a makeshift weapon. I used a sharp obsidian stone, which I found on the rocky patches of earth beside the pond. I caught the fish with my hands and then cut their heads off with the stone. Their small, slimy bodies darted away from me almost every time, making it a painfully, time-consuming hunt. Luckily the ponds were small.

I approach Lukas, seeing his shadowy figure lying still on the ground next to the fire. He looks so peaceful. A gentle face covered in cuts, bruises and dirt. I'm scared to think about how much I owe him. He could've given up on me at any point. Enyo never said both members of a Duo have to survive. Yet he kept fighting to keep me alive. And I didn't even know it.

Thank you, Lukas.

I always feel helpless next to him.

Maybe some people carry goodness within them, while others need to learn it. I know I don't have it. But I'm trying my best. I hope that's enough. I want to die a good person.

While Lukas rests, I leave to collect more firewood. My foot sears with agony every step, but I do my best to endure, stopping for breath whenever I must. I carve the ends of three sticks into sharp skewers to cook the fish. The embers pulse with orange sparks as the heat dims. I throw on new branches, and they catch fire quickly.

Black smoke swirls into the sky as I cook the fish, watching the flesh darken from blue-grey to a crispy brown.

I shake Lukas awake.

"Hey, I got us food," I say, showing him the skewers with an excited grin.

"It looks good," he replies, trying to smile and mask his suffering. I'm glad he's at least playing normal.

I hand him two fish and start eating my own.

"Why two for me?" he asks timidly.

"You have a problem with that?" I snap back, using anger to hide my embarrassment.

"No," he stammers, shaking his head. "I don't. I just feel bad."

"You get one extra for saving my life. Happy?"

"Oh… all right. Thanks," he answers, still uncertain. "But you would have done the same for me."

I don't dare respond to that. In truth I would've tried, tried really hard, but I don't know if I would've been strong enough not to give up.

"Just eat up," I growl, my stomach tightening with eagerness.

"Yes ma'am," he jokes, saluting me.

We eat in silence, savouring each bite. The fish tastes so good that I even eat the skin, enjoying each crunchy piece.

"I wish there was more," Lukas remarks, looking more relaxed.

I hope I managed to make him forget about some of his troubles, even if just for a little bit.

"You had two though… and that still wasn't enough?" I tease him, widening my eyes in exaggerated shock. He smiles.

"I'm sure both of us could've eaten more," Lukas says.

"Yeah," I agree. "Maybe we should check out the Care Point before getting some sleep?"

"I like the sound of that." Lukas stands up and gives me a hand. But the instant I put my left foot down, pain jolts through me. I lose balance and fall back down.

"I don't know if I can walk," I grunt, turning to him with blank eyes, already dreading what this means for the next stage of the Equilibrium. "I don't even want to look at it."

My foot throbs constantly. Lukas drops down and inspects it. His face stretches and winces in response.

"We'll go to the Care Point. It sounds like they'll have something to help," Lukas says softly.

I nod. "Okay."

Lukas cautiously wraps his arms around me and slowly carries me. The Care Point is that cabin I saw when I woke up. The red cross shines bright, illuminating a strange, human-shaped figure.

"What is that?" I ask, confused.

Lukas squints. "I think it's a who."

As we get closer, details come into focus. Black hair, green eyes and smart clothes. A red, long-sleeved shirt with a blast vest. A confident man. But something's off. His skin is overly pale, an unrealistic shade of white.

"Hello and welcome to the Care Point! My name is Ajax, and I will be your android assistant for all Safe Zones. How may I help?" The man's voice sounds human, but his monotone, rhythmic delivery is odd. There is a counter between us, like he's selling something at a market stall.

"What the hell is an android assistant?" I ask, bewildered by his clear, perfect skin.

Ajax slides to the side and projects an image of his blueprint from the countertop. The image shows metallic plates coming together like a jigsaw to form a robot that looks human.

"I am an artificial intelligence, designed to assist with medical treatment and to answer all your questions," he explains, his voice enthusiastic, yet still peculiar. Ajax tilts his head. "Is that a satisfying response to your question?"

"Sure, whatever," I respond, feeling slumped.

"Finished talking with him?" Lukas asks. "You're getting a little heavy."

"That's rude," I shoot, half-joking. I guess I'm not exactly as light as air. It's just frustrating not being able to stand on my own. "Okay, put me down."

Carefully, he sets me down against the cabin. His back is drenched with sweat. I need to thank him for taking care of me.

"So what can we buy here?" Lukas asks.

"Clothing, food and survival equipment can be purchased. Medical supplies are provided free of charge," Ajax responds, moving his hand through the air to change the holograph. "This is the list of obtainable items."

Lukas reads through each item and its summarised description. I see rope of different lengths, axes, knives and special equipment. Food varies from berries to canned meat and bread. There's clothes, too, from insulated shirts to fire-resistant or water-proof clothing.

"Lukas, what can we get?"

"I'm not sure..." He pauses and turns to the android. "Ajax, please explain the Survival Score System. How do we earn it?"

"Most certainly! Survival Score is earned as the name implies, based on survival. Score is awarded for staying alive through the Survival Zones of a Stage. In Stage One, 100 points are awarded per zone, this rises to 200 points in Stage Two, and 300 points in Stage Three. Your current Survival Score is 300 points in total," Ajax explains in a detailed manner, yet his words are *too* perfect. Despite knowing Ajax is just a robot, his kindness feels genuine, and his expressions all appear real to me, which makes him all the more unsettling.

"So we're always being watched?" I ask.

"That's correct, Aurora! Enyo, Milgram and other FORTE officials are always monitoring your activity. The main reason for–"

"Alpha–1. Shut down!" Enyo panics, her voice shaking with anger. Her shout echoes through the Safe Zone. "Obscure procedural information. Switch to Assistant Model."

Ajax freezes for an instant. His body hums and rattles with electricity. Then seconds later he appears normal again.

Lukas glances at me, his brows raised.

I shrug my shoulders in response. "I guess they didn't want us to know that we're being watched."

I always suspected it, but knowing there's nowhere I can hide to be alone is unnerving. My skin crumples up across my body like needles were pressing against my flesh.

"What do we need?" Lukas asks.

I bite the insides of my mouth until I draw blood. My foot aches like it's being chopped off. I need help, but I'm too ashamed to ask.

I don't want to burden him anymore.

"Water," I respond quietly.

"Anything else?"

I shake my head. "You choose."

Suppressing a groan, I crawl away from the Care Point, needing to stretch out. I lie down and spread my arms and legs out. The ground cools me.

I catch snippets of their conversation, as Lukas speaks in murmurs. Ajax nods and points to the sky. My eyes follow four white streams that shoot upwards, shatter into fragments and dissolve into the clouds. Silence fills the world for a moment. Then four blaring detonations rattle the air. Red sparks colour the sky in brilliance.

Ajax hands a matte white box to Lukas, who strides over to me.

"What'd you get?" I ask, trying to mask the pain twitching through my body.

Lukas doesn't respond. Instead he places the box beside me. He taps it, and after a second the box unfolds itself.

"Lift your foot," he commands, his voice tense. Startled, I comply. He gently takes my foot, rolls up my trousers to my knee, and pulls out a bag of bandages. He tears it open and begins wrapping my foot, layer by layer, up to my ankle. A small black box attaches to the bandage.

"I'd advise biting your shirt," Lukas whispers, worriedly. Fear stiffens my body as I bite down on my collar.

"Whad are ya doin?" I try asking, my voice muffled by my shirt. An electric burst rips through my foot, forcing it to quiver relentlessly. My vision blurs as I shriek in a smothered voice. I bite down even harder on the fabric until the buzzing stops.

I bolt upright, glaring at Lukas.

"What the hell did you do to me?" I shout, engulfed by rage. It's hard to breathe as the pain sinks down my leg.

"Stand up now," Lukas says, an acute softness permeating through his voice.

"What is wrong with you! You know I can't," I snap, my voice cracking.

"Just stand up. You'll see," he answers.

"If I stand up you're in for a world of hurt."

I rise up out of fury and hesitantly place both my feet down. I stop, stunned. My foot doesn't burn. I can stand on it.

"You won't feel any pain with the bandages on. It'll come off once the wound is healed," Lukas explains with a little chuckle in his voice. "Sorry for the shock. The bandage had to tighten to the wound and electrify your nerve endings."

"Ajax tell you that?" I ask, catching my breath.

"Yeah. I'm sorry I had to hurt you."

"Thanks," I reply, unsure whether to feel grateful or angry. "You didn't get anything else?"

Lukas smiles. "Your bandages were free, and we had enough to get these."

He reaches back into the box, pulling out a metal water bottle and a black cylinder.

"One hundred for the bottle, fifty for the purifier."

"That's a good deal," I say, smiling now. I notice the dryness in my throat. "I'd kill for some water."

"Then let's go."

I place both my feet on the ground and exhale in relief as I feel no pain.

We leave the Care Point and venture back towards the forest, towards our small campfire. We'll need wood to get it going again.

As we walk back, I catch a bright-red glimmer near the wall on my right. Curious, I approach and find a metal frame with a board attached.

At first the board is blank, but then scarlet letters slowly light up, revealing a message.

Wall of Survivors:

Lukas and Aurora.

Gyo and Zoe.

Todd and Amy.

Markas and Lina.

Aron and Ella.

Axel and Ivy.

I walk on, confused.

What's the point of me knowing this? It's cruel, but who else is dead or alive makes no difference as long as I'm still breathing.

Yet I can't help wondering how our deaths are viewed. Enyo kept mentioning the balance between the living and the dead. But does dying really mean anything? Won't there always be more dead than living?

I'm starting to think we're just resources for belief.

When we reach our campfire, I ask Lukas to gather more branches while I fill the water bottle from the pond and attach the purifier on top of it, which looks like the barrel of a rifle.

Lukas returns, dropping the wood into the circular pile of now ash. I hand him the flint rock I used earlier and within minutes the fire sparks to life.

We wait until the purifier beeps as a grey vapour oozes out of it and then take turns drinking until we feel refreshed. We lie down on the hard and soft grass, our heads opposite each other, separated by the fire. As the sky darkens, countless bright dots emerge, and we watch the stars in peace.

"Do you ever think about death?" Lukas whispers.

"Where did that come from?" I murmur in surprise. "That was sudden."

"When I threw you across the passageway into the Safe Zone, I thought I was going to die," Lukas recalls, his breath shaky, a hesitant fascination lingering on his face. "And ever since that memory, I haven't been able to stop thinking about it."

"What exactly are you thinking about? Are you afraid of it?" I ask. Death can mean a lot of things. I often wonder what happens after death. I've made it clear to myself I don't want to die in here. I want my memories back. I want to know who I am.

"I don't fear death, but obviously I'm not waiting for it either," Lukas says, chuckling lightly. "Back then, I asked myself, 'How would I like to die?' I've been trying to answer that question ever since."

I listen to the fire engulfing the twigs and branches, quietly snapping in a hypnotising rhythm. It's a gentle sound that feels endless and warm.

"I haven't really thought about that. I've been so focused on not dying that I haven't considered how I would want to die," I admit.

"It's a hard question. I guess we'll never truly know until our last moments," Lukas says, almost breathlessly, like he's desperate for an answer.

"And even then, you probably won't know you're dying. It will just happen," I add.

Lukas snaps his fingers. "Poof, just like that, and you're gone. It's scary to think about."

"So do you have any answers?" I ask.

"Right now, I feel like I want to die just knowing I meant something to someone. Knowing I did something bigger than just myself. I want to know I mattered. I guess purpose is what I want. Maybe I'm just lost."

"Maybe we're all lost, trying to find meaning." I meet his gaze, hopelessly smiling. A strange warmth spreads through me, soothing me. I want to tell him he means something to me. That he matters to me.

"So what about you?" Lukas asks. "How would you like to die?"

"I want to live a life of freedom." I pause for a moment, feeling my eyelids grow heavy. "The freedom to live how I want to live. If I want to work as a hunter, carpenter or whatever else, I want to be able to do all that. But freedom also means not being afraid of losing my loved ones. I want the freedom to love forevermore."

"Maybe our purpose is love then?" Lukas reflects.

"Maybe," I agree. "That's why I want to get out of here alive."

"Don't leave me behind," he says, averting his eyes nervously.

I turn over, my face flushed with embarrassment. Exhaustion weighs down my eyelids. My cheeks are red, and I'm not sure if it's from my feelings or the fire. I feel myself longing for him, even when he's so close. There's a terrifying confusion instilled deeply within me. Of him leaving and staying. It's the fear of hurting him, but the reluctance to admit I need him. I let the heat embrace me and close my eyes.

Softly, I whisper, "Then *stay with me*."

20

Lukas

I feel the sun's warmth on my face, gently piercing through the world, awakening me from a dreamless sleep. I remember Aurora's words from last night. We won't abandon one another. We'll be alone, together.

My legs ache, probably a feeling that'll cling to me for a while. I'll keep running into it, quite literally.

Birds chirp as the soothing breeze brushes through my hair. Ash sits firmly in the centre of the campfire. Aurora squints against the sunlight, eyes half shut.

At least I won't have to wake her.

"Do you know the time?" I ask, stretching my arms out until I'm more awake.

"I'm not a clock," she responds sternly. "Morning to you too."

"I'll ask Ajax," I say, noticing the steel bottle beside Aurora. "Any water left?"

"None." She smirks. "I'll refill it while you talk to your *new* best friend."

"He's just more interesting than you… what can I say?" I tease with a shrug.

"Take that back!" she gasps, pretending to be outraged.

"All right... all right." I smile. "He's not more interesting than you, and he's not my best friend. Now please get us some water."

"What was it you said yesterday?" She brings a hand to her head and salutes me. "Yes, sir!"

We both chuckle.

I head over to Ajax, passing the same blackboard from yesterday. The Wall of Survivors... seems to me nothing more than a way to make the subjects compete.

"Good morning, Lukas. How may I assist you?" Ajax sounds cheerful.

"Can you tell me the time?"

"Of course! It's currently 09:04 AM. The Constant is bound at noon, leaving you with two hours and fifty-six minutes to spare," Ajax answers while smiling.

"Thank you..." I nod, creeped out by his persistent, unnatural joy. "What's on the menu?"

Moments later, I return to Aurora carrying a paper bag.

"I saw the flares." Aurora's eyes look hopeful. "What did you get?"

I pull out two small loaves of bread. "Breakfast."

We eat in silence, preparing for the day ahead. A melancholy feeling lingers in the air, knowing these moments of peace are about to end.

"I needed that so much." I take a sip of water.

"Couldn't agree more. Thanks," Aurora replies, looking a bit less pale.

"Don't thank me... I spent all our points."

She tilts her head. "So we have none left?"

I sigh in disappointment. "Zero."

"Shame. At least we won't die hungry."

"I like how you think." I glance at her foot. "How's the leg?"

"Great, painless. Thanks to you again."

I meet her eyes with a smug grin. "You seem to be thanking me an awful lot."

"Don't get used to it."

We refill the water bottle and head towards the passageway.

"It's still early morning," I say.

She glances at me. "So?"

"We still have a couple of hours. We could enjoy the quiet for a bit longer."

"There's no point in waiting."

"You just want to finish this?" I ask.

Slowly, she nods.

The passageway is two grand white doors, like always. A hologram projects: "Start Stage Two."

"Do we shout yes or something?" Aurora growls.

"I think we just keeping walking."

Once we step past the hologram, the doors slide open, revealing a small, enclosed circle. We step forward, and the passageway doors shut behind us.

Tightness grips my stomach. I hunch over, feeling the same nervousness I felt in the memory. The same sensation that led to their deaths.

The air feels heavy, each breath harder to take.

"All over again," I whisper, my voice trembling.

"No," Aurora hushes. "This time will be different. This time we're together."

She strides ahead, fearless. At the sight of her concentration, I do the same. The ground shakes with rapid vibrations, like something was threatening to poke through the circle we're on. I stagger, struggling to calm the beating of my heart.

The circle starts to tilt side to side in an erratic rhythm. The ground keeps drumming, growing louder and louder like something's coming.

Aurora's face shrinks with horror. She quivers, "There's nowhere to run."

I repeat, "Nowhere."

Then the ground collapses, plunging us into a pit of darkness.

Water sputters out of my mouth. I cough and I cough. My nostrils burn with fluids oozing out of them. I shriek with each gasp for air.

Light shines down from the hole we fell through.

I hear the echoes of my coughs fading into the distance. Eventually, I recapture my breath.

We plummeted into this pit of water. I was sure I'd break my legs. I was almost sure we'd crash to our deaths. The water was deep, but easy to swim through. I climbed out of the water, shaking and sore, and I laid on the ground recovering.

It felt like we kept falling and falling. It was inescapable. I wonder if Ellis and Albert felt the same hopelessness when their necks were being crushed.

I can only wish it was quick and painless.

I stand up and look around. All I can see is the glimmer of light swaying in the water pit and a tunnel stretching out into a suffocating gloom.

"Aurora?" I call out to her. She should be here, right beside me. We had sunk into the water together. But all I can hear is my beating heart.

I yell louder this time, "Where are you?"

Silence fills my ears again.

"Aurora!" I shout, feeling a slow stream of panic begin to rise through me. Please be all right.

I hear sudden splashes as the inky outline of Aurora emerges at the edge of the pit. She gets out and drops to her knees. She coughs and spurts water out. I rush over and firmly pat her back to help.

"You all right?" I ask.

"I'm fine," she grunts, breathing in deeply a couple of times. She stays hunched over until she catches her breath.

"I'm glad." I exhale in relief. "Do you still have the water bottle?"

She taps her waist and water sloshes around. "Right here."

"And the blade?"

"In my pocket," she replies. "We have everything. Don't worry."

My constant overthinking is something I can't control. It's like breathing, often an unconscious mechanism.

"Welcome to the first zone of Stage Two!" Enyo's voice erupts through the dark.

Every time I hear her, it's become a habit to freeze and listen.

"Your objective is to survive the lasers. A mere brush against you will burn through you. Robots fire the laser rays at moving targets solely within their line of sight. Evade the lasers, then you'll reach the passageway. May you Blaze or Burn."

Enyo always finishes her report with the same phrase. She might as well say I hope you die.

"They're trying to burn us alive," Aurora declares comically.

"Next they'll freeze us to death," I add.

She chuckles sadly. "Don't give them any ideas."

Clanging footsteps shatter the ground, steadily approaching us. We silently creep to the edge of the tunnel and peek around the corner. Bright panels on the ceiling illuminate the dark. Three silver heads glare in our direction with bright, glowing eyes. The robots are human shaped skeletons, but much thicker, wider and made of metal. Their arms and legs are blocky. In the centre of each robot, there's a circular structure with a barrel in the middle. Synchronised with every step, they come towards us.

We look away for a moment, staring at each other.

"What the hell do we do?" she asks with doubt. She rests a hand on her utility belt. "I'm worried about where the laser will shoot from."

"We need them to fire it," I reply. "Then we'll know."

She puzzles, "So we need to trick them?"

"Divert their attention, yeah," I assure.

"Okay."

Without warning, she pulls out the Awareness tactical from her waist and inserts the syringe into her forearm, gritting her teeth as the serum takes effect.

"Why did you do that?" I stress.

Her eyes dilate. She takes out the empty syringe from her flesh and squeezes it in her hand.

I frown. "You should've said something before you used it."

Aurora looks around the corner. A second later, she grabs my shirt and yanks me forwards into the tunnel. I gasp in shock. A series of glints pierce the corner of my vision. Then she pulls me back to cover.

"Are you trying to kill me?" I snap.

"No."

Her eyes widen with concern. But not for me. She stares right past me.

I follow her eyesight, to find pairs of laser lines shining through the tunnel. After a peek, I confirm that the dazzling rays are emitted from the robots' eyes.

"Is that where they're looking?"

"That's their line of sight," she answers, then thrusts me forwards, sending me stumbling into the tunnel. She stays beside me. "Now duck."

Without giving me any time to react, she pushes me down and dives to the ground herself while tossing the empty syringe into the air.

A sharp gleam emerges from the centre of a robot's body and suddenly a beam vaporises the syringe. Ash crumbles to the ground.

My heart strikes my chest relentlessly, fear sinking into my legs. If the lasers can deteriorate metal and glass like that, then I don't want to imagine what it can do to me.

"What now?" I yell, my voice wavering as I pin all my hope on Aurora. She doesn't say a word. Should we make a run for it? Should we stay still? Beads of sweat roll down my face. My breath wobbles frightfully. "Should we go back to cover?"

A thought creeps into my mind... *If we move, it's suicide.*

"They want you to run," Aurora says. "If we crawl, they can't see us."

"You gambled our lives on that?" I stammer.

"It wasn't a gamble. Enyo said the lasers fire only when there's motion in the robots' sightline. As long as we don't move within those gleams from their eyes, we're safe."

"How can you be sure?"

"Only the syringe was disintegrated. That's because we weren't in their line of sight," she explains. "We just have to evade their sight."

I sigh in horror. "You want me to play dice with my life?"

I'm too terrified to move.

"Any better ideas?" she persists.

"None."

"Then I suggest we play dice."

I avert my eyes from the robots, trying to calm myself. I hate that she's right.

Aurora suddenly stiffens beside me. "Wait! Freeze! Don't move."

The buzzing of electricity shuffles as the footsteps grow louder. I glimpse ahead, catching sight of their red eyes going round and round, searching through the tunnel.

"They're looking everywhere!" I shriek.

"Stay still."

I'm starting to panic. "What do we do?"

She replies, "We need one of them to reach us."

Saliva builds up in my mouth. Each footstep shakes the ground like a short burst of an earthquake. My chest spirals out of control, forcing my lungs to expand and contract so rapidly that my vision blurs.

"Lukas, I need your help." Aurora meets my gaze.

The pounding of my heart intensifies. I feel my guts aching with worry. Sound becomes muffled.

The vibrations grow louder. The robots are close.

"Evade the eyes. Don't move if you think they're looking at you. When one of them gets close, I'll jump onto its back and turn its head to look in another direction. That's when I need you to spin the robot around."

What is that even going to do? The other robots will annihilate us.

I rage internally, unable to stop the rising terror clawing at my chest.

"Lukas, I'm going to need your help," Aurora says, her voice quiet and gentle. "Please."

I shake my head. "You're going to get us killed."

"Lukas," she speaks with warmth. "I need you."

There's desperation in her voice. Her face is caged with fearful confidence. I'm not the only one who's scared. There's softness in her call for me. I don't know why, but something about the way she looks at me makes the fear easier to deal with.

"All right. You've got me."

The electric hum from the robots crackles as they advance forwards. Keeping still, we stay unnoticed.

Cold trails of sweat trickle down my spine. My hands shake in terror. But Aurora shines with conviction. I think I can do this. Or die trying.

I sense the vibration of a robot's footsteps as it lingers right in front of me.

"Now!" Aurora hisses. In one sudden burst, she slides to the side, narrowly dodging the laser beam and climbs onto its shoulders. She grabs its metallic skull and yanks it away from us.

I push its body again and again, turning it to face the other way. The sharp flash of scarlet-orange darts in my peripheral vision, just barely missing me. Intense warmth flushes over my skin. A thunderous crash quakes the ground as large fragments of stone splatter all around us. A grey mist emerges from the destruction. It's hard to see anything other than rising waves of dust.

My heart races and my fingers turn sweaty. But I keep on slamming my weight into the robot, steadily tilting it around as its laser keeps on beaming into the wall next to us, sizzling like metal being torn apart.

"Don't stop!" Aurora screams with struggle, her voice flickering with horror.

My arms are heavy, tremoring with exhaustion. With every fleeting moment, I feel my strength diminish.

I ram my shoulder into the robot over and over again until I'm out of breath. Then I lean my weight against it and continue thrusting forwards. Fear blanks out my mind.

A sudden dryness in my throat forces me to cough. But I keep on shoving the robot, unsure of which direction it's going in anymore.

Disjointed shrieks and grunts come from Aurora, but I can't see anything. The electric hum grows into an accelerating roar. The echoing rumble of the laser drowns out all other sounds.

I keep on pushing the robot, my body fatigued.

Everything is murky within this impenetrable greyness. My eyes are itchy, and my throat ripples with the urge to cough again.

A final metallic bang undulates the ground, and the only sound left is the hiss of electric sparks.

Without hesitation I blurt out, "Aurora?"

The mist starts to glimmer with white light from the ceiling as the dust curls around itself and disperses. But the clouds of grey still make it difficult to see.

The robot in front of me is still standing.

I gulp, "Are you all right?"

"I'm right here," Aurora croaks, also struggling with the dust.

"Are you hurt anywhere?" I ask, feeling my nerves gradually die down. I can only see a vague outline of her.

"I'm fine… somehow," she replies in a raspy voice, then clears her throat. "And you?"

"Still alive."

She chuckles softly. "I'm glad."

"Did we do it?" I ask wearily. The tunnel is illuminated once more, as the mist vanishes.

"The other robots are down, and I cut the cables connected to this one's head. I think we did it." She gives me a lazy thumbs up.

I sit down next to her, catching my breath.

"How did you get the laser to fire at the other robots?" I ask.

"I lowered its head a little and kept shaking my hand in front of its eyes," she explains.

I raise my eyebrows. "So the laser was firing the entire time?"

She stares and doesn't say anything.

"I think I was right," I utter in surprise.

"What?" she groans.

"You're really going to get us killed."

She sighs. "Clearly I haven't tried hard enough."

I grin. "And please don't."

I lie down on the ground and close my eyes for a moment. I feel the tension in my arms and legs ease up a little.

"I just need a second," I say, feeling worn out.

Aurora undoes her shoelaces and checks the bottom of her left foot. "I thought I felt something loosen up."

"Did the bandage come off?" I ask.

"Mhm." Aurora smiles. "It's fully healed. Thanks again."

"I thought you weren't thanking me anymore," I tease.

She rolls her eyes. "Shut up."

"Well thank you too," I tell her. "I wouldn't have thought of whatever madness this was. You're crazy."

She flashes another smile. "You're welcome."

The tunnel grumbles, shaking violently as if it might tear itself apart. We're overcome with confusion.

Suddenly, cold water gushes around our ankles, quickly rising. The overhead lights flicker and sizzle, each burst of brightness forcing my eyelids to spasm. Then the lights die out and plunge everything into pitch black.

"What is this?" Aurora's voice is shaky.

I feel myself leaning forwards, a sinking sensation in my gut. The icy water clasps onto my calves.

Instinctively, I look down as the ground tilts beneath us, turning into a steep slope. Rapid waves of water sweep us off our feet and drag us down the slope.

Aurora crashes into the slanted floor with a sickening clang. She cries out in pain, but her groans are faint next to the rush of water.

An abrupt voice booms through the darkness. "Welcome to the second zone of Stage Two!"

21

Aurora

Nowhere in my skull does the pain stop, a relentless ache throbbing in the back of my head where I hit the ground after I slipped.

Damn, that burns! I fight to stay calm as the slanted floor digs into my spine. We're submerged into a smothering blackness.

Cold water slithers over my flesh, making me shiver uncomfortably.

I wiggle my feet frantically, attempting to shift my balance and stand back up. Yet the slope is nearly vertical, keeping me pinned down.

"I don't know what to do!" Lukas's voice quivers.

It's illogical for them to kill us, but the slope's steepness is like a death sentence. We can't save ourselves in any way.

"Lay flat, brace for impact!" I yell. There's nothing else we can do.

"Impact with what?!" His voice creaks with panic.

"How the hell would I know?" I shout back, trying to talk over the ferocious surge of water charging down the slope.

This feels grim.

I can hear Lukas gasping in crackled breaths, while water slops back and forth around us. The ground hammers into my back again and again, bruising me with every jolt.

"Can you see anything?" Lukas asks, distressed.

"Not even myself." I tremble in the cold.

He hesitates. "Please not yet."

The current hisses like a wild animal as it grows into a raging growl.

I sense a sudden shift, like the slope beneath us has curved, flinging me forwards instead of down. Then, with a vicious thud, I'm launched onto a flat surface, smacking face first into shallow water. The impact leaves my flesh stinging, as if the water itself struck me.

I roll onto my back, gasping. "Aw, ouch."

The muscles in my back flare as I try to stand up, the burn lingering like an aftershock.

"Aurora, are you with me?" Lukas howls frightfully.

"Right here," I manage in a whisper. I need a second to catch my breath, to push the scorching agony aside. I hear Lukas coming closer, as water lightly splashes against my legs with its frost.

"It's like they're trying to kill us," Lukas grumbles in a hush.

I sneer. "Yeah, they're definitely good at this."

"Hopefully not good *enough*," Lukas says, fuming. He's not amused.

In an instant, small blue dots light up on the floor and ceiling, illuminating the room in a sinister glow. I squint, my eyes adjusting. The tunnel we were propelled through seals shut with a grinding crunch, trapping us inside four walls.

"Welcome to the One Hundred Cubic Metres!" Enyo explodes passionately, her voice echoing off the walls. My body tightens, listening intently. "Your first objective of the second zone is to escape through the elevator doors hidden within the walls while the liquid level rises. Beware, every four ping, a sharp current will shoot diagonally across the cube from its corners. You can only escape when the elevator you're in lights up."

The walls clatter, and each wall shifts its middle bricks to the side, revealing two reflective elevator doors that are encircled in a blue gleam. Only one elevator glows at a time, shining in a vivid, eerie blue.

The room feels smaller with every passing second, as the water continues rising. I feel its coldness climb from my calves to my thighs.

"Once the cube fills, your oxygen will run out. Witness the instinct of fear. May you Blaze or Burn!"

Lukas leaps forwards to the glowing elevator. He's balancing on his tiptoes, trying to reach the edge of the elevator platform built into the wall. I bite back the cold and stagger behind him. His fingertips reach the platform and he jumps up, springing his weight upwards to haul himself up onto it.

With each stride I get closer to him, but the rising water slows me down. It's now above my waist. I feel my legs becoming stiff under the icy water.

"Hurry up! Get up here!" Lukas waves me over, a hint of urgency in his voice.

"I'm trying to," I blurt out thick with bitterness.

I march onwards, just a metre away from him. "I can't stop shivering."

Suddenly a screeching beep vibrates through the cube. Blue light ignites behind Lukas, encircling the elevator.

"C'mon, we need to get out of here." Lukas extends his hand to me. Another ping crashes through the cube. Ahead of me, the light disappears from the elevator.

The water is up to my shoulders now, making every movement a brawl against the stinging cold. I grit my teeth and reach upwards for his arm. Our hands meet, slippery and wet.

"Keep pulling!" I shout to Lukas, trying to grasp onto the platform. The third chime roars through the room, louder, more intense. My fingers finally grip onto the edge of the platform, and I squeeze it as tightly as I can, while attempting to pull myself up. Lukas stomps one foot up against a wall of the platform, trying to anchor himself.

The fourth beep shakes the walls, as a powerful, explosive stream of water blasts out from the corner of the room. It slams into me with brutal force, shoving my body violently upwards.

My fingers almost slip from Lukas's hand as he tries his best to hold onto me, his face contorted with concentration. But the current keeps bolting into me, until it flips me upside down in mid-air.

"I can't... hold on..." Lukas groans, struggling to pull me to himself. I grab onto the ceiling of the platform, trying to drag my body down to the elevators. "...much longer!"

Water thrashes me mercilessly. The edge of the platform digs into my fingers, as I fail to clutch it any tighter.

In the blink of an eye, the current stops, sending me hurtling away, as Lukas's hand slips away from mine.

I jolt upright and begin treading effortfully to him once again. But the water resists me even more, almost like it's heavier than it should be.

The water has now risen to Lukas's waist, filling more than half the cube.

We're going to die, if not now, then soon. I can't stop thinking it.

"Get back up to me," Lukas wheezes, dropping to his knees, reaching out to me once more.

"I can't." I shudder.

I use my arms to stay afloat as much as I can, as the water keeps climbing higher. A loud beep shatters the silence, the walls quaking with its force.

My chest tightens.

We're going to die. The thought keeps coming back. I hear the second beep, and my eyes snap wide in terror.

Reaching down to my zipped up pocket, I pull out the obsidian knife and swim the closest I can to the elevator where Lukas is waiting.

The third chime blusters ruthlessly, nearly knocking me off course.

Lukas's head pops up beside me, panting for air while he spits water out.

"What are you doing?" he yelps in a raspy voice.

"Hold on tight." I inhale, then drive the knife into the wall with all the strength I have left.

Lukas stares, confused, then scrambles for the ceiling of the elevator platform.

The fourth beep screams, jerking the room violently. An aggressive eruption of water flashes out of the upper corner of the cube, shooting down.

The current grazes me, swaying me off balance. My body tilts towards the bottom of the cube.

I hear a shriek to my right and turn to see Lukas swept away by the torrent. I can't help him.

My fingers start to tremble, weakening my grip on the blade while my legs dangle, half in the water, half in the air.

A merciless eruption of air and water knock me back as the knife is slung out of the wall and ripped out of my grip. The blade is thrashed away, deep into the water.

I'm flung into the water, and the current thrusts me rapidly to the bottom until I smash into the ground. My body is pressed down, as I fight to stay conscious, feeling a light ringing in my ears. A dark-blue glow illuminates behind me. I'm right below the glowing elevator. The current halts, releasing me.

I turn around to see Lukas hovering right beside me, his face pale and vacant. He's probably trying to control his breath.

A thin trail of dark liquid drifts through the water, barely noticeable. I dismiss it as dirt, too panicked to think clearly.

My heart shakes with a thumping pain as my lungs scream for air. I hear a muffled rumble of the first beep.

I lunge forwards into the elevator platform right above us, struggling to move as I hold my breath. Stretching my arms out in front of me, I push the water behind me in one synchronised motion, gliding forwards into the elevator.

Lukas stays close behind, and I reach for his arm and pull him into the elevator fiercely. The second beep reverberates through my ears, sending waves of alarm through me.

My vision grows dimmer, darkness creeping in at the edges. The third ping clangs through the room, yet our elevator remains still.

What the hell? My face turns red with fear. Bubbles escape my mouth, floating away as my throat tightens.

My eye sockets widen and freeze, threatening to pop my eyes out.

The silence I feel is heavy. My body turns rigid as my muscles loosen up with fatigue.

I close my eyes. I see nothing. I hear nothing.

Then, a faint screech echoes through my ears. And that's when the water in my throat floods out of my mouth as I catch a gasp of air.

In a flicker, I open my eyes as the elevator doors slam shut with a metallic rattle. The water in the elevator begins to drain, and I suck in air. The heaviness in my lungs slowly dissipates, and my chest starts to rise and fall rhythmically at a normal pace.

I breathe out in relief.

A violent thud shakes the elevator. I shift my gaze to see Lukas lying on the floor, eyes sealed, struggling for air.

"What's wrong?" I ask him, confused as to what happened. I chuckle. "Catching your breath?"

"Mhm, mry... opsid, niff..." He mumbles nonsense, his voice trembling.

"Huh," I mutter, and glance to his hands, which lay on his belly.

My heart skips a beat. I see the thick spread of blood dribbling from his fingers to the ground.

Lukas slowly looks down. The pupils in his eyes seem to multiply in size, before he freezes.

His eyes desperately stare into mine.

He moves his arms to the sides, revealing a stream of crimson gushing out of him uncontrollably.

Horrified by the dark stain on his shirt, I reach for it. I feel myself tremble.

Please be okay. Please be okay.

My hands won't stop shaking as Lukas's blood coats my skin. It's sticky and dark.

I lift his shirt.

Blood flows in thin trails from his sternum down to his stomach.

I see my obsidian knife sticking out from his chest.

Lukas's mouth falls open, but no sound comes out.

22

Lukas

Nausea scuffs the back of my throat. I feel like I'm being strangled. My lungs stutter, causing me to urgently wheeze for breath. It's like I'm still drowning, sinking into a darkness that won't let me go.

Tears rush from my eyes. It burns to look at the world. Everything looks twisted.

"Lukas, can you hear me?" I hear Aurora calling for me, her voice quaking. "Damn it, you're heavy."

I try to focus on her, but all I see is a haze of motion. To me she's a moving shadow.

My throat scratches with each cough. I want this to stop, but my stomach keeps on contracting. I crumple, helpless against the spasms tearing me apart. I inhale air, but my lungs howl for more. My heart pounds so heavily it muffles everything else. The sound of my pulse echoes like gunfire, firing in my ears.

I remember the blood. It was sticky, warm and all over my hands. My head spins. I feel sluggish, like I'm moving through thick mud. My sensations lag behind what I see. Sounds reach me as if through water.

"I'm going to pull you now. This might hurt," she utters, her breathing shallow.

A jagged surface digs into my lower back. It sears my skin, the ache spreading like wildfire. The pain creeps slowly, but my senses are dulled.

"Were you always this heavy? *Argh*," she groans.

Am I hallucinating? There was a pain in my chest. I remember the pummelling force of the water current, the way it slammed me against the floor. Whatever I did, however I tried to motion my body, it kept me pinned against the ground of the cube. I couldn't move. I remember a sharpness in my chest. It was like I needed air. But also like the throbbing of a bruise. After that, I remember following a shadow. I heard metallic clinks. I felt her touch me. My shirt was damp, sticky with blood. What happened after that?

Coldness radiates through my face, the light touch of a hand on my cheek.

"Lukas are you with me?" she pleads, quivering with fear. "Oh hell, oh no."

My eyelids droop down, plunging me into darkness.

"This is all *my* fault." Aurora lets out a stifled wail. Wet droplets drip onto my skin.

"C'mon," she whispers, desperation trembling in her voice. "I know you're still in there."

I try to wiggle my legs, but they're too exhausted to even rock side to side. I can't open my eyes.

I feel her hand slip into mine. Her grip is tight and shaky. A silent plea that makes me hate myself.

"I stopped the bleeding," she hisses, on the verge of collapsing into tears. Her breath is uneven. "What the *hell* am I to do? I don't know how to help."

My shirt is moist and gloopy. I feel it clinging to the skin around my stomach. There's a slight twinge near my chest. I think I'm okay. But my muscles are drained of energy.

"I, eugh..." She tries to speak, but her fractured breaths break into a silent sob. I can hear the heaviness in her exhales. It's like she's trying to hold back any further tears.

There's a rumble of madness in my head. I can't do anything. My muscles won't listen to me.

"Lukas, please don't leave," she whimpers, air catching in her throat.

She squeezes my hand tightly, refusing to let go. I feel her body tremble next to mine.

"Stay with me, please," she pleads in a sorrow mutter. Gently, she lifts my head and rests it on her lap. She mumbles, "You said you'd stay."

Darkness starts to intrude my mind, sinking me into a weak consciousness. I feel the inflexible need to sleep creeping in.

I'm meant to be strong, I think to myself, shame invading my helpless state. Strong enough to protect her and myself. Strong enough to drag the two of us to the light at the end of the tunnel. Strong enough to fight my past horrors. Strong enough to save us both. Yet, right now, I can't even stand on my own two feet. I lay here, whining to myself. I'm pathetic. I feel weak.

Aurora's hands softly brush through my hair, her touch slow and tender. She's delicate with me, patiently waiting for me to awaken.

But I don't know if I can get up.

"I think that if I got to know you, with all my memories... somewhere safe, faraway from here..." she stammers in a broken voice, at a loss for words. She hesitates, then mutters, "If I got to know you, I think we would have been friends. Really good friends."

Lightly, she continues to caress my hair, fighting her quiver. There's a dullness in my heart. I'm pitiful. My breathing begins to slow down, each inhale more painful than the last.

"I just want you to survive, damn it," she says, her voice

wavering. "I don't deserve to live if you die."

I don't want to leave her alone. There's a bubble of stress growing within me, but I can't get rid of it.

"I need you, Lukas," she mumbles under her breath, like a silent prayer. She squashes my hand out of dread. "I need you."

There's an empty blackness that seeps into my vision, silencing my thoughts. I can only feel.

"Please," she cries out in fear. "*Stay with me.*"

Numbness crawls into my fingertips. All I hear is the crushing weight of stillness.

I squeeze her hand, desperate to show her that I'm still with her. Then my mind drifts away into the dark.

The darkness is thick, shrouding my world in silence. I can't control my body. My muscles refuse to obey me, like they belong to someone else.

It's a strange state of consciousness. I'm trapped inside my mind, unable to sense the world.

I think I'm dying... I don't want to be alone.

My heart throbs, tight with guilt and despair. I fear being by myself. But death feels so close, so imminent.

Is this what Ellis and Albert felt? I see their pale faces in my mind. The terrifying stillness of their eyes as they accepted a punishment they didn't deserve still haunts me. Do I *deserve* to die?

I can't answer the question. That scares me.

Suddenly, my arms are pulled upwards.

"Argh, damn it!" Aurora shouts in a grunt, fury tinged within her struggle. She drags me.

"It feels like hours have passed," she pants, exhausted. There's a quiver that echoes through my body. My limbs twitch weakly. "We're finally at the passageway."

I hear a quiet thud beside me. Her voice is close.

"And here I am, talking to myself like an idiot," she says, trying to suppress a sigh. "I thought it might help you wake up."

Aurora's stomach rumbles. I can feel my fingertips tingling, so I force them to move, just a little. Slowly, my arms grow lighter.

"Oh hell, I'm weak. I'm so *damn* hungry," she complains to herself, as I hear another growl explode from her stomach. "Just a little more." She pauses before snickering. "One more zone to survive."

I hear the stretching of clothes, meaning Aurora must be shifting positions.

"Your face is pretty," she whispers, her voice shivering. Gently, she traces her fingers down my cheek. Her touch is soft, timid, sliding down my neck until she reaches my collarbone. A warm tingle radiates through my skin, leaving a trail of goosebumps.

It's a nerve-wracking, but pleasant sensation.

Heat rushes to my cheeks. I'm probably red.

It feels wrong to like this. I'm a little embarrassed.

"What's wrong? Do you have a fever?" She places a hand onto my forehead, trying to feel my temperature.

"I can't tell..." Her voice trails off in a confused tone. She wraps her arms around my neck, carefully lifting me into a sitting position. I feel safe in her arms.

There's a twitch in my feet as the numbness begins to fade. Slowly, sensation slithers back into my body.

I hope I can open my eyes soon.

There's a trickle of warm air that bounces against my face. It feels like steam.

Instinctively, my eyes fly open.

Aurora's lips softly touch my forehead, lingering for a couple of seconds. My cheeks burn hotter, my eyes locked on Aurora, mesmerised by the curves of her face, the delicate dimples, even the dirt that clings to her skin.

There's a rising ache in my stomach. I feel lightheaded, but not in pain. It's more like an emotion I can't unravel. I don't know what I'm feeling.

This moment feels like forever. And the growing twist of nervousness keeps my body still.

"You seem okay," she notes to herself, her voice sounding like it's wandering off elsewhere.

My heart races rapidly, a light drumming in my chest. I breathe out, shivering with anxiousness.

Then she shifts her gaze. Her eyes meet my own. She ignites with panic. She thrusts her hands onto my shoulders and shoves me back down to the ground, looking away from me, while settling on top of me. She's light.

Freaking out, she blurts, "You were awake?"

I nod, scared to anger her any further.

"The whole time?" she squeaks, her voice breaking off into a high pitch. Her face flushes too. She keeps her eyes averted away from me.

"N-no," I groan, my voice rigid with shyness. Maybe it's best I don't tell her I could hear her thoughts for a while. She'll get mad. I grit my teeth and sheepishly declare, "I just... just opened my eyes, and the first thing I see is... *you* kissing *me*."

"I wasn't kissing you!" she cries. Her face shrinks from timid to more embarrassed and self-conscious. She roars in a quiet hush, "I was checking if you had a fever."

"I know that now!" I answer, my chest tightening as if it might burst.

"Then don't say it like that," she hisses, still avoiding me, her eyes sharp with embarrassment.

My voice is low. "Sorry... I was just surprised." I don't know what else to say. Quietness closes in.

I rise to a sitting position and glance around, noticing the white panel lights hanging over our heads, a brick tunnel that stretches far away into the distance, and the colossal, white doors of the passageway.

She must've pulled me all this way, I realise, feeling guilty about her struggles. That must've been really hard.

"Hey, thanks for bringing me here... Wait! Woah! What are you doin'—" I'm spooked as Aurora's hands leap to my chest. She grunts in a breath of relief, rolling her eyes upwards to the ceiling before sealing them shut for a couple of moments.

She slams her palm into the ground, leaning over to look down at me. "I was so worried, you idiot."

A sniffle escapes despite her wincing to hold it back.

She wails, "You scared me so much."

Her face remains a contortion of rage and compassion.

Is this how Aurora worries?

It seems more angry than upset.

"I don't even know what happened," I respond.

"Erm..." Her voice gets stuck in her throat. She sighs, sounding defeated. She looks down at the ground and then reaches for her pocket and pulls out the head of the obsidian blade she had used in the Safe Zone. "This happened."

"Huh," I mutter.

"When I used the knife to cling to the wall, the current knocked it loose and it fell into the water." She continues, worry in her eyes. "I thought nothing of it, but when we were finally safe, this is what was in your chest. That's when you lost consciousness."

Impulsively, I bring a hand to my chest, checking to see if I'm okay. But it feels just like a bruise, which stings a little when you press down on it. I'm fine.

There's a snivel and she wipes her nose instantly, before looking up, frightfully.

"I'm sorry, Lukas." She breathes in heavily, unrhythmically. "It was my fault."

She wraps both arms around me. Her arms clutch me tightly, unwilling to let go of the embrace.

"Hey, everything's fine," I whisper, hugging her back, awkwardly. "I'm right here."

"I know," she whimpers. I can barely hear her.

I try to lighten the mood. "As long as you didn't *try* to kill me, it's okay." My attempt at humour is pathetic. But she still chuckles, though with a hint of sadness. Her laughter barely conceals the tears she's holding back.

She shakes her head, while gently laughing. "No, no, I didn't!"

She sounds so relieved to not blame herself, even if it's for a moment. And that makes me smile.

Slowly, she pulls herself a little away from me, until we're looking at each other side by side.

"I couldn't have tried to hurt you if I wanted to," she rejoices with a smirk. "We need to protect each other, remember?"

We stay in silence for a second. Aurora glances away. I catch my breath. All of a sudden, she pulls me back, her arms clinging to me.

"I don't want to be alone," she admits, her voice faint and quiet.

"Then don't let go of me," I reply.

"Just stay with me, okay?"

"All right."

I embrace her back. I pat her head, unsure of how else to show her reassurance.

After a couple of moments of looking at each other, giggling and smiling, we finally decide it's time to go.

"Pull me up?" I ask her as she stands first.

"After I carried you all this way?" She raises an eyebrow. "Absolutely not."

Her tone is teasing but sharp.

"Please?"

"Fine."

She gives me her hand and helps me, but as soon as I put my feet down, I feel a terrible wobble.

I stagger for a few steps backwards, nearly falling over. I stay still until I feel like I've caught my balance.

"Are you okay?" she asks, her eyes wide.

"I might need help," I reply, frightened by the overwhelming weakness I feel spreading through my body.

Unexpectedly, a buzzer sound echoes through the tunnel, loud and eruptive. Then a silent click continues to chime every other second. It seems familiar.

We both turn our heads round, confused by what this means.

"Do you hear the ticking?" Enyo asks, her voice ringing through the tunnel.

"Yeah, what the hell is that?" Aurora spits.

The white doors slide open, revealing three floating holographic images. Random letters, and a bunch of different shapes and numbers all hover within the air.

Aurora comes over to me, looking disgruntled, and places an arm around my waist, telling me to lean on her.

"Time is running out. Twenty minutes remain." The speakers crackle, cutting out with a hiss.

"Twenty minutes for what?" I ask, lost.

Fragmented noises engulf us.

There's a drumming emerging from the ground. The bricks I'm under rattle back and forth, then side to side. I feel my muscles stiffen instinctively as I recognise it. I know what Enyo's going to say next.

"The Constant is closing in! You have twenty minutes to complete your second objective," Enyo explains in a high-pitched voice.

It makes me feel uneasy.

The clock returns, loud and unmistakable. The ticking is invasive. I feel it echo in my skull.

While leaning on Aurora, I limp forwards, as we enter the room. It's similar to the cube room, a brick room with a high ceiling, except there's no water or dotted lighting. The room is clearly illuminated. In the middle of it, there are three black panels that have risen from the ground. The holographic images of letters, shapes and numbers all shrink and retreat backwards into the panels. Then the panels flash with the same blue shade from earlier.

My throat turns dry.

Above the panels, big red numbers float in the air.

The crimson digits form a timer: 20:00.

I gulp down on my saliva.

My heart beats faster.

Tick tock.

"The countdown has begun!" Enyo exclaims, and for the first time her excitement seems sinister. She sounds bloodthirsty.

Enyo sounds like she wants us to fail.

FEAR THE DEAD

Act III

Hiding the truth is not a lie.
It's the enslavement of your trust.

23

Aurora

I'm impatient. The ticking of the clock drives me insane until I feel like there's a short fuse sizzling inside my head.

Twenty minutes drop to nineteen, and the seconds keep falling away.

My limbs move like sticks. I feel stiff and slow.

To hell with death.

Lukas leans on me and we stagger forwards. My hair is soaked with sweat. My clothes are still damp, engraving my skin with a revolting itchiness. My body groans each step of the way to the panels.

I stop. "I'm going to set you down... okay?"

"All right, just, just..." He grunts, gripping his stomach. "Not too fast."

Gently, I ease him off me and shift his weight to the ground. I worry about each movement. I feel responsible... for everything. It eats at me.

"Better?" I ask.

"Yeah," he croaks. "Just need to catch my breath."

"I'm going to get us out of here."

Lukas's eyes widen, as if he's aching to tell me something. But it's a struggle for him to keep his head up, and after a few moments he gives up and lies down to recover his strength.

I approach the black panels in the centre of the room, their reflective surfaces like tinted mirrors.

The first panel shines with a radiant blue like it was luring me in. The two panels on the right display nonsensical grids, random letters, and numbers that rotate and move erratically.

On the first panel, there's sixteen random cards in total, in a four-by-four pattern. The cards are dotted on their backsides. At the bottom of the panel, along an answer box, there are instructions for what to do.

Objective: Identify the deviant in each category.
Rules: You may examine only one card at a time.

On impulse, my fingers fidget with one another. There's an overflow of thoughts that surrender my mind to panic. I try to ignore the gnawing cramp in my stomach by concentrating on what's in front of me.

I tap the glossy panel, and it reacts to my touch. The card in the top right corner flips around, revealing a Black Ace, with no suit, just two bold black **A**'s on opposite ends of the card. Then I tap the card below it, and this time it's a Red Queen, once again with no picture or suit, only a sharp red on opposite **Q**'s.

After I flip a few more cards, I start to suspect that every card is either a Red Queen or a Black Ace.

I go through all the cards, confirming this.

No suits, just Red Queens and Black Aces, scattered randomly. I try to find a pattern, looking vertically, horizontally, and diagonally at the cards' placements.

What the hell could it be? I feel taunted by my cluelessness. I look up at the countdown. Seventeen minutes now.

We still have time, but with each second that goes by I feel like I'm being pierced through the heart.

Grudgingly, I start looking at the design. Each card has a letter mirrored at the top and bottom. First, I compare the shades of red and black, but they all seem to be identical. The shape of the cards is the same, too, nothing noticeably different. I inspect every letter carefully, searching for anything distinct.

I examine the cards one by one, until I reach the last card in the bottom right corner—a Black Ace. My eyes narrow as I look closer. I compare the mirrored letters.

I squint.

The **A** at the top is normal, but the upside-down **A** at the opposite corner seems a little slanted, leaning off centre a bit. It's subtly placed.

Relief sparks through me, and my pulse quickens with hope as I rush back through the cards, focusing on all the Red Queens. But each **Q** looks symmetrical.

I run my fingers through my hair in frustration. If it's not the colour or the letter, then what am I missing?

The answer can't just be one card. The objective stated to find the deviant of *each suit*, meaning I'm not finished yet. I stare at the letter **Q** brainlessly, sighing in irritation. It's just an oval with a tail. What could possibly be written differently?

"Look at the differences in how they're written," Lukas grunts.

"You think I haven't done that?" I snap. "Lukas, please be quiet."

I go through the cards again, dissecting the symmetry of the ovals and the tails of each **Q**. Each oval appears to be written with the same diameter. It's not something I can be certain of just by looking, so I try to use my thumb and index finger to estimate each letter. Afterward I focus on going through each tail. I tap onto one Queen and then the next one, and the next one after that, until something catches my eye. I keep staring.

The sharpness of a tail draws my attention.

The **Q**'s tail grows thinner, but it doesn't come to a sharp edge. It's blunt. Unease slithers up my spine as I glance back at the last Queen to compare. The difference is minute. The other Queens have acute, pointy edges, but this one is pointless. The end of its tail is flat, almost rectangular.

A fractured breath escapes me. I drag the slanted Ace and the blunt Queen into the answer box. My hands are shaking. The box glows green, and the word "Complete" projects out of the panel into the air.

The middle panel lights up with a blue hue.

I can see a grid of squares materialise.

"I'm almost better. I'll come help you, I swear," Lukas mutters and sits up slowly.

"Lukas," I say, stepping aside to the next panel. My voice softens as I glance back. "Don't push yourself."

He stays silent. I think he's mustering the strength to get back up.

I shift my focus to the panel in the centre. A grey cloak of smoke disperses to the edges of the display, revealing a maze of jumbled letters that seems to be gibberish.

Objective: Find a three-letter word in the grid.
The word reflects what two subjects become together.

Rules: The letters must form a straight line.
This line can be diagonal, vertical or horizontal.

M	J	A	U	A	L	P	Q	Q	T	L	E	Y	U
J	B	M	A	S	T	X	E	M	Q	J	D	I	H
E	A	V	X	N	Z	N	X	S	K	E	Z	Y	G
W	K	M	V	T	F	C	N	K	K	A	B	N	I
H	L	W	D	G	C	J	I	V	S	U	A	U	E
Z	W	M	Z	M	B	J	H	F	P	F	U	V	F
X	K	J	G	N	R	E	T	K	K	O	I	D	N
K	S	T	H	I	Q	L	H	D	D	L	P	S	A
Y	L	E	W	T	O	U	D	V	V	G	Y	L	G
R	A	B	R	X	C	J	S	M	K	O	F	H	I
U	I	F	K	D	Q	R	D	O	V	F	M	N	Q
N	O	Y	W	Q	G	N	T	G	O	M	J	J	Y
J	U	T	V	T	W	S	N	Y	U	L	D	Y	C
O	N	N	J	F	Z	D	V	K	X	Y	G	G	V

How can a three-letter word reflect us, the subjects? What do we become together?

We become prisoners together. Prisoners who need each other. To survive.

Cold air floods my nostrils, shaking me awake. I can smell something salty, moist. Maybe it's our sweat.

There's a sinking feeling in my stomach. I feel heavy. It tickles my ribs when I breathe out.

I glance at the clock. Twelve minutes left.

A shiver churns from my gut to my chest.

I hear rustling behind me. Like clothes crackling against a hard surface.

Ugh, what the hell is wrong with me? I can't focus.

I skim through the letters from top to bottom, scanning each row. These absurd letters mock my confusion. Doubt creaks into my head.

Maybe I've missed something.

I wish that blade had pierced me instead. Then I wouldn't be standing here, trembling like a coward. It's like there's a stream of madness spilling through me. It hushes the world around me.

Pathetically, I attempt to read through the letters horizontally this time, seeing if there's anything I can put together. But the letters are just meaningless shapes.

My eyes jump to the clock. Nine minutes left.

Feelings invade my mind. I'm no longer concentrated on the letters. There's a little girl's voice in my head. She screams: "It's all *YOUR FAULT!*"

I shut my eyes and breathe in slowly, counting to four. Then again. And again. I must calm down.

This puzzle is such a mess. Everything seems so random. I go through the text sideways again, but nothing clicks.

"Aurora, what if…"

I grumble, "Just be quiet."

I gaze at the rules again. *A straight line.*

That string of letters can be backwards as well… so long as it's in a straight line. I haven't tried that yet.

I trace the letters diagonally, forwards and backwards. But I can't even find a three-letter word, let alone one that represents us.

Maybe specific words… but what could relate to us? I spiral through possibilities like end, die, or one. Maybe we become *one* because we rely on each other!

My forehead throbs with frustration. This is so damn illogical.

I start obsessing over the word one, finding every O and seeing what it may spell out with the other letters surrounding it. But nothing adds up. I rush through the text again. Up, down, nothing. Just more nonsense. It's like I'm missing the vowels to make a word longer than two letters.

My eyes flick to the time. Eight something left.

I search sideways, paying attention to the letters O and D, hoping that the word is one or die.

The first couple lines have nothing. Too many consonants. There's no words to form.

Next, I move to the middle section. Letter by letter, from one absurd cluster to the next. Until I read the letters O-U-D. That noise isn't a word, but it doesn't sound like nonsense. I reverse the letters. When spelt backwards it makes the word D-U-O.

We become a… Duo?

My face stiffens. I sigh in annoyance because it makes sense. They called us a Duo.

Damn it. I wasted so much time.

I tap the screen and draw a line through the letters D-U-O. The line glows green and the entire panel fades into a grey mist.

The image of the word puzzle disappears, replaced by floating letters that spell out: "Complete."

The third panel brightens with blue.

The screen flashes, revealing gridlines that form a table of words. There are sixteen words, all starting with the letter S.

There's no link between them… they're just words.

In the bottom right there's an answer box with a keyboard.

Objective: Create a sentence by taking one letter
from each word.

Hint: What is a sixtieth of a minute?

Stall	Seed	Sneak	Share
Swat	Small	Soak	Sequence
Sold	Sanctuary	Supper	Sriracha
Sruti	Side	Stab	Seas

I read the hint with a hopeless sense of confusion. One sixtieth of a minute is a second.

But what does that even mean? How is that a hint? How can a unit of time be the answer when the puzzle is made from random words? Time can't help me right now. It can only doom me.

I lock onto the words. I feel a vein popping out on my head. My eyes are numb and slow, tired of staring at a single point. I stumble over the list. I read it again and again, but it's just noise. It's like I'm reading without paying attention. The words start to blur together.

I read the words aloud, my tongue slipping and stuttering over the repetitive s sounds at the beginning of each word. It's all gibberish.

Maybe there's a pattern I'm missing. It might be the endings of the words. I go down in rows, taking the last letter from the end of each word. Nothing. Then I try the second last. But there's just too many consonants.

What the hell could it be?

The letter S must be important. My first thought is to go through the alphabet in numbers. S is the nineteenth letter.

So what? I can't do anything knowing that.

I scratch my fingernails in anger, steadily peeling off the dead skin around my fingertips. It's impossible to think. My concentration scatters into exhaustion.

I peep at the clock, dreading what I'll see. The numbers have gone from red to a dark and murky crimson. It's like sloppy blood floating.

Three minutes left.

Damn it.

Helplessly, I lift my head and look at the words again. My eyes feel empty as I focus on the hint.

"A sixtieth of a minute… a second… one single second," I whisper under my breath. I'm just trying to untangle the mess I'm in. Damn me.

I repeat the phrase over and over again in my head, until I'm sick of hearing those syllables together.

Out of panic, I start to read through the words in lines, going down in rows. The first word is Stall, so I start at the T and go down, connecting the second letter of each word. TWO.

My eyes glimmer with recognition. I feel a final spark of hope burn brighter. My eyes are locked in on the second letter of each word.

Second! As in place, not time. A single second meant read the *second* letter of every *single* word. My heart rushes with bursts of adrenaline as my eyes broaden with focus. A small breath of relief leaps out.

I trace the second letter of every word, trying to maintain my composure. My fingers rush towards the answer square, trembling as I tap the letters T-W-O.

The panel shakes beneath my hands, making my eyes scatter in fear, searching for the correct letters. The next word stretches across rows: R-E-M-A-I-N.

I can't stop my hands from shaking. But I have to finish this… O-U-T.

I fill in the last word: H-E-R-E.

As I release my fingers from the screen, all the panels swell with dark green light.

The glow isn't promising.

My heart rumbles in my chest. I slump forwards, hands squeezing my knees as my lungs drag in air that won't come fast enough.

The drumming in my ears fades. The weight in my stomach loosens just a little.

For a moment, I feel lighter.

"Lukas, I'm going to get us out of here." I whip my head towards him, but something flickers in the corner of my eye.

Numbers continue to descend... 01:37, then 01:36.

What the hell! I did everything they asked.

Time is still ticking.

Dread darts through me as the panels snap back to the same deep blue. I clench my jaw, my teeth grinding against one another.

I stare at the different screens.

Can it just stop? Please.

I don't want to know what comes next.

"There is a link between each answer you have solved," Enyo explains with a stale, lack of emotion. "A shared trait regarding quantity."

The clock freezes at 01:30.

The first panel displays the slanted Black Ace and the Red Queen with its blunt tail. The second panel shows the word D-U-O, each letter burning red. The third once again presents the same table of words, with the message "Two Remain Out Here" highlighted.

I rub my eyes, forcing myself to study all three panels.

Enyo continues, "You have ninety seconds to solve the numerical trait. Insert your answer at the passageway. May you Blaze or Burn!"

Every tick of the clock is a punch to the stomach. My heart thrashes violently, as if it might shred through my skin.

I hear a faint rustle, fabric brushing against the ground, but I ignore it. Focus. There's two cards. The word Duo. And that eerie message.

What do they have in common? I pause to think about it, but the answer feels out of reach.

"There's always at least—"

"Lukas I said silence!" I snap. My head stings with exhaustion, tension crushing my temples. Last thing I need is suggestions from someone who can barely breathe.

I look at my answers obsessively. They are cards and word puzzles. Are they games?

Each objective was a task, like an investigation… could that be a shared trait? I bite my tongue, unsure.

The pressure in my chest threatens to split me. My organs feel like they're shattering one another with every strained beat of my heart.

My eyes are glued to the panels, yet my mind stays blank. The walls start to shiver, shrinking within the incoming mist. Fragments of stones gallop forwards, twitching against the ground.

What the hell? Alarm bells erupt in my head.

The walls groan, shaking as though they are begging for mercy. A thick fog smothers the room. I blink, my eyes stinging, but the grey only deepens. The murk blurs the world into gloom. The timer's numbers pierce the dark like sharp blades of light. The crimson digits glare back at me.

Nineteen seconds.

A rattling hum bursts beneath my feet. The ground rumbles, fast and unrelenting, thudding like a heartbeat.

My body locks up, frozen in terror. It's coming.

My limbs won't move. Time suffocates me.

What the hell am I to do? I try to inch forwards, but each step is small and unsteady.

The faint shrieking of the room grows louder and more desperate as the ground shudders more rapidly.

The Constant closes in.

I stagger to the panel and stare blankly at the keyboard.

Two cards. Duo. The second letters forming the sentence "Two Remain Out Here."

It's all connected to the number two. It *must* be. But doubt coils around my gut.

What if you're wrong?

The Constant makes me feel like prey. My breaths are short, urgent gasps. Fear squeezes my throat. My fingers dig into the skin of my neck, desperate to exhale. The world grows dim.

Something hits me. Lukas stumbles into me, his body weak and trembling as he grasps onto a wall. He pulls himself up, whimpering with madness. His fingers slam into the screen. With his remaining strength, he taps the letters T-W-O.

The screen flashes green… "Access Granted."

24

Lukas

Numb fingers slip off the screen as I wobble to the side a few paces. The rumbling of stone approaches like a drum being played louder and faster.

I narrow my eyes as the world twirls and tilts around me. I rub my temples, trying to dull the heat throbbing in my skull. Adjusted to the brightness, I gaze into the new zone. Trees reach for the clouds with their branches, and leaves scatter the evening sun in dotted streaks. The sky glows with light blue, mixing with a yellow that you'd only find on sunflower petals.

Darkness is coming. Ahead, concrete blends into grass, which leads to trees and ponds. I sense familiarity.

Every step feels like nails are being hammered into my soles, as my skin stretches and stings and sears with blistering strain. I feel fragile.

"Lukas, wait! Stop moving, c'mon, stop." Aurora's voice is faint, fading like she's running away. After each stride I stop, take a deep breath and try again.

Birds chirp, critters buzz and other insects hum in a repetitive rhythm.

I've been here before. It's peaceful.

I believe I'm safe.

"Can you just *wait?*" she puffs, out of breath. Clothes scuffle as she stumbles. I keep moving.

"Lukas, wait up!" she bawls, her voice closer.

What does it matter?

"Lukas… what the hell is wrong with you?"

I just want to lie down.

I hobble forwards, my legs unsteady. I brace myself, expecting to crash into the ground.

Aurora grasps me tightly and lowers me down. My flesh relaxes into the concrete's warmth.

"Lukas, are you okay?"

"Safe Zone?" I whisper, but her response is swallowed by the breeze. Leaves bounce up and down with the wind. I see the orange giant in the sky.

I exhale, my chest rising and falling steadily.

There's a blur of movement within the forest. Sharply, I shift my eyes and try to follow the motion. Shadows lunge and sprawl across the trees.

I feel watched. It's the same feeling I had when I saw Ellis and Albert hanging. Their eyes were so pale and unblinking. Their gazes followed me.

Shivers of cold winds blow past me.

"Lukas, you're safe," Aurora says. Her voice is soft. I feel her warm breath on the side of my head.

My eyelids flutter lightly, growing smaller. Exhaustion crawls through my face. I feel my muscles loosen. Thoughts drift away. Soon enough, I'm alone all over again. And darkness triumphs before me.

"**N**ow we wait." The man lifts the cigar to his mouth and inhales deeply. His weathered, brown cloak hides his eyes. Across his lap lies a bow, an arrow ready on its string. After a short moment, he puffs.

Smoke curls slowly into the cold air.

My dad and I sit atop a hill, backs against a towering oak tree, taking shelter from the frosty winds.

Small white dots fall from the sky. Snow has embraced the world tightly, hardening the earth into stillness. Nature has lost its voice.

The trees below look lifeless without their leaves.

I look down at my feet, buried in the snow. I feel the cold seep through my leather boots, their brown colour turning into a soggy black. My coat is thin with holes near my forearms, and the biting cold makes it impossible to keep still.

"Dad," I whisper, fighting to stop the tremble in my throat. "Aren't you scared?"

"They're the ones scared of *us*," he scoffs, quietly. "It's the wolves you oughta look out for."

He stiffens, fixed on the trees ahead. His smirk flattens, as if he has remembered something. Something fierce. Something he fears.

"Why?" I keep my voice low, hissing with a gentle squeak. I'm small next to my dad. He's like a wall to me.

"Wolves know these lands better than us all. And they're starving just like us. But if a wolf's alone, you'll be fine. Just don't go near it. Ya hear me?"

I nod. "I won't go near it… but what if it's not alone?"

The man stays silent. Focused on the trees.

"Then get your blade out and stare 'em down like you're gonna *kill 'em*."

"I don't want to kill anything," I cry.

"Keep quiet, boy."

He refuses to face me.

I know he's teaching me to survive, but it feels like he's far away, leaving me alone to fear the world.

I hate that sinking paranoia. It's like you're being watched by something out there. But you don't know what it is.

My stomach tightens, rumbling with hunger. Numbness in my fingertips. Breathing burns my nose.

"Dad, how much longer?" I mumble, shivering.

"Shh-shh-shh. Look ahead, do ya see it?" His eyes point to the trees below us. I look down, seeing two deer emerge, a large one and a smaller one. Their breath visible in the icy air.

"It doesn't have any antlers," I say, staring in awe. The big deer leans its head down to the snow.

"Because she's a mother."

"Why is she sniffing the ground?"

"I left apples for 'em." He raises the bow from his lap, stands up and pulls the string back.

I feel a sudden rush in my chest. "Wait, no! You can't, Dad! What about the baby deer?"

"It's old enough to survive on its own," he answers harshly, without looking at me.

"Please don't do it, Dad," I plead, my lips shivering as I speak. I try to sniffle quietly, doing my best to keep my eyes dry. "The baby deer needs its mum."

"Quiet, Son."

My breath shakes, eyes burning with tears. But I keep my face tense. "Please stop, Dad. We'll eat something else."

"We have nothing else."

Dad's gaze doesn't leave his target. He draws the arrow back further, taking deep breaths in and out. His chest drops, free of tension.

"Please, Dad!" I yell, dread spilling out of me.

"You've caught its attention," he whispers.

I look around to face the deer. It has turned towards us, its feet light and ready to spring away. Ears stiff, pointing in our direction. The calmness within its eyes is contagious. A silent plea... as if she knows.

Then with a snap, the arrow thrashes through the deer's spine. The deer shakes and shrieks violently. She spins around, her tail flagging. She tries to hobble before her back legs give out, and she drops to the ground with a thump.

The little deer watches, ears perked, silent and tentative. After a few moments of stillness, it hesitantly hops towards its mother and leans its face against the mother's back. The baby deer tries to nudge its mother, as if urging her to get up. The snow around the mother starts to trickle with blood.

"We oughta finish it." My dad puts the bow on his back, his face overflowing with a sombre sense of determination. He starts to climb down the hill and shouts back to me, "Get up, Son. This isn't over."

The baby deer hurdles into the air, wheezing with fear. Its feet loop around and then it darts away into the trees. Quickly, the little deer vanishes out of sight.

I rise slowly, patting off snow from my trousers. Their wool is thick and itchy, but it keeps me warm... the only warmth I have. I was told my grandma had given these trousers to me. I don't remember her anymore.

She's been gone a long time.

I'm told the Arbiters hung her. I don't know why. My father speaks of her when he's bitter. I've seen him slumped in his room in the dark, his eyes flickering with rage but his face damp with regret. He thinks no one's watching. But the walls are thin. I hear his murmurs. I know he sobs by himself. I sense his emptiness. He's always cradling a half-empty bottle and muttering to himself when Mum's not home.

"Hurry up, Lukas," Dad calls me. I don't want him to yell. I stumble down the hill as fast as I can.

"What took ya so long?" He kneels beside the deer, pulling out rope from his bag.

"I was worried about the little deer." I don't want to be honest. He would be sad.

"The other one will be all right. Its mother taught it how to survive."

"How do you know that?"

"Because it ran away from us," he replies.

That doesn't make sense.

"What's the rope for?" I watch my dad tie it into a loop.

"To drag the deer home."

I mutter, "She'll be heavy."

"That's right, she will be heavy. We could cut her open and leave the guts behind to make it easier."

"Why don't we?"

Dad wraps the loop around the deer and tightens the knot at the end.

"You like the sausages mother makes, don't ya?"

I nod.

"The guts are needed. There's nothing we can afford to leave behind."

"Nothing?"

"Bones for soup, organs for hunting, deerskin for clothes. We use everything."

He prepares the rope, and we start treading through the snow back home. I watch the silence of the forest.

"Look, Son. Ya did good," he says. "I want ya to know. It's not about killing. We hunt to survive. But to take a life with care takes great strength."

"It's not fair!" I whimper.

"Maybe you're right," he remarks. "But one day you'll be the very soil that feeds a deer, the earth that flowers grow on, the dirt that ants and small creatures crawl through. Life gives and life takes."

"I feel guilty." The words slip out in a tremble.

You wouldn't think *anything* had died today.

"I'm sorry, kid. Give it time... you're gonna get used to it. It won't feel so bad."

I catch the little deer staring at us from a safe distance, behind some fallen branches that reach outwards like skeleton fingers. Its eyes are blacker than the night sky, and they bulge outwards.

I look up at my dad. "Should I feel bad?"

"No. That only makes things worse."

"**L**ukas, stop whispering." Her voice cracks with frustration. I feel her hands cup my face, soft and warm. "C'mon, just stop it already!"

Was that a dream... or a memory? Everything feels weightless, or as if I were floating. My legs feel steady, no longer wobbly or sore. Why did I remember my dad? I don't know his name. I don't know anything about him.

"Lukas, get up. Wake up already..." She nudges me repeatedly. Beneath me the ground shakes relentlessly. "Agh, damn you."

But we're okay... we entered the Safe Zone.

"Lukas! The hell is the matter with you!"

Aurora grabs my head and yanks it towards herself. I awaken, shove her off me and lean against the ground. I breathe out in rapid gasps, yearning for air as my lungs wheeze with pain.

"We need to go."

Why is she so urgent? I lightly shake my head, feeling my senses return to me. It's like I've just escaped a dream state. My head is still foggy, sluggish.

The Safe Zone stretches forwards with greenery, expanding into a forest filled with ponds and massive boulders. Just like before.

The sky has darkened into a deep blue, and the night is beginning to conquer the fading sun. A sharp breeze of icy air brushes along my neck.

Aurora clutches my face with both hands and pulls me closer to her face.

In a deep, raspy voice she hisses, "Lukas, listen to me." Her fingers dig into my cheeks. "We're in trouble."

"What? What is it?" I ask her. I spot the wooden cabin further ahead, with a small cannon on top of it that's aimed at the sky. It's the Care Point from earlier… where we bought food.

"What's the matter? We're in the Safe Zone, right?" I ask, my head lightly throbbing as if I were still in a daze. "Aren't we all right?"

"I don't know." She folds her arms to hide from the cold. I feel the ground quake underneath me.

"See? It keeps rumbling!" she cries, her voice breaking with dread.

It feels like the world is spinning around me. I try to look for the clock at the Care Point, but from here the red numbers are just a blur.

I look at Aurora. "Do you know the time?"

"Must be almost midnight. Why?"

"Oh no." My heart strikes ruthlessly, weakening my entire body. A slight quiver jumbles my legs. The ground doesn't stop shuddering. "When you were doing the puzzles, after I passed out, did it ever mention that we were in the third zone?"

Her eyes turn stiff with fear. She looks up at me. "I… I don't know."

Suddenly a roaring echo ruptures my ears as merciless winds pierce and slash through us. We turn back to the passageway through which we entered. Small specks of debris crash into my skin like a storm of sand and stone. The air smells crispy, like it's burning. The passageway doors burst off their hinges and plummet backwards through the air.

"We never finished Stage Two."

Aurora's face flushes with panic, suffocating in the chaos. She screams, "RUN!"

The Constant is right behind us.

25

Aurora

Growls of terror roar in my ears. My feet move on their own. The earth is crunched and shattered. Shards of sand and stone whip past my head like bullets.

"Don't stop running," Lukas shrieks, out of breath, his face red with fright.

My nostrils ignite with the stench of gasoline and chemicals. The smell clogs my throat. Each breath is a battle, making me drag my legs slower and slower.

This damn place just wants to kill us. I grunt as I bite down on my lips, sensing the taste of saltiness ooze onto my tongue.

I stumble in a straight line, evading trees and ponds with as little movement as possible.

A disordered spurt of colour engulfs the world, tinting the night's blackness into a yellow mist. Blinding flashes of purple lightning flare and crash throughout my vision.

The Constant relentlessly pursues us.

My chest hammers, pouring adrenaline into my limbs. I stagger forwards, feeling a cramp crawl through my ribcage, stiffening my lungs. My stomach contorts and throbs when I move. Each step is a deep breath of torment.

The trees appear like they're in a desert, with a weird, musty yellow hue coating them. The thought that the forest won't end gnaws at me. As I dash forwards, the trees keep on expanding, emerging out of the distant fog.

My lungs squeeze painfully as my breaths grow shallow. Groaning through my charred nostrils, I try to breathe through my mouth, but it only swells my throat.

"Hell," I blurt out.

Ahead I catch the sandy shadow of Lukas vanishing further away from me.

Don't leave me alone. Stay with me… please.

My eyes burn with acidic moistness. I tumble onwards, my entire body shuddering restlessly.

My legs grow unsteady. I can't keep up this pace. My body begs me to give up.

"Welcome…" A sizzling, different from the raging rustling of the Constant, squashes through the hailing chaos. Enyo declares, "…to the third and final zone of Stage Two!"

I shift my head to the Constant right behind me. The world is disintegrating. Trees are thrusted into the air, pulled out of the earth with their roots hanging, chunks of black soil falling off them. The trees snap like brittle bones and plummet into the mist. The walls collapse, and the impact violently wobbles the ground side to side, rocking my centre of mass. Tendrils of shadow puncture through the fog, reaching for me. I keep running, looking back, unsure of what they are. Spikes of brick flog towards me. Winds thrash my spine, echoing like ghostly hums singing in the madness of the storm.

My skin pops, as if fireworks were cracking beneath the surface. I fight the urge to claw my nails into myself, finding it more and more difficult to get air into my lungs. My nostrils tingle, failing to suck in any more air. Breathing is like an automatic motion I must perform but can't complete. I open my mouth, desperately gulping at the atmosphere, but only jagged gasps escape. My throat aches for breath, throbbing and pulsing from the inside as it feels like the inner walls of my neck begin to smother me.

The yellow haze thickens and turns murky. Dark-green specks shimmer like emeralds through the fog. Then flames leap from the ground, swinging hot sparks of black-orange onto my arms.

I watch the texture of my skin hiss and bubble into mushy lines of pink. It looks like pigskin.

I keep pushing my legs onwards, each step plunging weight up my hips. My body feels wrong, too dense, too sluggish.

The sky scorches the earth into spectral yellows. The air bleeds with sand. It stings, it strangles, it singes. I feel everything but can't react, my senses short-circuited by the gas.

Violet streaks flash through the sky, lingering like frozen lightning strikes. Thunder shakes the ground pitilessly. The fog lightens up in front of me... maybe I've started to outrun the Constant.

A straight path emerges ahead, surrounded by two rows of trees.

Every limb itches, weighing me down, tension slouching all over my joints. My knees tremble in opposite directions, toppling my body forwards. I slump to the ground, sensing the Constant's roaring vibrations leap from the earth to my chest.

Damp drops of leaf-coloured liquid fall from above. The skies stare down at me, like a grieving father failing to hold in his tears.

Desperately, I look up, my vision dimming with fatigue. The corridor starts to deepen, its transparency clotting into the same impenetrable yellow from earlier.

I'm not going to make it. A shivering voice creeps in my ears. A child's screech. Damn it. I'm doomed.

I sense the wind puff right past me, cold and fleeting, as it rushes into the sandy gloom ahead.

I try to get back up.

Slowly, I put one leg up but my other knee fails me, and it slams me to the ground, shooting a sharp pain up my back and leaving me kneeling. My eyelids flicker involuntarily, prickling my face. I shut my eyes, yet I still see the mist swirling around me. It's like the yellow sky has burned into my retina.

I bite my lower lip, unable to bear the aching torture of my skin being peeled away by the air I breathe.

Then I feel a rhythm of beats pounding the ground. The vibrations pulse through me at a sickening pace. The thudding grows louder. The Constant is here.

I breathe deep, squealing in terror to myself.

My eyes are forced open by a rising shard in my throat. My tongue stings with salt.

I cough and I cough and I can't stop.

I look down, seeing a sticky tangle of liquid dripping from my lips. Something wet streaks my trembling hands.

My skull is dizzy. Everything keeps on twirling. Nausea jolts to suffocate me. I shift my gaze to the ground and squint in still anticipation. I roll myself into a foetal position.

And then… silence. I can't hear myself breathe. I can only feel it. Air comes out in stutters.

Placing one arm in front of the other, I pull my weight forwards, slithering on all fours like an animal. My forearms sting with each movement. I can feel my flesh pulsing, but I'm too numb to care. My hair sticks to my face, leaving my skin damp and steamy.

I creep and I crawl and I'm hopeless. These frail arms, already weeping with fatigue, won't get me far, so I shift my eyes down to my knuckles. In this yellow tint it's hard to tell what colour they are.

The lumps above my fingers bulge outwards, as if the bones were poking through my skin.

My heart stops thundering. I feel at ease.

The silence becomes stiffness. Nothing moves.

I focus on my heartbeat, feeling the flow of blood popping in and out of my ears. The sky grows darker.

A tight grip grabs me around the neck and pulls me forwards into the dense swirl of sand. My eyelids won't stop fluttering. I sense itchiness on my face.

My skin bubbles up into blisters. It's texture twisting from soft into ragged and bumpy. I feel the searing sensation spreading through my chest, like a sickly warmth. My temples ignite rapidly, and the heat echoes through my head.

I can hear raspy breaths and frustrated grunts.

My eyes are narrow, facing the Constant, watching the world incinerate to ash. In frustrated heaps of breath, I groan, "You should've left *me*."

Dizziness inflates my skull, flaming my consciousness.

"You would've been better off… on your own." There's a damp quiver in my throat, and I sound manly from the deep growl I speak with. My vision blurs into a contorted flicker of yellow lines that look like fractured glass, like disconnected spider webs trying to cling to a surface.

A sharp prick digs into my flesh in my forearm. I feel the sloshing of liquid. Something flows into my blood. Blankly, I gaze down to my arm. A needle.

My chest is slammed with what feels like a hammer. My eyes snap wide. A surge of adrenaline floods my veins. I feel my breath become rhythmic.

The heat seems to drain out of my body through my fingertips. I rise, unsteady but upright. The twirling storm of debris stares at me. The lane has collapsed into a dim clutter of sand. The sky is blackening. Purple lightning zips across the sky and stabs the earth repeatedly. The inky clouds stretch thin and seep into the storm. The yellow tint of the world is fading, blending into a deep, dark brown. The colour of rot.

"Aurora, we need to get to the passageway!" The voice shouts with fury, its pitch breaking into a frightened squeal. I look down at my arm. My skin the colour of bone. There are small red bumps sticking out of my skin. My fingers twitch, desperate to scratch the irritation, but I resist the urge.

I see the tactical syringe bulging out of my forearm. I look at the letters that encase the plunger—B O L T.

That's not mine...

Tension fades from my legs, the heavy firmness of exhaustion loosening its choke over me. My fingers wrap around the syringe lodged in my arm. The sharp prick as it slides out makes me wince, but the relief is instant.

My eyes shrink. I feel Lukas's hands tugging at me. I toss the syringe aside.

"AURORA!" Lukas's voice breaks with fury. The shock jolts me back to my legs in a panic. My movements feel fast and excessively powerful. The skies crack with rapid bursts of lightning. Lukas rips the sleeve of his shirt and hands me the torn fabric. "Breathe through this."

His tone commands and doesn't suggest. I do as I'm told, pressing the rag to my mouth. My first breath is frail and shallow. The second stings less. A dry croak escapes my mouth when I try to speak.

I step forwards, biting my lower lip in fright. Once I start to transfer my weight from one leg to the other, I realise I can move just fine. I'm relieved.

Lukas watches me attentively, his arms out and ready to catch me. He lifts the collar of his shirt over his mouth and nose, trying to breathe as little of the gas as possible.

Lukas grunts, "Just follow me."

He leaps sideways, moving past a tree and then springs forwards. His movements are shadowy flickers within the storm's sandy fog. His prints are fresh and wet on the ground. I stumble after him, my steps clumsy at first. I can't keep up with him.

He runs in curves, weaving past trees and teetering on the edge of ponds. I stalk the prints on the ground, skirting over the edges of his steps while mimicking his path.

I want to collapse.

Branches snag at my arms and face. The dots on my skin slowly shred my flesh from the inside. But I force myself to ignore the agony.

I feel dreadful. Undeserving.

Lukas came back for me.

I don't know if I would have come back for him. This shameful thought twists like a knife in my gut.

My legs move faster than they should, propelled by the lingering effects of the syringe. I jump, hobble and evade the trees.

The mud in front of me grows dimmer, deepening into a suffocating brown. The fog blurs the earth, making Lukas's tracks look more like cracks in the surface. The more I breathe, the more I sense my body shutting down.

I pass by broken branches, cobwebs, bouncing pebbles and logs that have been flung across the forest. Without warning, lumps of wood shred off from the logs and lunge at me. I duck and dodge, but the clumps of wood and dirt graze my arms and face with little damage. The fragments swirl into the air, swept up by the storm that's behind me.

My hips and waist pulsate with smothering stabs. In frustrated gasps, I thrust my legs further, dashing through the forest erratically. I run fast, but my stomach thumps with scorching heat. I cough, inhale in a raspy squawk and grunt with every stammer of movement. I'm on the verge of losing balance with every sharp stride, but I keep upright, tottering ahead just barely. My arms twitch with fatigue. I drop the fabric from my mouth.

Burned air rushes through my nostrils. I feel like I'm breathing in ash. I pant and wheeze, then cough and dust flies out my mouth.

I force my body to move. Every limb retaliates in trembles. My feet are numb. I can't feel what I'm walking on, I can merely sense that I'm stumbling forwards.

I stop by a boulder and rest my weight on it. I choke on my own saliva, each breath a sharp jab at the back of my throat. I'm like a beast, growling for air.

"You're so *close!*" Lukas yells. Within the distorted hissing of the winds, it sounds like he's all around me.

I focus on the faint traces of his footprints that look like dried up puddles in the dirt. I walk away from the rocks and trees that entrap me. The forest thins, retreating into a barren path of dirt going straight.

Was this the road from before? But there were two lines of trees that surrounded me. The path stretches ahead, its surface obscured by the swirling mist.

With each breath my muscles squeeze more and more, as if the blood pumping in my veins stopped giving me air.

My vision begins to spin and displace the ground in front of me. Everything revolves in circles, leaving my head sore.

A sharp ache starts to rise from the pits of my guts to my chest. I gag, tasting scraps of bile on my tongue. One foot after another, I keep moving, I keep chasing Lukas's footsteps, steadily becoming overwhelmed by the sheer numbness of my body.

The spasm within my throat keeps me from breathing. My lungs squeal, stifled by the bronze gas.

I'm relying solely on the need to survive, my own spirit, my own willingness to live. But even my will to survive is starting to fracture, step by step, bit by bit.

Pain shoots up to my throat. I stagger to the ground, spitting and huffing for air at the same time.

A small clump of food bits and saliva trickle out of my mouth in a sticky string of dripping fluid.

My head slouches down. The temples on my face start to burn up.

"Aurora get up!"

Thunder roars across the skies, tinting the brown with streaks of crimson and purple. Each colour so dark it absorbs light and stretches into pitch black, like a dark wine. The Constant shrieks in destructive oscillations, shaking me to the core.

"I won't be able to hold the passageway any longer," he groans, impaling me with a wave of urgency.

I hear his trembling breath. He tries to silence his breaths, but that only makes him growl and puff deeper.

In anguish, Lukas squeezes the words out his mouth, "You *need* to come to me."

I drag my fingers through the dirt, gripping onto the remaining roots of trees that protrude from the withered soil. Pulling my own weight, my joints screech in agony, as dampness floods around my eyes.

I stretch my arms out and dig my fingernails as tightly as I can into the ground before pulling my body forwards. I yank and wriggle my feet. Every muscle in my body stings, like each fibre is on the brink of exploding with adrenaline.

The sandy taint of the world grows lighter in front of me, as if sunlight has pierced through the mist. Heavy and dizzy, I tramp ahead, dragging myself with every remaining ounce of strength in my body.

I catch glimpses of a shaky silhouette. The outline of the figure is blurry. I stretch my hands outwards and continue to squirm forwards. It feels like my ribs are tilting and stabbing through my flesh.

"C'mon, Aurora," Lukas snarls in a gruff voice. "Don't stop. C'mon now," he gasps. "Stay with me."

My hands vibrate in rhythm with the shaking of the ground. Steadily, the passageway breaks through the fog and enters my vision. The entire closing wall of this zone is transparent and glossy. At the bottom of it, one symbolic white panel acts as a door for the passageway.

Lukas's arms ripple in waves. His face wrinkles in dark-red colours of struggle. He holds up the white panel, his feet planted but slipping. His shoulders tremble.

Time is expiring.

I place my hands down and try to lift myself. My legs rock unsteadily once I place my weight on them. I scramble to Lukas, shuffling unevenly as my body limps forwards. Each step is a potential crash. I'm like a dead woman walking. Terror surges heartlessly across my bloodstream. Stride after stride, I reach him.

Lukas stares at me, his face trembling while veins swell in dark crimson lines, like coursing rivers. His biceps look like they're going to detonate from within. His legs are probably screaming in protest. His eyes yearn to give up. His spine begins to slump, as his knees buckle from under him. I see it all in a mere glance.

I march ahead, but my movements are sluggish. I duck down, stagger through the panel and crumple to the ground.

I can't feel my legs.

Snot rushes down my lips. I snort and grunt for breath as my lungs shake. In a hurry, I wiggle and turn my body so that I'm lying on my back.

We're in a forest, just like before. I sense the sun is vanishing from the sky, as everything dims.

The bumps on my skin rip apart my flesh. It feels like electricity is scorching holes within me. My chest rises in a thump, crushing the muscles in my neck, until I choke for air. I gurgle and moan helplessly.

Lukas shrieks, then grumbles as he lunges and stumbles away from the passageway. He falls to his knees and leans over, coughing in loud, explosive spurts like a dying animal.

The passageway seals itself in a rattle of metallic rustles. The glass wall surrounding the passageway door is engulfed by a brown, sandy whirling storm of debris. The world from before has been shattered, and now it spirals uncontrollably in an eruptive tornado. The brown gas weeps in black ghastly streaks.

What the hell am I look at? Why would someone create this? I don't understand how the Constant is a man-made storm. Its spinning and whirling create a relentless hiss that sizzles in my ears.

"Congratulations on completing Stage Two! And welcome to the Safe Zone." Enyo's voice booms everywhere around me.

Lukas won't stop coughing and wheezing, as if there's something in his throat. I want to help him.

My body rocks back and forth without my command, as the Realm continues to tremor.

The dark night sky plummets downwards with tiny white shards. Forbidden snowflakes land on my skin and then melt. My body hardens in the frost. The breeze howls slowly, gushing the world with snow.

Lukas whiffs air out in relief and lets his body fall beside me. He mutters something under his breath, but the words don't reach me.

My attention is torn to the glass wall once more.

I feel like the Constant could burst through at any second. A numb roar ignites within the storm. My ears crackle with the same crunching sounds. An awful stream of dust swishing around in circles fills the night. A never-ending hiss.

My blood freezes in my veins.

I close my eyes and sink into the cold.

26

Lukas

Obscure shades of yellow fizzle on the other side of the passageway. Crunching sparks pop out of the storm. The wind whispers gently through the grass on our side. It's quiet here.

"We made it," I grunt through long lumpy breaths, my throat grumbling with each puff of air. I rub my chest, flinching as the stiff flesh protests beneath my thumb. White dots sway down from above, softening into wet patches on my skin. My body trembles as dampness seeps into every pore. I inhale through my mouth, scrunching up my nose to avoid the frosty air. "We'll freeze out here. Let's find a place to rest."

Next to the passageway, two lampposts cast a warm ray of orange light. Aurora's head is tilted mostly into the dark. She seems to be gazing at the sky.

A gust of wind sweeps across my skin, making me shake off the cold. But the world stays quiet.

She doesn't move.

"Aurora?" I stand up and start walking over to her, half-limping from the rigid terror in my left foot. I notice dots on her skin. pink and bright-yellow bumps make her appear textured and sickly.

I ask her softly, "Can you look at me?"

But her neck won't turn, as if it were locked in its current slanted position. I wince as I slowly drop down to one knee.

"Please be okay," I mumble under my breath.

I reach out and gently turn her face towards me. Her eyes are sealed shut. Her skin is paler than the specks of snow drifting from the sky. My palm brushes her cheek. She's stone-cold, frozen stiff.

A crooked jagged gasp shoots out her lips, as if she were distressed. I look back down to her arms.

Blood trickles from the bulging spots, coating her arms in sticky streaks of crimson. Her skin starts to swell, cracking in odd lines like clay. Delicately, I scoop her into my arms. My feet wobble as I struggle to stand up while holding her.

Steadily, I spin around and scout the forest, gritting my teeth while I search for the Care Point. Pine trees loom over us, making the Safe Zone feel dark and endless. It's difficult to spot anything amongst the trees in pitch-black, but luckily I can see the faint glow of the red Care Point sign. Step by step, I stumble along the mossy patches of grass and approach the wooden hut.

As I near the Care Point, lamps flare up in a warm orange radiance. The gleam washes over the hut, illuminating its sturdy wooden boards that extend from the wall it's built into. At the front there is a counter, making it look like a rustic food stall.

"I need help," I croak. My body sways from foot to foot, stinging from the cold.

"Ajax at your service. How may I assist you?" The android beams with bright light as it comes to life, its upper body rising from its sleep state.

"She needs help," I blurt out, weak with urgency. "She's bleeding and it won't stop."

"Lay her down," Ajax replies, monotone yet assertive. "I will assess the injuries she has acquired."

Being deliberately slow and tender with her head, I lower Aurora's body onto the wooden counter. Her skin looks frozen, face stiff, eyelids pale. My breath hitches as I step back, unable to clear my mind. I can't keep my body still. I hear a buzz humming from the android, like the whir of an electric power line. A small hole opens next to Ajax's eye and ejects a thin, glass-like lens. The lens emits holographic beams of blue and green lines that hover in varying three-dimensional shapes over her body. Ajax moves from side to side, scanning her body with slow, methodical movements. At the end, cloudy white lines project from the lens, tracing the outline of Aurora's brittle bones.

She looks ensnared, her face ghostly.

"Scan complete," Ajax notes, and retreats into the back of his hut with a mechanical buzz. He reaches for the ceiling and opens a hidden hatch as wooden tiles slide to the side. A metal arm extends downward, delivering a syringe and a small black jar.

"What's wrong with her?" I gulp down my quivers. I stare at Aurora's blistered arms. The bumps scatter in a grid shape across her flesh. Beneath the swelling, her skin is chalky, and the slushy dots themselves protrude like veiny pimples.

"She's undergone exposure to inorganic arsine for a prolonged period of time. Her symptoms consist of pigmentation changes, skin lesions, muscle pain and nausea," Ajax explains in a flat pitch, making his words seem unconnected. His artificial face remains stiffly dull.

"Will she be okay?" My chest squeezes with worry.

"Certainly!" His lips curl into a jarring grin, one that's too wide to be human. Without hesitation, the android jabs the syringe into Aurora's neck.

"What are you doing?" I flinch at him, my knuckles tense with fright.

"This injection will neutralize the arsine's internal effects within ten hours," Ajax explains, his voice dreary and devoid of emotion. He hands the jar to me, and states, "Apply this cream to the affected areas of her body. It will dissolve the zit-like lumps of flesh and alleviate any discomfort. Immediate action is advised."

"Yeah, all right." My gaze drifts to her face, my heart thudding. I take the cream and slide it into my pocket.

"Please feel free to use the wooden cabin as shelter for the night. The snow will continue falling until the early hours of tomorrow morning."

Carefully, I slip one arm beneath Aurora's neck and the other under her knees. She feels heavier now... or maybe it's just the aching in my chest that won't stop. The small, wooden cabin is a single room filled with hay that merges with the Care Point's wall. The entrance doesn't have a door. As I step inside, an earthy and damp scent enters my nostrils, similar to freshly cut grass. At least it doesn't stink of faeces.

The room has no interior besides five large piles of hay at the very back. It feels more like a cattle shed than a shelter. Slowly I lower Aurora onto the haystacks, and then I crouch down and gather clumps of hay to cover her with.

That should keep her warm for now. Her chest rises and falls faintly, a fragile relief.

I take the jar out of my pocket, unbuckle the lid, and scoop some cream with my fingers. The dark cream is thick, yet smoothly textured like less viscous honey. I take Aurora's arm and gently stroke her skin, rubbing and spreading the cream until it seems to start dissolving. The cream's blackness sinks into her skin, leaving not a trace of its colour behind. I lift her other hand and do the same and then later gently caress the skin around her neck and face.

There might be bumps under her clothes...

My cheeks spark red with embarrassment.

I can't do that. I look down to the ground, lightly frightened of angering her. My palms tremble, unsure. But she'll be in pain if I don't.

Trying to keep my thoughts and feelings absent, I untie her boots and roll down her socks to check her feet. Her feet, thankfully, don't have any lumps. I put everything back on so she doesn't freeze.

Still unsure, I gently lift her shirt just enough so that I can inspect her lower ribs and abdomen and nothing more. My hands tremble. Her skin hasn't flared up and there are no bumps. Just pale, smooth skin.

She looks all right. She should be okay everywhere else too. I put down her shirt and cover her up with hay again. She's calmly asleep, her face softened by exhaustion. I take the cream and apply it to the itchiness on my wrist. It's the same arm from which I ripped the shirt sleeve. There are no bumps, but it throbs every now and again with a short, sharp spike of pain.

I can't bear to stand much longer. My knees bend and quiver from my weight. The blocks of hay are big enough for me to lay down beside her. Quietly, I climb on and lower my body next to hers. Keeping my body still I look up at the blank wooden ceiling.

I feel the occasional gust of wind surge into the cabin through the doorless gap, biting me with cold. The falling snow howls in a distant hush. Somewhere further away, the swirling rustling of the Constant can still be heard, echoing like a ghostly reminder of our fragility.

In the silence of the night, I find my mind wandering off. When I can rest, then I am free. That's what I'd like to think. But I can't call it free, when rest is an order, not a choice I made. I struggle coming to terms with this illusion of freedom. The only choice I can make is whether I will live or die. Everything else is decided for me.

Survival isn't freedom, it's instinct. I choose to live as much as I choose to breathe. I can try and stop but it doesn't matter. I impulsively desire air, just as I impulsively wish to live on. Can I call that a *choice*?

Somewhere within my blur of thoughts, my clash of beliefs and my lack of knowledge, my eyelids must've fallen, too heavy to open. Yet they feel light. Gradually the noises in my head grow quieter, fading into distant murmurs. Even breathing feels exhaustive, retreating into a subconscious rhythm I can't sense.

And then, there is only stillness.

"**H**mmr, huh, h-hold on!" A tight squeeze on my wrists jolts me awake. I blink in rapid succession, the patchy brightness of the cabin hard to get used to.

Get me the hell out of here," Aurora mumbles, her voice raspy, and slurred. She's twitching, flicking her shoulders up and down while her whole body shudders in short, erratic bursts. Aurora breathes out and then blubbers, "Don't leave me."

"I'm right here," I answer softly, hoping she'll wake up.

"No! Not again, *please!*" she shrieks, her voice splintering into a terrified screech. Her eyes flutter half-open, her pupils swoop up and disappear behind her eyelids.

"Hey, hey, it's me. I'm with you. Just relax," I plead, yet her face stays contorted in fear. It's like she's tense, expecting something to strike her.

"Help me!" Aurora croaks.

I try to wiggle my hands free, but her grasp won't let go. She tugs me closer to herself and buries her face into my chest. Her hands cling to my arms as if she'll float away if she loosens her grip.

"Please, please don't leave." Her voice shakes, as nervous fragments of air escape her mouth. Her breath is hot, damp through my shirt.

"Aurora, you need to wake up." I glance down, but I can only see the top of her head. Her hair is dark and dirty, but I don't really care. "You're all right. Everything is okay. Nobody can hurt you."

She rubs her face against my chest.

She whispers, "Stay with me, Lukas."

"I'm going nowhere."

Her grip softens, fingers falling limply from my arms. She continues to breathe in a constant rhythm. She's not waking up anytime soon.

My eyes stay narrow, still drowsy and urging me to sleep. With a tinge of guilt, I allow myself to close my eyes for a bit, as I revel in our shared warmth, her body relaxed against mine.

But my mind won't doze off again. I can't help but doubt where we're going. The Equilibrium is tortuous. The paranoia doesn't end. I keep waiting to die. For something to hit us, something that we can't escape, that we can't stop. We've been in the clasp of death so many times. We've gotten lucky again and again. But *that luck* will run out. Sooner or later we all get unlucky. When the time is right, we won't escape its pull.

I just don't know if I'll ever be ready for that moment. I have a feeling like I will lose everything. But I don't even know what I have to lose beyond my own life.

Aurora turns in her sleep, her breath brushing against my collar. I *can't* lose her.

The hollow pit in my gut deepens.

But what else is there? What else do I have to lose?

Maybe she's all there is. Maybe there's nothing else. *Maybe* that's enough.

Eventually, I can't help but drag my eyelids open. Impulsively, I look down at her arms, inspecting for any leftover bumps or bruising. But her skin looks squeaky clean. Not a spot... nothing. She remains a little pale. Probably not enough food.

I guess the cream really did work. The black jar is more than half full. I want to know if I can use it for other wounds too. I'll have to keep it.

"I'll get us something to eat," I tell her, my voice hoarse.

Aurora hums faintly in response, but she's not awake. Her face is a little crusty, slumped with exhaustion. The even shape of her eyes is charming. There's something delicate about the elegant lines of her face, something peaceful. I should let her rest.

With my ears perked nervously, I slide my arms up and twist my body around until I'm sitting upright. I unhook the water bottle from her trousers and attach it to my own. Then, I tip-toe out of the cabin, watching each foot, making sure to not step on any hay. Last thing I want is for her to wake up to the crunch of my steps.

Once I'm outside, I look back to check on her again, without thinking. It might as well be instinct.

Sunlight beams through the trees in bright golden lines. The scent is fresh and wet. It's like the air is full. It makes me feel awake. Birds whistle and chirp in cheerful tones. Along the brush of wind, leaves sway gently, rocking side to side in a flowy rhythm like they were dancing. The snow must've melted completely, because there are no patches of frost anywhere. It's like the weather completely changed overnight.

I crank my head side to side, lift my shoulders and bend to stretch my back. The sluggishness fades from my head the more that I move. I walk into the forest, looking for the nearest body of water. The mossy grass is puffy and sinks beneath my feet when I step forwards. The earth squeaks and sloshes with water. The dampness must be because of the snow. I shift my eyes to the left, where I see boulders lined up one after the other. They're fractured in splinters, with disjointed lines running down like broken spiderwebs. Beyond that the wind is weak. Yet I can pick something out. A faint hush. I walk ahead, lightly weaving between trees, trying to tread in whichever direction the noise grows louder.

I squeeze through a gap in the rocks, brushing past low bushes, as the swishing becomes clearer, a rhythmic shush. Trees curve, tilting towards something, and I find myself walking around a spiral of boulders. Right next to the ground I see water running down into the dirt. I can't see over the boulders, but the hissing of trickling water drowns out all other sound. Even when the grass squelches upon my step, I don't hear a thing. I only feel the dying vibration of air and water plunging out the bundles of moss.

Step by step, making sure not to sink into the ground or slip into any hole within the forest land, I head around the spiral, approaching the source of the noise. The rush of water surges into a greater hum. The grass becomes slippery and I slow down. The last thing I want right now is to be in wet clothes.

The rocks lead to a boulder enclosed patch of land. I trudge through the wet dirt, watching small streaks of grey mist twirl into the air, spreading warmth and humidity. My lungs take in more breaths. Deep-blue water rustles and breaks into white bubbles next to the muddy shore. My eyes sparkle, my mouth frozen and wide open in silence. I stare as massive waves of water lunge and crash into a lake. The hushing roar deafens everything else.

"I expected a small stream," I reflect, my eyebrows remaining arched upwards in astonishment. This might be a good place to clean ourselves.

I crouch down by the edge and carefully dip the bottle into the lake until it's full. The chill bites at my fingers, but it feels oddly satisfying. I attach the purifier and start the filtration process.

I won't be able to drink for a while. Staying steady, I reach down and scoop up water to wash my face. I flinch slightly at the cold but it feels rewarding. Within its dark-blue hue, I catch an obscure glimpse at my own reflection. My eyes look hollow, darkened by exhaustion. Besides that, my face looks skinny and sharp. Should be expected when you barely eat. My hair is frizzly, probably dehydrated. I splash a few handfuls of water over the top of my head and spread it across my neck and collar bone.

I grimace as the frost flows through me, exhaling in refreshing relief.

With nothing left to do but wait for the water to purify, I head back to Aurora, retracing my steps, making sure to remember the path for later.

By the time I reach the Care Point the mud on my boots has dried.

The android's gaze locks onto mine, its eyes unblinking yet watching vigilantly, unsettlingly alive.

"Good morning," Ajax greets me in his mechanical, neutral voice. "I hope you slept well."

"Not bad," I say, yawning. "I could use a couple more nights of sleep."

"Stage Three begins at noon, thus you still have three more hours to relax," Ajax suggests, his voice humming each word with a rising intonation that appears deliberately calculated, as if the android were trying to provide comfort with a warm tone it couldn't physically offer.

Three more hours is nothing. We need to eat. Clean up. Keep moving.

"That's not enough." I shrug, then narrow my eyes to focus in on his reaction. "I bet you could give us more time to rest."

Ajax smiles. "While I would love to, the parameters of the Equilibrium dictate all subjects must undergo controlled conditions."

I raise a brow. "Controlled conditions of what?"

"Everything. Examples include temporal elements, ecological balance and difficulty level."

"All right. Let me ask differently," I say, thinking for a moment. "What are these controlled conditions meant to achieve?"

"To minimize external influence."

"Influence towards what?"

"I have not been programmed to respond to that question." The unnaturally dark-blue eyes of the machine freeze stiff for a moment, as if it were stuck in deep thought. Ajax adds, "My only relevant code of instruction regarding your prompt is that I am unable to alter the Ceremony in any way, even if I'd like to help you. I may *only* provide medical assistance and allow you to purchase goods from the Care Point. I apologise."

I heave in disappointment. His apology seems soulless, more a repetition of coded manners than genuine regret.

Enyo is hiding something. The Equilibrium is meant to contain us. But why? Did we know something we weren't supposed to? Is that why our memories were taken?

"Show me the store," I say, hoping for something to chew.

Ajax projects a hologram from his palm, showing items available for purchase in a grid.

I press the grey bubble that says filter. The options... "Tools", "Clothing", and "Consumption" pop up vertically on the screen. I tap "Consumption" and scroll through different electrolyte drinks and water bottles.

The food items are all the way at the bottom—fruits, stew, cooked meat, grilled vegetables, and even soups but they all cost three hundred points.

"What's the purpose of the Equilibrium?" I probe, examining how he's programmed.

"To affirm if its subjects deserve life based on merits like courage."

"And how do you measure courage?"

Ajax pauses for a short moment, concentrating. "It's only when staring into the eyes of death, can courage be assessed." His voice sounds automated, almost like it was reciting a memorised script. "A coward shrinks and is hypnotised by his own demise. While a courageous man stares back at death, not permitting himself to be moved by the sentiment of his imminent end."

That's too vague. It's not an answer.

I ask, "So, what's my worth?"

"The Equilibrium has determined the value of a human life as strength," Ajax answers bluntly.

"And what is strength?"

"The reluctance to fail."

So they've thought of everything I could ask? I've failed to discover anything new.

I glance at the loaf of bread priced at seventy-five points. That's 50 percent more than before! I tense my jaw. My frustration simmers, but I keep my voice calm. "Why are the prices higher?"

"The prices of items increase steadily over the days of the Ceremony," Ajax explains, his robotic tone mimicking the cadence of a human. Too slow to sound authentic. Too perfect to sound human.

I tap on the loaf of bread.

If everything inflates, we'll start saving now, so that we can eat later.

If we *live* until later.

I make my way over to the cabin and carry the loaf of bread in my hands, seeing the faint trail of steam rising from it. The smell is warm. My tongue waters.

I approach the hay bale, watching my step and fighting the urge to gobble down the whole loaf.

Aurora lies still, her eyes squinting and her palm covering her face from the sun. At least she's awake.

"Hungry?"

"Where have *you* been?" Aurora hisses, her voice low and snappy.

I detach the water bottle from my waist and place it down on her stomach. "It's fresh."

She winces abruptly, squirming her body to the side. The frosty exterior of the bottle must sting. She rushes to throw the bottle aside.

"What the hell was that for?" Aurora grumbles, as she rises to a sitting position.

I fail to withhold my smirk. "To show you where I've been."

"*Tchh.*" She kisses her teeth at me. I suppose she didn't sleep her frustration off. She folds her legs, unscrews the cap and takes a few deep sips. After a moment, she breathes out in relief, wipes her lips with her shirt sleeve and lifts her head to the ceiling.

"That's really good." Her lips rise to form a smile. She brings her head back down and glances to me.

I smile back. "I'm glad."

"You sound funny. Have you had some yet?" she asks.

"Not yet," I sigh in a laugh, my throat dry.

"Oh, were you saving it for me?" she taunts playfully, her eyes glowing with anticipation.

I give in. "Something like that."

"Here." She hands the bottle back to me, a proud smile lingering at the edge of her face. That smirk broadens. Faint lines emerge on her cheeks.

I sigh out of irritated joy.

Why does she look so sweet?

I lift the bottle to my lips, embracing the coldness of the metal rim pressing into my skin. The water wakes me up, widening my eyes and getting rid of the crusty laziness I feel in my limbs.

I place the loaf of bread on her lap, and her eyes light up with delight.

"You've really taken care of me," she flaunts in a frisky cheer, lifting the bread like a trophy.

"I owe you," I admit. "For earlier."

"For carrying you *all* that way?" she asks, pleased with herself.

"Yeah, and for checking my temperature," I reply purposefully aiming to calm her down.

Her face shimmers beet red. In a hesitant manner, she shifts her eyes down, smiling with embarrassment. I climb the square hay bale and sit beside her.

"I didn't know you had dimples."

"No, I don't?" she rumbles, tilting her eyebrows downwards in confusion.

"Look for long enough, and you'll see," I reply, shrugging.

"Oh… so you've been taking long glances at me?" Aurora strikes right back. She's swift, I'll give her that.

"That's not what I meant."

She folds her arms. "As if I believe you!"

"Way to ruin a peaceful moment," I poke back, pretending to be annoyed.

"Hey! You brought it up," she fires back, cheeks still red. That's when her belly rumbles in a monstrous shriek. She squeaks awkwardly while facing away from me, "Sorry."

I choose not to tease her on this, as I'm starving just as much.

"We shouldn't let this get cold." I reach for the bread, grab it from opposite ends and gently tear it in half.

We grab one half each. I raise the warm, doughy texture to my lips and inhale in excitement. My stomach throbs in anxious desire. But I don't gulp it down. Instead, I eat slowly, small bite after small bite.

Aurora somehow eats it even more well-mannered than I, ripping off small chunks and then popping them in her mouth.

She finishes chewing and then stops eating for a second. Her eyes stay fixated on the ground.

"Thank you by the way," she whispers quietly.

"You're not the only one who's hungry." I take a large bite and groan under my breath in pleasure.

Everything is delicious when you're starving.

"Mmm." I chew in satisfied hums.

But I notice that Aurora isn't moving. She's narrowed her gaze down to the ground.

"Lukas, I..." she sighs, her voice quivering as she reluctantly takes a deep breath in. "I don't know how to say it. Just thank you for everything."

She pauses and we both stay silent. I feel unsure of how to respond. I feel the same way.

I would be dead without her.

She looks into my eyes. "I mean it."

"I know," I whisper softly. We stare into each other's eyes for a moment of solace. "I mean it too."

The cabin grows brighter as the sun rises further into the sky. Her eyes glimmer in a shade of gold. A dark-brown glow of sunlight, like the stones of amber.

We're lost, with no past and no set future. And yet, I find myself in her eyes. I find relief in being broken.

"You'll stay with me, right?" She asks the question again, like it's become our way of checking in with each other. Gently she leans her head against mine.

I close my eyes. "Always."

It's the only response there is.

It's human, this need to know, this need for reassurance. This weakness and need for one another makes me feel better. Less alone.

We stay like this, connected for a moment that feels suspended in time. I don't want to lose this.

I don't want to forget anything anymore.

I don't want to forget her.

Eventually, we separate and she takes another bite, nibbling in a hungry hurry.

She mutters, "My bread's gone cold."

There's disappointment in her tone.

"I told you to eat it quick." I smirk, continuing to munch away the remainder of my bread. My belly pleads for more, pulsing eagerly. But this is all we can afford.

Aurora says, "Some things are more important."

"I know." I nod at her. "But let's not leave with empty stomachs."

"Okay."

"I don't want to hear your stomach rumbling again." I laugh to myself.

"Okay I get it!" She nudges me out of irritation. Though I can see her grin. She rustles. "Shush already."

Having finished eating, I reach for the water bottle that's resting in between us. I drink, trying to get rid of the shallow huskiness in my throat.

Maybe if I fill myself up with water it will stop. But I need to save some for Aurora. We'll refill before we leave.

There's a splattering sizzle roaring outside, followed by the blaring voice of the announcer.

"Good morning to all subjects!" Enyo exclaims, a sense of thrill deeply submerged within her tone. "The time is ten o'clock. At midday you will have exactly until midnight to complete Stage Three. This translates to twelve hours, or more specifically four hours per zone. Once Stage Three concludes, survivors will be awarded one last Safe Zone before being led to the Final Act." Enyo then grunts in exhilarated relief and raises her voice to yell, "May you Blaze or Burn!"

This time the world falls into a rhythmic quietness without the crackling of the speakers. Birds continue humming, a cheery morning song echoing in the distance.

"Are you done?" I turn back round to her.

"Mhm," Aurora murmurs while drinking water.

"Then let's get going." I get off the hay bale, pick up the black jar, and ensure Aurora attaches the water bottle and checks that she still has her obsidian blade. Bubbling with enthusiasm, I say, "I want to show you something."

I grasp her hand and gently tug her along with me, retracing my muddy prints through the forest.

"We need to refill the bottle!" Aurora declares, puffing from the unexpected rush.

I tell her, "We will. You'll see."

The path is easier to track this time as the sun is almost directly above us, glimmering brightness onto us. The leaves scatter the rays of warmth, but only enough to faintly dim the earth below the pine trees.

The moss is dark green and bloated, making each step a light crunch. We evade fallen trees and cobwebs hanging from branches and bushes as we run across the pathless forest. Everything looks vacant, untouched by humans. Even the ponds look lively. Small grey fishes lunge away to safety in blurry groups as they sense our vibrations. The shimmering of green leaves fills me with hope, short bursts of peace.

Soon, we reach the trickling boulders.

"What's that noise?" she asks, her voice weary.

"We're safe, don't worry," I reassure her.

"Okay, but what is it?"

I glance over my shoulder. "Something beautiful."

We trod around the boulders and wriggle through the bushes, carefully watching our step to not sink into any mud. As we climb out of the wilderness and approach the tranquil hush I shift my eyes to her.

Aurora looks on silently, her mouth agape. She gazes to the waterfall, watching the burbling flow of water crash onto rocks and drizzle down to the lake. Within the dark-blue hue of the lake, the tall trees are mirrored in a wavy haze of sunlight.

"You weren't lying," she mumbles, her eyes broad and frozen in awe. Aurora bends down and drags her hand along the water. She looks back at me and smiles. "It's so pretty."

I crouch down by the water as well and slowly rub it into my face, arms, neck and chest in order to cleanse myself. Tension loosens from my skull, clearing my head and soothing my skin.

Water dribbles down from my chin, falling back into the lake. I turn my eyes to the tide of water sloshing down the rocks and crumbling into the lake in endless strafes.

Aurora comes by next to me and starts to lean over to wash herself as well.

"I never asked…" I hesitate, as she massages her face in round motions. "Is your skin okay?"

"Sort of," she replies, pouring water onto her arms.

"What do you mean sort of?" My face tenses.

"It still burns… in *certain* places," she whines quietly, sounding awfully self-conscious.

"Then why didn't you say anything? We still have the cream…" My voice trails off in bewilderment.

Did I do something wrong? I think back to when I applied the cream, trying to recollect if I made a mistake.

"Agh, I just didn't want to make a big deal out of nothing."

"It's a big deal if it hurts," I reply, firmly.

"Well, it's not like I was going to strip naked in front of you! Catch a hint," she bursts. Her face has turned red, and I can feel my own cheeks flaring up.

"Sorry," I utter timidly. Her arms look perfectly fine. "I checked your abdomen though… you were okay."

She speaks high-pitched, "I guess the gas managed to pierce through my clothes."

"I didn't want to take your clothes off while you were asleep," I tell her, slumping my shoulders sheepishly.

"It's okay. I probably would have shouted at you."

I take the cream out of my pocket and place it on the ground next to her. Then I walk away until I find a rock and sit down, facing away from her.

"What are you doing?" She chuckles.

"You should put the cream on now. It will only get worse the longer you wait."

"And you won't peek?"

"You have my word. I won't look," I tell her.

She warns me, "You better *not*."

I wouldn't lie to her. So I keep my head facing forwards the entire time, not daring to even move an inch, regardless of the swirling noises I hear splashing around from the water. There's something flustering about this whole situation. I feel shy.

I refuse to let my thoughts wander.

I sit there by myself, holding up my face in my arms. I can feel myself burning up, blushing red.

W̲e tread to the end of the forest, approaching the colossal white panels, which protect and entrap us simultaneously.

On the wall beside the passageway, there is a metal lever and a red holographic display. The lever can be lifted *open*. The red display shows the time—11:05.

We're an hour early. Best to start now and rest later. Whether that's physically or permanently.

"Should we go?" I ask her, my hand on the lever.

"Let's get this over with," she says.

I push the lever up. The white panels of the passageway screech with a mechanical rustling in its core, as if metal surfaces were grinding.

The doors open.

Before us there stand numerous pairs of walls, rising freakishly high into the sky until they graze the clouds. In front of us there are countless different entryways, kind of like tunnels or rather many individual lanes within one zone.

"What the hell…?" Aurora's voice trails off blankly.

"They all look the same," I mumble, scouting each entrance, with their grey walls and equally large entrances. The walls themselves are immensely thick. The entry gaps are so wide that when I try to look at the ones further out, a misty blur distorts the edges, making it impossible to see clearly.

We take a couple of steps forwards, unsure of what to expect. Metallic tremors ripple across the zone persistently.

The passageway to the Safe Zone closes behind us.

Suddenly, the familiar sizzling reverberates from all around us.

"Welcome to the first zone of Stage Three!" Enyo rejoices in a giggle. "The objective here is simple and clear. Find the passageway and avoid the obstacles. You may complete this while working together or separately. The choice is all yours!"

She pauses and inhales. I can sense the eagerness from her breath alone. Enyo shakes with venomous joy in her tone. "May you Blaze or Burn!"

I count the lanes. It can't be *just* choosing the right passage. And I can't help but fear the unknown obstacles waiting for us.

There is one lane in the middle, and then six lanes to both sides. Thirteen passages to choose from in total.

"Something feels off," I remark.

"It's too simple," she complains.

"Mhm." I nod.

"That means something is out there,"

I add, "And we don't know what."

I stare ahead into the middle lane, trying to see if there are any fluctuations in the straight pathway, if there's anything at all in the way up ahead. But it's like there's a limit to what I can see, as the grey bricks that make up the ground and the walls merge into a misty blur that I can't see past.

"Do you see anything?" I ask Aurora, doubting my vision.

She squints her eyes a little, trying to gape as far as she can into the distance, then says, "It's all fuzzy."

"I think we need to split up," I suggest, trying to figure how far we need to explore the lanes in order to decide which one is the right one.

"We'll be faster that way," she mumbles, reluctant but understanding what's best. "Let's not get lost."

I point to my right. "I'll take this side."

"What's the plan?"

"Run through a bit of each lane, try and spot any differences, and then meet here again."

"Okay," she agrees, subconsciously bobbing her head up and down. "But I don't want to be by myself for too long."

"I'll take that as a warning to hurry up." I laugh under my breath, trying to lighten the unease.

"You take that however you want to," she speaks, this time her voice low and serious. "You're not leaving me alone."

"All right. I wasn't planning on it."

"You better not," she persists, half-playful. We start walking away from one another, our footsteps echoing in distinct pitches. There's no other sound. Not even wind.

"Meet in the middle after," I yell out over my shoulder.

"I'll be waiting," she shouts back, putting inflexion on the last syllable to annoy me.

Yeah right… you're not faster than me.

I turn to enter the first lane on my side. Two parallel walls stretch onwards until they vanish out of sight. I can hear a faint rustling in the background, like metal clinking repeatedly. It makes me feel drifty, like when you're descending in an elevator. Maybe the air has gotten warmer. That's the only explanation I can think of.

There's nothing notable besides the dull greyness of the bricks. The sky is cloudy and very light blue, almost chalk-like. Somehow the walls don't cast a shadow, bathing the lane in an unnatural, even light.

I walk for about a hundred metres forwards. There are no irregularities. Nothing noteworthy. I jog backwards to the beginning of the first lane and venture around to the second.

While vague, the metallic clatters continue chiming. It's like the crumpling of metal is an echoing sound emerging from somewhere within the walls.

I sigh out of dreariness. I repeat this process over and over again, until I've been in all six lanes on my side. I turn back around and start heading to the middle, back where the passageway from the Safe Zone is.

The bottom of my feet are sore, likely from yesterday. Maybe I should've used some of that cream myself. I keep walking, not slowing my stride for even a moment. I'll just have to bear with the pain for the time being.

Once I start to approach the sealed white panels, I can tell there's nobody in sight.

"Hey Aurora! Are you here yet?" I call out but with no response. Maybe she hasn't come back yet.

I knew I would be faster.

To rest my legs, I sit down on the ground and stretch them out with my back against the passageway door. The white glossy panels are surprisingly not too rigid. It seems strangely flexible, as if it were plastic.

The seconds go by quickly, but each moment of waiting and anticipating feels like a short eternity.

I'm bored out of my mind. I listen to the metallic jingles, paying attention to its disorderly rhythm.

I wonder what could be causing the sound.

Sweat trickles down my forehead, aggravating my eyes. I use my shirt to wipe my face dry.

"Argh! Ergh!" I hear distant cries. They sound hoarse and croaky.

My face springs red with panic. She might be in trouble. I close my eyes and listen carefully.

"Ughh," the voice groans, in a deeply angered pitch. The noise comes from the middle lane, vibrating off the walls in a screechy echo.

She shouldn't be in there… I sprint towards her anyway, trying to ease my mind. I see her silhouette facing the other way. She's wearing a black cloak for some reason. She limps forwards, grunting in deep agony with each step. Something's off about her posture, the way she slants forwards. Even if she's hurt, it's unlike her.

"Aurora why would you come here?" I blurt out in frustration. My hands shake and I can't help but fume. "You had me worried sick. We said we'd meet back in the middle, not here. Why are you here?"

The more I walk into the middle lane, the more my breath quickens.

What could have possibly happened to her? I stress myself. Adrenaline pulses through me.

The figure in the black cloak turns around, filling me with dread. My fingers tremble. The silhouette faces me, sunlight flashing onto its body.

"How do you think we'll die?" a boy squeals deeply. He's around my age. His eyes are flaky, shifting rapidly from side to side. His brown skin looks frail, like he's feverish. Slowly, he takes off the hood of his cloak, exposing a bald, dotted scalp with pink scars. He shakes his head with great resistance, then croaks, "It's been following us every second since our birth. Patiently waiting for its moment." He pauses and then locks his eyes onto mine, as if he's staring straight through me. "We didn't know it was coming, but it's almost here now. Do you care how you die? I hope you don't... because you won't get to choose."

The boy bulges his eyes out at me and hisses in a ragged growl, "I *want* to die and I *want* it to be *quick*."

27

Aurora

Faint metallic clinks echo in the distance. It's as if metal were rubbing metal and scraping in gritty agitation.

Lukas is going to scold me if I'm late. The thought draws a brief smirk to my lips as I retrace my steps back to the passageway where we promised to meet.

I walk as the pattern of bricks repeats endlessly beneath my feet, their symmetry a tedious perfection to look at. Even the sky is hazy, a washed-out white, greying slowly, as if it were threatening to rain.

Just as I near the exit of the lane, I notice a round, shadowy tunnel inside the wall that leads this lane to the one beside it. The walls are massively thick, making the tunnel feel like a dark, narrow passage. Stripes of flickering light ripple at the far end of the tunnel, drawing me in.

The air shifts as I step inside, heavy and damp, smelling like wet grass after rain. My breath curls into steamy clouds that swirl up into the humid air. I brush my fingertips across the walls, and heat spreads into my skin, a stuffy warmth as if the rocky walls were breathing with a fever.

I'm not going to be entrapped in here. I speed up my stride and reach for the creases of light at the exit.

My palms press against the vines draped over the exit, their stiff, waxy stems resisting as I push them aside and slip into the new lane.

I feel a tug at my feet. My leg is swiftly raised, knocking me off balance and then the world flips. The ground looms above me like an inverted sky as I sway helplessly. I look down at my own body, seeing myself dangling from vines that coil around my ankles. They plummet from the wall tops, green hairy strings that loop and twist round one another.

My hands fly to shield my face, as I take in my surroundings. Leafy patches of moss protrude from the cracks in the bricks. The vines swamp the walls, making them look more like jungle trees than brick.

I try to kick my feet apart, but that only makes the vines cling tighter to my ankles. If I could reach the pocket below my knee, I could take out my obsidian knife and cut myself loose. With a sharp tension in my stomach, I fight against my weight to lift my upper body, but even when I do rise a little, my arms aren't long enough to wrap around my legs. I slump back down with a long, exasperated breath. My abdomen strains with exhaustion, but I can't waste time.

Rapidly, I swing forwards, the vines strengthening their grip over my feet as they dig into my skin. I rock more and more, my body swaying like a pendulum, whipping back and forth. Every time I hurtle closer to the tunnel, I can't help but wince out of fear, afraid my skull will smack into the wall.

My head buzzes, my eyes wide with confusion, as the world spins until colours and shapes grow foggy. I can't help but feel dizzy as I continue to thrust myself back and forth, hoping to build enough momentum to reach my pocket.

I shove my body forwards with as much force as I can gather, and then at the very peak of my swing, I hurl upwards and grasp my arms together onto the back of my thighs. I wait to lose speed, and once I do, I yank my arm up, reach for my pocket, pop the button loose and slowly wrap my fingers around the handle of the blade.

Using the sharp edge of the obsidian, I slash at the vines repeatedly, until small green tears start to peel away from where I'm slicing. I grunt with each cut, feeling the tension hardening around my legs and stomach. My arm aches as I ram it back and forth, slitting the vines with all my strength. I feel myself drooping lower and lower, until the bundle of vines snap.

Abruptly I plunge to the ground headfirst. I guard my face and use my hands to soften the landing, but the impact still batters the air out of my lungs.

I lay there, breathing heavy as relief flutters through my stomach. I sense the rigidness fading from my muscles. My knees, forearms and elbows sear from the fall. I turn to survey the lane, to make sure I'm safe.

But the emptiness of the lane bores my sight.

I look down at my palms, specks of dirt and gravel smearing my skin. I put my knife in my pocket.

A sudden surge of warm air grazes my shoulder, too fleeting to be the wind. My body tightens with fear.

"What the hell?" I leap up on impulse, jolting to the side defensively. A bundle of black fabric lies crumpled on the ground, rising and falling rhythmically. My heart trembles as I hesitate to step closer. That body is too slender, too small to be Lukas.

Cautiously, I approach and lift the black cloak covering the figure. I stare while staying completely still.

"Stop that." A soft whisper escapes a girl's lips. Her hair is a thick, inky black, falling down her back like a curtain.

Why would she not cut it off? Isn't that annoying? I frown in confusion. I couldn't maintain all that.

Her skin shines warmly in the sun, a reddish brown, glistening with sweat. Her clothes are messy and tattered, just like mine.

She shouldn't be here...

I need to find Lukas. Something's happening.

I gently reach for her shoulder and try to shake her awake.

"Hmph!" She curls her body, raising her legs until she's like a baby in a foetal position. It's as though she has a subconscious character.

I nudge her shoulder with my palm. "Get up."

She doesn't react besides making more frustrated hums. I grow agitated, and then grumble, "I'm not whoever you think I am. Hurry up and wake up!"

Still to no avail.

"Damn you," I mutter under my breath.

Out of frustration, I grasp onto both of her shoulders and wobble her body back and forth, repeatedly, until her eyes jump open. She stares at me, eyebrows slanted, her eyes wide with questions.

"Who in Statera's name are you?" she shouts, ready to pounce on me.

"Calm down." I signal my hands up and down, as I slowly back away from her. "I'm not going to harm you."

She remains quiet, keeping her eyes fixed on me. The girl rises to her feet, glaring at me with suspecting eyes the entire time.

"Do you need something?" I ask, disliking the contempt in her expression.

She shakes her head, her gaze following my every action.

"Then why are you looking at me like that?"

"I don't know you," she snarls.

She takes a few short steps in my direction. While her body may look timid, the hostility on her face doesn't fool me for a second. She's dangerous.

"My name's Aurora." I answer her previous question to hopefully get a conversation going. "I'm not here to hurt you. I just want to finish this zone."

"How did you get here?" the girl snaps.

I shrug my shoulders. "I don't know."

Fury teeters on the edge of her lips. She hisses, "Are you lying?"

"No!" I retort. I tell her the truth. "We came out of the Safe Zone, started Stage Three, then split up, and that's when I found you in this overrun lane. There weren't vines in the other ones, so I thought this path must be special."

Her face contorts with anger. "That's a lie."

"If we find Lukas, he'll tell you the same exact thing," I explain. Why is she so bold? It feels like I'm being wrongfully accused of something I didn't do.

Abruptly, she springs forwards, throwing herself at me, stretching her arms out towards my throat. She digs her fingernails into my neck, gripping onto me tight. Her shoulder slams into my sternum, sending a sharp pain rocking through my chest unexpectedly. I stagger backwards from the impact, lose my footing and collapse. It feels like air is being ripped out of my windpipe. I grunt with gurgling exhales as I prepare for the girl to jump on top of me. I lift my arms to protect my face.

"Why would you lie?" She grips my shirt and holds me up, her hands shaking with anger. She screams, "Is there anyone with you? Where's Todd?"

She squeezes harder and tighter, hoisting bits of my skin.

"I didn't lie," I groan, feeling the sting spread through my chest. I make sure she keeps her eyes on me and reach down into my pocket to grab the knife.

"Every lane is mossy and green. What nonsense are you spewing?"

I grip the handle of the blade, feeling the thumping in my chest accelerate.

"For Statera's sake, tell me the truth!" the girl grumbles, her eyes directed straight at mine.

In a flash, I swing the handle into her ribs, and thrust myself up, tossing her to the floor beside me. As she falls, I rush to jump on top of her, pressing my knees into her arms so that she can't move. I spin the knife around until I'm holding the blade inches away from her face.

Blankly, I watch her face burn up with shock as agony forces her to gasp desperately. She tries to bring her arms to her abdomen, probably to rub her ribs, but I lean forwards so that my bodyweight is all on my knees, crushing her forearms so that she can't budge.

I lower the blade to her throat, glaring into her stunned eyes. "Move wrong and you'll die."

Carefully, I apply pressure to the very tip of the blade so that she'll feel the cold touch of the obsidian gently prick her skin.

With very little tilts, she nods, too frightened to do anything else. Her face looks cloudy now.

I tell her, "I won't hesitate to take your life."

It's blunt but truthful. She didn't want to show me empathy. Why does she deserve it from me?

"Okay," she whispers, her voice wavering quietly.

Having total control over her, I take a short moment to inspect her face. I see small scars and bruises shrouding her otherwise silky skin. I'd bet she's scared. Yet still searching for any possibility to regain power. This needs to be settled, before I'm forced to stain my blade.

"I'm just like you. I just want to survive," I speak slowly, making sure she understands me. "I'm not going to hurt you if you don't hurt me."

"But you lied about the lanes…" Her voice trails off, bewildered and small.

"I didn't. I entered through *that* tunnel and then I found you." I look up to point to the path in the wall, but there's no hole. The vines are hanging over solid brick wall.

What the hell? Where did it go? I feel myself turning red a little, as I try not to freak out. The girl glances to where my finger confidently pointed to.

She arcs her eyebrows. "You couldn't have. That wall is the edge." Her face looks calm now, cheeks lifted with confusion instead. "We are inside the last lane."

Very slowly, I lift the blade away from her and then get off of her. But I don't put the knife away just yet.

"Then I guess I crossed into your side somehow." I gesture that she can get up. "The tunnel must've closed up. But I swear, I'm not lying."

She stands up and taps her clothes, flinging off any dust and dirt. The girl keeps her head down, looking sheepish.

"I… I believe you." She stumbles over her words. Then she points to the other wall of this lane. "Look."

New tunnels within the wall open up, light glinting through the vines, while the old ones seal themselves closed.

"That's… odd."

"Mhm." The girl fidgets with her hands, nervous like she was out of place.

"Do you know how to finish this zone?" I ask, unsure of how to make her feel better.

Maybe I shouldn't have threatened her?

Still, I won't put the knife away… I don't trust her.

She sways side to side, looking lost, while averting her gaze. I guess that's a no.

With her slender body and toned muscles, she looks tiny. She looks to be quite young.

There's this strange familiar sensation spreading through me. It's like warmth. A vague feeling of worry. It's like I must make sure she's okay. Like it's my responsibility.

"Do you remember my name?"

She turns to face me but refuses to look at me. Reluctantly, she bobs her head up and down.

She whispers quietly, "It's Aurora."

"What's yours?" I ask, keeping my voice gentle this time.

She mumbles, "Amy."

"Oh, both our names start with an A." I smile, trying to clear the air. I don't really know how to act casual. Technically I only know one person.

"Mhm, that's good," she murmurs.

I slide the knife into my pocket and approach her.

"Don't be afraid." I put my arms in the air to show I don't plan to do anything. "Remember what I said?"

"Yeah," she says, quietly. "I'm sorry... I was just scared."

Amy is a bit shorter than me. But up close, I can tell she's still a child. Probably around thirteen years old. I crouch down in front of her and softly take her hands. Her eyes are watery.

"I know," I assure her. "You just want to live."

Amy glances away, pouting her lower lip as she blinks stiffly, trying to keep the tears away.

"Hey, everything's going to be okay," I speak gently while catching her gaze. "Let's start finding our way out of here, mmm'kay?"

"Okay." Amy nods and wipes her eyes with her wrist.

She's a mere child. Why is she here? My blood boils at the thought of her getting hurt. Fairness isn't a quality that can be attributed to the Equilibrium.

We walk forwards, steadily heading to the end of the lane to see if we can find anything. With the cycle of reappearing tunnels, we can swiftly manoeuvre to the next lane if we find nothing.

"Amy?"

"Yes!" she answers sternly, turning to me with a serious expression, like a soldier answering orders.

I can't help but smirk. "You don't have to treat me like a general... calm down."

"But you're older..." she whispers shyly. She slouches, uncertain how to act.

Something about her shyness is sweet. It's such a distinct, familiar feeling that I'm anguished to not remember where it comes from.

Did I have a younger someone I cherished? A friend? A sibling?

If we talk normally maybe that'll soothe her a little bit. I ask, "Do you remember how old you are?"

"I don't remember much," Amy replies, her face blank. "I know stuff, but... not much about myself."

The girl stares at the ground. I can tell from the cloudiness in her gaze she's not lying.

You can't fake that emptiness.

The absence of what makes you... you. It swallows you from the inside, leaving nothing but a barren sinkhole where your whole life should be. It's hollow, that mind-numbing failure to recollect your past.

I try to steer her mind away from this and playfully ask, "So how do you know I'm older?"

"I don't." She shakes her head in denial. Her eyes flick up to mine for a second. "You just look older."

"Not sure if that's a good or bad thing." I chuckle.

"No, no! I meant like more mature and taller." She nervously smiles, panicking through her words. Amy turns away from me, her shoulders still hunched timidly.

I tap her shoulder and caress it, trying to reassure her. "You know, I'm glad you're here."

"I'm glad you didn't stab me," she responds instantly, her voice flat and serious.

I snicker, "I was close though."

"Hmm, yeah," Amy utters, so quietly her words almost vanish into the wind.

There's something so gut-wrenching about a child thanking me for not killing her. It all feels so wrong.

We walk in silence for a few paces, while the lane around us remains an expanding path of moss. Green colours cling to the grey bricks, growing darker and thicker near the base of the walls.

The sky is blue, full of soggy clouds that look like they're blackening.

Amy shifts her eyes to me before meekly glancing away, like she was afraid I'd tell her off if I caught her looking at me. That innocent fear in her eyes... its reminiscent to someone... someone I loved.

I just can't put a finger on who.

She's still a child. This is *so damn* wrong.

I feel shameful with her beside me. She's so brave, and yet I cower in fear of death. Not even knowing why I want to live so much. Is it just instinct?

Instinct means I don't need a reason. It just feels natural. Is that a reason in itself? If something is a part of your nature, does that mean you should do it? So, if wanting to live feels right, does that make it the right thing to do?

Amy clears her throat.

"Is there anything you remember?" she mutters, like a kid asking for her parents' permission, afraid they'll say no.

"I had a dream about my mother," I tell her, remembering the house I had seen in my sleep. The voices were familiar. The little boy wanted to be as tall as me. He had a bright smile. My pupils widen in recognition. "I *had* a brother."

So, Amy reminds me of my brother.

Amy's face lights up with sudden excitement.

"I remember my brother too!" she exclaims, her voice almost giddy.

"What was he like?"

"In my dreams I couldn't see his face, but he was taller than me and really, really bald!" She giggles, her lips curling into a smile.

"Really?" I smirk cheekily.

She raises her hands, drawing a massive circle in the air to illustrate.

"His head was like a ball," she says, grinning widely.

We both quietly chuckle, smiling at one another, sensing the fleeting moment of comfort passing between us. I must take care of her. I can't let that smile fade.

"Ya know my brother's just like Todd," she adds. "Todd's also bald, but his head's *really* sharp." She grins, then lifts her index finger upright, pokes the air and blurts out, "When you touch it, it stings you back!"

Her reactions are so genuine, full of pure emotion that I don't know what to do with myself. That smirk is so reminiscent it makes my chest ache.

I remember his face! My brother's smile pops into my head, as if it had always been there. My bones shake nervously, flooding me with a soft embrace of tickles around my nose. Warmth circles my eyes, making my vision a little blurry. I hide my sniffles. Remembering him has to mean something, *right?*

I steady myself and ask her, "Who's Todd?"

"My Duo," Amy replies. She looks up at me, puzzled. "Don't you have one?"

"Yeah, I do... his name's Lukas."

She smiles. "Oh, is he nice?"

"Maybe a bit... *too much*." This time I avert my eyes.

"Do you worry about him?"

"Yeah. I can't help it," I answer honestly. I catch her fidgeting with her fingers, staring at the ground again in a lost trance. I muse at the girl. "Are you worried about Todd?"

Amy hesitates, then nods stiffly.

"Is he in trouble?"

"No, nothing like that..." she stutters over her words, reluctant to say why. "It's just... just ya know, after swallowing some of that black liquid, he keeps talking about dying. He keeps saying if it wasn't for me he woulda gave up a long time ago."

I force myself to uphold my smile.

"Maybe you're his guardian?" I suggest to lighten the mood. The idea feels as empty as it sounds.

"I'm scared what he'll do without me."

I reassure her, "I'm sure he's trying to find you right now."

Amy smiles weakly, her eyes empty, drifting off into space. "I think he just wants everything to stop."

She sounds convinced.

What I don't want to tell the little girl is that maybe Todd has a point. Most of us are going to die. Maybe all of us. Suicide doesn't solve the problem, but when there are no solutions, cutting the suffering short might be the best thing to do.

But I can't afford to think like that. There's this discomfort I sense, somewhere deep within my subconscious that tells me this is wrong. That I must survive. It's weird. I don't know what my reason for living is but knowing that I have a reason is enough.

Amy snaps me out of my thoughts, pointing ahead. "Look! This is it."

I follow her finger to the flat wall at the end of the lane. "Dead end, huh?"

She nods slowly, humming, "Mhm."

Thick strands of vines entwine one another as they drape over the wall, concealing the entrance to tunnels that lead to other lanes.

Before I can suggest for us to cross into the next lane, a sharp rumble vibrates through the ground, nudging me off balance.

"Are you okay?" I shout but Amy doesn't respond.

The floor trembles in sharp jolts, like the ocean crashing against the shore.

"Why aren't you saying anything?" I ask, confused by her silence.

She steps back, keeping her body very still.

"Look over *there*," Amy grunts through tightly bit lips, her voice shaking.

A faint rustle of grass-like sloshy sounds swish from the walls. I shift my gaze to catch the vines slither upwards, revealing a second floor of tunnels.

"What the hell?" I mutter.

The new tunnels emerge in a staggered pattern, offset from the ones below. They're narrower, tighter, and just wide enough for a single person to squeeze through. There are small platforms protruding out of the wall that we can climb onto to reach the second floor.

"Aurora!" Amy's words are loud and urgent.

"I see them." I pause, paying attention to the metallic jerks I hear in the distance.

"Not there," she grumbles. "Behind you."

Why is she so mad?

I turn around, my forehead furrowed.

"What are you?" I stiffen, sensing my heart pulsing in my stomach. A dark, silver body tramples towards us, its lean figure shrouded in shadows. Bright-white rectangles glow where its eyes should be, glaring at us with malice. That thing is around three, maybe four metres tall. Its spine twists unnaturally into a metallic tube of metal chunks that imitate a torso and stretch thinly all the way up to its human-looking face.

"You are now *the hunted*!" Enyo's voice rings from the speakers, thrilled with suspense. "Your objective is to survive, hide and reach the passageway. Take a look at your predators. The Metal Grizzly is designed to follow, track and eliminate. Every three hundred seconds, one more Grizzly will join the chase."

A massive beam of light erupts into the sky, fading into the clouds above. It glints in a deep, sapphire blue, shimmering like a cruel illusion of hope.

"The passageway is located at the bottom of the beacon of light. Once there, escape the danger zone into safety. The hunt is on!" Enyo booms with excitement before preaching, "May you Blaze or Burn."

The Grizzly's legs are chunky poles that extend out from its spine and stretch into a triangle of spear tips that impale the ground with every step, clicking violently as they crush everything. Its steel body is stained with rust. Bright silver gleams from its feet where the metal has chipped away. Black, spherical joints connect the limbs, rotating unsettlingly in any direction. Instead of fingers, the Grizzly has thin daggers that clunk ominously as the creature treads towards us.

Terror crumples my bones.

What the hell is this thing? Alarm bells explode in my head, as I feel my heart hammering in my chest, making my breath grow shallow. That thing is a robotic monstrosity, yet it looks so human and animalistic. The ghastly smell of dread fills my nostrils.

"We need to run," I rasp. My eyes stay glued to the Grizzly. My breathing rattles me, but I still call out, "Amy! Get behind me."

She rushes over and digs her fingers into my shirt, her hands shaking as she does.

"I'm scared." Her voice is small.

"Just stick with me… okay?"

The Grizzly approaches us, steady and blaring in its path. Each step is ferocious, echoing back and forth across the lane, sounding like the banging of a drum. Its unnatural white eyes track us silently, its metal face vacant of expression.

"When I say now…" I pause, glimpsing to the side to see how close we are to the tunnel. It's right up ahead, a short sprint away. "…we run."

"Okay," she whispers, her breath thick with fear.

"Not yet." The Grizzly uses all three of its spear toes on each foot to thrust itself forwards. Its body sways back and forth in an unusual rhythm. I wait until the creature slants forwards, so that its weight is subsequently making it rock backwards.

I utter, "Now!"

We spin around and jolt to the tunnel. I hear the metallic clatters of the robot as it hounds after us. Its body snaps in electric buzzes with each movement. We plunge into the tunnel without looking back and run to the other end, then suddenly I grab Amy by the hand, forcing us to stop abruptly.

"What is it?" She lights up with worry, twitching with paranoia, looking back and forth.

Gently holding onto her forearms, I answer quietly, "We need to figure out how we're going to reach the passageway."

"Ya know there is a literal beam of light in the sky?" Amy grouses, her eyes bulging outwards, while she tries to keep her voice down.

"That only tells us where," I reply in a hushed voice. "We don't know what that *thing* is capable of."

"Don't we just need to run from it?" she mumbles, losing confidence in her flaming rage.

"What if it can outrun us? We need to be smart and stay safe." My tone softens as I see her shrink, fear flickering in her eyes. I take a deep breath in, then tug on her arms softly. "I'm not going to let us die, okay?"

"Okay." The little girl nods. Her eyes look determined, but beyond her gaze I know she's terrified. Her body trembles, nervously trying to shake her fears away. She's not alone. Sweat makes my palms sticky, as if fright were leaking out of me.

It's like I can hear those metallic clunks echoing in my head on loop.

Do we run? Do we stay? I question myself. I'm horrified with Amy beside me. Without her here, I'd act fast. But she's here, depending on me. My stomach tightens. I swallow dry saliva. *What the hell do I do?*

A sharp static hum pokes through at the other end of the tunnel. The head of the Grizzly leans in, searching for us. Its eyes shine bright, then they narrow and flare into a dark red. The creature digs with its sharp fingers, pummelling the ground into fragments of stone and dust. It flings its fingers towards us in a blurry motion, trying to swing the chunks of rubble at us, but they fall short.

Its blazing red eyes stare at us, as if it were studying our faces. Then it's gone.

Sharp thuds reverberate through the wall as the crashing sounds fade above us.

"He's climbing the wall!" Amy gapes at me, her face tense with panic.

I grab her hand and dash out the tunnel, heading into the new lane.

"Just run!" I scream, letting go of her hand and gazing out ahead to spot the next tunnel. The brightness of the sun stuns my vision, but I keep pressing onwards, swinging my arms and legs as quick as I can.

Rocks crumble and metal is crunched behind us. The brick walls plead for mercy, as bits and pieces are chipped off by the Grizzly's stomping.

I keep on sprinting, feeling a piercing sting tear my ribs apart. Amy stays right behind, doing her best to keep up. From her loud and vicious grunts, I can tell she's running out of strength.

Twenty metres ahead lies our next tunnel.

"Keep going!" I yell through my ragged breaths the best I can.

I risk a glance over my shoulder. The Grizzly's eyes radiate red as deep as the pulsing blaze of magma. It gallops after us like a wild gorilla, closing the gap a lot faster than I expected it to. A moment of silence passes in this discord. With a sudden rotation of my feet, I stop my momentum and leap sideways, closer to Amy.

"Just wait! Wooah!" she howls as I clutch her wrists and yank her forwards into the tunnel. I lunge right after her, skidding to a stop on my hands and knees.

"Run! Go, GO!" I roar in agony, trying to recover my balance.

Shards of rocks shatter through the air, ramming into my feet. I feel a wobble in my legs. A searing pain shoots through my ankle, and I fail to get back up.

In that split moment, Amy's gaze meets mine, her eyes terrorised with fear, as her eyes bounce up and down, fighting a rising panic. She opens her mouth to scream, but before I can hear her desperation, claws wrap around me and drag me out of the tunnel.

28

Lukas

"The hunt is on!" Enyo declares, her words dripping with amusement.

The boy glares at me, growling through his breaths, enraged like a rat with rabies. Veins bulge from his neck and forehead, ready to snap.

The predator creeps towards us, slow and calculated, its white eyes sharp with spite. The Grizzly screeches in crispy rustles with every movement. Its body a mutilated fusion of animal and machine. Wires dangle from its cylindrical spine. Rusty lumps flake off its steel limbs. The Metal Grizzly is a repugnant machine built for one purpose: killing.

A colossal string of dark-blue light beams into the sky, splitting the clouds in two.

How am I going to get to the passageway? The ground shivers restlessly, making me look back. The passage between the lanes is now a dead end. Tunnels open up within the walls. A second floor of tunnels looms above them, with platforms that we can climb onto.

Aurora. I *must* find her. To know she's safe.

"We should run," I call out to the boy, who's shaking with feverish giggles. The boy approaches me, his footsteps thudding unrhythmically.

I snap, "What is wrong with you?"

"Ya know, is there anything that ain't wrong with this place?" he croaks, his eyes wide. He steps closer, stopping a breath away from me, then hums gravelly, "*Hmm?*"

Like he was demanding an answer.

The speakers hiss in a familiar sizzle.

"May you Blaze or Burn!" Enyo's triumphant cry echoes across the lane.

I stare in utter disbelief as the Grizzly charges at us, slamming its arms down like a gorilla to propel itself forwards. The glow in its eyes shifts into a blistering red, like burning embers.

"I'm getting out of here," I mumble. I jolt my legs and head towards the wall as quickly as I can. My breaths come out in short gasps as I push onwards. I take a short glimpse at the creature chasing us. Its body is slim, tall, and broad, way too wide to follow us into a tunnel. Unless it can change form.

Just as I lunge towards the entrance to the tunnel, a sudden, rattling pull on my arm stops me. I flinch instinctively, as the boy yanks my body to himself, digging his fingers into my wrist. The Grizzly storms at us, its buzzing, metallic movements unnaturally swift.

Horror grips my throat. "What are you doing?"

"I told you," the boy grunts as he hauls my body and wraps his arms around me tightly. Without warning, he turns us both to face the incoming creature and snarls, fury laced in his voice, "You don't get to choose how you die!"

My heartbeat pops in my ears, like a bomb ticking down to detonation. Under his smothering hold, my body quivers, nausea surging through my skull. A sour taste of breakfast oozes in the back of my throat.

I exhale in short, ragged bursts of air.

The Metal Grizzly closes in. Its claws, razor-sharp, gleam with venomous intent. Its demented eyes flare in crimson. Ready to carve us into blood puzzles.

I shake my shoulders, loosening his grip a little bit.

I squeal, "You don't have to do this!"

"I… eugh, I…" he babbles, saliva dripping from his lips. "I have to. For *her*…"

The boy chuckles and mumbles in relief, believing I've accepted fate. In a twist of my torso, I drop low and ram my elbow backwards into his sternum. A crack erupts from his chest, and his mouth drops open in a startled gasp, struggling to drag air into his lungs. Without a second to spare, I hook my leg behind him and shove hard. He crumples. I ignore his groans and gagged breaths. I grab his hands and haul him across the harsh bricks. Just as the Grizzly bounces off the ground, plunging directly at us, we disappear into the tunnel. Behind us, an ear-shattering crash shakes the ground.

Everything darkens. Light pokes through the tunnel's ends. With a squawking buzz, two red dots peek into the tunnel. The rocks roar with a crunchy hum as the Grizzly grinds against the wall, trying to squeeze into the tunnel. The scarlet hue dulls as the creature exits, its shoulders too wide to fit in here.

I drop the boy's arms and let him fall to the ground with a fierce thud that kicks up a cloud of dust.

The boy croaks in a broken laugh. My veins are racing. I feel my jaw tightening with anger.

"Why did you do that?" I whisper, restraining myself from hurting him.

"No, no, NO!" he screams, his voice scratchy. I can barely see anything in the misty tunnel, but I hear him turning over and getting up. "The question is, why did *you* stop *me*?"

I feel myself throbbing with rage.

I want to hurt him.

I grind my teeth. "What is the matter with you?"

"Ya know, I think your question oughta be why I accept what's coming to me," the boy mocks me, his tone condescending. He pokes my shoulder with a finger. A finger he might lose.

"Yeah," I reply, quietly. "Whatever that means."

"Because all this means *nothin'*," he stresses. "Nothin' at all."

My face slants in confusion.

"You don't know that."

"I'm the *only* one who knows," he howls.

I won't try to change his mind. I know I can't. When he talks, there's this conviction in his voice. And his muddy eyes believe it too.

"I'll let you die," I answer, walking away to the other end of the tunnel. "Just leave me out of it."

"Don't you see?" he asks, high-pitched in disbelief.

I don't say anything. I just keep walking.

Firm and heavy, his footsteps ring behind me. Growing louder.

"Don't you see?" he asks again, quieter this time.

"See what?" I finally respond, agitated. I don't have the time for this. The Grizzly has probably figured a way to reach us by now.

"Don't you see?"

"Again, see what?" I turn around. His lips curl into a lustful grin. His fist stabs into my belly, sending a sharp pain wobbling through my gut. I pant instinctively, staggering backwards to get away from him. I shield my abdomen, and that's when he thrusts his palms into my shoulders and drops me.

"Open your eyes," he squeals, reaching down to strike again, while I scramble. My hands burn as I stumble, pushing my weight off the ground and lunging back. A few punches reach my ribs, stiffening my core until I gasp in huffs. His shadow looms over me, his face twisted with bloodlust. "Don't you see it now?!"

"What? See what?" I cry out in anger, lifting my legs to protect myself. I kick at his arms, aiming for his knuckles.

"I'm just ending your misery," he hollers, enraged. Determined, he lurches after me, using his forearms to block my kicks, trying to find a way to grab me again. The tunnel starts to grow brighter behind me.

I squirm and wriggle backwards, but I only hurt myself more the more I try to get away from him.

"It's nothin' but a favour," the boy screeches. I look above to check behind me, noticing I'm a metre away from the exit. That's when he grips both my feet and swings my legs apart. In that instance, he leaps down and wraps his hands around my throat. My skull trembles as he squeezes. "You won't have to suffer."

"Sta-op," I stutter in exhausted puffs.

His nails dig deeper into my neck, as my skin is stretched with strain. He doesn't say another word. The light coming from the end of the tunnel illuminates his face. His eyes bulge with exhilaration. Sweat dribbles from his face onto mine. A tremor shoots through the walls, the vibration rippling down my spine.

The boy's eyes flick to the tunnel exit. Instantly, I pull on the collar of his shirt and slam my head into his face. The collision echoes through my skull. A numbing sting blinds my vision for a short moment. But there's relief in my throat as air rushes down my windpipe. The boy is on his knees, leaning against a wall, both hands pressed tightly to his face.

I lean back and peep out the tunnel. I look at the sky and my face freezes in terror. A pair of red dots gleam back at me from the top of the wall, its stare stiff with menace.

"It has climbed over the wall," I stammer, my chest pounding so hard air gets stuck in my lungs. The creature springs down the wall slowly, its metallic legs shattering bricks with each gallop.

Steadily, I stand back up. One final deep breath.

I turn the corner, exit the tunnel and sprint ahead. He'll follow if he wants to live. Fear propels me forwards, my body moving faster than my thoughts. The beam in the sky looms closer now, guiding me to safety.

The boy's footsteps stay right behind me, his intentions unclear.

"You shoulda let it kill us then," he spits.

I glimpse over my shoulder. Blood gushes from his nose, streaking down his mouth. His legs stumble, but he doesn't stop.

"I promised Aurora I'd stay with her!" I recount. "You can leave your Duo to die for all I care," I yell at him, my voice jumpy. "I'm finding mine."

The boy falls silent. I race forwards, refusing to loosen up, unwilling to give up. Each step is a battle against the fire ripping through the crest of my legs.

It stings to breathe.

Reluctantly, I glance back to see the Metal Grizzly leap from the wall with unnatural agility, and transition into a brutal predator pursuing its prey.

We approach the end of the lane, and I dive into the nearest tunnel. I slump to the ground, recovering my breath. The boy scuttles in after me.

"I oughta kill you for what you just said back there!" He coughs in raspy, puffing bursts.

My eyes meet his. For a split second, recognition flickers in his eyes. The flaming dullness still resides, but buried beneath the rage, glitters a hint of humanity.

"We're almost there," I pant, my heart pummelling my ribs, threatening to break free.

A thunderous blast interrupts us as the Grizzly's claws tear into the tunnel, smashing the floor right beside us.

"Get away from 'em!" the boy gasps.

I scurry away, my head spinning as the walls around me quake violently. The creature starts to dig erratically, breaking the tunnel from the inside.

It can't reach us…

The cracking grows louder. Black, crumbling lines splinter across the bricks of the walls enclosing us.

"It will collapse!" I shout, scuffling to turn around. Chunks of stone crash down.

Shivers clash through my legs, while I leap forwards in frantic hops, trying to evade being flattened to death. In a rattling dash, we vault out of the tunnel just as the walls cave in, a roar of dust and debris erupting into the air. The ground churns violently, sending me toppling over.

C'mon, get up, get up! I whimper to myself in a panic, scrambling to my feet. My head darts towards the demolished tunnel, seeing the Grizzly crawl through, pushing the debris backwards like a dog digging in the dirt. Glowing blue particles spiral upwards, merging into a tower of light. I limp to the passageway. It opens into an empty room enclosed by three walls. The ground inside the next zone is marked by a bold, red rectangle, labelled in yellow hazardous letters: "The Danger Zone."

The boy comes up behind me, his legs bruised, shoulders slouched with fatigue.

"We need to cross over." I hobble forwards, feeling my legs ache relentlessly.

The boy stays quiet. Once we've stepped beyond the red rectangle, a static noise sizzles in the room.

"The hunt is complete! The hunted survive!" Enyo declares with a sinister hint of anticipation.

The next zone is eerily still, an empty room with no visible exits except the passageway we came through.

"Why are they not here?" the boy quivers, his face frowned with true fear for the first time since I met him.

"Elevation commences!" Enyo announces through the speakers as the passageway separates from the previous zone, closes up with four walls and starts to rise up. Wind rushes past as if we were in an open elevator. My legs wobble anxiously.

"Where is she?" the boy screams repeatedly, his eyes watery, charged with fright. He drops to the ground, his body twitching.

Suddenly the platform rocks to a halt. The passageway doors and the beacon of light return.

"You are now connected to the zone of your fellow Duo's. You are not permitted to reenter the zone. Wait for them to enter the passageway and exit the Danger Zone," Enyo says.

My chest tightens with terror.

"They'll be here any second," I say, breathing heavily.

"I just want it all to end!" the boy shrieks like he was witnessing a murder, his eyes aghast, flowing with tears.

I kneel beside him. "What happened?"

He doesn't answer. Just whimpers quietly.

"I still don't know your name."

"My mother named me Todd," he sniffles, wiping his face. His breath catches, light and shallow, and his eyes shoot upwards like he's chasing the tears back where they came from. He presses his lips together, his voice trembling. "She told me it meant good luck."

"I'm Lukas. Just breathe… all right?"

"Lukas… I'll call you Luke."

"All right."

Todd breathes heavily, his eyes trying to hold back the flow of tears like a dam.

"This is why I want it all to end!" he cries, his nose thick with snot. "Ya know." Todd turns to me, red with pain. "They killed my mum, they killed everyone, they killed 'em all." His face tenses like he's about to burst. Then he wails, "They shoulda killed *me too*."

"Who killed them?" I ask, holding him up slightly, trying to calm him down. "Slow down, you're not making sense."

"Luke, they took it all from me!" he mutters through fractured huffs and puffs, while his face creases, struggling to speak. "She's the last of my family. I've got nothin' left."

"Todd, look at me. What are you talking about?"

"They killed 'em all right in front of me, Luke!" Tears roll down his face, his voice quavering. "At least I covered her eyes. I swear to Statera, I tried to cover her eyes."

Hopeless, he just stares at the ground like he's seeing it all over again. I lift him up to a sitting position.

My voice barely a whisper. "Todd...?"

"I remember!" he sobs, wheezing helplessly as he does. He presses his palms against his hairless head.

I frown, dread gnawing at me. "Remember what?"

"My family," he squeaks with a lump in his throat. Todd looks up at me, his eyes bulging wide with fear. "Luke, I remember what they did to my family."

29

Aurora

Harsh slices rip through my torso, the pain spurting out faster than the blood. The Grizzly's claws clench in a metallic rattle, tossing my body to the side like a pit bull spitting out a chew toy. Stone grates my flesh as I slide across the ground. My shoulder aches in burning throbs. My clothes are moist with my blood.

The creature's head jerks around to find me again. The deep blaze within its eyes seems to burn redder the longer it watches me. I struggle to my feet, my hips cracking. The dark lines carved into my abdomen sting deeper with each movement.

I need to run. At the nearest wall there's an elevated tunnel. I'll just need to climb onto its platform.

In a burst of motion, the robot slings its body forwards, leaping off its legs and knuckles like a monkey sprinting to show dominance. I feel my body go cold.

I hobble backwards, my feet staggering unsteadily. Each time I put my weight down on one foot, my abdomen thumps in a scorching twitch of flesh. Step by step, I totter away to the wall. The Grizzly looms over me, casting a dark shadow that dulls everything. I stumble over and my body slams into the wall.

The creature buzzes and screeches. I turn back to see it lifting its arms, ready to shoot its claws through me. My eyes shut on their own, and my body flinches into a ball, my arms shielding my face.

"Hey! Over here!" Amy yells, tinged with rage.

What is she doing? I glance over to see her jumping up and down and waving her arms around erratically. The Grizzly snaps to face her, leaving me alone for a moment. That girl... why would she do that?

I owe her now.

"Over here, you metal freak!" Amy screams.

My heart hammering with relief, I keep thanking Amy in my head and force myself to get up, unwilling to waste a second. I wrap my arms around a clump of vines and climb it like a rope, trying to reach the platform a couple of metres above me. My arms quiver weakly. I grunt under my breath and reach for the ledge of the platform.

"Are you going to keep standing there?" Amy howls, her breath whimpering with terror. "For Statera's sake, choose who you're going after!"

Once I have a firm grip, I release the vines and push myself onto the platform. The ledge lightly brushes against my torso, prickling my abdomen with tearing pains. My stomach is warm with blood.

A trembling squeal erupts from Amy's lips. "Aurora, go now!"

The Metal Grizzly whips its head back to me. In a blur of motion, it hurtles towards me, propelling itself into the air, claws ready to slash. I roll over and, with all the strength I have left, explode into a dash and lunge deep into the narrow tunnel.

Behind me, the creature smashes into where I stood moments ago, shattering the platform into a cloud of mist. The crash seeps through the tunnel, the ground shuddering ferociously, nearly knocking me off balance. The ceiling wobbles like jelly, threatening to cave inwards. I hear a scream.

Amy?! Is she okay?

I totter forward, my body lagging behind my mind, as if my muscles were failing to read what I command. I press my palm against my stomach, lightly rubbing it to try and numb the pain away.

I need to get to Amy.

The tunnel is dim, with light poking through at the other end. Leaning against the wall, I limp to the exit, each breath stabbing through my gut. I peer out the tunnel cautiously, scanning the next lane. The wind whistles in loneliness, nothing in sight.

"Amy? Can you hear me?"

"Aurora?" Amy rejoices in a shrill gasp. The girl hesitantly pops her head out from a tunnel below me. "What do I do?!"

"I'll come down to you," I croak, my lungs shaking in agony.

"I'll help you!" she says.

I stick my palm out. "Don't move."

Her eyes glisten with a bright willingness. She bites down on her lower lip in displeasure. I grip the vines and lower myself to the ground, my waist searing intensely like someone was tearing off flesh from my bones. Am I losing too much blood? I don't believe so.

I'm worried that we're taking too long. I don't want more predators hunting us.

"I don't understand you. I'm not a little kid, ya know!" she grumbles, almost pouting in frustration. "You should have let me help."

"I know you can help," I tell her. "But, you—"

A sharp jolt of pain rumbles through my gut, forcing me to clench my teeth and close my eyes.

"Get in the tunnel," Amy commands, her face stern with determination. "Let me see how bad it is."

"We can't," I fight back, my breaths shallow.

"But if you can't run—"

I raise my voice. "There's no time!"

"Okay but listen!" she persists.

"We'll die if we stop now."

"Look..." she reaches into her pocket, her face creased in distress, desperate to show me something.

I shout at her, "We'll die."

"Then listen to me!"

"What?"

"We'll die anyways if you can't move!" Amy snaps. "I'm not going to make it alone."

"One of us is better than none."

"Just listen, you selfish pig," she grunts, exasperated. "Nobody needs to die."

Before I can answer, Amy shoves me into her tunnel. From her pocket, she pulls out a roll of bandages, unravels it and tears off a strip with her teeth.

"Hold still," she orders.

The bandages sting as they stick to my skin, but her movements are quick and practiced.

"Where'd you learn that?" I groan, quietly.

"My Duo is stupid and reckless," Amy sighs. "Just like you."

"I'm not—ouch!" I yelp as she pulls the bandage tight, her small hands tugging with no mercy.

Amy scowls. "That's for being stupid."

I blink at her, in terrified awe. She's too witty for her age. It's like she's being strong for the both of us. I breathe deeply, my pain softening into a damp throb.

I care for her more than I do for myself.

I want her to survive. I want her to keep that gentle, innocent smile. She's too good... too good to not live. Amy—the girl of love.

"Thanks," I say, swearing to protect her.

"*Mhm.*" She grins smugly. "That's what I thought."

"We need to hurry."

I peek out the tunnel, holding my breath as I inspect the new lane. The wind shivers across the grey, the vines swaying rhythmically. My stomach tightens. Silence crushes my nerves. But nothing stirs.

"Are we almost there?" Amy asks.

"Almost." I look up. "Let's move."

The beam grows brighter the closer we get. We maintain our stride, weary not to exhaust ourselves. Every few steps I look over my shoulder.

"I think… we've… escaped it," Amy mumbles. She must've noticed my constant turning.

Distant metallic crackles echo like faint whispers.

"*Maybe,*" I answer, my eyes cold with doubt. Having crossed the lane, we enter another dark and narrow tunnel.

"Is this the last one?" she asks with a hopeful smile. She stares at the daylight coming from the exit.

"I think so," I reply, my fingers trembling. The wind blows in bone-chilling slashes, prickling my skin.

Amy speeds up her pace, chuckling lightly as she heads towards the white light.

"C'mon, this is the end!" she encourages me like a cheerful bird singing and vanishing into the clouds.

"Careful!" I growl. "Wait for me."

I burst out the tunnel, panting and alarmed. But Amy stands still, gazing at the sky like she was hypnotized by the colossal beacon of light.

"It's the colour of a dove," Amy says calmly, her eyes glistening in wonder.

Below the beam, two white doors are illuminated. We're a minute's walk away. I just need to get her there.

"Three hundred seconds have passed!" Enyo's voice booms. A croaky slowness seeps into her tone. "Another Metal Grizzly joins the hunt."

Damn it! I yank Amy's hand and drag her forwards. Enyo's words dig into my skin until I choke on my own breath. We scurry to the passageway. The ground beneath us wobbles aggressively, as vibrations shudder and slosh through it. My legs squeal as I try to stay upright. Each stride squashes the flesh of my torso.

Behind us, the ground crumbles into a swirling pit of falling bricks, forming a gaping black pit. Sparks and screeches reverberate like thunder.

The second Grizzly rises from the hole in the ground. Brick dust shimmers within its skeleton of steel. Its slender limbs unfold like a scrunched-up flower petal, claws stabbing the walls to lift itself out of the ditch.

Instantly, the creature locks onto us and charges forwards. The creature uses all of its limbs as legs to vault towards us, chasing us down the lane like a spider crawling down its web to stalk its prey.

Amy's fingers squeeze my hand so tight her arm starts to tremble. A pulse of terror pounds in my chest. I can feel the bandages grow heavier as they soak more and more blood.

The wall to our left wails in a bone-rattling creak. Bricks hail from the sky like it was raining. I shift my gaze up and my pulse surges in disbelief. The first Grizzly hurls itself headfirst down from the wall, crashing into the ground with a blaring impact. The air stutters as a cloud of debris shoots up, buying us only a few moments of safety. Shudders shoot through the ground. My neck hairs stand up straight. I don't dare to stop running.

We're nearing the passageway, just around sixty metres left to go. The white doors slide apart, opening an escape path. I grip Amy's hand tighter, feeling as though if I let go, I'd lose her.

My ears wince as the rustling of metal joints haunts me. I whip my head back, catching one Grizzly rotate its upper body in a full circle, like a corpse being wrung out, round and round, its bones cracking with every turn. Two metal creatures storm after us, tauntingly glaring at us like feverish predators.

"Keep running!" Lukas yells, his voice breaking in terror. My heart flutters in relief as I spot him inside the passageway. Another boy is beside him, frozen still. I clutch Amy's hand and continue to sprint ahead.

"Behind you!" Lukas screams.

Two killing machines gallop in a clattered blur of movement. They charge like gorillas. The ground ripples to the rhythm of the Grizzlies' steps.

The passageway is just twenty metres away now. But the gap between us and the Grizzlies is closing. Adrenaline floods my veins, leaving no choice of giving up. Amy's slowing down. I'm dragging her more than she's running. Her frail body is shutting down.

"C'mon, Amy." I utter, out of breath. The grinding of metal grows louder. The ground quakes beneath our feet. "One last push."

Amy's legs stagger onwards as I pull her with me. A Metal Grizzly propels itself into the air and almost leaps over us. It lands right behind us, its claws ripping into the ground where we were a moment ago.

"I'm slowing you down," she groans, her voice filled with sorrow and exhaustion.

The beast slashes the air above us, narrowly missing us by inches.

"You're not!" I shout. Tremors bolt through my chest. I keep drawing air. But it's never enough.

I struggle to keep dragging her with me.

"Hurry up, Amy!" the other boy croaks. "Get past the gates. You still need to get past the red rectangle!"

Amy starts jogging, struggling to heave enough air in. She's too weak to run.

The creature springs ahead and pulls its claw back, ready to strike.

"C'mon!" I grunt, stumbling forwards, tugging Amy along with me.

"Ya know, you're like a sister to me," she mutters, letting go of my hand. "But I'm a big girl now. You don't have to lie to me."

"What?" I stammer.

She stays with me for a couple of paces, but as soon as I see the Grizzly begin to thrust its claws at us, Amy shoves me past the beam of light with all the strength she has.

I stumble for a couple strides and then collapse.

I look back at her, my chest rumbling with fear.

Amy smiles at me, her face young and innocent. The light shimmers around her, truly brighter and paler than the white feathers of a dove. She's like an angel.

The Metal Grizzly rams its claws and knocks Amy to the ground. She drops backwards on her head, and her arms fall to her sides, resembling the shape of a cross.

"Amy!" I scream. No, no, no. Not her. Not the little one. Not the girl of love.

Amy, I swore to protect you.

I will fight for you.

I stagger to my feet, running back to her.

In a split second, the creature grabs Amy and wraps its claws around her chest. Another arm snatches her legs. Dark colours ooze across the air. The Grizzly jerks both of its hands in opposite direction, tearing Amy's body in two.

30

Lukas

Even the wind holds its breath. The creature extracts its claws from the girl's corpse, metal rumbling as it fades out of earshot.

I hold Aurora tightly, making her look the other way. She sinks into my embrace.

"She was just… a little girl," Aurora says.

"I know," I whisper. "It's not right."

Crimson dribbles down the walls, dripping through the cracks in the stone. I can't look away.

Tissues and organs droop down the white passageway doors, leaving a trail of black and red goo. A bowl of flesh squelches, oozing out fluids through its veiny holes. Webs of blood vessels stick to the ground, wet and slithery like slugs. Strips of guts curl away from her open torso, twitching restlessly, as if her body were still pumping blood.

Her body snapped quickly. I just hope it was quick enough.

I help Aurora lie down. She squeezes my hand. "Let me be by myself. Just for a second."

"All right."

The boy shakes as he gets up. His feet edge closer to the red rectangle.

"My baby girl," Todd whimpers, short-winded.

"Don't you think about it," I tell him.

"Why should I not?" He glares, his face twisted with fury. "I have *nothin'*."

I step closer. "Are you going to let her death be for nothing?"

"Ain't I just ending my own misery?" Todd puffs out, his voice brittle, as if he were holding something in.

"Maybe." I nod. "But is that all she meant? A reason for you to die? Is that everything?"

Todd leans back, shoulders sagging.

He whispers, "She *was* everything."

"Then let her be your reason to live," I plead.

I step even closer.

Todd looks at me, his lips trembling, unsure. "How?"

"Fight for her."

His voice breaks, "Why?"

"She wouldn't want you to die."

"Oh *yeah?*" He takes a step back, his voice shrill. "I didn't want *her* to die either!"

I stay quiet. I just keep my eyes pointed at his feet.

"And ya know," he wails, the pain he had been holding back this entire time leaping out of his eyes. "That damn bloody mess of her is all I have."

I look down at Amy. Blobs of dark blood have drizzled into a pool. A triangular organ slops in streaks of yellow and green.

"You're allowed to grieve," I say, moving closer to him. "But it's no reason to die."

Todd turns back to Amy, his posture hollow.

"Why'd she die like that?" He shakes, sniffling repeatedly like he was trying to stop himself. "I wish I could have given her flowers. She loved flowers."

"Tell me more," I urge him on.

"She loved poppies. She used to pick them in May, when they bloomed pink and red."

At the mention of those colours, I can't help but to stare at the string of guts, carved out from her insides and tossed out. I feel a throb of acids rising in my mouth.

"I'd bring the vase, and she'd put water in it and gently place the flowers inside," he recounts, tears spilling down his cheeks. Slow breaths strain his voice, like he had a lump in his throat. "Every day of the summer our kitchen was bright with colour."

I walk up to him from behind and put my arms on his shoulders.

"Hold onto that memory," I say softly. "I'm sure she'd like that."

"Hmm, okay," he blurts out in between sobs. "Then I'll try."

We don't say anything for a few moments. Todd remains standing, his body sagging. He tries to be quiet, but the tears won't stop falling. He shrieks and weeps and shakes.

The stench of exposed meat crawls into my throat. I gag involuntarily, trying to gulp down the bile burning at the back of my mouth, but the uncomfortable protrusion stays there.

Todd steps back from the rectangle. I follow close behind him, hands stiff at my sides, ready to catch him. He staggers towards the end of the room where Aurora lies still, her face splattered with drying blood.

A smothered squeak rips from Todd's throat, "Oh God. Why?"

"What is it?"

His lips quiver, strained by the thought of what he's about to say. He swallows hard, hesitating.

"She died not knowing I'm her brother." Todd weeps and closes his eyes. He lets out a long, broken breath as if the air itself hurt to release. His eyes stiffen, lost in thought. "I never got the chance to tell her."

"Oh." My voice wavers. I don't know what to say.

Aurora glances up, like something's caught her attention. She wipes her face with her sleeve.

Todd crumbles to the ground and sags against a wall. He clasps his palms to his face, as quiet sobs escape his mouth, unrhythmic and ragged. He whispers, "I have no family left now."

I crouch down beside him, my chest limp with grief. My lips shuffle back and forth, dying to say something. I look at Todd, my gaze hollow. His fingers lined with scratches, his skin rough in brighter patches of dots where he's bruised himself.

"I feel like I abandoned her," he spits, choking up.

"You didn't."

He lets his hands fall. His eyes turn watery again. Then he groans, "She died not knowing I'm her brother."

"But she remembered you," Aurora snaps, her voice sharp. "She told me about you. Her brother."

Todd flinches.

"She died thinking of you," Aurora says, and this time her voice softens. "So please, stop talking."

Todd's body tightens up, like he doesn't know whether to cry or smile.

Aurora meets Todd's gaze, her eyes narrow with sorrow. There's a sparkle within them, like tears will gush out at any moment.

"She saved me," Aurora grumbles. "It should've been the other way around."

"That's the type of girl Amy is," Todd says. "She would help you with all her might even if she don't know you."

Aurora hesitates, "She was unafraid to love."

The silence that follows feels like a farewell, a memory working hard to be sustained, unforgotten. After a while, Todd's breath becomes steady again. He rubs his face and slowly stands up, like there's still an ounce of regret in his step.

"I'm going to say goodbye," Todd frets, a quiver of anger coursing through his voice. He adds, "Alone."

"I can't trust you by yourself."

"That don't matter."

"But…"

"Just please."

Todd looks at me, his eyes begging for solitude.

"All right," I reluctantly agree. You can't make someone want to live. They have to find that for themselves. "We'll wait."

Todd carefully teeters next to the red line, getting as close as he can to Amy. Steadily, he shrinks down to his knees, his hands trembling. He starts speaking to her, his words fading into distant hisses before they reach me.

Todd reaches for Amy's utility belt. Maybe as a final memory.

I turn to Aurora, catching her drying her eyes with her sleeve again. She notices me staring.

"I'm okay."

I raise my eyebrows. "Don't lie."

"I said…" she sighs in response.

"C'mere." I wave her over. She hesitates, then steps forwards. I embrace her, feeling the smallness of her frame as we share our warmth.

She shivers in my arms, her body light and gentle like it could collapse at any second.

Aurora's breath stammers, "She was so… small."

"But you tried for her, didn't you?"

"Maybe not enough?" She looks up, her face slumped.

"You did all you could."

"I don't know… I…" She leans her head against my chest, then heaves a sigh of relief. "I think I did."

I run my fingers through her hair. "If you did everything you could, then you did everything you should."

"But it doesn't feel like that." She gulps down a sob, her voice wobbling in a whisper.

"I know."

"Why did she let go?" Aurora gasps quietly, tears lingering in her eyes. "Why did she push me?"

"I don't know."

Aurora stays silent for a long moment, then buries her face deeper in my chest. "I should be dead."

I growl, "Don't say that."

She pleads, "You won't let go, *right?*"

"I'm right here."

"You'll stay with me?"

I pull her closer, afraid to promise something I can't keep. I utter again, "I'm right here."

All three of us are sitting up against a wall, trapped inside the four walls of this passageway. Todd won't shut up, even when no one talks back. He rambles about past memories, shouting that we live in wastelands.

I try not to look at Amy. My stomach clenches searingly, not enough of anything to throw up. My head feels dizzy from the stinging whiff of blood.

"I ain't lying," Todd blurts out. "We're fighting tooth and nail to scratch our way back to the surface. For what? To go back?"

I sigh, "You said this already."

"And still no word out of her."

"You're telling us dying is better than living," I retort, my skull aching with frustration.

"No, no!" he scoffs, a pitiful grin clinging to his mouth. "Luke, you ain't living. You're surviving and barely at that. There's a difference."

"Yeah," I mutter. "You would know."

"I remember our home," he fumes. "It ain't worth this struggle."

"What if everyone thought like you?" I ask.

Todd looks around, deep in thought.

"We'd all be better off," he preaches, his face rigid like he was a mad prophet.

"Was Amy better off?"

Todd doesn't answer. He stares at me, his pupils thickening. I don't let go of his gaze.

He's wrong and he's refusing to see it.

"I don't know if I have a family," I breathe in, my chest tight with the only memory I have. I still feel like Ellis and Albert are watching me. "But I want to survive to find out. And if I have no one left, then I'd survive to carry their memory into the future, so they'd have someone who remembers them."

"You won't even die for *yourself*?" Todd raises his eyebrows. "Luke, you just suffer and suffer, and it ain't for you. Pitiful."

"I survive so that I can live. That's reason enough."

"Having a reason don't make it right."

"I have a reason to survive. I don't have one to die."

"Ya know, that's because you ain't thinking, Luke." He puts a hand to his chest. "You're letting the human in you..." Then he points a finger at me. "...talk for you."

"I have purpose," I hiss, twitching with agitation.

"Purpose. Is that what I need?" Todd mocks me.

"Nobody but you can remember Amy," I snap at him, my patience thin. "She dies with you."

Todd's smile drops. His voice turns gentle, and he asks, "Suffer for her?"

"Would you not?"

He mumbles softly, "Always have."

"Then live to carry her memory. Is that not enough?"

Before Todd can say anything else, I feel a sharp scratch scraping against my back. I whip my head round to see the wall we were resting against lower into the ground.

"Three questions, three doors, and one choice!" Enyo's voice cuts through the silence, making me jump up to my feet. "Welcome to the Triad of Fear! Once you choose a door, the objective will be issued."

The wall sinks into the ground, seamlessly aligned with the bricks on the floor. We leave the passageway and enter a room that looks like a hexagon split in half. At the end of it, there are three walls, slanted at different angles with a translucent door in the middle of each. We walk forwards, noticing the inky black letters above each door.

The door on the left states, "Do you fear burning?"

Todd squints at the words. "What in Statera's name is this?"

The middle door queries, "Do you fear drowning?"

The shape of the letters has changed, almost like they're bubbly to resemble water, while before they were rounded and sharp.

Todd sighs, "We're only here to suffer."

I snap back, "Then suffer in silence."

"Just wait and see," Todd hisses, disgruntled.

The last door has scrawny letters, making the ink look like disfigured bones.

The final door questions, "Do you fear falling?"

I turn around to look at Todd and Aurora.

"Any preferences?"

"We even get to choose how we suffer." Todd chuckles.

"Is this how you mourn?" Aurora finally lashes out, glaring at Todd with a venomous spark. "You just remind everyone else of how short life is and keep on repeating the same damn nonsense over and over again!"

Todd slowly looks at Aurora, blank of expression.

"Nobody is dying with you. We want to live," Aurora shouts out, fury edged in her voice. She pauses. "Get that through your *damn skull.*"

Todd looks down.

"Mourning the dead is meaningless," he rumbles. "It won't bring them back."

Aurora's head shakes as she asks, "So you feel nothing for her?"

"What I felt for my sister don't matter no more."

I tilt my head towards him. "You cried for her though? You're not weak for wishing she was still here."

"Did it bring her back?"

"That's not the point," I fire back, my head dazed.

"There shouldn't be any other point."

I frown in disgust. "Something's wrong with you."

"We're wasting time," Aurora cuts in, grumbling like she's about to explode. She turns to me, her eyes frustrated. "He can die on his own if he wants to."

The instant she's by herself, her eyes wander off again, lost in her thoughts, like she was elsewhere. Tension lines her face into a statue. While staring off into empty space, Aurora starts to scratch her nails aggressively, ripping slivers of flesh away.

I focus on the doors again, considering our choices.

"Burning ourselves is the worst thing we can do right now," I say. "I know water sounds bad." I nervously glimpse at Aurora. "But it might be the safest option?"

"Lukas," she calls out, her eyes sharp like they were warning me not to anger her.

"Falling could mean anything?" I stress.

Aurora grunts quietly, "I am not in the mood."

"All right fine." I turn to Todd. "Any objections?"

"Ya know I don't care."

I read the text a final time. "Do you fear falling?"

I pull the handle and nudge the door open.

Flat rocks float through the air in swirling motions, lightly shaking in ripples. The right half hovers onwards, while the left half glides towards us and then loops around to repeat its journey.

With a small step, I peer down into the fall. The black glimmer of water looks back at me, its tint muddy.

Enyo announces, her tone proud. "Welcome to Saturn's Rings! As a continuous current of rocks levitate round and round, you will have to choose the right ones to cross over to safety!"

"I ain't tell a single lie," Todd whispers. "There ain't nothin' but suffering for us in this world."

Aurora groans, "Quiet."

I watch the stream of rocks sail through the air. Some are larger, steadier, while others tremble nonstop.

"Each rock has a specific weight capacity that it can hold. This is determined by size, density and sturdiness. Your objective is to judge wisely, select your rock, and then drift over to the passageway. Once you're safe, you can't go back to help your fellow subjects or the rock you're on will drop..." Enyo pauses, her words tingling with elation so much that she exhales in relief. "If you fall, you'll land in water. In fact, you can even climb back up..." she sneers. "But only if you're fast enough!"

At the edge of the cliff, metal bars descend into the dark.

"Beware, this water is far worse than the Great Waves. It's mixed with arsenic *and* epinephrine stimulants. Pure insanity in liquid form. It triggers hallucinations, impulsive behaviours and finally your heart slows and slows," Enyo intonates with anticipation. "Until it stops."

"Suffering, suffering, suffering," Todd mumbles.

Enyo roars with joy, "May you Blaze or Burn!"

I crouch at the cliff's edge, getting as close to the passing rocks as I can. I tap a few randomly, studying how much they wobble and how firmly they resist my push. The rocks closer to us are smaller and thinner, but the ones further out are thicker and shake less.

"I oughta ask, you learn anything?" Todd asks like he was interrogating me.

"Don't pretend you care," Aurora grumbles, walking past him to get closer to me.

"We don't need to rush." I swerve the conversation elsewhere. "We need to choose one and mark it,"

"Any winners?" Aurora raises her brow.

"The ones further out."

"My sister's bandages woulda been good markers." Todd shakes his head, his voice scratchy.

The boy squats down, both hands stuck to his scalp, squeezing himself until he glows pink.

"I might have some," Aurora whispers in my ear. She rolls up her shirt, showing me her waist. White bandages curl around her abdomen, stained in dark streaks of red.

"Are you all right?" I murmur, noticing the three separate lines of blood. My eyes shrink with worry. "Claws?"

"It was a close call. I got lucky."

There's no such thing as luck.

I brush my fingers against the Band-Aid and ask, "The girl?"

"Mhm," Aurora closes her eyes, twitching as she breathes out in fear. "Amy patched me up."

Gently I press the back of my hand against her ribs, a little distance away from her wounds.

She flinches hard, gasping. "It *hurts*."

"You still need them."

"But if we have nothing else?"

I assure her, "We'll think of something else."

"Fine," she mutters in frustration.

If we're just marking a rock, we can use a shirt or anything that stands out. But we're trying to leap onto the ones further away from us. We need something to hold on to.

I turn to Aurora. "Do you still have your knife?"

She hands it to me. I test the blade against a small rock floating near us. A small dent cracks in the middle.

"All right, listen," I call out to both of them, as my heart beats faster. Aurora seems to have caught the idea. But Todd stays on one knee, panting relentlessly. His hand tugs at his chest, tightly digging into his shirt.

"Todd?" I step towards him. "What's wrong?"

"Please stop this," he wails quietly, his head slumped over while he trembles. He wheezes, "They *won't* stop shooting."

"Todd look up."

"Make them stop!" he howls.

I grab his head and tilt it up to me. "Look at me."

He gasps abruptly, his eyes contracting.

"You're with us. You're here."

"They won't stop coming," he mumbles.

Aurora comes over. "What's wrong with you now?"

Todd looks up, his face crunched with exhaustion, as if he were defeated. He grunts, "I keep remembering."

"We need you with us." I help him stand up.

"Okay, thanks." He shakes my hands off himself.

"I'm here, ain't I?"

"Listen up," Aurora orders.

Once I'm sure he's found his balance I take the lead. All three of us walk over to the cliff edge. My fingers quiver as I tighten my grip around the handle of the blade.

"I'm going to go first," I say, watching the swirling oval of rocks glide round and round. There are waves of static, humming like the lone shivers of a forest talking back to you. You feel like nature's watching you.

"And we just sit around waiting for you?" Todd asks, a tight scowl over his face.

Aurora clicks her tongue in irritation.

"If I get this right," I exhale in a stammer, looking down at the sunlight fading into the murky pit of blackness, "we'll know where it's safe."

"How?" Todd spits, unconvinced.

"If the rock doesn't tip over with me, it won't drop either of you," I explain. "The knife will mark it."

I take a step back, controlling my breath as I prepare to throw myself forwards.

"Lukas," Aurora calls out. I look back, seeing her face sharp with determination. "Don't fall."

"All right."

"I got nothin' for you, Luke." Todd gives me a quizzical look. He half-shrugs. "Good luck or whatnot."

The rocks drift slowly. I keep watching until I spot a wide rock steadily soaring over to me.

Mostly flat and should be thick enough to hold me.

I puff air out over and over again, lightly bouncing on my feet, ready to jolt into a full sprint. The rock starts to swerve around the corner, shifting course to drift away from us. I bend my knees for just a moment and explode forwards. Once my feet are at the very edge of the cliff, I leap ahead, raising my right arm into the air, ready to shove the knife into the rock.

Air swishes against my face. I slam my arm down, targeting the very centre of the grey rock. The tip of the blade skates against the rock's surface, failing to pierce it. A sharp pain clangs up my abdomen, as my body crashes into the rock. My ribs rattle from the impact.

In a hurry, I grasp the top of the rock, my fingers unsteady. My feet dangle in the air. My grip loosens up as sweat precipitates along my hands. Inch by inch, I start to slip, while my skin grates against the jagged stone. I reach for the edge of rock with my other hand. But it's too far.

The blade stops moving. Then it sinks deeper into the rock. In a panicked shuffle, I grab the blade with both hands, my chest choking me with fright.

The rock tilts beneath me, its far end rising, threatening to tip over.

A strangled gasp jolts out of my throat.

I throw myself on the rock. It slants back down, wobbling side to side like it was deciding if I'm too heavy. I stay crouched, trying not to move a muscle. Shortly after, the rock stops shaking, stabilising into a steady drift.

"*Don't look down...*" I repeat to myself, freezing my head as I stare at the approaching platform. A quiet hum of air whistles past me.

My feet jiggle slightly, my heart trembling at what's beneath me. Everything in me is screaming at me, reminding me to *look down*.

The new platform is almost in range. I rise up, my knees wobbly, threatening to buckle. Once it's right in front of me, I hop on over to safety. My chest falls with relief once my feet touch the ground.

"Who's next?" I shout over.

"I'll go last," Todd yells back.

Aurora waits for the stabbed rock to float back to her. I watch her fixatedly, unable to stop the twitching in my belly. She runs, jumps and scrabbles onto it. The rock balances out, gliding along unshakeably.

Each breath is a tortuous wait. I wipe the sweat from my hands onto my shirt, but they won't dry.

The rock she's on starts to close in, swirling around the corner now. Without looking down, Aurora stands up and leaps over to the platform. I grab her arms tightly and pull her further away from the ledge.

"You all right?"

Aurora mutters, her breath weak, "I'll be fine."

I pat her back gently.

Then we wait for Todd. Once the marked rock is back on his side, he dashes at full speed and springs off the cliff's edge. His upper body lands at the jagged rim of the rock, both his arms squeezing onto the sides.

"For Statera's sake!" he yells, squabbling for breath. After a few moments of shifting his weight side to side, the rock begins to lift upwards at the far end, slumping him lower and lower, second by second. My head spins, dazed from the rush of terror. Todd grips the handle of the knife and swings his right leg back, then forwards, and then thrusts it up to the opposite end of the rock, flipping it back into a stable position. He climbs up and squats down, groaning with each exhale.

"Ya know, I thought that was it," Todd calls out, wearing a prideful smile.

"It's not over. Be careful," I warn him.

He tugs on the knife handle. "I oughta bring the blade back, right?"

"There's no need!" Aurora tells him. She walks up beside me. "Just get over here in one piece."

Todd chuckles, "It's nothin'. I'll do it."

He wraps both his hands firmly around the hilt of the knife and pulls. The blade doesn't budge.

Todd's face flushes in dark red as he grunts in failure, "How'd you get it in there so deep?"

"Just leave it," Aurora barks.

"I ain't quitting."

Todd realigns his feet, shoulder width apart, and yanks the knife with all of his weight, leaning backwards as his shoulders hunch forwards. The rock flutters erratically.

"Todd, stop that!" I scream.

He starts to approach us. The rock cracks sharply, like it might burst. But there's no visible damage.

"You have to jump soon!" I shout.

Todd's legs tremble, his knees crumpling as his body slouches down like he was collapsing in on himself. Todd shuffles in a clumsy panic, unable to find his footing.

He rips the knife free.

The rock snaps in half. The force hurls Todd backwards, and his body smashes into smaller rocks that can't hold him up. Todd slams his head against a stone. For a silent moment, he hangs there, limp. Then his body rolls over and slips away into the dark.

"Todd!" I gasp, lunging to the edge, staring down, trying to spot him.

We don't even hear the splash when he hits the water. Bubbles pop up amongst the black flicker of waves. Soon, they also disappear. The water's surface smooths over, frozen again, like nothing had ever happened.

31

Aurora

Ensnared by instinct, Lukas leaps to the cliff's edge. He stares into the dark. His eyes wander restlessly, as if he expects Todd to rise above the waves. But the water ripples like honey, viscid and rigid. By now, Todd must've sunk to the bottom. Swallowed by shadows.

"I told that damn idiot to stop!" I grumble.

Lukas grips the cliff, his arms trembling.

I mutter, "I don't understand him,"

Lukas slams his palms against the ground, grunting in frustration.

"Pointless," he spits.

Amy's smile crawls into my mind. Mentally, I try to put her back together. Stranded flesh that was once her, pale eyes, twisted bones and a growing puddle of blood. I grit my teeth. The girl of love won't leave.

"He didn't even get to talk to his sister," Lukas hisses, his voice cracking.

"She loved him."

"Did..." he hesitates, "...did she say that?"

"I could tell."

Lukas finally turns away from the cliff. "How?"

"The look in her eyes when she spoke about him."

"What did you see in her eyes?" he asks, brittle and unsure.

I recall the wide glint within her eyes. How her face arched into an immediate smile when she spoke of him. She longed for her brother because she was scared.

"She missed how safe she felt with him," I answer.

Lukas wags his head slowly. He bursts, "She was just a child."

"I think her brother was too," I note.

Lukas's voice shatters, "Aren't we all?"

"Maybe when we're scared."

Lukas stares at me, his fingers squeezing the rocks beneath him. "You're not scared?"

I place my hands on his shoulders, gently pulling him back from the ledge. He doesn't resist.

"Did you see him?" I ask, crouching beside him. His nose is stuffy, surrounded by puffy skin.

"I just saw bubbles." He sounds groggy.

"Did you hear him?"

"I can't hear anything from down there. I can barely see a thing," he replies.

"Do you think he's coming back?" I caress his shoulder with my thumb.

Lukas shakes his head.

The sky loses its brightness, darkening into a deep blue with hints of fading pinks and yellows. Clouds glow in an orange shadow that spreads across the horizon.

"Let's say goodbye," I say, patting his shoulder.

But as I turn to leave, his hand catches mine and pulls me close. His fingers are ice.

"What if that was me?" he asks.

"You wouldn't do something *so stupid*."

"But if I did?" His eyes plead for an answer.

I don't hesitate. "I'd jump in the water."

Lukas goes silent for a moment, his face narrow with frustration, like he's struggling to form his words.

"I feel like I left him to die," he whispers. "I feel guilty because…" He pauses. "I'd jump in for you, but I didn't want to jump in for him."

He swallows back his tears.

"Did Todd want to live?" I ask.

Lukas shrugs his shoulders. "It feels wrong."

"Did he ask you to save him?"

Lukas clenches his jaw. "No."

I glance up, watching the last of the sunset bleed into the night. The dark will haunt us soon.

"But he could still be alive," Lukas says, his face stiff with tension.

"Then he'll find us, won't he?" I soften my voice.

"I'm scared he'll think I betrayed him."

I frown. "You *can't* betray the dead."

His eyes find mine. "I think you can."

"Todd won't come back," I snap. "He wanted his misery to end. Let him have his wish."

Lukas watches me for a while, then nods. "All right."

Without another word, we head for the passageway. The white panel doors glide open with a whoosh, and a sudden breeze of cold air slams into us.

The sky drifts into a deep blue, only a small flicker away from blackness. There are no more clouds.

Fog seeps in through the Realm, blurring the night with misty air. My breath leaves my lips in ghostly puffs.

"Why is it so dark?" My voice shakes.

"It's winter," Lukas says, blowing hot air into his cupped hands and rubbing them together. "It always gets dark quick."

The murky haze engulfs the world, like someone had replaced the atmosphere with steam. Except that steam is cold and silver. I can't see what's ahead. We walk forwards, slow and weary. The bricks on the ground splinter into a terrain of mush. Wet dirt with stones and sand. Small cracks echo beneath my feet.

"Keep close," I say.

"I keep thinking about them." Lukas sounds like he's speaking more to himself than to me.

"I miss Amy," I say, remembering her tenacity to help me. The persistence to do what's right in the face of fear.

"I feel wrong," he frets. "Moving on so fast."

"You're not leaving him behind," I tell Lukas again, but the words feel flimsy.

"It feels like I am."

"Look." I turn to him. He gazes at me with droopy eyes. "You want to die with him?"

His face locks up. He doesn't answer.

"We can't think about them right now," I stress. "Unless we want to join them."

"I know."

"We make it through this and then we'll make them something."

Lukas raises a brow. "Like a grave?"

"Something like that." I nod. "To say goodbye."

He breathes in slowly, exhales, then mutters, "All right."

With only the sounds of each other's breath, we tread forwards, cautious with our steps. The air thickens, like there was less of it. But the further we walk, the more my skin itches with warmth.

Wind vanishes into a distant howl.

The grey blur suffocating us starts to disperse. Dark-red spots pierce through the mist. I can't tell if it's flames or a pack of animals glaring at us. The claggy brightness of the red dots looks like a dying flare in water. You can see the colour clearly, but it barely lights up anything around it.

"The ground is different." Lukas stomps his foot, and the thud echoes back and forth. "A lot more solid."

"We've entered something," I say.

A hiss spirals around us in circles, growing louder by the second. Then, a voice erupts from nowhere.

"Welcome to the last zone of Stage Three!" Enyo cheers. "Introducing the Jaws of Fire! Inside this mineshaft, pressure plates are hidden beneath your feet, that when pressed will exhaust the oxygen with shooting flames. Your objective is to follow the trail of red torches before you're smothered by the heat and smoke. May you Blaze or Burn!"

The hush disappears into a murky stillness. I can hear the jumping crackles from the torches. My own breaths echo in my ears. Nothing moves except the wavering flames. Black and red is all I see. The rest is shadows.

"Really wish I had a syringe for night vision right now," Lukas complains.

"What the hell do we do?" I ask, feeling my lungs tighten up.

"What choice do we have?" he answers, gravelly.

"None."

"Not when we're this close." He walks in front, stretching his palm out to me. "C'mon. I'll go first."

I take his hand. I can't stop myself from sweating. We interlace our fingers together, and he squeezes my hand once. Like a little push of good luck.

He gently pulls his hand away.

With this surge of reassurance, I tread carefully behind Lukas. Soon, the mineshaft's walls start to thin into a slender passage. I keep my arms by my sides, not touching anything unnecessarily. Every couple metres, another torch flickers to life above us, switching from right to left. There are many flames, but the light from them is too weak to illuminate the mine.

Lukas walks with bent knees, his posture small and hesitant. He takes one step at a time, persistently using the tip of his foot to brush and scan the ground in front of him before he decides to move.

He lifts a hand. "Wait."

"What is it?" I whisper.

Lukas whips his head around, struggling to make out the details of the cave.

"That's a nasty crawl," he says and shifts aside so that I can see past his frame. The mineshaft comes to a dead end. There's a small gap near the base of the wall that emits a faint red glow.

With a lazy slump, Lukas lowers himself to his knees and taps around the entrance of the narrow passage.

"We'll fit." He goes prone, heading in arms first, ready to slither through the tight space.

"Is it long?" I ask. The floor crunches and shifts under my weight, like it was made up of wet sand and gravel.

"I'd guess about twenty metres!" His voice reverberates in the cavity, sounding muffled and hoarse.

I crawl in, using my hands to pull myself forwards, while also shoving with the tip of my feet. My fingers clamp to damp surfaces, brushing past granular drizzles of stone. My chest is constantly squashed, forcing my heart to ripple. Each breath is shallow, dying short of fulfilling my need for air. The cave walls compress my limbs, pushing my arms in front of me, like I was in a streamlined position at the start of a swim.

"Everything all right?" Lukas shouts over. His voice sounds muted as if I had earplugs in.

"In a tight spot right now," I grunt.

"Try to shake your belly and push forwards at the same time," he suggests.

I bump my feet against the ground and wiggle onwards, passing through the narrow squeeze. Relief spreads through my ribs instantly, a lightness that allows me to move again.

"That actually worked," I utter.

Lukas says sternly, "C'mon, keep moving. I'll pull you out."

After a couple of thrusts forwards, the red light sparkling near my face tells me I'm at the exit. I grasp Lukas's hands, and he gently drags me out of the passage.

I brush the dirt off my knees, arms, and stomach, while whining, "Damn it."

"My shoulders might pop off," Lukas groans, steadily rotating his arms, his face wrinkled in agony.

"Make sure you don't leave them behind."

His face stays expressionless. But when our eyes meet, we burst into a quiet chuckle.

I get up to my feet, then crack my neck side to side, the sharp tingle of pleasure shooting through me.

Lukas takes a couple steps forwards, staying light on his feet, but then there's a click and he freezes. He turns his head slowly, his face shrouded.

"What is it? I can't see," I say.

"I've stepped on something." His words are disjointed murmurs, like they weren't a part of the same sentence.

"A pressure plate?"

"I don't know what else it could be," Lukas mutters.

I just nod unsurely. "Okay."

There needs to be something we can use to keep the pressure plate pressed down. It might require the same weight, or it might just require the necessary force to make it click. Steadily, I lower my knees to the ground and start dragging my fingers across the surface.

"Aurora, you should—"

"Before you say anything stupid…" I cut him off, my voice flat, but sharp, "…I'm not leaving you."

"But there will be fire," he complains.

"I know." I continue searching the ground.

"If you go up ahead, you'll be safer," Lukas explains, his voice strained in protest. "I'll catch up."

"You can't promise that."

"I can try," he says, earnestly, his voice shaking with worry.

"Look," I hiss back in retaliation. I glare up at him, my patience crumbling. "If I keep asking you to stay with me, that also means, I stay with you."

Lukas falls silent.

Besides a wall, my hands stumble upon fallen rocks. They must've come off the mineshaft's roof.

"Then what do we do?" he asks.

I lift the biggest rock there is, my back tilting downwards under its weight. "I'll place this down on the pressure plate, and you'll move your foot at the same time."

"And if that doesn't work?"

I breathe out, as a cold rush tingles down my spine. "Then we run."

Slouched over, I heave the rock towards him.

I look into his eyes. They stopped trembling a while ago. I guess teetering on the line of death for long enough makes you a little numb. You either deal with your problem and live, or you fail, and it's no longer your problem to deal with.

"Ready?" I ask him.

He nods.

"On the count of three," I say, stooping down as low as I can without dropping the rock.

"One." My heart slams against my ribs. "Two." In that split moment, I uncurl my fingers from the edges of the rock. "Three."

I let it drop, and Lukas leaps away from the pressure plate. And then it's silent.

"Did that work?" I ask, panting heavily.

"I don't need to know," Lukas replies, waving me over. "C'mon."

I hop over the pressure plate and stay close behind Lukas as we prepare to escape this passage. Heat sweeps across my back, like someone was puffing hot air onto me. A hum surges out in an electric buzz and then another click rings through our ears.

Suddenly, the red torches above our heads slant down in a bumbling vibration. Once they're aimed at the ground, they stop.

Lukas grabs my hand and pulls me with him as he storms ahead. We tumble across the irregular curves of the cave. The walls thunder and shake like they were screaming. The tunnel threatens to collapse with us inside it.

A ripple of tremors ruptures the stillness of the mineshaft. Flames are spat out from the torches in vicious, shimmering stabs into blackness. Pulsing swirls of amber curl across the rocky ground. The darkness ignites into an orange passage of uneven steps and crooked shadows. The air thickens, growing hot with smoke and vapour. My lungs croak in desperate squeezes for breath.

I feel Lukas's fingers crushing my palm.

The fumes brush past my ears like a rope whipping the ground over and over again. Every couple seconds, the same torch vomits out a spiral of scorching heat. Sweat trickles down my forehead, and my shirt sticks to my skin. My nostrils turn dry and stuffy, each breath searing the insides of my nose. The cave smells like charcoal, ashy and humid. All I can hear is the sizzling bursts of shooting flames.

Lukas grabs my shoulder and leans down, one hand tugging his shirt up to his face. He grunts, his voice a muffled squeak, "Cover your nose."

I lift the collar of my shirt over my mouth and nose and keep my hand pressed against the fabric.

"When the flame dies, we move on," Lukas says in between gasps. I nod, seeing no other way to escape.

The torch in front of us falls quiet, and the fire vanishes. We lunge forwards and head on to the next torch a couple of metres further down the mineshaft. Again, we wait for the molten flames to fade before we move past it. Then we do it again and again and again.

I lose count of how many torches we've passed. But the longer we're in the mineshaft, the harder it becomes to breathe, as if my lungs were being crushed from the inside. I feel like I'm drowning, like my throat is being ripped out by the heat.

Sparks spray violently into the dark.

We keep moving in between the gaps of fire, but I'm struggling to stay balanced on my feet, swaying side to side so much that my legs are threatening to topple over.

"The Jaws of Fire will swallow all prey in thirty seconds!" Enyo's voice echoes up and down the mineshaft in an eerie stillness.

We sprint ahead, stop by the flames being spewed, then once the fire dies, we rush forwards all over again. My heart starts to drum, the thudding ricocheting around my body. My skin burns from the air that pierces my flesh with ash.

"Twenty seconds left," Enyo warns us.

The torches shift. No longer predictable. They twist at erratic angles, spraying fire at the ceiling, ground or straight through the air.

We duck, then crawl and get up again.

"I can see the passageway," Lukas wheezes. "C'mon, almost there."

My stomach flares up, a stitch paralyzing my lungs. Breathing is asking for agony.

"Ten seconds remain," Enyo speaks again.

A cloud of sparks swirls behind us. I peek over my shoulder, seeing the tunnel erupt into a growing fireball.

Lukas hauls me by my hand, and we stumble over uneven stone as we leap to the passageway. Even in the darkness, its white colour gleams bright.

The passageway starts to rise from the ground, opening horizontally upwards this time.

I feel my arms throbbing with sweat.

"Open, damn it!" I slam my fists against the passage doors.

"Five."

I turn back, seeing the blaze growing into a spinning cloud of fire, its shade bright and deep crimson all at the same time.

"Four."

White dots flicker off the inferno.

"Three."

A trembling wind shoves me up against the half-open doors.

"Two."

A sudden gust sends me hurling backwards through the air into the Safe Zone. I crash into sand. The impact knocks all of the air out of my lungs, forcing me to gasp helplessly until I start to cough out the stuffiness impaling my throat.

"One."

My ears ring, muffling everything else.

I stare out through the open passage doors, watching in utter disbelief as the blaze reaches the end of the mineshaft. Blackness lights up into red, air vaporising into a growing ball of flame. Streaks of fire climb up the walls until the rock itself begins to drip in sizzling bursts. The beaming glare of the firestorm ignites into one eruption. I squint and blink involuntarily, bringing a hand up to my eyes, unable to gaze directly at the flash. I press my hand against my eyes, and I begin to see my bones through my skin. Then a hollow whistle lashes through the Safe Zone, and the flames die out into dark. The mineshaft still stands, somehow. The passageway doors fall to the ground with a massive crash. And I stay lying still, refusing to move.

My leg won't stop throbbing, like someone had put a burning cigarette to my skin and kept it there. I feel my lungs grow lighter, each breath a little less painful.

I hear my name being called. But only gargles and raspy gasps escape my throat.

Fatigue engulfs my eyelids, making my mind dreary and silent. I drop my shoulders, and the tension trickles out from my neck. I feel myself fading, but I can't fight the exhaustion any longer.

My eyes slump into blackness.

A thousand dots of light dance across the night sky. Chunks of sapphire melt together into a swirling cloud that looks like it's been frozen in time. Leaves sway gently in the corners of my vision. The darkness up above taints into brushes of purple and pink, almost like someone had painted the sky.

The cold doesn't bite, it crushes.

Am I dreaming? I ask myself, trying to shrug off the shiver slithering down my body. My eyes still feel stifled, like they may pull me back to sleep at any moment.

A campfire, filled with dying embers, illuminates the room a little. I'm lying up against a haystack, a shirt thrown on top of me to keep me warm. The cabin is full of hay and wood, but there's no roof this time around. I see the branches of trees drooping over the cabin.

Beside me, Lukas's shirtless body is curled up into a ball, his arms wrapped around himself. Next to his hands, I see a transparent tape and bandages. His head twitches in his slumber, his forehead wrinkling up with fear and confusion over and over again. Restless even in his sleep.

In that moment, a dying whistle echoes in my ears. A giant crash pummels the ground like an explosion. I stare out into the darkness beyond the cabin, where the suffocating stillness of the night glares back at me.

My neck hairs stand tall.

It's like I can see something out there. And it, too, can see me.

I feel like someone is watching me.

"Now that everybody is in the Safe Zone, I'd like to inform all subjects that the Final Act will soon commence. Everyone will be woken up by a gong," Enyo announces, a sombre tone shaking on the edge of her tongue, as if it were about to turn a lot more sinister. "To blaze or to burn… that is the question."

Her final words are like a prophecy of a choice we will make, regardless of whether we want to or not.

In his sleep, Lukas turns over to me and mutters something under his breath. I almost leap up to my feet, when I feel Lukas's arm gently embrace my waist. He wriggles closer to me in his sleep, as if he were searching for warmth. I let him hold me. I feel my face burning up. But it's the only human touch I have. And warmth is nice. I like how the heat spreads from his skin to mine.

I try to move my leg, but there's tightness around my ankle, like something's restricting movement. I reach down, only to feel the silky touch of fabric swaddled around my foot.

That explains the bandages beside him.

The grass dances with the wind. When I look back into the dark, I don't sense anything anymore. It's all black and foggy and cold. I must've been paranoid.

Quietly, I inspect Lukas's face, then his arms, and slowly I move my way up to his chest. His shoulders are bruised, his palms and knuckles rough to the touch, and the wound in his chest is enveloped with a scab. I pull his shirt over his head and gently push his arms through the sleeves, tugging it down until he's wearing it properly. I wince nervously, hoping I haven't awakened him, but he doesn't budge.

He sleeps completely still. Only his chest rises and falls, alongside the faint sounds of his breath.

I lie down next to him, letting us press against one another for warmth. I lean in towards his face. Watching him breathe in and out. The peaceful emptiness that engulfs his expression makes me smile. I glide my hand down his cheek. His skin feels cool and smooth. In the cold and the dark, with nothing but the hum of nature, I can confess this much to him, *Thank you, for everything.*

My head feels dizzy again. Heavy with fatigue.

Once again, I sense myself fading in and out of consciousness. At one point, I hear the cracking of flame. Lukas throws more wood onto a small campfire he started inside the cabin. He sits on the ground and hugs his knees, rocking back and forth, his breath erratic and shaky. Lone by the fire, his shadow flickers behind him.

"Forgive me," Lukas shrieks, his voice watery. It's like he's screaming and hushing himself all at once. "Back then, I couldn't save anybody," he hisses and trembles. "And now I'm still the same. Forgive me."

Lukas stays by the fire, slouched over with sorrow, looking out into dark, his body stiff like a statue.

Snow begins to fall. The flakes that blow into the cabin melt as soon as they touch the ground. Lukas shuffles back up and collapses beside me. Eventually his breathing slows, steady again.

"Stay with me," I whisper, clinging closer to him.

I long for warmth.

Last thing I can recall is the leaves swaying in rhythm with the wind.

32

Lukas

Nearby the air clangs and ripples. A gong screams. My eyelids press down tightly, unliftable. I can sense the slothfulness stuck in my muscles.

Fatigue drags me back to sleep.

A tremor bursts through the ground, disrupting my stillness. Then the gong bangs again.

Adrenaline stabs through my veins, forcing my eyes to flutter open. I can feel my mind wobbling in a panic, struggling to come to its senses, still dreary and tired. My eyelashes distort everything into a shimmer of blurry shapes and colours. A resonant clangour rumbles through the air again, pushing me awake.

I spot lines of red light glinting at me. A small clock hanging on the doorway reads 02:44.

I look outside. Darkness caresses the landscape of the Safe Zone. Snow has piled up overnight. The wind howls and shoves the frost inside. A small campfire sizzles in the middle of the cabin, its embers glowing red, specks flying across the room like petals.

"Have you come back to the world of the living?" Aurora speaks softly, getting off a haybale behind me. "That gong's been shouting for quite some time," she adds, getting closer. "You were as dead as a rock."

"Why didn't you wake me up?" I groan, sitting upright to stretch my neck.

"You looked tired." She smirks, crouching down beside me.

"That doesn't matter, you know…" I trail off, startled by her gaze. She leans in. Her hot breath bounces against me. Heat rushes to my face. I drop my head.

"What?" she asks, clueless.

"Nothing," I mutter. "Thank you then."

Aurora waves her hand, as if to say *don't worry*.

"We're even," she says, pointing to her foot.

I've barely registered what she meant before she moves closer and rests her head against me.

"What are you doing?" My heart pounds faster.

Aurora chuckles. "Stealing your warmth."

I don't say anything for a moment. Her head is light on my shoulder. Her hair tickles my neck. I stiffen my frame, afraid to disturb her position. My mind is fuzzy, stinging lightly from the lack of sleep. We watch the fire crackling in front of us. Its flames dazzle in orange flickers, slowly shrinking from the cold.

"How much time do we have left?" I ask.

"Until three," she drawls.

"All right."

We'll have to visit the Care Point before leaving. Maybe get some water or something to chew on.

Suddenly, Aurora lifts herself off my shoulder and straightens up, her eyes never letting go of the fire. She wraps her arms around her knees. In a reluctant sigh, she opens her mouth like she's about to say something. But nothing comes out.

"Something bothering you?" I ask, quietly.

Aurora finally shifts her gaze to me, her voice shy. "Remember I promised we'd say goodbye?"

I nod.

"We can't do much" She hesitates, then lifts the hem of her shirt. The bandages on her waist are stained a rusty crimson. "But maybe we could burn these bandages Amy gave me. As a farewell."

"All right," I reply. "Let's send them off."

Slowly Aurora peels the bandages off her torso and wraps them into a ball. Then she drops it on top of the flame.

A final reminder that Amy and Todd were here.

Red sparks rise from the fire. The corners of the fabric wrinkle up and shrivel in the heat, its colour fading to black.

Aurora looks down, her hands unsteady. Under her breath, she whispers, "Now we carry you with us."

I breathe out.

"I hope they find peace." My voice shakes. "May they find each other again." I pause, my eyes quivering. "To tell each other everything that was left unsaid."

Aurora trembles with every breath. "I hope Amy can keep smiling."

I know she's holding back tears.

I take her by the hand. "She will."

Our eyes meet. Aurora's fingers close around mine, squeezing me as tightly as she can.

"Those around us make us who we are," I tell her. "That's why we live on through each other."

Aurora keeps looking at me, her face a little calmer. It's like she's still scared, but she's strong enough to acknowledge it, strong enough not to hide.

"So, we become memories, and we live on as memories," she says, her eyes longing for an answer. "And I guess we'll all be forgotten one day. We die as memories."

"That's how it's meant to be," I reply softly. "Our memories and feelings will always have existed." I pause, smiling gently. "But we belong here, where we are right now. Not later. The future is for the future."

She nods and after a moment of silence, confesses, "I guess I just want to be remembered."

Aurora looks at me with glossy eyes, eyes that shake with terror and gleam with hope.

"Being forgotten sounds scary," I agree. "But I don't need to remember you if you're right here. I don't want you to become a memory. I want you *right here*."

She squeezes my hand even tighter.

"Don't you dare let go," she says sharply.

"I won't."

Aurora looks deeply into my eyes, her fingers trembling as they squash mine. "Stay with me."

"Always."

Our unspoken wish is an empty promise. But that emptiness clings onto hope. So I cling onto our promise.

We stay connected in silence. Holding onto the moment while we still can.

"Ten minutes remain until the Final Act." Enyo sounds too indifferent. The lack of explosiveness in her voice makes it seem like she's bored of waiting. That leaves me unsettled. As if something's not right.

In the sky, red lines fizzle into sparks, like someone had just bought something from the Care Point.

"What hell was that?" Aurora winces in confusion.

"I think it's to start our ten minutes," I say, rising to my feet. "We should head over to Ajax anyway."

"I guess so." She gets up.

The snow compresses beneath our feet, crunching smoothly with each step. White flakes invade the night sky, drifting down like they were falling in slow motion. I rub my arms together, fighting off the shivers. Even without the wind, the air stings us with its icy touch. Misty clouds of breath escape our mouths. But the night isn't so dark anymore. It's quiet and vivid. The trees look frozen, their branches entrapped by the frost. The Safe Zone is a small lane this time, with only a cabin, the Care Point and the final passageway. It doesn't look any narrower than before, but there's no forest to hunt in anymore, just a few trees perching along the path to the exit.

The moon glows bone white, with patterns of cloudy ridges carved into its surface. It's full, looking like a smaller sun. A hopeful glint in the dark.

"Welcome back, Lukas and Aurora! How may I be of assistance?" Ajax buzzes in his usual, unnaturally bouncy voice. His counter is fresh with slashes, like wild cats had clawed away at the wood. Before I can ask what happened, Ajax unfurls his fingers from a balled-up fist, and the holographic store flares to life.

"Your Duo has acquired a Survival Score of 1,050 points. Is there anything you wish to purchase?"

I look through the items, which range from water to food to clothing and a new category called specials.

"What the hell is that?" Aurora points to a special item, a syringe with a red vial in the chamber. She reads its name aloud, "The Resurrector... damn nonsense."

There are three special items, a rifle, a pistol and this syringe. The Resurrector's description states:

> Heals wounds, bruises and biochemical damage.
> Overwhelms the user with adrenaline, optimising

decision-making and unlocking full physical capacity. However, Tactical Syringes cannot be used alongside the Resurrector as an overflow of performance enhancing narcotics will cause an overdose. In such a scenario, the nervous system will shut down resulting in brain death.

It's basically the ultimate tactical syringe.

I check my belt. "I still have one syringe left."

"I still have t-two," Aurora notes, shivering.

"Then we don't need it."

"But why would we need weapons?" She tilts her head uncomfortably, her brows furrowed. She stomps her feet.

"*Ajax?*" I muse.

"The laws of the Final Act paradigm declare..." Ajax freezes, and his eyes flicker. "I'm not permitted to answer."

"Never mind," I mutter. "Something warm would help, right?"

"Hur-rry up," Aurora grumbles, her voice quivering yet still angry.

I swipe to the winter clothing options, which range from fuzzy jackets to shoes of leather or fur, to heat-sustaining shirts, to scarves and gloves. I spot a black turtleneck that is described as a thermal.

Our cargo trousers and boots are a good fit for winter. But our thin, long-sleeved shirts... not so much.

"Is this okay?" I tap on the turtlenecks, which are five hundred Survival Points each.

"Yeah, anything warm." Aurora trembles.

I press the plus symbol once to make it two turtlenecks and select "Purchase."

Red flares shoot into the sky, dying out in a zigzag of shimmers.

"Give me one already, damn it!" Aurora moans, unable to stop pounding her feet on the snow. I shift my gaze back down to the front desk, seeing Ajax holding out the two turtlenecks.

I grab one and throw it to her. "Put it on before you turn to ice."

"I'm going back to the cabin," she insists, pressing the turtleneck against her chest. "Don't follow me."

"All right. I'll wait at the passageway."

Once she disappears inside the cabin, I strip off my own shirt, wincing at the touch of the fabric as it grazes my shoulders. The unnatural heat on my neck and shoulders feels like it's searing through my flesh. Burns.

Snowflakes brush against my skin, leaving the sensation of a cool breeze.

I quickly put on the turtleneck, stretching out my arms in an effort to get used to the skin-tight squeeze it imposes on me. My neck throbs uncomfortably, itching from the material. But I'm warm, almost like my body heat can't escape.

I make my way over to the passageway. The white doors stand pristine, yet I feel so grim next to them.

Aurora strides through the snow, looking a lot better now than before. The turtleneck clings to her slender figure, accentuating her densely muscular frame.

"Are you ready?" Aurora asks, as she takes her final steps towards me.

"How can I be ready?"

She smirks. "Because you always look so brave."

"Not brave." I shake my head. "I'm just scared."

She gazes deep into my eyes, her face not happy but heavy. Like she's dying to tell me something.

"I'm scared too, Lukas." She grabs my hands and looks down. "But when you're the face I see after each time I escape death... when you're carrying me when I'm hurt, holding me when I need you," she says softly, dropping her head against my chest, unable to stop herself from shaking. "When we're together like this after everything," she murmurs. "And when I still see your face now…" Her voice trembles, but she looks up and our eyes connect. "…I feel *hope.*"

I stay quiet. I don't know what it is I feel, but my lips form a nervous smile on their own. Suddenly the fear twisting in my gut uncurls into a light warmth.

I rest my head against hers. And I clutch her tight, afraid of the moment when I'll need to let go.

"I feel it too," I whisper. I wish I had the courage to tell her everything I feel. To promise her that I'll always stay with her.

But in this moment, our shared warmth and our fears and our hopes just feel right in silence. A final plea to see each other again after this is over. In my short memory, this is the first time I've felt it. I don't know if it's out of care, or out of fear. I don't know why or how. But I know this feeling is love.

"Ten seconds remain until the Final Act!" Enyo exclaims, a sense of thrill surging through her voice once more. "From this point onwards, each subject is on their own. Survival is individual."

The passageway doors slide away from one another, revealing an opaque wall with three different silver doors.

"One subject per entryway," Enyo instructs us, her tone flat.

"There's only two of us," she says with hesitation.

I just shrug, as confused as she is.

"Anyway, it looks like we're being separated," I note, glancing at Aurora, my chest beating slowly.

She looks at me, unwavering. Her eyes glimmer in the moonlight, filled with desperation, overflowing with dreams. I can feel the air shiver as I breathe out.

I'm scared… all right? I'm more scared than I've ever been. I think we're both terrified of what's to come.

For a moment I feel like I've been here before, like me and her have met eyes while being separated once before. Sometime before here. Yet the suspicion vanishes away as quickly as it had come.

"Good luck, Lukas," she whispers. "I guess I'll see you on the other side."

"You will."

Aurora glances at me a final time. "Remember your promise to me?"

I nod.

Aurora turns away to face her door. Her expression hardens into concentration. Her voice goes almost silent. "Don't break it."

The silver doors click open and we step inside, leaving each other alone. I swear I can hear the thudding of distant footsteps behind me. Then, they also disappear. The silver door smacks shut behind me, the slam echoing like it had almost flown off its hinges.

"Follow the light," Enyo orders.

A white dot sparks to life in the distance, illuminating the dark passage. I skid my fingers against the walls, feeling their smooth and slippery texture. Everything around me is made of colourless glass. Nothing to be seen through it.

The instant I catch up to the spark, the tunnel flickers to black and another dot lights up even further away. It feels like I'm chasing a butterfly.

"Let the light guide you."

The longer I walk, the harder it becomes to stay calm. I don't know what's waiting for me. And that makes everything so much worse.

I reach the light, and the world dims to blackness. Suddenly, I'm submerged by clicks and clangs, but I don't dare move. It feels like I'm swirling, like the ground beneath my feet is spinning. The walls hum with electricity, the buzz rotating as if it were constantly swinging close by me and then away from me and then back to me. A screech pierces my ears, like glass had shattered all around me.

"Congratulations. This is the Final Act of the Equilibrium."

Glass bursts into shards like thin sheets of ice cracking over and over again. It's still pitch black. Breath by breath, my chest turns heavier.

What is happening? My eyes widen, alert and paranoid.

"Without further ado, I'd like to welcome you…" Enyo jabbers. "To the Maze of Nightmares!"

Her scream echoes up and down the passage.

My skin swarms with goosebumps. I hold my breath in anticipation.

Then, a dim light bulb flashes above me and stays on. The room is ghostly white, as if the air itself had turned into a milky powder. I glance up and my eyes turn to statues. I see myself staring back at me.

Rapidly, I turn right to left, but no matter how much I turn or where I look, all I see is myself. The walls crook at odd angles, parts of it slanting up, parts of it drooping down. But no matter where my eyes go, my own reflections stalk me.

"Your next enemy is yourself. Escape your own mind," Enyo declares. "Shake through your worst fears and quake through your cursed tears. Your nightmares are here!"

Lightbulbs dangle from the ceiling, flashing in waves. Bells ring again and again, like I'm in a funeral march. I don't want to die.

"The 99th era of the Ceremony of Equilibrium. May the Final Act restore Statera," Enyo roars with passion, an eruptive tremble darting through her throat. She says, soothingly, "May you Blaze or Burn."

The lightbulbs stop flickering, shifting into a sickly red that mimics the colour of blood.

Footsteps thud towards me, reverberating across the passage. I turn round and round, but I can't escape these copies of myself, spinning with me, unsure and heavy in their movements. I look at my face. Dark-blue circles stain the skin beneath my eyes.

"Audra," a man says, his voice croaky and lacking energy. Once again, I can't see anybody else around me, except myself. "What should we do?"

Droplets drip onto the mirrors, running down the glass like rain. But in the red glimmer of the maze, they look like driblets of red paint.

Nefarious images course through the mirrors all at once. I see open flesh, blood bubbling out of holes and bones as grey as the hollow carcasses of festering animals. I walk closer to the mirror. Tension lines the pits of my belly, warning me. This feels familiar. For a second, I gasp out of terror at the recognition. I don't remember what this sight means, but I know it's mine... I know that it's a memory.

Then I hear a sob, and I'm brought back to wherever I was before. The weeping is soft and quiet, as if someone is covering their mouth.

The mirrors shift into a shaky image of a living room. The walls and the ceiling are connected by cloudy wooden logs, where it looks like the brown tint has started to fade through the years. The table in the middle is scratched, and one of its legs is split in two, being held together by a thin piece of plywood held on with nails. The chairs are dented inwards from prolonged use. On one of the chairs, sits an older woman. Her arms are bulky, and her shoulders are unusually broad. I'd have expected her to be slender, like most of the people from my dreams, who are always starving. Now that I think about it, all my dreams of past memories have included food. From the deer to Albert and Ellis.

Why does she look so strong then?

"Audra, you hear me?" the man speaks more fiercely this time. He stands above her, his shirt off as he holds a wet towel to his waist. The bleached colour of the fabric slowly seeps with red.

The woman squeaks, trying to wipe her sniffles with her sleeve.

"I don't know," she mutters.

I get a closer look. The lady has dark-brown hair just like mine, but hers is long and wavy. Her eyes are puffy and tired. Their colour drained into an empty blue, like the sea during a storm. Both the man and the woman are wearing all black, their arms covered in bruises and mud.

"We need to do something. They saw us!" He hushes himself, demoralised.

"Did you take off your helmet?" she asks, her tone hanging in suspense like she's realised something.

"No," he answers, his head snapping back in confusion.

"Not once?"

"I told you I *didn't.*"

The woman's eyes trail off, deep in thought. Slowly she nods, her breathing growing heavier.

"You're not going to like it," she warns him. "I'll confess to the captain that they saw me." She pauses for a moment. "Alone."

"I can't let you do that," he scolds her, his voice breaking up. He turns around, scrunching the ridge of his nose, trying not to cry.

That's when it comes to me. From the wide jawline to the brown darkness of his eyes. That man is my father, which makes her… my mum.

"We don't have another choice." My mum's face turns watery, the tears teetering on the edge of her eyes. She looks like a balloon that's about to pop.

"I already lost my mother, I can't…" He inhales sharply, huffing air out in rapid bursts, holding himself back. He whispers, "I can't afford to lose you too."

Tears spill down my mum's cheeks. She gets up and wraps her arms around my father.

"I know, darling," she comforts him. "B-but," Mum stutters, trying to stop herself from trembling.

"But what?" Father turns around, showing her his soaked face. One hand stays pressed on his hip with the blood-soaked towel. He uses his other hand to gently wipe away her tears.

"But our children can't afford to lose both their parents."

"Then let me go instead of you," he snaps. "They need you so much more than me."

This time the tension rips, and I can hear my father begin to weep.

"That's not true, honey." My mum holds him tight. "That's not true."

My father tries to withhold himself, spinning his head from side to side. But the tears don't stop.

"They saw *me*," my mum reiterates. "The Arbiters will know it's me. But they have no way to track you. We can't let them find Viper."

"Don't you know, I can't live like this?" he bursts.

"I know you, Arthur. You're strong." Now my mum wipes his tears, but she's crying too.

"I'm not strong without you."

"You'll be strong for *them*," she demands, half-wailing, half-serious. She mimics him, "*You hear me?*"

Father sniffles, pain shredding his mind undoubtedly. He answers, "Yes ma'am."

Something pushes against me. I don't know if it's an artificial wind or if I'm falling involuntarily. I try to stay upright, but after a few instants of fighting back, my knees hit the ground and the mirrors fracture.

I look up and my mum is staring at me, her eyebrows bent in confusion. She swiftly wipes her face with her forearm and walks over to me.

"Sweetie, why are you still up?" she asks, worried.

It's not like I can respond to her. I'm watching a memory. I stay on my knees, cautious of what's coming.

Then I hear a young boy's voice. "Can't sleep."

It's me. I can't be older than ten. The voice sounds screechy and high-pitched. Nothing like mine now. Yet I still recognise that it's mine. A foggy familiarity.

"Me and Daddy are just talking, my sunshine," Mum whispers, trying her best to form a smile. But even then, I could probably see the agony hidden in the lines of her face. "Why don't you go to bed and wait for Mama? I'll tuck you in."

"Why are you and Dad crying?" the younger me squeaks, with an uncertain stutter in his voice.

"You're a burden, Son," my father growls in monotone and leaves the room. He doesn't sound like himself. This doesn't feel right.

"What's wrong?" the younger me mumbles, panting. But that doesn't sound right either.

My mum looks at me, and it's like I can feel her glare through the glass, beyond the passage of time. For a split-second, tears dribble from her eyes, run down her face, and hang from her jaw before falling to the ground. Wrinkle by wrinkle, her expression folds from sorrow into anger. Except it's unnatural. It looks like someone is poking at her from inside her skull, repositioning the skin that lines her face.

"Mum, what's wrong?" younger me shrieks.

The lights flicker. Each time there is a flash of light, I can almost make out the outline of a person in the mirrors. But before I can figure out who it is, the silhouette disappears every time.

The room turns red again. The air feels misty. Then, I hear the cracking of glass, like the mirrors were smashing to pieces. I hear the hissing of gas.

"You should have died instead of me!" Her voice rages all around me, bouncing off every surface of every mirror and shooting right back to me.

A figure stands before me. My chest rattles violently like a bird trying to escape the cage it's trapped in. I gulp down saliva, but my throat is smothering dry.

"Remember me!" My mum towers over me, her eyes firm with determination. She's set out on a goal. Me.

I lunge to shove her away, but my arms pierce right through her, and she scatters into the mist.

"What?" I gasp. Slowly I pick myself off the ground.

"My *sunshine*, did you forget your manners?" Mum grunts, the syllables sounding disjointed and unhuman. She reappears before me, her eyes pale and hollow, lacking life just like Ellis's and Albert's.

She's just a hologram, I tell myself. But the truth doesn't get rid of her. And it doesn't stop my heart from shaking.

I can't stand this much longer. I whip my head round, studying the walls of mirrors. The closer I get to them, the more unsure I am if they are in front of me or away from me. An illusion. I stretch my arm out and slowly walk into the wall. Except I don't touch anything. My reflections extend outwards into a tunnel. I'm in a maze of mirrors.

Before I know it, I'm on my feet and getting as far away from my mum's hologram as I can.

She's not real, I tell myself again.

"Don't forget to bring flowers to my funeral," my mum howls at me from behind. Her inhuman voice echoes across the passage.

Identical images of me move with me, blurring my surroundings into faint streams of motion. These are distorted memories. I know that. So what do I do?

The walls ahead of me rotate and slide to the side, uncovering different passages. I shift to the opening on my right, stretching my hands out in front of me so I don't throw myself into solid glass.

At the end of the passage, I run into a room with a brown coffin in the middle. The lights glow orange, losing their crimson glint. Rain hisses in the background, water dripping down the glass again. I don't pay any attention to whatever memory this is and start searching the walls for other openings. I just need to keep running. I'll find my way out of here eventually.

My hands brush across the smooth, yet awkwardly slanted surfaces of the mirrors. The walls are uneven.

Feeble footsteps tiptoe behind me, ticking lightly on the floor.

"You're the reason they died," a little girl utters, her voice cracking. I spin around instinctively, and a small child, maybe twelve years old, stands before me. Redness seeps through her eyes. Fury rushes down her face. She quivers with hatred and then screams at me, "It's all YOUR FAULT!"

The words ring in my mind, a vague familiarity.

Her hair is braided in a ponytail that swoops down to her waist. The bones of her body are outlined on her skin, sharp and bold. She's too pale, too scrawny.

"My father should have lived." She reaches for my collar and, though her little hands dive right through me, unable to actually touch me, I can't help but leap back in terror. She spits at me, "Damn you."

It's Aurora… as a child. Her father died because of me? I really hope not. I don't want her to hate me.

She's all I have.

Aurora walks over to the coffin and squeezes down on its edge, her little fingers grasping the wooden surface as tightly as she can.

The ceiling breaks into shards, but the falling glass descends in slow motion. Just in case, I swipe my hands through them, but I don't touch anything. The shards must be holographic as well.

I trod as slowly as I can towards the coffin, my gut uneasy. I'm not sure if I want to find out what's inside.

But when I glimpse inside the open casket, it's filled with purple flowers. They resemble lavender in colour, but they're not quite the same. The texture is velvety, and the petals curl out in little stars.

"It's purple hyacinth," the little Aurora mumbles, sounding flat and devoid of humanity. The girl turns to me, her brown eyes appearing half sunny from the orange gleam of the lights. I notice the shards are just about to graze the ground. "These flowers," she croaks unnaturally, "are a dead woman's specialty!"

The ground splinters into dots, and the glass collapses like it was rain. I'm sent flying down in shock. My feet crash into the ground, and I lose balance immediately, falling over to my knees. The breath in my lungs gushes out of me, and the impact leaves me gasping, holding onto my stomach in terrified emptiness.

As I'm hurled over, the wind tickles the back of my neck. I look up to catch a pair of feet dangling above my head. I jump back, my eyes wide. The feet belong to my mum. Her body hangs from a rope around her neck, as she swings back and forth. I feel weak, like I'm about to faint. There's no life on her face, and her skin is whiter than chalk.

"I'm sorry, Lukas."

I turn around to see my father, looking on with wet eyes. His nose is moist and swollen, probably from his failure to stop crying. I don't blame him.

I just wish I had never forgotten.

My gut twists. I want this all to stop.

Father tightens his grip on the glass bottle in his hand and takes a large swig until the spirit inside starts to drizzle in large gulps as it comes out. He lets out an *ahh*, before sniffling, wiping his face and turning around. Then he starts to walk away into the dark.

"I can't be the father you need me to be."

"But I love you, Dad," younger me shouts out, panicked.

"My love died with her," he spits, refusing to turn back to her hanging corpse. "I don't have any left to spare."

After a few more steps, he comes to a stop.

My dad grumbles under his breath, but his words echo through the walls.

"I told her I'm not strong enough."

The bottle drops from his hand and breaks into a million pieces.

He cries out, "Forgive me, dear."

The faint outline of his figure vanishes into the mist.

The glow of orange steadily brightens into a bright yellow. I check behind me. My mum is no longer there. Good. I can't bear to see her anymore.

For a second, my chest loosens up with relief.

Sounds of a fire sputtering and crackling emerge quietly. The mirrors fog up with a dark shade of grey, the same colour as steam. A few red and orange sparks flicker across the glass, bits of flame leaping from the fire. Finally, the blur disappears, and I can see a thousand pairs of hands holding brown envelopes. That's when the mirrors flash with white light and readjust into forming one massive screen.

A child's hands tremble as they grip the edges of a brown envelope.

"What is *this*?" a younger me whimpers.

Slowly, he rips the top of the envelope and pulls out a sandy sheet of paper. Its corners are folded. Uneven lines crease the paper through the middle, making it look old. The boy unravels the paper and straightens it out.

There's writing on it. It's short. And I recognise it immediately. I don't know how, but I do.

It's my mum's handwriting.

To my sunshine, my son. This is far too short to tell you everything. But I need you to promise Mama that you won't give up on Dad. He will be broken for a long time, but slowly he'll start to pick up the pieces and put himself back together. He'll just need a little push.

I want you, sweetie, to promise me you'll give him that little push.

Tears fall onto the page, leaving dark wet spots.

"I miss you *Mama*," the boy squeals under his breath, his fingers shuddering as he grips the paper.

I don't know how I know, but I do. And I know this hurts. Because I never said Mama, I always called her Mum.

But there's more. The boy breathes in heavily, withholding his sniffles. He looks at the bottom of the paper and reads quietly.

Grow up to be brave, to be strong, to be good.

If you can't do it for yourself, do it for me.

Do it for Mama.

I love you, Lukas, my sunshine.

Remember.

I will always be in your heart.

Always.

I can't control it. Ripples of tears leak from my eyes. I'm trying not to scream. But these memories are coming back to me. And so are my emotions. The guilt. The loneliness. The pain. I feel useless. Helpless.

I squeeze my chest. "You're still here, Mum."

In the distance, I hear a scream. It sounds like my own. I'm on my feet and running before I can process it. I squeeze through a narrow passage, watching my reflection in the mirror struggle and wriggle.

The lights have shifted from yellow to white. Everything is illuminated. I push through and enter a room that's shaped like a dome split in half. There's one flat wall at the very end. Here I see a hologram of my current self. I'm yelling in my father's face. His blank expression arches into fearful for the first time I've seen.

"You didn't raise them. I did." I watch myself shout. There's pain in my voice.

"I know, Son," Father whispers like he's afraid.

"I will be gone..." I say, trying to keep my voice from breaking. "They are your responsibility now."

"I know."

"Don't mess up," I snarl. And then my hands grab his shirt. "I will haunt you from the grave if I have to. Don't mess up."

Father nods.

There are two other figures behind my hologram and his, but they disappear before I can see them.

I watch myself hug my father, anger quivering through my face.

A whisper cuts the silence. "I love you, Dad. Really, I do. So please don't let them down."

"I won't," he answers, a desperate smile clinging to his face. I think I gave him the push I promised Mum.

The outlines of me and my father fade away into the dark. For a moment I'm left all alone. My heart accelerates, making me feel like my chest is going to explode. My eyes sting. The salty taste of pain trickles onto my lips. Drawing breath is slow and unfulfilling.

Images start to bounce onto the mirrors. My reflections disappear as snapshots of my past, and my fears are displayed back to me. Sounds from the memories bring a tingling feeling to my eyes.

I see a glimpse of my mum smiling and laughing, as she reaches out her hand to me. In another my father is helping me hold a fishing rod, as I spin the reel with all my strength.

"*You've got it!*" he cheers.

We must've caught something.

In another, I'm walking across grass, holding onto the hands of two little girls. Do I know them?

Next, I'm in class getting scolded by a teacher. She yells something about homework, her nostrils flaring up. After I'm back home, Father is cooking by the fire while Mum cradles a bundle of clothes gently in her arms. She looks at me and smiles.

"*Isn't she just adorable?*"

The past flashes by me. The woods, the lakes, the school, the town market, home. Faces I recognise. Faces I don't. But these memories are for me and only me.

I don't care if I don't remember it all.

Nobody can take this away from me.

My heart falls weak with fear and joy. Finally, I wipe my face dry. These memories slowly settle into place, like a key turning the right lock.

I run my palms across the flat wall. The glass is smooth and even, but I can sense it's hollow. I can almost hear the faint whistling of the wind on the other side.

Around me, I keep hearing the voices of my mum, my father, myself and others. But I ignore it all. My body surges with chaos. Tightness grows in my lungs, making breathing harder than ever before. I step away, until I'm as far back as I can get from the flat wall.

Without thinking, I bolt forwards, passing by my memories one last time. I bring my arms up to protect my face, grimacing as I prepare for impact.

I leap ahead. The glass shatters, and a thousand fragments hurtle with me. I'm bracing for pain, but instead I land and sink into something cold and soft. The wind grovels across my feet, introducing me to the frosty air. I'm in the midst of a blizzard.

Snowflakes plummet from the sky in hordes, hardening once they touch the ground and coating everything around me white.

It must be dawn soon. It's not completely dark.

I think I can hear the thud of footsteps creeping nearby, but I don't know if it's just the wind or my imagination. I gaze on ahead, but the blizzard's white fog blinds my vision. My mouth is dry. Beads of sweat drip down my spine, but the cold air still leaves me shaking. My skin crawls into itself.

The wind whispers and flicks across the air like a whip smashing into the ground. It doesn't take long before my fingertips start to quiver, overcome with numbness. My earlobes burn, probably turning bright red. I stagger forwards, hoping to find shelter from the cold.

Out of nowhere, a hand clamps over my mouth. Ice sinks into my skin. A blade presses against my throat. Frigid and sharp.

Warm breath brushes past my ear.

"You oughta stay quiet, *Luke*."

33

Aurora

Dawn breaks the night. The sun waits behind the horizon, but for now the sky is bruised in black and blue.

Cold wind blows against my face. A storm of raging snowflakes diffuses into my vision. Above it's dark, but everything around me is smothered in an empty fog. I trudge through the snow, in long, exasperated steps, trying my best not to topple over. I hug myself, shoulders hunched, trying to guard what little warmth I have left. I can't feel the ends of my fingers. I think the frost is beginning to seep into my bloodstream. I can't fight the whimpering.

Every time my body trembles, my mind can't help but to go back to those damn stolen binoculars. To how my hands trembled as I held them. To the sight of the little boy calling for his mother and holding her tightly. And then to the bullets that entered him. And the puddle of blood. And how much he reminds me of... my brother.

The past is like a broken puzzle being put together; too many pieces lie in a cluttered mess. The frame is there, but the picture makes no sense.

I'm becoming scared of who I am. Who I was.

Why is there so much pain in my chest when I remember? Why is there so much death in everything I see? My mother's words echo in my head: *What happened to the little girl I used to know?*

I don't know what to tell her.

Don't think about the maze. Don't think about the nightmares. Don't think about the past. Think about now, I instruct myself.

In between the howling gales, I swear I hear a cry for help. Then an odd burst of laughter. I need to move faster. I need to find Lukas.

"You have now made it past the first wave of the Final Act. Congratulations to the remaining seven survivors," Enyo announces, her tone beaming with sadistic joy. I imagine her lips curving into a cruel grin. "The second and third waves of the Final Act will begin simultaneously. Please pay attention. This is of critical significance."

I feel the air slowly growing thinner, like my lungs are losing the ability to breathe. My ears tighten up uncomfortably, and for an instant the world goes silent. Then I grab my nose and squeeze air out of my ears until they lightly pop. The ground wiggles beneath me as if stirred by some unseen force. I plant my feet to steady myself.

"Right now you are standing on the very heart of Statera itself, the Yin and Yang. This platform is being lifted into the skies to honour the Trinities of the Elect."

No wonder my knees feel weak.

"Here life ends and life begins. To survive the second wave, you must perform the neutralisation. The Great Constant has hunted you this entire Ceremony. Now, you must destroy the core of the Constant and resolve it into nothingness. The core lies at the top of the Central Atrium. Your objective is to neutralise the core."

I take note mentally. Reach the Central Atrium. Destroy the Core. But what comes next crushes me.

"And most excitingly, the final wave. Life will be given to one boy and one girl. As per the Yin and Yang, life must be taken and life must be given. Out of seven, only two are permitted to survive. One boy. One girl."

Stride by stride, my feet slump along the snow, heavy and desperate. Breath leaps out in stutters. Suddenly, I feel puny, frail. My chest aches in horror.

I don't want to kill. I don't want to die.

There is no giving of life! There is only taking. Only killing. My eyes narrow in horrifying recognition.

I have no weapons. I am now prey.

The blizzard freezes, snowflakes hang suspended mid-motion, like the weather is being controlled by a button. The fog dissolves. The snow continues falling.

I see clearly now. The platform is a flat land of snow, at the centre of which lies a tower. That must be the Central Atrium. The other end of the platform is black and ashy, contacting the snow in an odd *S* like curl. That's when I realise the ground is the literal image of the Yin and Yang.

"May the passage of time restore Statera," Enyo declares in celebration, her voice booming around me. The plummeting flickers of snow bring me back to what's important. I must find Lukas. Any chance of survival I have is together with him.

The last words Enyo says have been carved into my skull. The same persistent phrase that has haunted me and brought me fear every time. I'm more afraid than I've ever been before. And yet, somehow, I feel relief in knowing that this is the last time I'm going to hear it.

"*May you Blaze or Burn!*"

I keep my pace cautious. Already paranoid. Anyone could be watching me, waiting for me. Thousands of flakes drift to the ground, creating the false illusion of cover. But I'm dressed in all black. My appearance is almost flagrant, like I'm trying to be noticed.

Two bangs burst through the silence. The gusts of wind return almost instantly, like nothing happened.

"Subject Markas has been eliminated. Statera welcomes his sacrifice to restore the balance of the living." The announcement rattles me. The voice sounds indifferent and non-human.

Seconds later, another pop explodes. This time I see the short glimmer of flame fizzle out into the sky.

"Subject Lina has been eliminated. Statera welcomes her sacrifice to restore the balance of the living."

It's already begun. The thought twists and wrings inside my head. I quickly grow short of breath.

There is a killer here... with a gun.

But there's nothing I can do but stay vigilant. So I keep moving, ignoring the violent throbbing in my chest.

In the distance, the Central Atrium rises from the snow, its tinted-glass body stretching upwards in a dark cylinder. An orb sits on its peak.

A henge of stones surrounds the tower. Each structure is strangely assembled, with two legs and a horizontal slab balanced across the top.

As I approach, a low-pitched buzz thrashes my ears. It's like electricity is coursing through the ground beneath the Central Atrium. The hum muffles everything else, forcing me to concentrate gravely just to hear the sound of my own steps.

I sneak around the stones and tiptoe towards the tower. The ground splits in a curve, half snow, half ash. Four columns stand in a square, arches connecting them to form four distinct entrances. Inside there's a spiralling staircase leading to the orb. The roar of electricity still hasn't died down. I walk inside. That's when I hear the crunching of snow.

I spin to the entrance from where I sensed the footsteps. Just in time to see the pistol and the spark.

I dive towards the stairs and roll over on the ground. The bullet whips past me. A metallic clank jams the gun. The girl has to reload after each shot. Relief hitches in my throat. My heart races, packing me full of dread. But I can't force myself to run, it's like my body has been paralysed with terror. Instead, I look back to study who they are. There's a boy with the girl, but he's so short and skinny that he must've been merely eligible for the Ceremony. My heart quivers as I think of Amy. Both of them small and afraid. But courageous.

This is unfair.

The boy's dark skin contrasts with the pale and famished appearance of the girl. She towers over him like a protective polar bear.

"Stay down here. Hide in the stones," she orders, her voice sharp and stern, like an older sister's. "I'll be back to get you, sugar."

"I'm scared," the boy squeaks, teeth clattering.

"Hey, hey, look at me."

The girl crouches and wraps her arms around the boy, turning her back on me. Clearly, I'm no threat.

"I don't wanna lose you," he mutters.

She pulls him closer. "You won't."

I don't know why I don't run. But I can't help watching. Guilt twists in my gut. *I couldn't save Amy.*

The boy glances at the ground. "What if the others come after you?" He pauses. "And I can't help?" He looks back at her, his face trembling with terror. His voice cracks as he cries out, "Then they'll kill you. And then they'll kill me next, and—"

"Axel, look at me!" she snaps, cutting him off. "That's not going to happen. I promise."

The girl's voice is steady and full of conviction, like a general giving commands to her soldier.

"You promise?"

"Have I ever lied?"

The boy shakes his head. She hugs him again and pats his head.

"Remember what we say when we're scared?"

"Yeah." His voice is muffled in her shoulder.

They sing the rhyme in unity: "Until the day we fall, it's Ivy and Axel."

This lightens the mood, and the boy named Axel quietly lets out a giggle.

"Better?"

"Yeah!" Axel rejoices.

"That's a good boy," she says. "Now go."

Axel creeps back into the cold and disappears into the shadows cast by the stones. He's so young and innocent. Lukas won't save himself if it comes down to it. I feel a tremor in my chest. A distant longing, as if he were already gone. This isn't right.

"This isn't personal." The girl sets her sights on me and heads for the stairs. Her hand dips to her waist, and I don't need to linger around any longer to find out. She's going to reload and shoot me.

I leap up the stairs, two or three at a time. The staircase spirals around the edges of the cylindrical tower, each step suspended with open air between the treads. One slip and you're gone. There's no railing to keep you safe. My pacing is erratic, but all I can do is run and keep my breathing in check to stop me from falling to my knees and screaming until I meet death.

At least it will be quick.

Light skids across my vision. The eruption of the bullet slipping by me punctures my ears. I flinch instinctively, ducking for a second. I'm alive by inches.

My brain stutters in thought.

Run. Just run. And don't stop running.

"You're only making this harder on yourself, sugar." She's brutal. Her voice reeks of exhaustion, like she's fed up that I'm still breathing.

Unlucky for her I won't give up so easily.

"One of us *must* die!" she growls, as the metallic click of the gun tells me she has loaded another round. "You can still die with dignity, of your own choice."

She quietens down and waits. The only sounds are the stomps of my feet on glass.

I shift my gaze up. Light pokes through the entrance to the orb. Just ten metres. A few more steps.

"Fine. You'll die like a dog."

The gunshot rattles the glass underneath my feet. I stumble over my steps, lose my balance and crash into the sharp ledges of the stairs. My heart pounds, my abdomen screams and my head spins. Gasps drizzle out desperately from the back of my throat. By instinct, I start tapping my stomach, checking for any patches of blood. The girl climbs up the stairs at a steady pace, her footsteps ringing through my head like lethal warnings.

Get up. You must get up. She's hunting you.

Another *click*. She's getting closer.

I dash to the top of the Central Atrium and hide inside, unable to come up with any way to help myself. In the centre of the orb stands a glass podium. A chrome ring floats above it, rotating on the spot. Below, far off in the distance, green streaks and sandy lines interweave the brick lanes that constitute the Realm. I see a ring of diamond-blue passages right below this platform that must've composed the Maze of Nightmares.

In the snow beneath the Central Atrium two figures wrestle, trying to overpower one another. From his light-brown hair, I know one of them is Lukas. But I can't see the other's face. Lukas tilts backwards, gets kneed in the stomach and loses his footing. He staggers to the ground. The other figure still looks blurry from here. I can't recognise him. All I can see is that there's no hair on his head. The stranger pulls a knife from his belt and lifts it above his head.

"Lukas!" I shout out on impulse, my eyes flinching at the sight. But right before the figure brings the blade down, he turns around and begins to run, leaving Lukas behind in the snow.

The Great Constant closes in from the edges of the platform. It glimmers in a toxic mix of green and yellow, like sun-scorched grass rotting in the summer heat. In the corner of my eyes, a flicker of colour flashes. The ring above the podium shifts colour, matching the Constant's glow. I freeze, my eyes open wide.

The ring is the core of the Constant. I must destroy it. But before I can move, the girl tramps up the last couple steps and enters the orb. I lunge to the middle and press my back against the podium, trying to protect myself the best I can.

"I'm sorry, sugar," she whispers, circling around the podium in slow steps. I keep peeking through the sides, shuffling around to stay away from her. "I have no other choice. It's you or me."

I swing myself round and sneak a peep. The girl is aiming the pistol at me, its barrel shaky. The room flashes. The bullet ruptures glass, splits popping out in a circle. My forearm throbs with numbness. I feel the trickle of warmth running down my elbow. Once I raise my left arm, I feel the searing heat begin to surge through me. A hole gapes below my wrist, lines of blood spilling from it. Shreds of flesh curl around the wound, pink and fresh. Mangled skin flops onto the wool of the thermal I'm wearing.

"I know it hurts," she murmurs with a poignant tone. "Don't suffer. I'll make it painless."

I gulp down the taste of acid in my mouth and hold onto my left arm with my right hand. Just rotating my wrist lights up every nerve with fire. I'm trembling in agony. I'm going to die here. Right now.

"You won't feel a thing. I don't want you to suffer."

I hear a pocket flap open and clothes rustling. No time to think. I spin, rise to my feet, and sprint straight at the girl. If she loses her gun, we'll have to fight hand to hand. I'm at a disadvantage, but it's my only chance.

I reach her in two strides. She's still fixated on opening the chamber of her pistol when my knuckles thrash her jaw. Her neck snaps sideways, and her legs quiver before she tumbles down. The pistol falls from her grasp and slides across the ground away from her.

A sharp jolt tears through my arm. The short run drained more blood than I thought. I fight the dizziness swirling in my head. I look at the girl lying motionless on the ground, her eyes grey and half-shut. Unconscious. A revolting thought crosses my mind. I have to kill her. To survive I must do it. And from the memories in my sleep and the nightmares in the maze, I know it wouldn't be my first time. But I can't bring myself to do it.

I spot the glint of a knife on her belt and reach for it instead. I unsheathe the blade, slice a long strip from her shirt, lift my sleeve and then wrap it around the hole in my arm. I create a loop with the fabric, bite down on the corner poking through the ring and tighten the knot with my teeth.

Sparks pop and sizzle. It sounds like bombs are raining from the sky, detonating on impact.

I glance outside. The green wall of gas is devouring everything. The Great Constant encircles the Central Atrium. If I don't break the core everyone will die.

In an instant, I grip the knife stronger and make my way to the floating core. I take a deep breath in. Then I plunge the blade as deeply as I can inside the ring, interrupting its rotational orbit.

The ring begins to vibrate, and the entire Realm shakes with it. Suddenly the ring loses its glossy texture, shrivelling from chrome to dust. Then it bursts into pieces and scatters into the air. Dark bubbles ripple across the Great Constant, its viny, green tint undulating to black. The walls of gas shatter like glass, splintering into a flurry of sparkles. A rumble rips back and forth across the Realm. The remaining sparks of the Constant ricochet in reverse, retreating from the platform.

The glass quakes beneath me, and the tower begins to slant.

"*Arghh*," the girl groans as she crawls across the floor to reach the gun. I back away, pressing myself against the rounded wall of the orb. She clicks a bullet into the chamber and snaps it shut. Heavy grunts seep out from her. The girl cocks the pistol towards me, preparing to take aim. The Central Atrium bolts sharply, slowly sloping to the ground. Gravity tosses me forwards, and I slam into the podium. She fires. The bullet flashes past me, fracturing the window behind me. Out of instinct, or maybe spite, I throw the knife at her. The blade spins through the air and then thrusts into her chest. The knife sinks into her lungs. Blood oozes out. The girl glares at me, her face cracking with fright.

"Tha-the boy," she gargles, running out of air. Her eyes turn watery. "Let him live. Please."

My heart shakes. I nod. Trying to make her passing peaceful. She croaks with each breath.

The Central Atrium continues leaning over, bound to crash any minute now. I see the girl's head flop down.

The announcement chimes overhead. "Subject Ivy has been eliminated. Statera welcomes her sacrifice to restore the balance of the living."

I fumble at my belt for the tactical syringes. My fingers are slick with sweat, almost dropping them. In one motion, I inject the Mobility and Stability syringes into my thigh at the same time. My right hand trembles from the strained resistance of the plungers. Soft breaths slip from my nostrils. My mind clears into silence. Even the tower plummeting with me in it doesn't upset me anymore. My vision narrows, growing sharper. I throw away the syringes and stand up.

Once the tower collapses, everything inside will come crashing down. Then it hits me. I can use the tower's fall to break my own.

I sprint to the fragmented window with the bullet hole and ram my shoulder into it. The glass separates at the lightest touch, and I leap from the orb, landing on the cylindrical shaft of the tower. Energy jolts through me. The tower begins dipping closer and closer to the ground. I propel myself ahead, jumping greater distances than I should be able to. I run along the body of the tower, each step steeper than the last. I speed up, running along the reclining tower with every bit of strength in me. Fatigue doesn't concern me, but my breaths become faster, shorter and emptier.

Wind smacks and strafes against my stride, but I don't slow down. My heart ticks like it's on the brink of exploding. But I don't stop.

Just keep running. You'll make it. Keep running.

I'm drawing closer to the rim of the tower's body, preparing myself to jump off, trying to reckon the safest landing. The Central Atrium slumps into the platform and crumbles on impact. A rumble of fissures echoes up the glass, biting my heels. The round exterior of the Central Atrium bursts into bumpy and dented fractures. My feet sink into the uneven surface of the tower, and I can sense it could cave in on the spot, dropping me with it. I build momentum with one final dash and vault into the air as the tower breaks apart beneath my feet.

I fly over the henge of stones, lost in motion, my face hurdling towards the snow. The wind slashes my body. Breath spills out from my lungs in a panicked rush. I begin to shudder as I plummet into the cold.

I look down below myself while diving through the air. The Central Atrium creaks and crunches before it all stabs into the ground in a violent crash. Debris disbands. Shards of glass stick out from the ground.

The cold slaps my face. My chest crumples into the snow and then the rest of me follows. I wince at the stinging frost coursing through my limbs.

The aching in my chest weakens. The effects of the tactical syringes must be wearing off. Everything feels slow. I feel like I'm going to pass out. My forearm sears.

"Ya know, you can't hide in the rubble forever."

What? My mind blanks. My pupils shrink. That voice... my body trembles... it can't be.

He's not dead? How in the hell? I mourned him.

"I'll end your misery," Todd roars, his voice exploding in a guttural wail. "I promised you, Luke."

I can't stop shaking. I resist the daze taking over me. I fight the cold spreading through my bones. I get up, my legs and knees wobbling. And I hurry towards the henge of stones, my eyes searching for Lukas.

I must save him. Just as he's saved me over and over again. Lukas stands for what's right. He listens. He tries to understand. But there's no understanding a man that only wants death.

"It ain't right if you live, *is it*?" Todd shouts from the outskirts of the henge. Maybe he *wants* to be heard. He must be armed. I need to stay low. Strike first. "It wouldn't be fair and you know that's true."

I see figures leaping in and out between the stones, their bodies too blurred from the falling snow to figure out who is who. Hopefully the fog will conceal me. Light on my feet, I creep to the nearest stone and hide.

"You left me to die in that ditch," Todd shrieks, a little closer now. "Drowning in that black goo." I see him circling the stones. "You betrayed me!"

I can't figure out what to do. I need Todd to be closer to me if I'm going to take him out.

"But ya know what? It's all okay. I had taken Amy's tacticals from her corpse. Arms Blazing and Awareness. They oughta help I thought. Once I shot them into my veins, I climbed out quite easily really…" Todd trails off, like he's lost in thought. "My throat was a little scruffy though."

His footsteps approach me. I crouch down, pressing my ears to the edge of the stone. Nearby I hear the light scrunching of snow. Lukas, or the little boy Axel, is close to me.

"And the two of you were nowhere to be found. Both of 'em bailed on me! The pair of 'em lied to me. Lied to my face!" Todd shrieks.

The ground crumps alongside his voice. Todd will be here any second now. I start to rise to my feet again.

"I ain't forgotten what you told me, Luke!" Todd's voice crawls closer. "Live for others, was it? Live for loved ones? To remember them?"

I glimpse over the edge of the stone for a split second. Todd walks slowly, half stumbling, yet his posture is straight and steady.

He looks drunk. His original outfit is tattered, strips hanging from his chest. The last thing I notice are his bloodshot eyes.

"I know y'all ain't love me… but you two sure moved on fast. Cuddling up beside the campfire in your sleep. Maybe I shoulda cut your throats then?" Todd says, enthusiastically considering the possibility.

A sudden scream cuts his monologue.

"Gotcha!" Todd groans.

"All right. I'm here in front you." Lukas leaps out, already trying to break the tension. "Just let the boy go."

My heart trembles, realising Lukas will do whatever he has to, to save the child.

"Not so fast, you pushover," Todd snarls with disappointment. "The girl as well. Come out now."

He's talking about *me*.

"I saw you peeping!"

Damn it. How? I reveal myself from behind the stone and walk closer to them. We form a triangle. Lukas and I side by side, Todd facing us. He's got Axel in a headlock. In his other hand, a steel blade catches the dim light. Todd looks at me, his eyes raw.

"That's close enough. You shoulda stayed hidden."

"What do you need me to do?" Lukas asks without hesitation.

"Kneel before me," Todd orders, jerking his head side to side, like he's trembling with excitement.

I want to tell Lukas to stop right now. But I know it won't help. He gets on his knees and glances up at Todd. This seems to appease Todd as his lips stretch into a disgusting smile.

"Remember you said you have a reason to live, but not a reason to die?" Todd stares down at Lukas, his grip on Axel growing stronger as shades of blue start to emerge on the boy's face. "Well, ain't I great? I got you a reason to die."

Todd tosses Axel to the ground. The boy gasps, hands flying to his neck as he trembles uncontrollably.

"It's you or the boy," Todd whispers. "Choose."

"How do I know he's going to be all right?"

"You don't. You just need to trust me," Todd snickers. "There ain't no other choice."

"All right," Lukas utters quietly, his breath unsteady. "Just don't hurt the boy."

"Ain't you righteous?" Todd scoffs. A short chuckle slips out, then his face loses all expression. He grabs Axel by the hair and yanks his head up. The boy winces, his eyes quivering, wet with tears. Then blood shoots from his mouth. The knife enters his neck, and I see the sharp end of the blade pierce through the boy's throat. Before Todd can pull the knife back out, Lukas pounces on top of him. They scuffle in the snow, squeezing, smashing and grabbing one another.

I rush to Axel and scoop him into my arms.

"Hey, hey, everything's going to be okay. Just stay still, okay? Don't move. Just breathe." I try to press my palm to the hole in his throat to stop the bleeding. He looks at me, his eyes drooping and vacant. Warm blood trickles out in spurts, spilling down his body, painting his dark skin with crimson. I can't stop it. I can't stop the flow of blood. He gurgles horrifically, choking between coughs, drowning in his own blood.

"Stay with me. Don't close your eyes. Don't fall asleep, Axel. Just keep breathing."

But the gurgling doesn't stop. His shirt clings to him, sticky and soaked. The boy gazes at me, his eyes small and unfocused. His chest pops up and down in a spasm. Axel squeals and gasps on empty air, unable to breathe it in. Slowly his little body stops shaking.

"C'mon Axel. Don't fall asleep… stay here." My voice cracks, and I feel the burn of tears encircling my vision in a blur.

I quickly wipe my face and hold the poor boy in my arms. The weight of his head sends throbs of pain pulsing through my wounded forearm. But I don't let go of him.

Blood stops spilling from his neck. Axel stares at me with dull eyes. Then his gaze drifts off into the distance and turns stiff.

"I'm sorry, Axel." My hands tremble, trying to sniff back my tears, forcing them back into my eye sockets. "I'm really sorry."

Enyo announces, "Subject Axel has been eliminated. Statera welcomes his sacrifice to restore the balance of the living."

I hope he didn't suffer long. That's all I can think. And horribly I feel relief. Lukas can still live.

"Argh!" Todd howls like a wounded animal.

I lay the boy down gently, trying to avoid looking at the puddle of red growing in the snow. Todd stumbles backwards, dragging Lukas in a chokehold. I follow them, my boots crunching through the snow. Todd leads us to the edge of the platform.

"Now where was I?" he barks, squeezing his forearm under Lukas's jaw, trying to lock his arms together. However, Lukas doesn't let go of Todd's hand, reaching a stalemate. "I'm done with Luke and now that brings me to you."

I stand in front of him, breathing heavily, trying to calm my nerves. I can't look weak in front of him. I can't let myself cry. I need to fight him.

I need to kill him.

Lukas pulls on Todd's arm, tucks his chin down and tries to elbow Todd in the chest. But they're too close. So instead, Lukas grabs ahold of Todd's utility belt and rips it off his waist.

The belt hits the snow with a thud. Inside, I see one syringe with an empty, red-tinted vial.

"Too late for that," Todd rasps and strengthens his hold on Lukas. "The Resurrector is in my system already. I injected it right before we reunited," he squeaks and shifts his arm from the front of Lukas's neck to the back, digging his nails into the flesh. I lunge forwards. Just before I reach them, Todd flicks another knife from his pocket and waves it around Lukas's head. "Atatatata. No you don't."

"How?!" I scream in confusion.

"Familiar?" Todd grins, clutching the obsidian knife even tighter, pressing it to Lukas's skull. The knife he got from me. The knife he should have died with.

To hell with you.

"Ya know, Luke, you also said Amy can only live through me. That she dies with me," Todd says, calmly. "But that ain't true. Aurora knew her too. She grieved my dear little sister."

"We mourned both of you," Lukas croaks.

Todd just ignores him. "So, I thought I oughta solve that problem while sticking to the rules."

Something in my head starts to click, like the gears of a bike shifting. I glance at that red vial.

"What are you saying?" Lukas wheezes, gasping for air. We lock eyes.

"Aurora will remember us. You, me and Amy. We'll all live on through her."

I remember the words floating at the Care Point: "*Tactical Syringes cannot be used alongside the Resurrector.*"

I glare at Lukas, trying to figure out how to signal this to him without making it obvious. Me and Lukas keep our eyes settled on one another.

"The rules stated they permit one boy and one girl to live. Not that there must be one boy or one girl. So if you and I jump, we'll die together," Todd shouts. "Aurora will carry us on with her. Ain't I great, Luke?"

Todd's gaze is preoccupied with Lukas, as he plays with the tip of the blade, dragging it along the side of Lukas's face. I must be a smudge, an empty blur in the corner of his eyes.

"I told you I'd end your misery."

I mouth the word *Resurrector* and subtly point a finger down to my belt, tapping the empty tactical syringe slots and signalling for him to do it.

Lukas's eyes widen in recognition, and he nods.

Todd tilts his head in bewilderment, Lukas's nod having caught his attention. He follows Lukas's line of sight and spots my hand lingering on my belt. His eyes narrow, then his entire face stiffens with anger, realising the hint. But before Todd can react, Lukas swings his hand backwards, stabs the syringe into Todd's gut and smacks down on the plunger.

A sudden wheeze escapes Todd's throat.

Todd looks at me, his eyes wide, almost protruding out of his skull. His pupils look like a ring of blackness amongst the redness in his eyes. Then they shrink.

An explosive gargle darts out from Todd's mouth as he stumbles forwards, grabbing Lukas in a desperate cling. He wobbles in place, gripping onto Lukas tightly in order to stand up straight. But his knees twist inwards, and he falls backwards into the snow.

Purple flushes across Todd's face as tremors erupt through him, rattling his body frantically. Veins swell and coil, growing and spreading under his skin like a tangle of spiderwebs. Todd trembles in the snow, his limbs jumping then flopping back down. The outline of his skeleton grows clearer and sharper, as if his insides were deflating. Todd starts to turn a darker shade of purple, verging on an inky blackness. The veins poking through his skin start to twitch and jerk his body into unnatural shapes.

Todd's lips rise to form the silhouette of words. I believe he's trying to mouth Amy's name. But no sound comes. His red eyes turn cloudy, their shape hollow and hopeless. Then he stops shaking and sinks deeper into the snow.

"Subject Todd has been eliminated. Statera welcomes his sacrifice to restore the balance of the living."

After a pause, the announcement comes.

"One boy and one girl remain. The Yin and Yang give life to Lukas and Aurora. You have *blazed* and restored Statera, while the rest *burned* and restored the scale between the living and the dead."

"So what *now?*" I ask, my voice rising in confusion, as I turn to Lukas and freeze at the pale sight of his face.

"Aurora…" He drops to the ground. His hands clutch his lower abdomen, right where the obsidian knife is buried. I look on in horror, unwilling to believe what's in front of me. Refusing to believe. Without another word, I run to him and fall beside him, hauling him up in my arms and letting him lie down on my lap. I don't know what to do. A dark pool spreads around the knife handle sticking out of his sweater. I push down on the wound, but my hand sticks to the wool, stained with blood. I try to stop the flow.

"I thought I lost you," Lukas murmurs, looking up with a soft smile.

"I'm not in the mood!" I howl at him, tears flooding my voice. "Just keep still and don't speak."

It's too late. My eyes shake and the teardrops burst, spilling down my cheeks.

"Don't cry." His voice coarsens.

"Just shut up, okay?" I plead. "You're not dying."

"I'm not." He chuckles, coughing and grunting to conceal his agony. "Just stop the bleeding for me."

"Yeah, I'm doing that," I say as my voice cracks from the tears. I swallow hard to get rid of the lump in my throat.

I curse Todd in my mind, again and again. Every fibre of my being burns with hatred for him. Vile creature. He's not human. I'm glad he's dead. I'm glad.

I notice the snowflakes gliding across the sky. I had completely forgotten about the blizzard.

That might work.

I scoop up as much snow as I can and gently pat it down onto his wound. I can almost hear the snow hissing as it pushes the cold down onto his flesh.

"Thanks." Lukas breathes, his voice relaxed. "That's a lot better."

"I'm not letting you die."

"I know."

"Lukas, you don't have my permission to die," I cry out. I fight the urge to scream. I feel myself erupt inside. Emptiness swirls in my gut. I hold him there, pressing my hand down on his wound, while the other softly strokes his hair. "You're going to be okay."

"I know." Lukas pauses. "Because you're right here with me."

We lie in the snow, coated in drops of blood.

"Why the hell would you scare me like this?" I weep, my eyes swelling from the stinging of the tears.

I can't hold them in any longer. I let them fall.

"I didn't mean to… all right?" Gently, he brushes his fingers along my face, trailing to my chin. I can't help but smile. Yet my breath is shattered, and I keep croaking when I try to say something.

The skies have cleared. Helicopters soar above me, their rotors a distant hum. Ladders and ropes drop to the floor, as Arbiters dressed in red and black prepare to climb down.

"The moon is beautiful, isn't it?" Lukas remarks, gazing at the giant up above.

I look up too. "Mhm, it is."

The sky starts to brighten from a dark, deep blue into something lighter. I catch the rounded edge of the sun begin to rise.

"And so is the sun," I add.

I feel Lukas's touch on my cheek, as he gently brushes my skin. He gazes at me, his eyes narrow and wondrous. I squint and wince to get rid of the wetness from my face.

"What is it?" I ask, my cheeks turning red.

"And so are you," he whispers.

A tremor of heat burns inside me. I want to tell him that I need him. I want to tell him how I can't live without him. I want him to know my feelings.

So I lean down to his face, and my lips reach for his. We kiss.

And just for a moment, I believe that everything will be okay. Warmth spreads from my chest to the very edges of me. Then I kiss his forehead, and I hold him tight.

I feel connected. I feel hope. But I'm lying to myself. The Maze of Nightmares brought back more than I wish it did.

I know I'm never going home from the Equilibrium.

No one ever returns.

His eyes drift down, and I can tell he's weakening, losing blood and slowly losing consciousness.

I can't lose him.

My heart pounds with terror. I don't want him to die. I want him right here with me. We promised each other. He promised *me*! The cold from the blizzard has left me numb. Tears collide from our faces, falling to the snow.

"Aurora, I remember their faces!" Lukas gushes, his face shivering with recognition. "You made me remember them. I used to kiss them like that every morning before I left." He trembles. Then his voice saddens. "My family... *my sisters*... they were real, and..."

He falls silent, realising we're never going to see them again.

I nod, my eyes red with pain. "I know."

I don't know what to tell him to ease the misery. The terror of what's coming to us.

"Please don't go, Lukas," I beg him, pleading while I refuse to loosen my grip, fearing that the second I do, someone may tear him away from me.

He smiles gently, like he always does.

He says, "I'm right here."

Time passes on. The sun climbs over the horizon, its light dim and hopeless. Behind us the moon shines bright, illuminating the fading night. Arbiters start to descend from the ladders. But I only hold on tighter, dreading the moment they take him away from me. Dreading the moment he's no longer mine.

I squeeze his hand, incapable of letting him go.

I glide my fingers through his hair. I feel for his heartbeat. Helplessly, I lean in and whisper to Lukas. A final wish. A warped and self-serving conclusion.

"*Stay with me.*"

Acknowledgments

First and foremost, I want to thank the people who helped shape my creativity. To the English teacher who inspired me to delve into the world of literature, Amy Druce. You showed me how stories can change lives. For your guidance and goodwill, I deeply thank you. To Alberto Gonzalez, whose humour and compassion fostered my confidence and belief in myself. Thank you for teaching me that creativity thrives with courage. Lastly, to Bronagh Maquire, the first reader of this manuscript—your faith in my work and dedication to helping me refine it gave me the strength to keep going. Without the three of you, I might never have discovered this passion.

Thank you to designer and artist Calla Sawyer for the most incredible cover that captures STATERA's heart and tone so perfectly. Thank you to fine artist Pernille Caprioli, whose phenomenal attention to detail brought this world's architecture to life.

To my greatest friends—Aaron, Amy, Lasya, Alex, Rafid, Mindaugas, and Emily—thank you for your patience, belief and laughter along the way.

I must pay tribute to my editor, Ian Graham Leask. Without your insight and guidance through the polishing process, this book would have never found its place on the shelf. I'm deeply grateful for your time, expertise and care.

There aren't enough words to express the gratitude I owe my family. Thank you to my Grandmother for always encouraging my passions. I hope I've made you proud. Thank you to my Aunt for your eternal bravery. Your compassion makes me strive to be a better person. Thank you to my Sisters who have taught me what it means to cherish and protect; you two little troublemakers bring me joy like no other. Thank you to my Father for your wisdom, discipline and strength. Your love made me a man I'm proud to be. Lastly, thank you to my Mother—my truest teacher. You taught me how to think for myself and how to fight for my dreams. Your unwavering expectation of greatness allowed me to strive for success. Your love is the reason I have so much determination. Thank you for being my Ma. To my family as a whole, the words I truly mean but never say enough: *I love you all.*

And finally, I'd like to thank you—the reader. Without your imagination bringing this book to life, it would be nothing more than mere words on a page.

Until we meet again,

Adrijus Kveda

About the Author

Adrijus Kveda is a 19-year-old writer born in Alytus, Lithuania. He currently lives in the United Kingdom, studying Psychology and Language Sciences at University College London (UCL).

Passionate about creative writing, theatre, martial arts, debating, basketball, and video games, Adrijus draws inspiration from both art and human nature.

His love for storytelling stems from a deep fascination with resilience and human emotion, shaped by Lithuania's history of exile under the Soviet Union. His key literary influences include Ruta Sepetys' *Between Shades of Gray*, Cormac McCarthy's *The Road*, Marie Lu's *Legend* series, and Suzanne Collins's *The Hunger Games*.

He believes stories exist to give power—and a voice—to those who don't have one.